THE TIME BETWEEN US

MARINA MCCARRON

First published in the UK in 2021 by Head of Zeus Ltd
This paperback edition first published in 2022 by Head of Zeus Ltd,
part of Bloomsbury Publishing Plc

9 7 5 3 1 2 4 6 8

A CIP catalogue record for this book is available from the British Library.

ISBN PB: 9781801104425
ISBN E: 9781801104418

Head of Zeus
5–8 Hardwick Street
London EC1R 4RG
www.headofzeus.com

Printed and bound in Great Britain by
CPI Group (UK) Ltd, Croydon CR0 4YY

For A.C. and J.C.S.

PART 1

PROLOGUE

OMAHA BEACH, NORMANDY. JUNE 6, 1944

Bullets sing. He never knew that. If he listens closely he can hear every single one of them. He wonders, just for a second, if one will sing for him. The mortars fall around him: the percussive drums of this violent opera. They hit the beach and the earth explodes. Sand flies up, sticking to his body, coating his eyes. He wipes it away and keeps walking, grateful to be out of the freezing water and moving.

He'd gone over the side of the landing craft the moment he could. Better to take your chances and brave the Channel than to be a sitting duck on the boats. The captain gave the order. No time to hesitate, to question the insanity of walking into a wall of bullets. Over he went, holding his rifle above his head so it didn't get wet, catching his hip on the side. It hurt like hell until the iciness of the water numbed him. So cold for June. The sea was filling with the blood of the soldiers who had gone before, great patches of crimson filling the waves and crashing into him. But he couldn't think about that now. Ahead, on the hill above the beach, the enemy was well protected, hiding behind concrete bunkers, their massive guns pointed directly at them. He pushes forward.

Two years of training but he was not prepared for this. The noise. The metallic smell of blood; like the buckets of nails from his grandfather's workshop. He lowers his head and keeps walking. How far is it across the beach? Will he make it? He thinks of the beach back home, the run he took the last morning before he shipped out. The sun was just coming up. He remembers walking out into the early morning, catching the screen door so it wouldn't bang and wake his parents and his little brother. Who else was there that weekend, to see him off? His aunt and uncle. The neighbours came by, briefly. Their boy had been one of the first to go. Their country had been attacked. They knew what they had to do. Still, it was an ugly affair.

Another step. One hell of a roar. The earth trembles; it feels like an earthquake. In front of him a man is engulfed in flames. A human torch he's close enough to touch. He can feel the heat stinging his own flesh as he tackles him, forcing the burning man into the water, using his helmet to drown the flames encircling the soldier's head like a glowing crown. He looks away, closes his eyes for a brief second. The smell. Like a barbecue. A smoky October night. And something else he's never smelled before. His stomach turns.

'You're alright, you're alright,' he yells although he knows it's not true. What else can he say? The man probably can't even hear. Artillery rages around him. He has to get across the beach. Moving backwards, he shoves the burned man toward the closest obstacle, the metal structure their only cover. They remind him of playing jacks when

4

he was a kid. Why is he thinking about that now? He leaves the burned man slumped in the sand and turns back to the job. They have to scale the cliffs. The sand and waves pull at his legs and he falls backwards into the water. Lands on his butt. He'll hear about that later. Can almost hear Hank saying something about sitting down on the job.

Hank. Where is he? He can't see much, with the sand flying into his eyes as the earth is pulverised.

He stands, aware he is a larger target now. Secures his helmet strap. 'I'd like to live,' he whispers, like a small prayer. He has a lot to live for. A family. A girl. But he won't think of her. He doesn't want to bring her into this nightmare with him. She doesn't deserve that. His boots seem heavy now; maybe they're filled with water. He's not sure. It takes a second to get his bearings. He feels dizzy and has to concentrate to get his legs working. One step. Two. He thinks he can hear his name being screamed over the whistling bullets. He takes another step.

'Medic! Medic!' he hears. He knows that voice and looks around trying to find where it is coming from. Something warm and wet sprays across his face. Blood. His own? No time to check. Another step. Something is in the way. He stumbles, looks down. A leg. No body attached. The flesh all torn. He knows what it is, can smell the blood, see the bones, but it might as well be a car tyre or a birthday cake for what he takes in. Now he is walking on flesh. He can't think about it, has to keep moving. They have to clear the beach. It's their job. It's what they have to do. A few more steps, and he'll be safe. He'll have made it. But the cliff is hazy in the distance now. It feels like it keeps moving further away, like a mirage.

The noise is unbearable. The shells hitting the ground

send shocks through the earth, making his body vibrate, lifting him momentarily off his feet. He struggles to keep walking. He sees Hank in front of him. They've been together since basic training, and he'd know the slope of his shoulders anywhere, the strange way he runs, with his body bent so far forward you think he's going to fall over.

The smell of the water fills his nose, his lungs. It reminds him of the ocean spray in Cape Cod. If they survive he'll take Hank to Cape Cod. They only live a few hours apart, but never would have met, except for this war. Now, they're friends. They'll go sailing and eat oysters. Lobster. He'll show Hank home.

The smell of the ocean is stronger now. It makes him think of pearls. Of walks on the beach. Of his girl. The life they had planned together. He can feel it slipping away.

The noises are not so loud. He is getting colder. Who knew it would be this cold in France in June? How much further is the sand bank? He can rest there for a moment and wait for orders. He slips but doesn't look down. He doesn't want to know what he's stepped on this time. He keeps slipping, and he's on the ground. Funny, but he can't get back up. He grips his rifle tighter, pulling it into his chest. He's being dragged. Can hear his name being said over and over. He knows the voice. He needs to stand up. But he can't seem to move. Someone puts his helmet back on his head. He didn't know it had fallen off.

'It's okay, buddy. It's okay.' It's Hank.

'I've been hit,' he says to Hank. He's almost surprised. For some reason he'd thought he might make it. But he knows that will not be. The feeling of home grows stronger. He can smell bacon, eggs, cinnamon, and the light scent of the ocean that always filled the air. Can hear his father whistling as he reads the paper, the sound of his mother in the kitchen. The thump of a ball hitting a glove, years and years of playing catch with his little brother, who had absolutely no hand-eye coordination. How he'd teased him. He feels badly about that now.

The pain he hadn't felt slices into him, making him gasp. He tries to move his hand to his chest but the simple action is beyond him. He won't see her again. Won't taste the sweetness of her kisses. Won't hold her in his arms. He feels tears come to his eyes and doesn't bother to blink them away. Doesn't think he could even if he wanted to. He knows he's made it out of the water, but still, it's like he's drowning.

He feels arms gripping him.

'You're okay,' Hank says again. But he can see the panic in his friend's eyes. Above him someone yells for a medic. Or maybe Hank is yelling. But he needs to stop that. Hank needs to stop yelling because before he dies he has something he needs to say.

'Hank,' he says, trying to talk over the chaos, trying to be heard. What he has to say is important. He reaches for Hank's arm, grabs him, and his friend looks down at him, forcing a smile.

God, it hurts now, not from the wound, but from thinking of all he has lost. Hank grabs his hand, holding it tightly, like he is trying to keep him here by force. Pull him back from the void. But there's something in his throat. Blood, he thinks. When he speaks, his words feel like he is talking through a fountain.

'What we talked about, my girl? You'll take care of her?' His gurgled sounds are desperate, anguished.

'You're gonna be okay.' Hank's words say one thing, but

his eyes something else. His grip is slipping. His hands are too cold to hold on, but he feels Hank's grasp – sure, solid, strong.

'Hank,' he says, trying to get his hands to work. Hands that took piano lessons for years. Hands that held drafting pencils, sketched houses, buildings, stroked her face. Hands that he thought would hold children. Now he can't get them to work.

'Of course I will. Of course I will. I promise.' Hank's wild eyes betray his sure words.

He feels better. Hank will take care of her. He sees her before him now, as she was that night in Paris, in that simple cream dress, alive with energy and beauty and love. He hopes she can feel how much he loves her.

'You need to go sailing, in Cape Cod, like we talked about,' he says. He closes his eyes, takes what he knows will be his last breath. He would have liked to live, he thinks again. There was so much he wanted to do. So much to live for.

'Take her sailing, too.' Hank grips him tighter.

It's quiet now, the shelling, the gunfire, the sound of bodies being ripped apart. The screams of men. One of the bullets was singing for him after all.

ONE
ESPERANCE, FRANCE. SPRING 1937

Elise can feel the sun on her shoulders as she walks to the bakery. Can hear the wind through the leaves of the trees. Sycamores, poplars. In the distance Monsieur Gravel's wind chimes and their soft tinkling sound that always makes her think of fairies. It is a beautiful spring day, a perfect day, and she is turning sixteen, so she is going to the bakery to buy a cake. She's not had a cake in three years, not since Papa passed away. Even though she knew her maman would not bake a cake, the night before she had found herself hoping to discover one on the table, sitting on the cake stand, protected by its green glass dome, the red of the cherries shining through like patterns on the glass. A present, or presents nearby, depending on how Maman was feeling. Papa singing to her as he drank his *café* before work.

Having a birthday had been fun when he was alive. Everything had been better. Not perfect, but better. Things were different now. Papa was gone. Her brother Philippe was studying in Paris – and he had changed so much since Papa died, he was a stranger, lost in a world of drink and cigarettes. Now it was just her and Maman. She tries not to think about it. She looks again at the leaves and concentrates on the sound of the fairy chimes.

The walk to the bakery is not long, so she slows her pace; there's no reason to rush, and it is nice, being on her own, away from the house. Down the streets lined with houses, along the main street, past the shops. Too soon she finds herself standing in front of the little stone building that is the village bakery, across from the park. She stops for a moment and breathes in the scent of freshly baked bread. It is so thick and heavy around her she feels like she could reach out and butter the surrounding air. The idea makes her smile as she goes up the three smooth steps to the entrance. A tinkle of bells sounds as she opens the wooden door. Behind the counter Monsieur Allard sees her and a big smile replaces his usual fixed look of concentration and impatience as he does three things at once. He is always delighted to see Elise, and she feels the same way about him.

'*Ma belle*,' he says, raising his arms toward her in greeting, despite the big wooden counter that separates them. He bumps into it, making them both laugh. Elise has the sneaking suspicion he goes out of his way to do such things, just to make her giggle. In the village he has a reputation for being a bit grumpy, but Elise knows this is not true; it's just his way. She laughs now to make him happy.

He pulls a face, as if surprised the counter is there. Quickly he turns and walks toward her, his steps graceful despite both his size and his foot, twisted from some child-hood disease.

'*Bonne fête, chérie!*' he says, pulling her into his arms.

She feels the thick cotton of his apron, and his warmth from working with the oven. He smells of doughy bread and sugar and cinnamon. The aromas comfort her as much as his embrace, and she feels as though she is being hugged by a large cinnamon bun, straight from the oven.

Elise's cannot believe he remembered. It makes her want to cry. Instead she hugs him back, fiercely. He is so large that she can only get her arms halfway around him, and she ends up mostly squeezing his sides. This, too, makes her laugh.

Keeping one arm around her, he shepherds her behind the counter, and up the narrow stairs to their little house above the shop. The door swings open and she sees Marianne, Monsieur Allard's wife. She says something Elise does not understand, and then laughs, a quick, precise laugh.

'That is German, for happy birthday.' Marianne is from Munich, and it was the talk of the village when she arrived. A new person was always good for gossip. So much talk of Germany these days, and its little leader. Elise doesn't pay much attention. He is an ugly man and she has no interest in him. Besides, what does Germany have to do with France anyway?

'Thank you,' she says. '*Danka*, right?'

Michel, their son, is perched on Marianne's hip. He is staring, mesmerised at the fiery tip of the match as Marianne lights the candles until he sees Elise and reaches for her. She scoops him into her arms. A look of relief settles on Marianne's face. She looks tired, Elise thinks. She will have to see if she can help with some more babysitting so Marianne can rest. Monsieur Allard's hands are on her shoulders, urging her to sit. Elise is laughing, as is Michel.

Such a happy baby. She grabs his hands and peppers them with loud kisses, making him laugh more.

'Attention, attention,' Monsieur Allard is saying. Elise looks up at him as Marianne places a cup of coffee in front of her. The breeze from outside catches the white muslin curtain in the window and it floats dangerously close to the lit candles on the cake. Elise pushes it back, a small crisis averted. 'Today is a very important day.' He clears his throat, puts his arms behind his back. Elise gets the feeling he has been rehearsing this, and it makes her love him even more. 'Our beautiful Elise is turning sixteen. A woman now!' he says and for some reason this makes her blush. 'No more will you be interested in my jam tarts, or squeezing the warm custard from the pastries.' His voice is filled with mock despair and Elise thinks instead of being a baker he should have been an actor. Marianne is staring at her big bear of a husband as though she is thinking the same thing.

'Before our eyes you have turned into a beautiful woman. A beautiful woman,' he says with more force. 'May the coming year be the best one yet! Happy birthday, Elise!'

Marianne gives her a warm, motherly peck although she is only five years older than Elise. Monsieur Allard puts his big warm hands on her cheeks, pulling her toward him and giving her not one, not two, but three kisses, until Marianne laughingly says, 'Enough!'

'Make a wish!' she is told. Elise complies, closing her eyes. A moment of sadness steals over her. She knows what she wants, for Papa to come back, but she knows that can never be. So she makes another wish, a crazy, ridiculous wish for love and adventure, which she can't see coming true in this quiet little place she calls home. Placing her hand over Michel's small head, she cradles him closer to her chest, keeping him safe from the wax as she blows out the candles. As tiny bits of smoke twist into the air, Marianne starts cutting up the cake, putting it on small white plates decorated with bright red roses and gold trim. Elise knows it is her wedding china, and the fact that Marianne is using it makes her want to cry. She pulls Michel even closer and buries her face in his warm baby smell.

'Eat up!' Marianne says, rubbing Elise's hand in a gesture that says, *I see your sadness and wish I could help.*

Elise takes a mouthful of cake and a sip of her coffee. Monsieur Allard takes out a bottle of Calvados and pours small aperitifs for everyone. The bells over the door tinkle, indicating someone is in the shop below, and Monsieur Allard springs to action.

Elise picks up her glass of Calvados. She has never tasted it before, the apple brandy everyone in her small village drinks. She takes a small, hesitant sip and feels the burning in her throat.

'Oh,' she says, reaching for her cup of tea to clear away the taste and the awful sensation. Michel looks up and laughs at the face she is making.

'You get used to it.' Marianne shrugs.

'Why would you want to?' Elise laughs. But it is true, what Marianne says. You get used to terrible things and accept them. She may only be sixteen, but she knows this.

'Right,' says Monsieur Allard, coming back into the room. 'Time for some seriousness. Life can't always be parties.' He looks at Elise. 'Now that you are a young woman of the world, you will be needing spending money,' he says, putting his hands in his apron pockets.

Elise thinks he is going to ask her to mind Michel. She likes the idea but is not sure how Maman will react. She is not prepared when he says, 'I am hoping you might like to work at the bakery, mostly on Saturday, but after lessons as well?' He looks at her hopefully.

Elise beams, overwhelmed. A job in the bakery. Money! She can buy a new hat, go to the pictures. But reality settles over her like a bucket of wet cement, cold and sticky and paralysing. There is no way Maman will agree. She will say Elise is needed at home. After Papa died she started to depend upon Elise more and more. Now she can barely let Elise out of her sight.

'I would love to work here. How I would. But...' Her voice trails off. Elise has tried to keep it a family secret, but, well, secrets in her town are impossible. Monsieur Allard knows, she thinks, but she does not want him to know just how bad things are. Papa had left a trust to pay bills, and his parents had, too. There was some money, to keep her and her brother in school. But the house needed repair. Maman doesn't get dressed most days. Elise is embarrassed, as though the woman herself has suddenly appeared at the party in her ratty bathrobe, and colour rises in her cheeks. She can feel it burn, not a harsh sting like with the Calvados but somehow worse. A burn that does not go away. A burn that creeps into every part of her life, with no end in sight.

'I have spoken to your maman.' The dark light of anger shines quickly in his eyes, but he hides it as Elise's heart starts to thump double time. Was he at the house when she was at school? In what state was Maman? Surely she hadn't gone to the bakery? She has not left the house in two years!

'Your lovely maman said it was fine. She understood a

young woman needs to start making her own way in life. And she knows we need the help.' He waves in the general direction of the kitchen, but the large arc of his arm also incorporates Marianne, who smiles brightly at Elise, as if to say, *It's okay. Have faith.* But still Elise's mind races. Was Maman dressed or wearing that awful brown nightdress when he arrived? Monsieur Allard puts his large warm hand over Elise's. 'It is fine. All is good! You will start next week, yes? All day Saturday?'

Elise wants to jump up and kiss this lovely man. But she has the baby in her arms, and coffee in front of her, as well as the niggling fear Maman will somehow ruin this for her. Still, right now... it is something. She has tears in her eyes when she looks up at Monsieur Allard and says, 'Thank you.' Her words and the light in her eyes soften him and he looks at Elise with the tenderness of a father. Elise barely remembers such looks.

The bells tinkle in the shop and Monsieur Allard hurries down the stairs to serve his next customer. Marianne moves toward Elise and says, 'Is he too heavy for you? Do you want me to take him?'

Elise shakes her head. 'No, he's perfect,' she says, nuzzling the top of his head.

'So, sixteen. Any big plans?' Marianne settles into a chair and smiles at Elise.

'Philippe is coming,' she says, trying to make it sound like he is coming for her birthday when in truth her brother probably has no idea of the date. But it is good that he is visiting. It perks Maman up.

'That will be fun,' Marianne says. 'And next week you will start work here. It will be so nice to see you more often!' She dabs some icing from Michel's face.

Elise suddenly thinks of the time and shifts in her seat. 'I must be going,' she says, but she stays seated, not wanting the good time to end. Not wanting to go home.

'I shall wrap up your cake for you,' Marianne says.

Elise thinks of the few centimes she has in her bag. Now she could put it toward a new winter coat. She outgrew her last one and is wearing her father's now.

'Are you sure? Maman would like a slice with her tea.'

Marianne takes out a piece of brown paper and starts to wrap up the plate.

'I can't take your good china!' Elise exclaims.

Marianne waves off her concerns. 'You'll bring it back.'

Elise hands Michel back to Marianne as she takes the plate. She gives the baby a kiss and Marianne, too, and walks out of the shop.

'Thank you for my cake,' she says to Monsieur Allard, asking for a baguette, and handing over some coins.

'Not on your birthday!' he dismisses. Although she knows it is hopeless she tries again, but he is adamant.

More kisses and she is out the door, the tinkle of bells going behind her. She hurries now, keeping a tight grip on the plate, the paper already sticking to the frosting. As she walks along she wishes so much that Papa was alive so she could tell him she now has a job. A familiar pain nudges at her heart, as though she needed to be reminded he is gone. She walks faster, as though she can outrun it. The wind is picking up now and Monsieur Gravel's chimes are peeling away, like they are heralding a great arrival or announcing an important event.

Elise can picture him, looking out his window, the stump of his left arm, which he lost in that horrible Great War, twisted behind him, worried his chimes may blow away. The neighbours, tired of the incessant tinkling, would not have similar concerns.

Up the path to her house, stepping carefully on the stones that get so slippery. She opens the door with one hand and a push from her hip, then sets the cake on the small table in the entryway, catching her reflection in the cracked mirror above. As she unclips her hair and shakes her head, she sees her brother's brown leather satchel on the floor. It is so worn at the corners she would know it anywhere. It is not old but neglected. Philippe does not take care of anything anymore. Not even himself. There was a time when he was charming, vain, quick to laugh. Fun. Those days are gone, but Elise hopes they will return. Next to it is a navy-blue case, smart and new. Who does that belong to? Quickly she ties back her hair and picks up the plate, starting toward the kitchen.

A few steps, and she sees Maman standing in the parlour. Something about her is different. She touches her hair with her hand, as though trying to make it look better. A smile plays with her lips and the rarity of it stops Elise. As she watches, someone new steps into view. A tall man in lovely clothes. Who is he? From where he is standing Elise thinks he must be looking at the portrait of Papa. Her heart starts to beat faster as she watches, silently. The man towers over Maman, even over Philippe, who is the tallest person Elise knows.

Still holding the plate, still motionless, she stares at the stranger. He's wearing soft grey trousers and a crisp white shirt that shows his broad shoulders. His dark hair catches the little bit of light that comes in from the window, and the glossiness of the colour reminds Elise of the bark of trees after a heavy rain. As Elise stares he slowly turns around.

All of the air seems to leave the room and her grip on the plate tightens inexplicably. He is handsome, no, more than that: he's beautiful, with large grey-blue eyes, the colour of the ocean before a storm. He's looking at her and smiling. At her. Elise feels a jolt run through her, remembering the wish she made before blowing out the candles on her cake. Could it be?

The back door clangs and Elise knows her brother is outside, having a cigarette. '*Minou!*' says Philippe, walking toward Elise. 'We were wondering where you were. Ah, what have you got?'

Elise knows her brother is speaking to her and that she should reply. But she can't seem to get her mouth to work or to stop staring at his friend.

'Elise! Your brother is speaking to you!' Maman sighs, and a look of surprise crosses the man's face. Elise is used to this, for Philippe is Maman's pride and joy and can do no wrong, unlike Elise. You dislike the person you depend on, she is learning.

'Cake. Monsieur Allard baked me a cake for my birthday,' she says in a high, slightly warbly voice that doesn't sound like her own.

'Ah yes, happy birthday,' says Philippe. 'I have something for you.' He pats at his pockets as though a gift might appear. 'In my bag.' Elise doubts this very much. Philippe has always reminded her of puff pastry: sweet and lovely on the outside but empty on the inside until filled with chocolate or lemon. Lately nothing fills Philippe but cigarette smoke and drink. She waits to be introduced to his friend, but nothing is said.

'Would anyone like some cake? Shall I make some coffee?' Elise recovers, already walking toward the kitchen, her steps jerky from the pounding of her heart. In the kitchen she sets down the plate and takes a deep breath. Then she peeks around the corner of the door to see him again. Maman is speaking to him and he leans forward to hear, a lock of hair falling into his eyes. He looks like Jimmy Stewart. As Elise watches them chat his dark eyes narrow into seriousness and Elise can only wonder what Maman is saying to this man. Without warning, he looks up, and sees her watching him. He smiles directly at her, showing a mouthful of white teeth and a glimmer of something Elise doesn't recognise in his eyes. His hair falls forward again and he pushes it out of the way.

Elise is mortified to have been caught staring at him, and spins quickly around, her back now to him. She uncovers the cake and tries to make it look nicer on the plate, getting frosting on her hands. As she licks the icing from her fingers, she spies a tray on top of the cabinet. It's never used but she thinks it is big enough to carry the cake and the cups and plates. Standing on her tiptoes, stretching, she carefully pulls it down, catching a glimpse of the old green cake plate and dome behind it. Grabbing a chair and climbing up, she balances carefully as she pulls it down, too. It is caked in dust.

When was the last time they used it? Not since she turned thirteen. A terrible year, but on that day, her birthday, they did not know what was in store. She rinses it in hot water, and wipes it dry, then she puts Monsieur Allard's cake on the plate and covers it. The pink roses don't shine as brightly through the green glass as the red cherries did, but still, it makes her happy to see it. This is what she wanted. Well, mostly. But when the tray is all loaded she finds it is too heavy to lift.

'Philippe,' she calls, poking her head around the door. Her brother is not to be seen.

The man walks toward her, his movements easy and his strides confident. With each step that brings him closer, Elise's heart beats faster. It is so loud she wonders if he can hear it as he stands beside her.

'Can I do something to help?' His voice is warm, courteous and kind. Elise is again speechless, but for an entirely different reason. That lovely accent of his! She could listen to him all day. He is American, she thinks, although his French is lovely.

'Um, could you, could you carry the tray to the table, please? I'm not sure where Philippe is?'

'Outside having a cigarette,' he states, lifting the tray effortlessly. Elise knows that Philippe will give up going outside soon and Maman will say it is fine for him to smoke in the house. Elise's lungs already tighten at the thought. They never remember that it brings on her asthma. But Philippe coming home is rare, and Maman dotes on him, her firstborn, when he does.

'After you,' he says, giving a tiny bow. Elise, thrilled, walks in front of him, wishing furiously she had worn her smart navy skirt instead of the drab grey one.

'I'm Elise,' she says. 'Philippe's sister,' she explains.

'And it is your birthday today. Happy birthday. I'm William.' He sets the tray down and extends his hand. For a moment Elise is not sure what to do. Tentatively she reaches out but then the door flies open and Philippe appears in a cloud of smoke that immediately hits the back of her throat. She withdraws the hand that almost touched William's and coughs into it. William's forehead creases, just for a second, and she is embarrassed. How vulgar to cough into her hand! But it is her brother he looks at, not her.

Glasses clatter together as Philippe rummages in a cabinet for something.

'Ah ha!' he says with a flourish, pulling forward a bottle of red wine and a bottle of Calvados. The tea is ignored.

They all sit at the table and for a moment, a delicious and delightful moment, her leg rests against William's. She can feel the smoothness of his slacks, the solidness of his leg underneath. The warmth of him. He moves it away quickly, giving her a sidelong smile, part apology, part shrug, and her heart starts a rapid, fluttery beating. Really, turning sixteen has been the best thing ever.

TWO
BOSTON. SUMMER 2009

It's a beautiful summer day and instead of walking through the Commons or sitting by the river, Lucy is drinking water from a measuring cup and waiting for the movers.

Why had she packed all her dishes first? She wasn't even sure where the measuring cup came from. It might have been here when she moved in. She drops it in the sink and looks at her watch, then out the window. For two years she's had the same view, spending countless hours staring at the trees in the distance, like they were old friends offering comfort on bad days. Answering all the questions she's had, like whether she should take a semester off. She had decided not to go to commencement as the first buds appeared on the northern red oak. A tree, her granddad told her, more likely to be struck by lightning than any others. She will miss watching its leaves turn to a flaming red. She will miss autumn in Massachusetts. Already she misses her grandfather's endless bits of trivia. But the trees have no answers for the questions in her head now. And granddad isn't here to ask.

Turning away from the window, she looks at her life, all neatly packed in storage bins and suitcases, filling one corner of her tiny studio. Her bed and desk, the table she was supposed to eat at but actually used as a second workspace, and a couple of chairs are all grouped in the middle, like some sort of furniture sports huddle. She's putting it in storage until she moves to the West Coast. She just has the rest of the summer to get through now.

The buzzer startles her, the loud, shrill sound like a million angry bees. No matter how many times she's heard it, it still makes her jump. She won't miss it. Lucy looks out the window, making sure it's not Hal, desperately seeking forgiveness she can't give him. She's both relieved and slightly disappointed when she sees that it's not him.

The movers seem annoyed to see how little she has.

'This is a job for just a couple of friends and a van,' one says, like they're admonishing her for wasting their time.

'Well, I don't happen to know anyone with a van. And I've already paid. So can you take this stuff or not?' The harshness even shocks her. She's tired. Overwhelmed by everything, she consoles herself.

The one who made the comment just looks at her, while the other says, 'Of course, miss.'

It takes them two trips. As they leave she asks them if they want the four bottles of Sam Adams in her fridge. It's been there for weeks, and she knows she won't drink it. They take it and leave.

Lucy looks around at her now almost empty apartment and decides to go for a run.

The summer sky is filled with light and the promise of more light to come. It has a golden shimmer to it. She loves running along the quiet streets lined with old trees. By the end of the summer some of them will have leaves the size of frisbees that will make a swishing sound on windy nights. Already, she misses that, and she finds herself saying goodbye to her favourite homes as she passes them. She likes to think about what they looked like inside, about the lives being lived. To think about how the road she runs on was once a field, then a dirt path, before being widened to use for cars, and then finally paved. She likes to run in the early morning or early evening, as she is now, when there are fewer people around and it is just her and the road. She paces herself, hoping to do a good distance, to make up for all the hours spent sitting in a library.

In the end she runs eleven miles, returning home in the dark. She sees it immediately, something on the step, flowers wrapped in paper. Her heart both sinks and jumps.

Breathing heavily after sprinting the last part of her run, she bends down and picks up the bouquet, sees the note sticking out of the top. Her name appears, written in black ink, the block letters so familiar to her. Three years of birthday cards, Christmas cards, Valentines. Her very first love letter. Now, apologies. Appeals for forgiveness. Forgiveness she refuses to give.

She looks around, thinking about taking it straight to the trash, but the flowers are so pretty, a spring mix with yellows and pinks. She pulls out the note, then heads to the apartment beside hers and knocks on the door.

Lucy hears the familiar sounds coming from inside and listens as the volume of the radio is lowered, as though how loud it is has some impact on what happens at the door. Lucy knows the TV will be on, although muted. Her neighbour told her she likes to think of the people on the screen keeping an eye on her, visiting her, although she doesn't care for what they have to say. 'Too much bad language these days.'

The door opens.

'Lucy!'

'Hello, Mrs Morgan,' Lucy says.

'Come in, come in. You look sweaty. Do you want some water?'

'I'm fine, thanks. I just wanted to bring you these flowers,' she says, showing them to the elderly woman. 'Do you want me to put them in water for you?'

'You know where everything is,' she says, moving back toward her chair.

Lucy walks to the kitchen and opens a cabinet, pulling out the plain glass vase she always uses and filling it with water. Mrs Morgan is standing behind her, watching.

'Your young man sent you flowers again, did he?'

Lucy turns and looks at her.

'You don't miss much, do you, Abigail?' She had told Lucy to call her Abigail years ago but Lucy falls between the two, not wanting to appear overly familiar, and not wanting to make her feel old. Lucy knows she is the only person in the building who checks on her, and her son lives in Seattle. Lucy is both her friend and her guardian. She has no idea how to address a person who fills such criteria, so she covers all the bases.

'Pour us both a sherry, and let's have a chat,' Abigail says.

Lucy needs a shower; still she does as asked, not wanting to go back to her empty apartment.

Abigail settles into her chair as Lucy brings the bottle of sherry and two glasses.

'What does this note say?'

Lucy had appeared teary-eyed at her door after an endless barrage from Hal, a call from the woman who was once her best friend saying she hadn't meant for it to happen. All Lucy could think about was them together while she'd buried her grandfather. She felt like the entire apartment building had fallen on her when she knocked on the door.

'I haven't read it.'

'Well, read it now.'

'I'm sure it's the same as the rest. He's sorry he hurt me. Blah blah blah.'

'Does he want you back?'

'He wants my forgiveness. Is that the same thing?'

'You forgive for your own health, not for his.' She takes a sip. 'But take it from someone who's been around a lot longer than you have, he's no good. Be grateful you learned that before you married him. And that friend of yours? Trash.'

Lucy winces at the statement. She had loved Hal, even though she knew her grandfather didn't like him. When Abigail had warned her. But Molly has said she was lucky, that Hal was a dish. Lucy wonders if she is capable of judging someone, knowing the tinsel from the gold as granddad used to say.

'I don't want to think about him, but I can't seem to stop.'

'It takes time, but you'll forget about him.'

'Have you ever had your heart broken?'

'Many times. By men I met before my husband, by my husband repeatedly, by friends and family. Life, Lucy, is one big heartbreak.'

'So I'm just getting started, am I?' Lucy jokes, but inside, something clicks into place. Her grandfather had said something similar to her, about learning to navigate through the heartbreaks of life. She wishes she could remember exactly what he said now. Why hadn't she paid more attention?

'You know, Granddad said something like that to me,' Lucy says. 'Just before he died.'

'Your grandfather was a wise man with a good heart. That's important. He's shown you what a good man is.'

Lucy blinks the tears that always seem about to fall away.

'He was a good man. I miss him so much,' she says.

'The pain weakens but the memories grow stronger,' Mrs Morgan says. 'That is life.' She drains her glass. 'When are we losing you?'

'I have to clear out day after tomorrow.'

'Where will you go?'

'The house in Florida.'

'I don't like to think of you alone.'

'I have the ocean for company,' Lucy says.

'You should take a trip. Do something fun. Have you been to Las Vegas?'

Lucy laughs. 'I've been to Vegas. Once was enough,' she says. She'd gone with Hal, but doesn't want to say his name out loud. They had stayed at the Paris Hotel, both of them too busy with studies to go to Europe like everyone else seemed to be doing. Lucy feels a jolt as an idea comes to her.

'Granddad wanted to take me to France and show me where he fought. Where my grandmother came from. The

27

first time he asked I had signed up for summer classes and was working at a bar. The second time I wanted to spend the summer with Hal.' She stops. 'It's one of the things I hate Hal for most, now.'

'Dear girl, don't let yourself hate. It will only make you sick.'

'I wish I had gone,' she says. Regret sucks at her chest, fills her lungs with some sort of emotional cement.

'So, go now. What's stopping you?'

A little burst of life stirs her.

'Go to France?'

'Why not? Planes go every day. You've got enough money.'

Lucy's not sure how Mrs Morgan knows this but she's right. Her grandfather left her well off, to quote his lawyer.

'Go see where he fought. Go see where your grandmother was born.'

'Maybe it's a way of atoning,' Lucy says.

'The guilt you carry, I can't believe you're not Catholic.' Abigail shakes her head. 'A change of scenery will give you a new perspective on things. Do you know where you grandmother was born?'

'I know the town, yes. Not much else. I'm not even sure of her last name. But I know my granddad's best friend is buried at Omaha. He wanted to visit his marker.'

'So you go, and you walk the land. And your grandfather will be with you in spirit. Then you come back, you go to graduate school, and you meet a good man. Soon, this will all seem like a bad dream.' Her words are so certain, Lucy thinks she might just do this.

'You'll find, Lucy, that life is a never-ending bunch of

decisions to make. You'll make some good ones, you'll make some bad ones. Learn and move on,' she says.

Lucy isn't sure how to take this. What is there to learn from Hal breaking her heart? From all she has lost? If there's a lesson to learn, she'd like to know. Maybe it would stop all the death that surrounds her.

'Now fill up my glass again, dear. It's the last time we'll be meeting like this.'

Lucy does as she is told.

* * *

Mrs Morgan falls asleep after her second sherry. Lucy tucks a blanket around her, turns the radio on low, lets herself out, as she has dozens of times before. A different feeling of sadness tugs at her, knowing this will be the last time. She reminds herself to buy Mrs Morgan a bottle of sherry before she leaves.

Her empty apartment has a spooky feeling when she returns, like it's not really hers anymore, like she's already gone. She turns on her computer and looks up flights to Paris, France. There's one leaving the day after tomorrow that is not outrageously expensive. She takes it as a sign and books it, then finds a cheap hotel near Gare du Nord. A long-missing sense of anticipation nudges out some of the grief and sadness she's been carrying as she heads to her tiny bathroom and takes a shower. Wrapped in a towel, she walks to her kitchen and drinks more water from the measuring cup, rinses it, and leaves it on the counter for the next resident.

She sees the note from Hal and thinks for a second. Picking up her phone, she considers texting him. But no, she can't. She won't. Setting the phone down, she picks up the note and throws it in the trash.

'Thanks for the flowers, Hal,' she says to the trees. Without them, she never would have thought about going to France.

THREE
ESPERANCE, FRANCE. 1937

The cake is gone. Philippe had eaten the last slice. Now, he is asleep in a chair, head falling on his chest, making horrible snoring sounds.

Maman has retired, claiming a headache, but Elise thinks it is exhaustion from trying to be normal for Philippe's friend.

It is just the two of them. William is looking out the window, and Elise is watching William, his long, lean frame outlined, almost ephemeral in the soft evening light coming in.

'Would you like to take a walk, see some of Esperance?' she asks, trying to sound casual and failing.

He turns from the window, becoming more solid as he moves toward her. 'That would be great,' he says, walking past the sprawled-out Philippe as though he was not there.

Elise slips on a sweater as William opens the door for her. He walks behind her until they make it to the street, where he falls in step beside her, his arm brushing hers softly. They move along quietly, Elise trying to think of what to say. As they turn toward the town centre William says, 'There is a church here I'd like to see. I read about it in a tourist book.'

'Oh,' is all she says. She's seen the outside – it can't be missed, the way it dominates the town, built when it was a bustling mercantile centre, the mill churning out textiles. Now it is more a village than a town, the industry long gone. There is nothing much of note now, except the church, too big, too grand for its surroundings.

Strolling along in the golden evening air Elise tells William she's never actually been inside the church. 'Maman has not gone to church since her two brothers were killed during the Great War, and Papa preferred to read on Sunday mornings.' Elise knows it is a sensation in Esperance; that they do not go to church. She hopes she has not shocked William and decides to change the subject by asking him what part of America he is from.

'Massachusetts – have you heard of it?' he asks, and Elise gives a delighted laugh. 'Like my favourite poet, Emily Dickinson.' As she speaks the first star of the evening appears, and she makes a wish.

'You like Emily Dickinson?' She can hear the pleasant surprise in his words.

'Papa taught us English by reading poetry.'

They turn a corner and the church appears, the limestone shining under the slowly emerging moonlight. It looks heavenly, ghostly. Ethereal, she decides, for she has always liked that English word. It took her ages to learn how to pronounce it.

'The church always makes me think of Quasimodo, although it is not so grand as Notre Dame.'

'You like Hugo as well?' William turns his gaze from

the church to her, and she feels herself warming under his gaze.

'I like reading.' She shrugs, trying to seem casual, and thinking, just for a second, about telling him of the time she spends alone with Papa's books. Would he think her strange? Best to keep quiet, she decides.

'Philippe has changed since I saw him last,' William says.

'He has changed a lot since Papa died.' She makes an attempt at an explanation, and to defend him.

As they cross the street a cyclist, not paying attention, careens toward them, a basket full of bread, eyes on his cargo, and William puts his hand on Elise's arm, to stop her from walking into his path. His touch is brief, but even after he takes his hand away, she can feel it, some wonderful energy zipping through her.

'The entrance is around here,' she says, moving around the side of the church. The spires reach so high into the purple evening light, the tips blend into the sky. Someone has a fire on, and the smoky scent wraps itself around the village. It is a beautiful night, the air filled with peace and possibilities.

William pushes the heavy door open and holds it for her. Elise ducks by him, catching his scent again, reminding her of the forest after it rains. They walk slowly together, Elise marvelling at the space. The church looms over the village, big and imposing, but inside it seems even larger, grander. All of France could fit inside it, she thinks. And the windows! They seem to tell a story, and their colours remind her of the jars of hard candy in the apothecary's shop in town.

She watches William move through the church, his

arms loose by his sides, his trousers still pressed sharp even after his long journey. He tilts his head back and slightly to the side, studying something. He catches her watching and motions her over.

'This is a beautiful example of Norman Romanesque architecture,' he says. 'We have nothing like this at home, nothing original at least. This building has stood for a thousand years!' In a low whisper he points out how the altar is neoclassical as Elise memorises the term to look up in the encyclopaedia at home. She is more interested now in the sound of his voice, the way he draws out his vowels, the way his minty breath falls warmly on her cheek, causing her heart to go faster than it ever has in her life. The church is beautiful, with its blue and gold ceiling glowing softly in the fluttering candlelight. But it is seeing how happy it makes William that causes a swell of pride that she calls this place home.

'The church was built when the town was an important source of trade. It is far too grand for the village now,' she says. Her father said this once, and so she repeats it, as though she knows something about local history.

Elise hears the big wooden doors of the church open, and Clotilde and Brigitte France enter. She watches the two sisters haltingly making their way down the aisle, then kneel slowly, as though they are hundreds of years old. The evening is cool but they are dressed for far colder weather, in layers of itchy wool and old clothes. She sighs softly to herself. The sisters are legendary in the village. They had been engaged to two brothers, both killed in the Great War. Elise knows they visit each day, have done since their loss. She turns her head, averting her eyes from their grief and loneliness. Silly women. They need to move on.

As William studies the church, Elise studies William. What is his life like in America? Where does he study? What are his parents like? A feeling of dread fills her, like noxious gas invading a room. Does he have a girlfriend? Somehow, she has to find out.

Elise sits in one of the pews, waiting for William, who is sketching something in a small pad – wishing, hoping he does not have a girlfriend – until he makes his way toward her and says he would like to see the crypt.

'I did not know there was one. It must be underneath?'

A smile plays with his lips as he ushers her ahead of him, and they find the steps leading down to the darkness. She does not even like the word, crypt, and is nervous until a huge space, filled with paintings on the walls, opens up in front of them. The colours surprise her, the reds still deep and the blues still strong, brightening the space. Funny, she lives so close, and knew nothing about this; an art museum of sorts, under the church.

'I had no idea this was here,' she says as they wander, staring, studying. 'It is extraordinary,' she whispers.

'Yes,' he agrees. 'It is. Such beauty and such skill, for it to have lasted a thousand years.'

There are fancy columns with lots of details at the top. William, standing behind her, tells her softly the style is called Corinthian. Elise listens closely, while studying the painted angels. Male angels, shirtless, very muscular and with enormous wings.

'I always picture angels as being plump, not ready to box one another,' she says.

William laughs softly. Then he points out how they painted the halos, like semi circles around their heads, so long ago.

Elise sees an angel who looks particularly powerful. Strong, like he could simply lean against the church and push it off its foundation. There's something about him, and she knows she will return to visit him.

'Beautiful. Just beautiful,' William says, as he follows Elise up the stairs, through the church and into the night. Elise sees this part of her home in a new light and is delighted at how impressive it is to this handsome American man.

Standing on the steps, she looks up into the sky for the star she had wished upon but can't find it among the thousands now shining, so she offers up a second wish to the Heavens: *Please don't let William have a girlfriend.* She stops for a second, then adds, *unless it is me.*

'Would you like to look around some more?' she asks.

'I would, but you look cold. What do you say to a hot drink first?'

'There's a nice spot close to the waterwheel, and you haven't seen that yet.'

'Lead the way,' he says, in his lovely accent.

It is now dark out, but Elise feels like the stars are lighting the way.

FOUR

ESPERANCE, FRANCE. SUMMER 1937

Nine weeks and four days after William leaves, Elise finds a package waiting for her at the post office. A parcel! She never gets parcels. She does not recognise the writing and looks for the return address. When she sees the name she lets out a gasp. 'William Hardwick.' Instinctively she pulls the brown crinkly paper into her chest. What on earth could he have sent her? Shaking with excitement, Elise does not even hear Amelie, the woman who runs the post office, shouting after her that she has forgotten the rest of her post.

She flies down the street and is halfway home when she abruptly stops. Will Maman want to know who has sent her a package? She thinks for a second about going to the bakery. But how would she explain wanting to open post by herself? How she wishes she had a bag she could hide it in. She remembers her papa's satchel, hanging on a peg by the back door. If it is still there, she will use it. Now, all she can do is hide it under her thin jumper and hope

Maman is upstairs in her room when she gets home. She starts to run again, excitement moving her faster than ever before.

Elise flings open the front door and races up the stairs. From the kitchen she can hear her maman call to her but for the first time in her life, Elise ignores her. Closing her bedroom door, she cautiously slides a chair under the knob. Still shaking she sits on her bed, setting the package carefully in front of her. For a moment she simply stares at it, drinking in its magic. A package for her, a present that his fingers have touched! Gently she traces his name and address with her fingertip. William Hardwick. She has thought of nothing else since she met him. As she works in the bakery, sits in school, the memory of their time together is her constant companion.

She looks at how he has written her name: *Mademoiselle Elise LaCroix*. With a sigh of delicious anticipation, she picks up the package and tugs at the string. Nothing happens. She tries again. Nothing. She will need something to cut it with. Elise looks wildly about her room. Her gaze falling on her nail scissors. She had bought them with her first pay from Monsieur Allard. Jumping up, she grabs them from the little bowl on top of her vanity table. They are so small they can't cut through the string and she has to saw through it, desperate to see what is inside. Eventually it gives way and she opens the parcel, pulling out something solid, heavy, but wrapped in delicate tissue paper. The first corner pops open just as an almighty bang comes from downstairs. Elise hesitates. A second passes, then a minute. Should she go check? She waits, listening fiercely, desperate to unwrap her gift. A few seconds tick by, and a few more. Nothing. Then the familiar sound of Maman shuffling about lets Elise know she is okay. Gently she pulls the paper away to reveal an envelope and a book.

Poetry, by Lord Byron. Elise plucks it up, staring at the dark leather cover, the gold-embossed title, before pressing it to her chest. It is the loveliest thing she has ever seen. Then she picks up the envelope. The paper feels thick and creamy in her hand. It's not sealed, so she slides the letter out, unfolds it carefully as though it were breakable.

Dear Elise,

I wanted to send you a book to celebrate your sixteenth birthday, and to say thank you for showing me around. It was kind of you to take the time.

I hope you like Byron as much as I do.

Best wishes,

William Hardwick

He'd bought her a birthday present! She can't believe it.

The memory of that night with William fills her as she gazes at his unexpected gift. She had never dreamed of something so magical. With the book resting in her lap, she pulls the paper that had protected it to her chest, grasping it tightly as another memory, the best one, fills her. When William left the next day, he had taken her hand in his own, bowed deeply and then lightly kissed her on both cheeks, saying that sadly, this was not done in the US. Her first kiss. Even though it wasn't on her lips it still counted! The memory is so strong she can almost feel his lips on her cheek now as she reads the simple note again and again, marvelling at the precise way he wrote his name, the soft blue of the ink. With a deep breath, she folds the letter and puts it back into the envelope, gently placing it under her pillow as though it is as fragile as a spider web and as valuable as diamonds.

She takes up the book again. It looks... expensive to her. The pages are like tissue and the edges gilded in gold. The black leather cover says simply *The Collected Works of Lord Byron*. With softly trembling fingers she opens the cover and starts to read. The words flow over her as she pictures William choosing this book for her. She is lost in dreamy thoughts, her heart racing, when she hears steps on the stairs outside her room. Quickly she hides the book under her bedspread.

'Elise, what are you doing in there? It is getting late.' Maman rattles the locked knob. Elise has never disappeared to her room before and Maman does not like breaks in routine. But Elise wants to keep the present, and William, to herself. It's too special to share.

Energetically she flings open the door to see her maman standing there. Instead of offering an explanation she moves past her, heading to the kitchen, already thinking about the letter she will send to William as she heats the lentil soup she made the day before, and puts bread and butter on the table. Maman will not eat much and will push the food around. Perhaps smoke. It's the smoking that bothers Elise the most, but tonight, the whole house could burn down and she wouldn't care as long as her book – and her letter – are safe. She eats quickly, makes a pot of tea, pouring some apple brandy into her maman's cup.

With her settled in front of the fire with her drink, Elise waits silently for her to fall asleep. She knows the signs, the hand weakening around the cup, her head dropping to the side, caught – it seemed to her – from snapping off her bony neck by some invisible force. When Maman's mouth drops open Elise gently takes the cup from her hands, stands and heads silently to her room. A stair creaks with a sound no louder than a kitten's purr, but to Elise it sounds like someone has dropped a piano. 'Please let her be asleep.' One second passes, then two. Nothing. She walks even softer, trying to be weightless, opening her bedroom door an inch at a time. Sitting safely on her bed she takes out some stationery, the pretty blue paper that Papa had given her for her birthday all those years ago. What will she write? Her gaze falls lovingly on the book, as though it holds answers. Plucking it from where she hid it, she carefully flips through the pages, reading until she finds a short poem called 'She Walks In Beauty'. When she is done, she reads it again, wondering what it would feel like to have someone feel this way about you. About her. She reads it again and again, until she has it memorised. Taking the first sheet of paper she begins, 'Dear William'.

Thank you for the book. When I got the package I had no idea what could be inside and it was exciting to open it. I've looked at a few of the poems and so far I like 'She Walks in Beauty' the best.

Elise nibbles the end of the pen as what she wants to say to William takes shape in her mind. Since they met she has passed endless hours thinking about what he could be doing, reliving their evening together. No, she won't tell him of those things. She remembers the walk to the church and almost telling him about the time she spends in the woods. She will tell him now. In a letter it is easier to be brave.

I took a walk in the woods on the other side of town,

close to the train station. It's not near the church and you didn't see them when you visited, which is a shame. It feels like its own little world, and even though I can see the tops of the roofs nearby I pretend I am all alone in the middle of someplace magical. There's no real path but I always walk the same way, over pine needles and bracken, and each time I walk it I see a path beginning. I know it is my creation, and I like this.

The other day I went for a walk just after it rained and discovered a tiny patch of bluebells. The petals were wet and glossy and I thought, just for a second, about picking them. It seemed somehow sad that they were hidden in an area and no one would see them but me. But the fact that they were there at all was enough. Besides, they seemed happy where they were, and would have wilted quickly if I picked them. They belonged where they were.

Tell me, what are the flowers like in Massachusetts? What about your land inspired the poetry of so many greats?

Dreamily, Elise reads what she has written, thinking of both William and the flowers. It would never occur to her to tell anyone else. Her friends at school would think her crazy, but with him it feels right. Thinking of how he studied the roof of the church, she knows he will understand. She jots down a few more words before picking up the book and reading. As she turns the pages she forgets the time until the chime from the downstairs clock startles her. Slipping the book away, she makes her way down the stairs to Maman, who is still asleep in the chair. Every night Elise wakes her and puts her to bed, but this time she lets her sleep. Covering her with a blanket, she checks the fire, making sure the grate is in place, then goes back to her room to read some more poetry. And to think about what else to write to William.

She sighs. What a perfect day it has been.

FIVE
NORTHERN FRANCE. SUMMER 2009

The wind catches Lucy as she steps off the train in Normandy. It's cold despite the clear sky and bright sun, and it feels, somehow, like two days in one. Pulling her knapsack over her shoulders, she walks down the ramp to the parking lot. The first thing she sees is a billboard advertising tours to the landing beaches. It makes her stop, just for a second. To the left of it are some tall trees swaying in the wind as though they are waving a greeting to her. In the distance, rising above the town, are the spires of a church. She's been here five minutes, and already she loves Normandy as much as she loved Paris. She continues walking.

The street divides ahead of her, a fork in the road. Without thinking she heads right, happy to wander if she is wrong, but feeling instinctively she is on the correct path. She walks past houses with window boxes filled with red flowers, shutters open. So pretty. Like she pictured it, she thinks, a quintessential French village, a French town. A little like the village from *Beauty and the Beast*, or at least the pictures in her storybooks.

The smell of baking bread drifts toward her as she crosses the street. She feels the uneven grey cobblestones through her trainers. A bakery appears and then another, and another. They are everywhere, it seems, like in Paris. She'd spent a week there, feeling each day like a new and better person, discovering there was more to life than university and heartbreak. There were grand old cathedrals with gargoyles, corner bistros where famous authors once gathered, winding streets filled with boutiques, hotel rooms that looked out over a river that had carved its way through the most beautiful city in the world. Paris both took her breath away and filled her up, with a joy she had never experienced before.

Hal had texted, but after a few days she didn't even bother to read them, just deleted them. Apologies were useless. And she would never understand how he could claim to love her and do what he did. Paris distracted her, and she was grateful.

It had been hard to leave it, but she had promises to keep, both to herself, and to her grandfather. And that can only be done here, in the land where D-Day was fought.

On a corner she sees a sign for her hotel, and an arrow. She follows it and finds the building, small and white, just off the main road. It looked so much bigger online. There's a bakery beside it, with a yellow and blue awning rippling in the wind. Lucy takes a minute to look in the big window at the croissants and pastries. She thinks about getting something to eat, but decides to wait until she checks in. She has too much to carry right now.

Inside and grateful to be out of the whistling wind, she

digs out her reservation, handing it to the girl at the desk. She has glossy black hair cut into a bob, perfect red lips and black glasses, the kind with thick rims. She looks like something out of a magazine. Her eyes narrow as she looks at Lucy, wearing a sweater that belonged to her father, and carrying her grandfather's old satchel, like someone from another time. Her lips are slightly chapped, too. She needs to buy some lip balm. A quick look in the mirror behind the desk shows the wind has done some wild things to her hair.

'*Bonjour,*' Lucy says. She'd been surprised in Paris at how much French she understood. She had taken French as an elective at college but hadn't really spoken it before. The Parisians did not seem impressed by her efforts, but Lucy had felt a sense of ease with the language she hadn't anticipated, and she wonders now if it's because of her French genes.

The clerk – a little white tag says her name is Helene – speaks to her in slow, precise French, about the stairs to her room. Lucy is surprised at how easily she understands. She hands her a key, a real key, heavy and old, with a red tassel on it. It doesn't fit with the clean white modern lobby at all. Lucy puts it in her pocket and makes her way to the stairs. They are covered in an ugly red carpet with some sort of black design, and Lucy thinks they must be renovating as they go. Maybe that was why it was the cheapest place she found, right in the town centre.

On the third floor she turns on the landing, looking up and down the hall before she sees an archway leading to a twisting flight of small steps. They must be the ones she was warned about, leading to her room on the fourth floor. They are small, the hallway claustrophobic, like something that would lead to an attic, and Lucy struggles with her case, banging it into the wall twice. At the top is a door, the only one. Lucy opens it to a drab, shadowy place, like a crime scene from an old movie. There's a darkness that no number of lamps and light bulbs can fix. The single window on the far side of the room looks like a postage stamp on a large letter. It's not big enough to be of much help.

She clicks on the light and a depressing glow fills the room, showing ugly forest green carpet and a bedspread in an orange colour that makes her think of the horrible marmalade with the stringy bits that Granddad used to put on his toast every morning. A faint scent of mildew hangs in the air. She crosses to the tiny window and after a few attempts manages to open it, then looks down at the small parking lot below. In the distance, toward the train station, there are more trees and houses, a long line of connected rooftops forming an arc. They look like a shield.

Lucy tosses her bag on the bed and unzips it, rummaging around until she finds her toothbrush and heads for the bathroom. Unlike the dark old-fashioned bedroom, it is bright, filled with sunlight. The walls and the floor are lined in glossy white tiles. There's a large white tub, the kind with claw feet and a stand-up shower in the corner. The room feels like they started to remodel and then gave up.

Back out on the street, not far from her hotel, she sees another sign advertising tours to the landing beaches, and heads into the shop. An old-fashioned bell, attached to the top of the doorframe, tinkles as Lucy catches her satchel in the door, pulling her up short, causing her to give a little yelp of surprise. She has to wrestle herself free. When she looks up she sees a man walking toward her. He's her age, maybe a year or two older, with large grey eyes like nothing she's ever seen before, the colour of the sea on an overcast day. Between his eyes is a small crease, like a paper cut. He tilts his head slightly, acknowledging her, looking like he's about to laugh, and Lucy feels the effects with her entire body as she struggles to get the strap of her bag out of the door handle.

'Can I help?' His American accent surprises her. Lucy looks up as she manages to unhook her bag.

'I'd like to book a tour, please.' She'll pretend the catch did not happen.

He nods, like he's in on her plan, then he turns, heads to the counter. Lucy finds herself looking directly into his back. She's five seven and figures he must be at least six four or five. Lean, like a runner. Taller than Hal. More attractive, too. The thought surprises her.

'We have morning and afternoon tours to each of the beaches, but many are sold out. Is there one in particular you want to see?' He takes out a pamphlet detailing all of the tours, laying it out in front of her. She sees Omaha Beach, and points.

'Here.' She presses her fingertip to the spot on the map. Her grandfather's friend is buried there. She knows granddad landed there on D-Day. She doesn't know much else, but she's hoping the land jars some forgotten memories loose.

'We have one space on a tour going out in the morning. Does that work for you?'

Lucy nods, and opening her grandfather's old satchel, she takes out some of the euros she bought for the trip.

'Just you?'

'Just me,' she says, giving him her name.

'Someone will pick you up at your hotel in the morning. Where are you staying?'

She tells him, glancing again at his eyes. It was not a trick of the light. She can't figure out what colour they are. But she looks away. The first thing she noticed about Hal was his eyes. She won't make that mistake again.

'Thank you for your help,' she says, and turns to leave.

'Careful with the door,' he replies.

'Ha ha,' Lucy says, over her shoulder.

She makes a show of letting herself out, grasping her bag to her chest, stepping around the door, then turns to give him a smirk. She is pleased when he laughs.

The town centre is so quaint. Everything so close together. She meanders, looking into shop windows, trying to figure out what to do next. On the corner, she stops in front of a leather shop. A leather journal, the colour of a perfectly toasted marshmallow, catches her eye, and Lucy goes inside. The floor is made of rough timber, and there's a man in an apron of some kind sitting at a sewing machine. He looks up at her and she asks about the journal, pointing to the window. He nods, setting down the belt he is working on and pulling the journal out, wiping the cover with a cloth from his apron pocket before handing it to Lucy. He tells her it has been in the window a while, and the sun has bleached it. He offers her a discount on the price and Lucy laughs, as the different hues are what caught her attention.

'I'll take it,' she says digging out some more euros. He wraps the journal in tissue paper, and then puts it in a brown bag, the kind with twine handles. They always make her think of Victorian Christmas celebrations. Of Dickens. She takes the bag, almost forgets her change, then heads into the waning light. She looks in the window of the jeweller's next door, and then a boutique that sells scarfs and purses, before stopping at a bakery and buying a baguette with cheese. She sits in the park across from her hotel. Protected by an enclave of three large trees, Lucy takes out the journal, to make a plan of what she can do now that she is here, where Granddad met his wife, in this little place in Normandy.

* * *

In the morning, Lucy heads to the lobby early, hoping she can grab a coffee before being picked up for the tour, but when she reaches the bottom step, she sees him, talking to Helene, who is wearing what Lucy thinks is a seductive smile along with her hotel uniform. Like a vixen in the romance novels she used to read in secret, knowing her grandfather would never approve.

The slope of his shoulders, the way his black hair catches the light. He could easily be a hero from one of those novels. As she stares, he turns and looks directly at her.

'Hello,' he says, crossing the lobby. 'Are you ready?'

Lucy nods, hoping he did not see her looking. He holds the door open for her, and she squeezes past him, noticing his scent – clean and soapy and something else. Something minty.

'We're in the white van.' He steps ahead of her and opens the passenger door. 'We have three couples coming so you have to sit up front with me.'

'Okay,' she says, as he closes the door for her.

Lucy feels the bumps as the tyres move slowly over the

cobblestones that make up the old road. The same road she walked yesterday. The same road her grandmother may have walked, many years ago. Maybe her grandfather, too. She wishes she knew.

* * *

'Our first stop is Pointe du Hoc, where the Americans came ashore on D-Day,' Rob, as he has introduced himself, begins once all the group is in the van. Lucy listens as he tells them about the US Rangers, and how many of them died scaling the cliffs they're about to see. She pictures the opening scene from *Saving Private Ryan* and wishes she had watched it with her grandfather. Instead, she rented it with Hal.

The sun is shining and the sky cloudless. She looks out the van's window at the French countryside, dotted with farmhouses, barns, cows. It's hard to believe a war was fought here. It's so peaceful, so uncluttered. At home there would be billboards telling them where to eat and how far they were from Pointe Du Hoc. There is none of that here. Unlike the town, where everything is compact, here there is space.

Then Rob is turning, pulling into an empty lot where he stops and parks. Wordlessly they all get out of the van. The brightness of the sun fooled them into thinking it was nice out, but it is cold at Pointe du Hoc, with a wind her granddad would refer to as raw coming from the Channel. Lucy wishes she'd brought a heavier jacket as she follows Rob, walking toward the water, the cliffs. They are getting very close to the edge when Rob turns and starts to speak about Operation Overlord and how many men were involved, of the events of D-Day that took place right where they stand.

Lucy knows her grandfather was one of those men. She wants to tell the group that, a burst of pride filling her, but she stays quiet, looking at the landscape, as ominous as any military force. To the left the cliffs continue, and she sees them across the rough Channel waters. Sees how high they are, and the sheer drop of them into the sea. Soldiers had climbed them while having mortars, bullets, shells lobbed at them. It's a miracle any of them survived.

She can hear the chop of the water on the rocks, and even though she's five feet from the edge, Lucy feels nervous. It's like she's standing in war-torn France and the very air is unleashing a war cry, the crash of the waves the sounds of artillery around her. The wind is picking up, its wail increasing as it blows around the group huddled on the cliff, making jackets flutter like sails. Dust gets into Lucy's eyes and they start to water as she wraps her arms around herself, trying to warm up, to create a barrier to whatever is attacking her.

Rob has stopped talking, and looking up, she sees he's walking toward her. When he's a step or two away he lifts his hand and unzips his fleece. In one smooth movement it slides from his shoulders, revealing a grey V-neck sweater over a white cotton T-shirt. He reaches around and drapes his fleece over her shoulders. Warmth from his body envelops Lucy as his scent fills her senses, clean and comforting. She breathes it in as she slides her arms through the sleeves. They're miles too long and hang past her hands and she lets them, feeling something more than warmth from the gesture.

He continues talking about Hitler's plans, the Atlantic Wall, the weather on the coast.

'If everyone is done here, we'll head out for the next stop,' he says, raising his voice above the wind. Everyone heads back to the van, Rob leading the way. He opens the door and again takes out a little stool for the women to help them into the van, offering them each his hand.

'Such a gentleman,' says one woman, grasping Rob's hand tightly as he helps her.

Lucy sees Rob blush. He catches her eye and they share a brief smile, before climbing into the van to continue their trip.

* * *

Pointe du Hoc is four miles from Omaha Beach. The wind seems to be pushing against the van, and it is too loud, too aggressive, to have the windows rolled down. No one in the van is speaking at first, until one of the men asks Rob to show them a hedgerow.

'Beside us. Everywhere.' He points, and Lucy looks at the thick green tangles of tall shrubs, heavy and formidable, lining the side of the road.

'What's the significance of them?' a woman asks.

'The Allied invasion was held up due to the thickness of the hedges that lined the roads. They hid the German tanks, so it was slow going for the Allies.' Rob lifts his arm, pointing toward a farmhouse. 'See the fence. What it's made of?'

There is movement in the van as everyone shifts to see where he's pointing.

'The Allied planes landed in fields on wire that had

been rolled out, making a landing strip of sorts. If you look there, see?' He points to a fence that looks like it was made of some sort of barbed wire. 'The fence is made from the material they used for the landing strips.'

From the back a female voice says, 'It's lasted so long.'

The fence disappears as the van moves along, sunlight appearing and disappearing behind the hedgerows, casting shadows on the road ahead. Lucy wonders what Granddad would think, seeing this place now, how different it would look to him.

And then another parking lot, huge this time, with rows of tour buses. It takes Lucy a minute to realise they're at Omaha. The American Cemetery. The beach where Granddad fought. The cemetery where his friend is buried, the one he wanted to visit all those years ago. The reason she came on this trip. If there is anyway her grandfather can send her a sign, she hopes he does now. Hopes he guides her to the marker he wanted to visit.

Rob parks, and they step outside, to the solid ground of the parking lot. The wind has softened, and Lucy can feel the sunlight on her face.

It's not how she pictured it. But she had pictured Capa's photos from D-Day, as though history was still playing out, that one day being repeated over and over.

Now it's a sunny day in August, but it still feels dark. And haunted. Maybe that's what violence does to the land.

* * *

Rob gathers them in a little group. 'At this part of the tour I usually let people wander. You may have a stone you wish to visit or spend some time in the chapel, and you may want to walk on the beach itself. There's a path that takes you there. It's a big area, and you have two hours. Please be back here at the van then. I'll walk you in.' And then they are part of the crowd, walking quietly, some with heads already bowed, toward the land France gifted to the USA.

Colleville-sur-Mer cemetery, where ten thousand soldiers are buried. Some Lucy's age, or not much older. Some younger. Lucy thinks about the day she spent at Père Lachaise in Paris, the elaborate tombs to the artists and writers. The famous who were buried there had lived their lives, been singers, artists, writers. Here, the only story the dead have to tell is how they died. They had not had the chance to write their own stories.

She is not prepared for the sheer magnitude of it. The way the gravestones stretch into the distance, shine in the sun. Rob is ahead of her, walking purposefully toward a marker. It feels intrusive, but she watches him as he stops in front of a stone, placing his hand on top. She thinks she sees his lips moving, like he is saying a prayer. He dips his head, his hand still resting on the stone.

She reaches out and touches the marker beside her. It's cool under her hand, despite the sun, and she is surprised by this. Moving softly along, she whispers the names she sees. They are not buried according to name or rank. She's not sure how the markers are placed. She'll have to ask Rob.

Then she sees a Farrell, from Rhode Island, and stops. She was born in Rhode Island. If Granddad had died, there would be a marker that said Corrigan, Rhode Island. If he had died, he would not have married, had her dad. Lucy would not be here now. It all feels so arbitrary, so tenuous. So random. She wishes again that she knew the name of Granddad's friend, so she could place her hand on his marker. Pay her respects. Somehow, she hopes her granddad knows she is here, that she is thinking of him. She should say a prayer but has no idea how. She waits a few seconds, before turning away from the sea of markers, toward the sound of the waves. The English Channel, which divides England from France. Part of the Atlantic Ocean, the same ocean she lives on thousands of miles away. It sounds different here, louder, but she doesn't stop to wonder why. She simply responds to the siren call of the waves.

* * *

There's a path that goes from the cemetery to the sea. It starts out as large smooth stones, then changes to a wooden walkway, like the beach boardwalks in Florida. Lucy sees a sign in French saying it is a protected area, just before the walkway ends and the sand of the beach begins. Saltiness hangs in the air, waves break gently on the shore, and Lucy sees the English Channel before her. She moves toward it, the earth under her feet both solid and uneven at the same time, the mix of sand and sea. War and peace. Past and present day.

She looks around, trying to figure out where Pointe du Hoc is in relation to where she is standing. Where does Omaha end, and where do the four other beach heads begin? The Americans fought here, and at Utah. The Canadians at Juno, and the French and British at Sword and Gold. She turns in a circle, trying to sort her cardinal points. Facing the land, Utah is to the left of Omaha. She wishes she could so easily figure out where her grandfather had walked.

Making her way to the water, and seeing no one nearby, Lucy slips off her shoes and socks. The sand is cold under her feet, and the water splashing her toes makes her gasp. She stares down, as though she may see blood. What did it feel like for these young soldiers to jump from the landing craft, wade into the frigid water, the sounds of artillery filling the air, the ting of bullets bouncing off the landing craft? Being cold was probably the least of their worries. As the water numbs her feet, she tries to picture what took place in this spot, all those years ago, what it must have been like for the young men who walked into bullets as thick as flies on a hot night. But there are some things no one can imagine.

SIX

ESPERANCE, FRANCE. 1937

When Elise wakes to the sound of the rain on her windowpane she feels a jolt of appreciation run through her. The forest was tinder-dry, the reservoir as well. A nice rainfall was needed to remedy both situations, but it is not for those reasons she is pleased. Staring at the rain as it dances on the streets, she has a feeling of hope. Maybe the bad times are being washed away, and new, better times are coming. She slips from bed and takes a bath, then quickly twists her hair into a bun and pulls on a dress and stockings, then her papa's raincoat. It is far too big and she had to fold up the arms but it keeps her warm and dry. She had planned to buy a new coat with the money she made at the bakery, but discovered she likes wearing the coat. It has his scent. It makes her feel safe, like being wrapped in one of his hugs. And it is warm. She cannot get a cold. There is simply no time to be sick.

She checks and sees Maman is still in bed, sleeping. The lines that cut her face are softened in rest, and Elise hopes she awakes feeling better. Grabbing an umbrella, she steps onto the slick steps and walks purposefully to the bakery to start her shift.

'Bonjour, Monsieur Allard. Bonjour, Marianne.' The bells above the door tinkle as usual, announcing her arrival. She pauses, enjoying the smell of bread. She loves the aromas in the bakery and often jokes with the large jolly baker that she can smell icing.

'Bonjour, chérie,' his voice rings through the room. You always knew where he was. It was one of the many things she loved about him.

Making her way to the kitchen, she slips on an apron and asks what needs to be done. As he wildly gestures she finds she is already thinking about her lunch break, when she can run to the post office, across the park. Somehow, she knew today was the day, and that a letter would arrive. She fills the baskets with bread, frosts a cake. Michel visits and she sits with him for a few moments, feeding him a tart she'd broken when taking it out of the pan. Then she washes baking bowls and trays, usually her least favourite part of the job but today she does not mind. As she works, the soap flakes making her sneeze more than once, she pictures Amelie at the post office, with her big mane of red hair that would be so frizzy with today's rain, handing her William's letters in that coy way she has. Finally, as the arms fall into place on the large clock above the counter indicating it is two o'clock, Elise asks if she can pop out for a few moments.

Monsieur Allard frowns. 'Is something wrong at home?' He looks out the window at the rain.

'No. I would like to check the post. It has been a few days.'

'But of course. Off you go.' He gives one arm a wide

swoop, sending her on her way and making her laugh. Monsieur Allard is so filled with energy and life.

Elise races to the post office, the rain continuing to dance about her, the old raincoat keeping her dry. Once inside she notices the quiet. For a moment her happiness falters and she steps toward Amelie with a wobbly smile. Elise notices she has a headband trying to control her crazy red curls – trying, but not succeeding. What if he hadn't written? What if he never wrote again? The thought does not sit well with her. She'd only spent a few hours with him but somehow those hours seemed the most important in her life.

A few men are huddled around a paper, talking about Mussolini and Hitler. They seem afraid of Germany's leader, afraid of fascism. Elise is not even sure what that is and has no interest in politics or Germany or Italy. Life has enough challenges in her tiny part of France without worrying about things she can't control.

'Lots of post today.' Amelie grins as she hands over a neat stack of mail tied with string. On the very top sits a blue air mail envelope. She knows the paper. She knows the handwriting. Excitement thrums through her.

'Thank you.' Elise blushes, grabbing everything up in her arms but only noticing the one small envelope.

'And how is your mother?'

'Good, thank you.' She must get back to the bakery. And she won't be able to read William's letter until later this evening. Still, knowing it is in her satchel makes her giddy for the rest of the day. As she watches the minutes tick by, the rain gives way to a rainbow, and she smiles.

* * *

At home Elise goes straight to her room and sits on her bed. She looks at the envelope for a moment, maybe two, before carefully opening it.

William's letter is two pages long, on thin blue paper that matches the envelope. She marvels again at his neat, perfect writing.

Dear Elise,

Thank you for your lovely note. I am pleased my book arrived, and that you enjoyed it. It was the least I could do after my visit. It was kind of you to show me around.

Your time reading in the woods sounds delightful. During the summer I like to sit with a pile of books on the beach, next to my parents' house. When the weather cools, I like to sit at the library. I have a favourite spot, close to a window where I can see the trees. I am sitting there now as I write this, taking a break from the rigours of studying.

You asked about the poets inspired by my area of the world. That is a difficult question to answer, since I do not have a creative bone in my body. But I think people connect to the land in different ways. My mother can spend hours watching the hummingbirds at the feeder, while my father probably is not even aware there are hummingbirds – maybe even birds at all – around. But on the rare occasions she gets him to go for a walk, he always comes back with a stone in his pocket. Sometimes he knows what they are, other times he looks in a large book he has. In a different time I think he would have been an archaeologist.

People are so different, in their interests at least, and who knows what spoke to Whitman, Dickinson, even Hugo. I will say that each place has its own beauty, but you would be hard pressed to find a spot more beautiful than New England when the leaves change.

I am reading a book by Pearl S Buck, called The Good Earth. *Have you heard of it? It has won the Pulitzer and I can see why, although the story is sad. Some people have such challenges in their lives. If you have read it, do let me know.*

Best wishes,

William Hardwick

Elise reads the letter three times, from start to finish, but lingers over the part about letting him know her thoughts on *The Good Earth*. Surely that is an invitation to write back. It almost makes up for the 'best wishes'. Holding the pages gently to her heart, she looks out the window and dreams. Of seeing him again. Holding his hand. Falling in love... After folding the letter up she carefully places it in the envelope, then sets it in her father's old steamer trunk she has dragged from the storage room, under the steps. The noise she had made caused Maman to yell, but she wants to keep the things William gave her safe. She sets the new letter inside then gently closes the lid.

Tomorrow, she will go to the library and get a copy of *The Good Earth*.

SEVEN
OMAHA BEACH. 2009

Bending down, Lucy puts her hands in the water. She thinks again about soldiers jumping from the landing craft, up to their necks in the icy water now stinging her own skin, and walking toward bullets. *Granddad was one of them.* How do you go from high school or college, to fighting in a war? And then she thinks about where she is standing. What was it like to have your country invaded? A cold feeling of dread that has nothing to do with the water grips her, and she shivers slightly as she stands, moving away from the ebbing waves, thinking. What if she got up one morning, opened the back door to the porch *to let the sunshine in*, as Granddad said, and there were a bunch of soldiers walking across the sand, toward the house. Where do you hide? How do you survive? And how do you go on, after?

She rubs her hands together, trying to get them warm, and looks down the beach. Someone is coming toward her.

Rob.

'Hello,' he says softly, just loud enough to be heard over the waves.

'Hello,' she replies, his presence pulling her from her imaginings. 'Am I running late? Were you waiting for me?'

'No, we have time. I just... I saw you on the beach, by yourself, and wanted to check on you.'

'Oh,' is all she manages, caught off guard by his simple kindness, and feeling silly pulling her socks on her damp, sand-coated feet.

'That's nice of you, thanks. I'm fine.' She wobbles slightly as she stands and he offers his hand for support. She takes it, feels the warmth from him. Her hands are so cold.

'Are you travelling on your own?'

'I am, yes.'

He nods – she can tell by the way his head moves in his shadow on the beach as she straightens. Together they start to walk.

'What part of the States are you from?' she asks.

'Massachusetts. You?'

'I live in Florida but was born in Rhode Island.'

'We were neighbours, then.'

'I was very young when I left,' she says. 'Do you live here?'

'For now. When did you arrive?'

'Here, yesterday.' She pauses. 'Seems longer, though.'

'What brings you to this area on your own, Lucy?'

'My grandfather fought here.' It's not the whole story, but it is the truth.

He waits, as though he knows there is more.

'And he met his wife here.'

'In Normandy?'

She nods. 'Did you have anyone fight here?' she asks, remembering him resting his hand on a marker at the cemetery.

'My grandfather lost his older brother. He tells me all the time how much I look like him.'

They move from the beach to the path, the sound of the waves mingling with the swoosh of the swaying trees, their gentle tread on the wooden planks. The cemetery appears again, as overwhelming as the first time. One of the men from the tour joins them by the reflecting pool, asking Rob questions, and Lucy is left to her own thoughts.

She walks to the shimmering water, which is glowing in the strengthening morning sun, then turns toward the ocean of markers. Her wonderful, kind funny grandfather, who she loved more than anyone on earth, survived. And she is so grateful.

EIGHT

ESPERANCE, FRANCE. 1937

It does not take Elise long to read *The Good Earth*. Not because she loves it, in fact she finds it very sad, but because she knows she can write a letter to William when she is done and tell him her thoughts. She does not talk to Maman, and Marianne is always so busy. There is a new girl in the village; she's come from Brussels and lives with her aunt and uncle, close to the library in town. Genevieve is her name. There is something both captivating and frightening about her. She has black hair and green eyes and is very beautiful. They have spoken at the library, when they meet. She is a keen reader, sharp as a dagger, and Elise watches her pore over atlases, planning something. A trip, yes, but something more. An escape. Elise knows, because she feels the same way. Genevieve is not like the other girls in town. But then, neither is Elise. Perhaps that is what draws them together at the library.

In the twilight, in her room, the sky that whitish colour it takes on as the days become colder, Elise sits at her desk and writes to William. She knows every word of his last letter but has still taken it from the trunk and set it beside her. Her copy of *The Good Earth* sits next to her as well.

Dear William,

I hope this note finds you well.

I have just finished reading The Good Earth. *Not for the faint of heart, is it? I was not sure what the Boxer Rebellion was, so went to the library to look it up. Did I tell you I am working there now, as well as at the bakery? Just a few times a week, and I really like it, especially when we receive new books. Sometimes I think it would be nice to live in a library and look up whatever you want to know, whenever you want to know it. But we must be grateful for what we have, especially compared to poor Wang-Lung and his wife. When O-lan kills her baby after birth to spare her a life of poverty and pain, I had to set the book aside for a few hours and just think about how badly some people have it. I was horrified reading about the Boxer Rebellion. Imagine having jewels and fine things while others around you starve. Terrible.*

So, hasn't this note taken a cheery turn!

What is it like in Massachusetts now? Are you still reading on the beach or are you inside, cosy and warm? Do you have snow? We get what I would call gentle coatings of snow, and it is very pretty but I would love to see a big snowfall, with drifts and covered roofs and sparkly lights reflected from the silvery whiteness. What is a big snowstorm like, with towering snowdrifts?

She takes a sip of her drink. It is time to change the subject before she sounds like a weatherman.

You must be studying now. I am sure it is stressful, but it must also be satisfying, learning something new and proving you know it to others.

Elise wants to train as a pastry chef, but there were no places nearby, and Maman could not be left alone. She does not tell him this. She used to dream of going to Paris, but now she dreams of Boston, but that might as well be the moon.

What is your favourite part of being a student? I would like to know.

Ending the letter, she folds it up, putting it into an envelope. She will mail it tomorrow, before she goes to work at the bakery.

* * *

As the days grew shorter Elise thinks about sending William a Christmas gift. One day, when the air was so cold Elise had to snuggle into her scarf when she went outside, she walked by a shop and saw a leather-bound journal in the window, a soft colour that reminded her of the bales of hay in the farmer's fields nearby. Somehow, she could see William sitting in a chair by a window, a pen in his hand, writing in it.

She was saving her centimes when Marianne said one Saturday when work was quiet and they were sharing a hot drink that it was always a good idea to make men work for your attention. Elise had never spoken of William to Marianne but knew, somehow, why this advice was being handed over. So she kept saving her money and stopped walking by the shop with the journals in case she weakened. She did buy him a nice Christmas card depicting the waterwheel in town decorated with ivy and red berries and wrote a cheerful message inside in her best flowing handwriting. Then she waited. And waited. As she walked to the bakery and worked at the library, and cleaned the house and cared for Maman, she waited.

Nothing. Perhaps it was all over. Perhaps he did not agree with her thoughts on *The Good Earth*. But no, that would be ridiculous. Perhaps a new girlfriend now takes up all of his time. The thought makes her insides go cold.

And then, two days before Christmas, as the wind blew and large snowflakes fell, Elise makes her way to the post office. From the big smile on Amelie's face she knows something is waiting for her. She had never spoken of William to Amelie, but somehow, in her town, everyone knows everything.

'Bonjour, Elise. Happy Christmas,' Amelie chirps, handing over a brown paper parcel with the now familiar writing. Simple joy floods her and with softly trembling hands Elise slides the parcel and the other post inside Papa's satchel. The worn leather and the smell, deep and rich and earthy, reminds her so much of him. Smiling brightly at Amelie, she closes the bag; then forces herself to be still and chat for a few moments, trying to both contain her excitement and be polite. The post office was so jolly this time of year, and everyone in good spirits. It is funny, but Amelie's hair seems even redder during the holidays.

'Is Philippe coming for Christmas?' Amelie asks, cutting brown paper for a parcel. Elise nods, although Philippe had not yet shown up and they had expected him the day before. Maman is in despair; she is always worse at holiday time. Elise did her best, with a small tree and a rum cake, a gift of some soap for Maman, and socks for Philippe, but she knows there will be nothing for her. Philippe, if he shows, wouldn't bother and Maman does not leave the house. The post office fills up so Elise steps away, giving

Amelie a cheery wave before setting off for the boulangerie. Feeling the weight of the parcel now resting on her hip, seeing the size of it, she has an idea of what it may be, and already she is filled with anticipation. How she'll be able to stop tearing the wrapper off as soon as she gets in, she doesn't know. But she wants something really special to mark this first holiday of knowing William, something for herself, so she will save it for Christmas morning. She will resist.

The tinkle of bells above the door sounds particularly jaunty and festive, as Elise steps inside, a whirl of wind and snow making her entrance dramatic. The smell of pastries and cakes fills the air and customers fill the shop. Quickly she steps into the back and pulls on an apron, noticing Marianne is nowhere to be seen, which is odd.

'*Alors, bon,* you are here,' says Monsieur Allard. 'You wait on customers and I will refill the cabinet.'

'Of course.' Elise steps easily into his spot, wrapping up baguettes and packing up Christmas cakes. The fruit had been soaking in spirits for weeks and seeing the finished product only adds to her happiness. The bells over the door ring constantly and Elise never stops, even as she thinks of William, and her parcel. They work well past closing time and only shut the shop door when there is nothing left to sell. Monsieur Allard is beaming.

'Alors, bon!' he declares as he locks the door with such force the bells jangle and seem to dance. Crossing the floor he pulls Elise into his arms, as though they, too, are about to dance.

'*Merry Christmas, lovely Elise!*' he cries. Elise feels the heat from the ovens and his hard work. She is trying not to be smothered in his embrace when Marianne appears with

Michel beside her and says, 'Put her down before you suffocate the poor girl!' but she, too, laughs. Single file, they climb up the windy stairs to their flat above the shop. Elise lets out a small gasp at what she sees. Although she had been expecting something as Monsieur Allard believes in celebrating, she revels in the rich aroma of food. Marianne has laid out a spread for them, with bread and cheese and the rich beef stew that is her husband's favourite. The delicious smells, the satisfaction of hard work, the anticipation of what her parcel may hold, all make Elise light-headed with pleasure.

'We'll have a small Christmas party, just us.' He beams.

'After you.' Monsieur Allard waves her to a chair, pulling it out for her. Elise sees a parcel in bright glossy paper on the seat and knows it is for her. She has a small trinket for Michel of course, but nothing for Marianne and Bertrand. A tiny bit of guilt mars her happy mood.

'A little something from Michel for all the time you spend tickling him,' Marianne pipes up. 'Why don't you open it now?' Marianne always knows what to do, in any situation. It is a gift Elise wishes she had.

'The paper is so lovely.' Elise is careful not to rip it as she slowly peels the tape away. It crinkles as she pushes the ends apart to find something soft and pink. It's a large scarf, a shawl. Holding it up she sees dainty threads of burgundy and gold stitched magically into the shape of butterflies and wildflowers.

'Oh, it's beautiful,' Elise breathes, carefully touching the silky material.

'Bertrand got it in Paris. None of the girls here will have anything like it. You will be unique.'

'She already is!' Monsieur Allard beams over his shoulder as he ladles up dishes of stew.

Elise has never seen anything so pretty in her entire life. Standing, she wraps it around her shoulders and looks in the tiny mirror over the sink.

'It looks pink in some lights and blue in other. It shimmers,' she says, turning around in the light. She feels so pretty with it wrapped around her. 'Thank you so much.' Bending she gives first Marianne, and then Monsieur Allard, kisses. Then she sits and eats, feeling safe and happy as the snow continues to fall outside.

By the time Elise is ready to leave it is snowing so hard Monsieur Allard declares he will accompany her. He reaches for his heavy overcoat, but Elise stops him, placing her small hand firmly on his arm.

'Don't be silly – stay inside and warm with your family. I'll be fine.'

'At least take my hat, and scarf.' He wraps his long woolly knit scarf, bigger and thicker than her own, around her neck. The wind grabs the door and she is grateful when he pulls it back. The snow feels like ice, stinging her eyes and her cheeks. She can't remember it ever being this cold or snowing this hard. The walk takes twice as long as usual, as she battles a wind that feels like it is both grabbing her and holding her back at the same time. She pushes on, trying not to think about what lies ahead. When she reaches her house her heart sinks. It looks so dark and ominous. There's no holly wreath on the door, no porch light casting a welcoming glow, not even a glow of light from a window. It feels like a mausoleum. Gloomily she opens the door, knowing Philippe is not there. Maman is sitting alone in the dark, a bottle of

Calvados beside her. Elise grits her teeth and lights a fire silently.

'There's no way Philippe will make it in this weather,' Elise says, looking out the window. Even though it should be dark out the sky is white with snow and cloud, creating a ghostly grey colour. She closes her eyes and reminds herself that behind all the snow and clouds the moon is out, watching over her, the way Papa used to tell her when she was little and had bad dreams. She turns to set the table and sees Maman asleep in her chair, her head bobbing, her legs splayed at grotesque angles. Suddenly it is too much for Elise, the never-ending sadness, the dark empty house, the lies from her brother. A log in the fireplace crackles and snaps, making Maman jerk slightly, but she does not wake. Elise sees she has drool on her lip. Her stomach tightens in revulsion, but she swallows it away, reminding herself of how this woman used to be, not maternal, but so alive, and the good times before Papa died. It must be a horrible thing to lose the husband you love so deeply. And before that, she'd lost both brothers in the war.

But still, she has Elise and Philippe. They are important, too! Elise closes her eyes and pictures William standing in this very room, the way he had when she first saw him. How is he spending Christmas Eve? She bets there are lots of people at his house, and much excitement. His younger brother Aaron is just eight years old, a great age for Christmas. Elise pictures a large tree, decorated with lights and colourful baubles, candles filling the room, a fire crackling. Friends stopping by with gifts. The house scented with cooking. Joy filling the air.

She puts the guard in front of the fire, locks the door and crawls into bed. Sleep claims her the second her head touches the pillow. It had been a long day, and she was so very tired, but the promise of William's gift keeps her going.

* * *

A world of snowy whiteness and the promise of sun greets Elise when she wakes. The parcel! Instantly she is out of bed, pulling it from her dressing table drawer where she had put it the night before. As she does with his letters, she runs her finger over his writing first, before opening it. Sitting up in bed, heedless of the cold of the room, she cuts the string and, she cannot help it, tears into the brown paper. Inside she finds another parcel, wrapped in a deep cranberry paper and tied with an elegant gold ribbon. It is so beautiful! She undoes it gently and then unwraps the present without tearing the paper. Inside she finds a book, with the same cover as the Byron title he sent her, only this time it's Wordsworth. Now she has a set!

Her happiness makes her tremble and she finds her hand is shaking as she plucks up the card and opens the creamy envelope. It's a Christmas card, with a deer running through the snow. Above the printed message on the card in his careful script he's simply written, 'Dear Elise,' and after 'Best Wishes, William'. There is no letter, and she realises how much she had been looking forward to his news. And the card, well, the card makes her see that he thinks of her only as his friend's baby sister. Humiliation creeps over her. He feels sorry for her. He saw Maman and knows what Philippe is like. Realisation hits her like a broom to a carpet being beaten for dust.

She looks out the window. The bright morning sun is

now cloaked in clouds, and the sky has taken on a greyish heaviness. How quickly it changed. She thinks for a second. She will have to change William's thinking, let him know that she is not a little girl. In the back of her mind she wishes she had someone to whom she could speak of such things. Maybe Genevieve. Yes, she will know what to do. Elise is not sure she wants to talk to her about William, but sacrifices must be made.

She slips her treasures inside the trunk and makes her way down the stairs to light the fire.

NINE
NORTHERN FRANCE. SUMMER 2009

Lucy is getting ready to go to the library when the phone in her room rings. She scrambles to answer it, surprised to be getting a call.

'Hello?'

'Lucy, it's Rob, the guide from your tour yesterday?'

'Hi,' she says, wondering if she left something in the van.

'I'm calling because we have space on the morning tour to Juno. I thought you might like to come?'

Lucy thinks for a second. Yesterday Rob had said Juno was where the Canadians landed. She should go to the library, do some local research, but she had such feelings at Omaha yesterday, feeling she had never expected. She wants to see this part of D-Day.

'Absolutely! I'm on my way.'

'See you soon,' he says.

Remembering the wind off the Channel, she wishes she had a coat and doubles up on layers, hoping that helps.

She sees Rob's fleece, and brings it with her, wishing she had time to stop for coffee.

When she gets to the shop, Rob has one waiting for her. She is touched again by his simple kindness.

'Thanks.' She takes the mug. 'And for this, too,' she says, handing back his fleece.

'Do you think you may need it?' He motions to the fleece as he pushes sugar packets toward her. She shakes her head at the sugar.

'I'll buy a jacket somewhere.'

'Keep it, until you do.'

'Are you sure?'

He nods. 'I have so many. My mom buys me a new one each Christmas,' he says.

Lucy pulls it on as they walk to the van together. 'Thanks for calling me when you had a cancellation,' Lucy says.

She climbs into the little van, same one as the day before. As the tyres pass over the same bumpy stones, she looks at the shops as they pass by. Later, she'll do some shopping, find a jacket. Work a bit more at being a fashionable Frenchwoman. After all, it is her heritage.

* * *

The tour starts at the Canadian Cemetery near the villages of Bény-sur-Mer and Reviers. Rob tells them it's where the 3rd Canadian Infantry landed and that in the nearby cemetery Canadian, French and British soldiers rest.

The sun's so bright her sunglasses don't offer much help. Rob's just a soft shadow in front of her. She looks around, hears the gentle whooshing of the sea. The cries of seagulls. Cars in the distance, carrying people going to work, coming home, running errands. Lucy wonders what it must be like to pass by the remnants of a world war every day of your life.

On the cliffs above are large square buildings that might have been family homes before the war. Summer homes, perhaps, for those fleeing the heat of Paris. Standing with her back to the water, she looks at them now, thinks about her grandmother's family. They may have visited this same seashore. Maybe they had ice cream where she stands. Photos from history books appear in her mind, and she sees the same buildings bombed to bits, shells of brick and smoking wood, and not the solid stone structures there now. How do you go from being a quiet, coastal seaside community, to being in the theatre of one of the greatest battles of all time?

Rob gathers them in a small group and tells them about the soldiers who landed where they now stand, of the Royal Winnipeg Rifles and the Queen's Own Rifles of Canada.

'Fifty per cent of them did not make it off the beach,' Rob continues, saying that weather conditions caused problems with the landing. Pointing, he tells them about the five different beach heads, and how they had planned to link up on D-Day. Lucy remembers this from the last tour, about the weather conditions, the sheer scope of the operation. About the fact that the Germans were not expecting the invasion from Normandy. Different weather, different military decisions, an entirely different outcome. Hitler a world leader. It is scary to even consider.

People are asking Rob questions. Someone read a book where they tested the soil, before D-Day, to see if tanks would sink in the sand. Had he heard of this? He must hear the same questions every tour, but he answers as though it's the first time he's been asked.

From the beach Rob walks them to the Juno Beach Centre, a big silver building that shimmers in the sun.

'You have forty minutes to visit, and then we will continue the tour.'

Lucy nods and follows the group through the entrance doors. She has never been to Canada, but she's met lots of Canadians who travel to Florida for the winter. Snowbirds, they're called. She's always pictured Canadians as being sixty-five and over. Reading about its history now, she had no idea it was so young, less than 150 years old. Played a major role in the Great War and lost an entire generation of men. So much sadness and so much she doesn't know about the large country to the north.

Lucy is reading about the Royal Canadian Air Force when Rob approaches her and tells her they are moving on, speaking quietly, like they're in a library.

'I've learned more about Canada here than I have in my entire life – and we're neighbours!' she whispers to him.

'I know. Same thing happened to me,' he says.

They walk outside together, Rob holding the door for her.

'Careful,' he teases.

'I've got the hang of French doors now, thanks.'

He gives a half-grin, and again she notices his eyes. Today they almost have the smoky blue hue of Wedgwood china. With his black hair and pale skin, he really is beautiful, she thinks. And he seems really nice. But she thought that about Hal, too. Besides, she's not here for a holiday romance. She's here to connect with her past. She's just not sure how to do that.

'Our next stop is Ardenne Abbey,' he says. 'It's eight hundred years old and has seen a lot.'

Lucy likes the fact that he's personalised the abbey. Anthropomorphised, that's the word. Giving living qualities to a non-living entity.

'In the twelfth century, a couple from nearby Caen had a vision of the Virgin Mary,' he begins. Someone makes a joke she doesn't hear, but no one laughs except the teller. 'They built a priory, which is basically a monastery. The building collapsed killing twenty-six monks but was rebuilt. Wars were fought around it and over time the building was abandoned. It was sold during the French Revolution, and an Englishman bought it to live in. In 1918 it became a historical monument.'

He stops, gearing down behind an old tractor on the road, before speeding up and passing it. 'Now it is best known as the scene of a war crime.' Rob stops speaking as he turns and brings the van to a stop in a small, dusty lot. Again, they step from the van.

There is a feeling in the air that Lucy has not felt before. A deep, all-encompassing quiet. No birds chirp; there is no sound of traffic or life. No sound of waves. It is unnaturally still, like the house after Granddad died. The sunlight bounces off the buildings as they walk toward them, making the sand-coloured stones almost white. Rob turns to face the group, pointing to the abbey. 'During World War II, the building was owned by a member of the Resistance, who stored guns here. Later, it was occupied by

German soldiers who used it as a lookout point. From the top—' he points to a window in a tower '—they could see everything for miles. They watched a group of Canadian soldiers coming from the direction of the beach.' He stops and looks momentarily into the distance.

'It was June 7, 1944, the Day after D-Day. The abbey was in the possession of Kurt Meyer, commander of the 25th Panzergrenadier, now a convicted war criminal. The young Canadian soldiers who walked up this road were captured and taken prisoner to the abbey. Over the following few days the men were marched out one by one and shot in the back of the head. Twenty-seven of them all together.' He pauses. 'It is said they knew what was coming and shook hands with their fellow soldiers when their names were called.' Lucy feels sick at his words.

'The bodies were discovered when a local noticed a border of flowers that had been disturbed, and they dug up the land. Eventually Meyer stood trial for war crimes and spent nine years in a prison in Canada.'

'Nine years. That's six months per dead soldier. That's nothing,' a man's voice drifts toward Lucy just before his wife hushes him.

'There is a memorial to the fallen men, just inside,' Rob says. But he does not move through the arch that marks the entrance. He is staring in the distance, and Lucy follows his gaze, wondering what he is staring at. All she sees is an open field, filled with blue and yellow flowers. They move softly in the wind, like a gentle dance, a waltz of sorts. A blanket of beauty, so close to the scene of an atrocity. Lucy gets the quiet now, the sadness. It's like the land remembers, and will never be the same.

'I'll wait here while you visit the memorial.'

The group files past Rob, sombre and silent.

She walks to Rob. 'Not going in?' She tilts her head to the archway.

'I've seen it several times,' he says.

'You said their pictures and their names are listed?'

'Yes,' he says. 'You should see it. It is poignant, but it's also really difficult, and I don't want to see it so often I get complacent about what happened.'

He reaches up and gives her arm a gentle squeeze of support. Lucy feels the kindness in his touch, and is surprised by the small burst of energy, the little bit of happiness it gives her.

She turns away from him and moves to the memorial to the men executed.

The first thing she sees is dozens of little Canadian flags, placed in the earth where they died. The round flower bed where their bodies were discovered. It has a border of tiny white flowers now. She's not sure what they're called. She sees their names listed one after another. Their photos, along an outside wall of the abbey. The ones where they are serious make them look older, less vulnerable. The ones where they are laughing hurt the most to see.

Then she thinks about the local man who noticed the border of flowers had been disturbed. Why would he notice something so simple, when the land around them had been torn apart by war?

With a final look at the young men, long gone but forever remembered here, she turns and heads back to the car park, and to Rob. As her feet move over the dusty ground, she thinks of all it has seen. About how much there is to see in this world. And maybe how the more you see, the more you are changed. Maybe her grandmother saw something like this. That would be hard to live with, Lucy thinks. Maybe even impossible.

TEN

ESPERANCE, FRANCE. 1938

It is the talk of the village, how Elise is corresponding with the American. Elise suspects that Amelie at the post office is counting the notes that have gone back and forth; she gives Elise a knowing look whenever she shyly drops off a letter to post to William. They talk about books, mostly. Elise is surprised to hear that even he is reading *Gone with the Wind*. They have debated whether it is primarily a romance novel or a historical novel. As she reads it Elise thinks of how cruel the war was, and fate, too. One minute Scarlett is laughing and having fun, and the next she is hungry, making her way across a war-ravaged city she loved, trying to save her life as well as that of Melanie and her new baby. A baby she had with the man Scarlett loved. As Elise reads she has to remind herself it is fiction. After all, how much can one person take?

Elise does not tell William that she sees a lot of herself in Scarlett. That she sees her mother in Mr O'Hara. That even with their weaknesses it would be nice to have sisters. If nothing else they could help with Maman, and Elise could move, get her life going, especially if one is hung up on a soldier who died in the war, as Scarlett's sister is, and does not want to leave his nearby grave. The story lingers, taking up space inside her, and she must remind herself that wars are now a thing of the past.

But then something occurs to her, a thought that makes her stand still in the street. If Papa was alive, Philippe would not be the way he was; at least, Elise does not think so. Philippe would be studying, having fun, not drinking so much. Her papa would not stand for it, first of all, but mostly, Philippe changed so much when he died. It's like he decided to throw his life away, like it no longer made sense to do a good job at living. Before that, her brother had been clever, had worked so hard.

And then, another thought occurs. Perhaps in this other life if Philippe had come home with William, Elise would have been out in the village with her friends for her birthday. There would have been a party at home, but would she have shown William around? She doubts it. He and Philippe would have gone into town for drinks, to see his friends. He'd had them, once. Elise herself might be dating one of the boys she grew up with, like so many of her classmates were, and still are.

She did not realise until this very minute, standing in the very street she and Papa used to walk together, Elise holding his hand as they made their way to the bakery, to the library, to the woods to listen to the trees, how much losing him had altered everyone's lives. It wasn't just dealing with the sucking, dragging-down feeling of grief that never goes away, it was how his death had changed all their lives. Papa was not some famous scientist who may have cured cancer, or some philanthropist who might change the lives of millions through charities. He was a hard-working man who had a wife who both adored him and depended on him, a daughter and son who loved him. Friends who had come to the house for months after he died, trying to help, only to be rebuffed by Maman. Elise winces at that memory. It was like once Papa was gone, she didn't know how to act, how to behave, how to live anymore.

All their lives would be so different, had Papa lived. Despite it all, they must, she must, go on.

It will soon be Elise's birthday, and the one-year anniversary of the day she met William. She is wondering, hoping, praying he remembers. Each day she finds a reason to visit the post office, no matter how demanding Maman is. Most days she is in town, at work at the library or the bakery, and someone covers for her so she can run over. Genevieve waves her away as she sits and reads, telling her she can help whoever comes in, even though she does not work at the library. Elise has no doubt. Her friend is very capable. Nothing shakes her. Elise is not sure if this is good or bad, and wonders more each day about why she left the bustling city of Brussels for this little place, barely a dot on a map.

Each day passes, with no note. There is an increasing heaviness to the air, and Elise is hoping it rains as she walks to the bakery. She likes the sound it makes as it hits the street, coats the windowpanes. Elise remembers sitting outside with her papa, watching storms together. How he would hold her hand when the thunder crashed nearby. She would pretend to be afraid, but really, she loved the boom it made, like the whole world was being commanded to pay attention. When she gets to the bakery she sees she has a few moments, and decides to check the post office one more time.

She knows from Amelie's beaming face that something has arrived from America.

'It is heavy!' Amelie announces, pretending to be straining under the weight of the package and laughing. Elise's heart is beating so fast she feels almost dizzy. Others in the queue are whispering, and grinning. 'A present from America! Lucky you!' Amelie hands her the parcel, and she knows by the feel of it he has sent another book. Slipping it in her satchel she speeds her way to the bakery, keeping her package snuggled into her chest. She knows there will be cake and a party. It will be lovely but she wants to open the package so much it hurts. She desperately hopes there will be a longer letter this time, perhaps a kiss next to his name. Oh, but that would be asking too much! She is seventeen now and must be realistic.

She lets herself into the bakery, savouring the warm, sweet air and the joy in the shop. Pulling on an apron, she starts serving customers. Monsieur Allard whistles as they work side by side. Soon the shop is almost empty of its goodies, and the door is being closed.

'Alors, bon! Now it is time for a little party!' Monsieur Allard grabs Marianne, dancing her around the small space as Elise holds Michel, getting the toddler to laugh as she spins him as though they are dancing as well. It is both silly and wonderful, such small moments creating the magic in life.

'Come, come,' he says, ushering them up the stairs to where they live.

Although Elise knows they will celebrate her birthday in some way, it still brings a tear to her eye as she sits at the table, Michel beside her. They start with toasted cheese sandwiches, Elise's favourite, with mustard and a small tomato salad. Perfection.

'This is so kind of you,' Elise says, her parcel not forgotten, but enjoying herself very much.

When they are done Marianne clears the table, before moving the cake front and centre. Michel claps his little hands when he sees the gooey cake, smothered in thick white frosting. Marianne cuts big slices for everyone, pouring out both tea and Calvados. Taking a seat, Monsieur Allard leads them all in a loud, if off-key rendition of *'Joyeux Anniversaire'*. Then he reaches into his apron pocket and takes out a small box. With a flourish that for him is commonplace, he sets it down in front of Elise.

'You shouldn't have. Really. It's too much.' A tear threatens at the corner of an eye and she blinks it away. Slowly she opens the box. Inside, resting on some creamy-coloured tissue paper, is a beautiful silver bracelet, set with sparkling blue stones. As she lifts it up the light from the small window catches it. Marianne stands and crosses to where she sits. 'Here, let me.' She takes the bracelet from Elise's hand and slips it on her wrist, finds the clasp and fastens it shut.

'It is so beautiful, really.' Elise holds her wrist up and shakes her head, nearly overcome with emotion. 'You're too good to me.'

'I just know this is going to be a good year for you,' Marianne says, nodding. 'I just know.' She kisses her on both cheeks, Michel pressed between them.

Then Marianne hands her something else. 'This is from your friend, Genevieve. We asked her to come, but she is working at the bistro.'

'She works a great deal,' Elise says, taking the small parcel. Inside is a barrette for her hair, silver with a gold design, a wave of some kind. She knows the shop it came from. It is a lovely present.

'Oh my,' Marianne says.

'So pretty,' Elise agrees. 'I am being spoiled today!'

'Why don't you open your package from your young man?' Monsieur Allard suggests impishly.

'How did you know?' she exclaims so loudly Michel looks up from the cake he is eating, momentarily alarmed.

'I've seen you hold Michel as a baby with less care than you were holding something against your heart when you came in.' Marianne laughs.

Elise is delighted they think of William as her young man, and blushes as she brings out the package. Carefully she cuts through the string with the cake knife and opens the brown paper. Inside, another volume of poetry. Shelley this time. She lifts it up and runs her fingers over the gold-embossed cover, finds the silky tassel inside that marks pages and runs it through her thumb and forefinger. William has touched this book. The thought thrills her. As Elise gathers up the wrapping paper a small box slips to the table. She gasps. Two presents!

'Open it,' says Marianne, just as excited as Elise.

Elise lifts the cover off a small white box and sees, resting inside, earrings. Gold, with tiny clusters of milky pearls that make her think of anemones.

'Oh my,' Marianne says. 'They are stunning,' she whispers as Elise plucks the earrings from the box.

'The backs are different.' Marianne's eyes narrow as she studies Elise's gift. 'There are no posts for pierced ears.'

Elise picks up the letter and scans the familiar, and

precious, straight up and down writing, each word a gift to her.

Dear Elise,

Happiest of birthdays to you! To think that this time last year I met a lovely young lady who took the time to show her brother's friend around when she could have been out celebrating. That was so very kind of you.

I am sending another book of poetry for purely selfish reasons – I enjoy hearing you tell of your favourite poems and why they resonate with you. Poetry can be such a personal, emotional thing. Have you ever read e.e. cummings? He's a Harvard lad, doing very well. His stuff is very modern and innovative but still manages the romance of a ballad. Do let me know if you've read him.

I am also enclosing a small trinket. These new clip-on earrings are all the rage here, and I thought you might like a little piece of American fashion.

I hope the angels in the church are still well, and I hope you have a lovely birthday.

William

She sets the note aside, knowing she will have it committed to memory soon, but for now, she has friends who want to celebrate with her. It means so much.

'They're called clip-ons. Apparently, all the women in America are wearing them.' She picks one up and opens the back, clips it into place. It pinches briefly and she thinks of her maman once saying 'beauty must suffer' as she pulled a hairbrush through Elise's hair. That was a long time ago, when she was well. As Elise clips on the second earring, Marianne pulls a mirror from a nearby drawer. 'They really suit you, chérie. See?'

Elise looks in the mirror, thrilled at how the earrings

catch the light. She pictures William at a shop, buying them, thinking of her. Or maybe he asked his mother, or a female friend to pick them out. Elise does not like to think about him spending time with other women. The thought makes her stomach ache.

'Your young man is really something else. Tell me, with all the letters going back and forth, does he ever mention coming to visit again?'

Elise gives a sigh and instantly Marianne regrets bringing up something so impossible.

'Not yet.' Not yet. A range of emotion in those two simple words that Marianne cannot fully understand but one she does recognise: hope.

* * *

A week after her birthday, Elise makes her way to the woods. The sun is at its best and brightest, just approaching two o'clock. The air around her shimmers. In her satchel she has a flask of water, a baguette and some cheese, a tiny bit of wine, some paper, an envelope and a pen, William's latest letter, and a blanket under her arm. As she walks the bag thumps rhythmically against her hip. Her mouth is set in a determined line, but her insides are a jumble. How do you tell someone you like them, *really like them*, without actually saying it?

She turns the corner and strides on, seeing houses now. She knows who lives in every single one of them. What must it be like to live someplace where you met new people? Live in a place where it is possible to have secrets? This makes her think of Genevieve. She's a girl of secrets, but then, she is an outsider. Outsiders can have secrets.

Elise is fascinated by her confidence. Her complete indifference to the people who think her too much.

There is a coolness in the woods that Elise enjoys. It greets and comforts her like an old friend. The earth is still damp from the memory of snow and rain, and it is too wet to sit, but she doesn't mind. Under her favourite trees she spreads her blanket, the movement making the birds take flight.

'Sorry to disturb you.' She laughs. Her time in the woods is her own, away from her responsibilities, away from work and Maman. Settling down, she opens the wine, takes out the paper and the book she will use as a desk.

Dear William,

Thank you for the book and for the lovely earrings. It was so very, very kind of you. I know I shall be the envy of every girl in the village when I wear them, but for now I am saving them for something special. A trip to Paris perhaps. Or Brussels. I know you have been to a lot of places. Do you have any favourites? If you tell me about them, I can begin my travels through you.

Elise hesitates for a moment, and then forces herself to be brave. Her pen shakes slightly, making the D look awkward, as she begins:

Do you have any plans to come to France? I could show you the rest of my village, and perhaps take you to nearby Caen. It is a lovely city close to the sea and I know how much you like to walk on your beach back home. Tell me more about your beach. Is the sand white and sugary? I've heard you have beaches like that in America. We have lovely coastal villages, but the water is very cold. Some people swim but I am not that brave. I do not like being cold. A warm beach must be magical.

The wind has just picked up and seems to want to whisk this letter away from me. The leaves are making that magical sound as the wind whistles through. If I listen closely I can hear children playing in the street, children I've known my whole life. Do you know everyone in your town as well? Somehow, I doubt it, as I picture America being a very large, very spread-out kind of place.

I will say adieu *now. I have some bread and cheese to eat and want to do some walking. If I am very quiet I might stumble upon the fairies who live in these woods. Perhaps they will invite me to tea.*

It would be really nice to see you again.

She stops and thinks, just for a second, then takes a deep breath and writes:

Love,
Elise

ELEVEN
NORTHERN FRANCE. SUMMER 2009

'Do you have plans for the rest of the day?' Rob asks, dropping her off at her hotel.

'I was thinking of going to the library, but now, I'm not sure. I feel kind of...' She looks out the window of the van, at the white walls of her hotel, as though the right word will appear. Empty? Hollow? Despairing?

'I like to wind down from the heaviness of the tours sometimes with a cold beer followed by a short nap. I recommend the same for you.' His voice is a mix of gravitas and light, and she feels better just hearing his words.

'I don't like beer,' she says, but his comment, and the cheerful lilt of his words, makes her push away some of the darkness.

'There's a really good pub nearby, one without tourists. I think you'll like it.'

'I'm a tourist,' she says.

'Not when you're with me,' he replies.

'Okay.' She laughs.

'I'll pick you up after work, if you'd like to go?'

The idea of hanging out in her hotel room all evening no longer appeals.

'Yeah, I think so.' Lucy hears the weakness in her voice, in her words. She will not fall for another Hal. But Rob, he's been so nice. No talk of his parents' estate, as Hal called his parents' home in Newport. Rob has a grace Hal lacked. Why is she only seeing that now?

'See you around six.'

'Thanks,' she says.

She gets out of the van and makes her way through the lobby. In her room, suddenly cold, she turns down the blankets, crawls into bed, curls up in a ball trying to get warm. The room is still; there's no noise from outside. So much is running around in her mind. Lucy thinks about the area, all she has seen. All it has seen. And of her grandmother, who must have experienced so much. And she grows even more curious about the woman herself. Did she work with the Resistance? Had she been to Ardenne Abbey? If she was alive, would she have remembered the story, told her grandfather? It seems so wrong that all she saw has been lost. She allows a memory she has been holding at bay to come forward. She needs to know now.

She closes her eyes and remembers waking to the scent of bacon frying. Moving to the kitchen and seeing Granddad cooking. He never cooked. They'd lived on spaghetti, frozen food and takeaway until she was thirteen and took over in the kitchen.

Pulling a sweatshirt over her pyjamas, she had started for the kitchen, then turned back to her room, pulled on a pair of socks. Granddad liked for her to have her feet covered. Lucy wonders now if this had something to do with his time as a soldier, how they always wore those heavy boots.

'What's up?' She was momentarily stunned by all the smoke in the air. He wasn't frying bacon so much as cremating it. Lucy moved to the stove, turned down the heat under the frying pan. He'd set the table, and this worried her. Usually they ate on the back deck, not at the kitchen table.

'Everything okay?'

She could hear him settling at the table as she cracked eggs into a bowl. He loved scrambled eggs with onions and peppers. What was he saying? She grabs a pepper. It's seen better days, but she can salvage most of it.

'So what do you think?'

'Sorry, I had my head in the fridge?'

'I was thinking you might like to go to France with your old granddad this summer. See Paris. A bit of Normandy. There's a few places I'd like to show you.'

She drops the pepper in the sink.

'Granddad. That would be amazing. I'd love to see it. But I'm taking a summer class, and Molly got me a job at the bar where she works. I was going to stay in Boston for the summer.'

Sitting in France now, the memory so fresh she can feel the pepper in her hand, smell the charred bacon in the air, she realises he never said his friend's name. Never mentioned his long-gone wife. At least, not that time. All the questions she has and no way to get answers. If she had gone with him that summer, her whole life might be different. Instead, she worked at a bar and took a class. All the time they had together, why did he choose the summer she planned to study?

A fresh wave of regret hits her, and she feels it settle deeper into her body, seep into her organs. Make itself at home. Grief hollows you out. It bends you and it breaks you slowly. It sucks the marrow from your bones, leaving you somehow empty yet filled with a sharp pain. Regret is different. It fills the empty spaces with poison, until you can feel your insides corroding.

She stands and looks out the tiny window in her room, until it's time to meet Rob for dinner.

* * *

The sky is clear, a soft bluish grey. The air is refreshing. It's Lucy's favourite kind of evening, and she can almost smell woodsmoke in the air, reminding her of Hallowe'en when she was a kid in Providence, before everything changed. It's comforting, after the emotion of the day.

'I didn't think it would be this cool here, in summer,' she says to Rob.

'It's being close to the Channel, I think.' They're walking so close their hands touch. There's something about the brief contact that gives Lucy a pleasant sensation of connection, welcome after the loneliness of the last few hours.

'I didn't pack for it. I didn't even check the weather in northern France.'

The main street is lined with restaurants, and people are sitting outside, surrounded by heat lamps, eating, drinking, laughing. A full, generous chuckle wraps itself around her, making Lucy feel wistful as she looks for the source – she'd like to know someone with such a laugh.

'Oh, wow!' She stops.

Rob turns his head to look at Lucy, who has stopped speaking, stopped walking. She is staring into the distance. He follows her stare to the church.

'Impressive, isn't it?' he says.

'It's incredible. The size of it, and the windows, they're beautiful.'

'It dates back to Roman times, the original structure, but it's been rebuilt.'

'It's lucky it wasn't damaged during the war.'

'No, this area was relatively untouched. We're too far inland, and there was no industry to attack. An old mill town with its glory days behind it,' he says. 'The church is a big tourist draw, how old it is, the artwork. Apparently a knight templar is buried there as well.'

Lucy continues to stare.

'It's closed now, but the inside is pretty incredible. It has the highest ceiling I've ever seen. I'm not religious, but I like sitting inside, in the quiet, thinking.' He gives an embarrassed shrug, and Lucy is charmed.

'We'll have to stop back later, when the outside lights are turned on. The place seems to glow. It's impressive.'

'I can't wait.'

They continue walking, moving past the church, as Rob ushers Lucy down a side street. It's narrow, only a few steps from the main street but isolated. She sees a light above a door, advertising some sort of beer, she thinks.

'Okay, it doesn't look like much...'

'Looks can be deceiving,' Lucy says, walking past him into a dark room filled with old round tables and mismatched chairs, the kind you'd find in a summer home. The lights are weak, but the candles on the tables highlight

the imperfections. It is dark, but cosy, and she likes it immediately.

Rob ushers her to a table, in the middle of the room,
close to the bar.

'Yeah it's a bit of a dive, but the food is great and
cheaper than the places that cater to tourists.'

A man in his forties, looking ridiculously dapper in
jeans and a blue Oxford shirt, walks over and offers his
hand to Rob, greeting him like an old friend, before
handing them menus. 'This is Lucy. She's visiting from
America.'

The man swoops down and kisses her on both cheeks,
surprising her.

'Bonjour,' Lucy says to him. He asks what they'll have
to drink, and Rob orders two pressions. 'A draught – is that
okay?' he asks Lucy, who nods. When he steps away she
leans toward Rob. 'If a waiter did that in the US someone
would sue.' She laughs, opening her menu.

'You get used to their ways. It's nice, I think.'

'It is, but totally different.'

Rob motions to the menu. 'They do a great croque
monsieur.'

'I had one in Paris. A grilled cheese in a tuxedo, but it
was good.'

Rob laughs. 'Sounds about right.'

The waiter reappears with their beer as well as a small
glass of something. 'A small aperitif, to welcome you to
France.' He winks and sets it down in front of her and takes
their order.

Lucy looks suspiciously at the yellow-coloured liquid
in the stubby glass.

'Calvados,' Rob says, as though he is reading her mind. 'An apple brandy Normandy is famous for.'

Lucy is sceptical but picks it up and takes a small sip.

Rob laughs as she makes a face, covering her mouth with her hand. But after the burning, the taste is okay. She takes another sip.

'Easy,' he says. 'It's very potent.'

She nods. It tastes like something familiar. Like the molasses taffy handed out at Hallowe'en. Funny, to think about Hallowe'en again.

She takes another sip. Rob doesn't say anything but moves his chair closer to her as he looks around the room.

'Are you planning on going on any more tours?' he asks.

Lucy nods. 'Yes. But after today... I think I'm going to wait a while.'

'Yeah. What those Canadian soldiers went through, it bothers me every single time.'

'I don't understand how something like that could happen,' Lucy says. 'The planning of it. Seeing the man walk toward you, how you can say, "Turn around so I can shoot you"?' She shudders.

'It's a process, I think. A person sees so much violence and becomes desensitised. You're constantly being told your enemy is subhuman, you start to believe it. Maybe you start to believe you are superior. People can be manipulated.'

'It's hard to understand how you can change that much.'

'Think of how young the kids were when they became the Hitler Youth,' Rob says. 'Think of how he played on people's fear. One on one, I couldn't convince you of any of his beliefs. But the group mentality is something completely different.'

'I doubt it could happen today.'

'You'd be surprised,' he replies.

Lucy is about to ask what he means when their food arrives, smaller portions than in the US and on mismatched dishes, but it looks delicious. The waiter sets a steak in front of Rob, and a mound of fries. Lucy has a weakness for fries – skinny fries, curly fries, chunky fries. She loves them all.

'Your fries look good,' she says, and he pushes them toward her. Lucy pops one in her mouth. It's hot and she makes little waving motions in front of her mouth, like that might help. Rob laughs.

'Have you seen much of France?' she asks, when she can speak.

'Not as much as I would like, but a bit. I loved Paris.'

'Paris is different. Like it's saying, *Take me or leave me, it's up to you, but I know I'm special.* I like its confidence.'

Lucy nods, understanding. 'It has a more settled feeling, like it's been at this living business longer and knows how to proceed. I like it. I may buy a beret next. It's part of my heritage, after all.'

'Really?'

'Through my grandmother. I never knew her, I don't even know her last name, but she was born here. It's crazy to think I might be walking by someone related to me, however distantly, and have no idea.'

'Can't you ask someone back home?' He cuts into his steak.

Lucy shakes her head no. 'My parents died when I was a kid, and my grandfather raised me. I'm on my own.' She is embarrassed to say this, as though she has any control over the string of deaths that decimated her small family.

He sets down his knife and fork. The paper-cut line between Rob's eyes appears and she can tell he is thinking. She hopes he does not ask about her parents.

'That's rough, Lucy. I'm sorry about that.'

A small silence. Lucy hopes she hasn't made him uncomfortable.

'What about your family? You told me about your grandfather,' she prompts.

'My parents. My little brother Alex. That's it.'

'How old is Alex?'

'Twelve.'

'Do you keep in touch?'

'We email, mostly about basketball. I miss NBA games. When I graduated from university, Alex took me to a game as a present. My parents paid but it was his idea. He was more excited than I was.' He takes a bite of steak. Chews. 'What did you do for your recent graduation?'

'Nothing,' she says. 'I didn't even go to the ceremony.'

'Hang on. You didn't go to graduation?'

'There was no one to see me cross the stage.' She shrugs, hoping it doesn't sound as pathetic as it feels. She doesn't tell him about her break-up with Hal, about Molly's parents sending her flowers at graduation, the card with no mention of their daughter. About her neighbour Abigail Morgan saying she would love to see her cross the stage.

'You need to celebrate.'

'My trip to Europe is a celebration of sorts.'

'No desire to mark such a momentous event?'

'I graduated with no student debt. I think that's pretty

momentous. Besides, I've got years of education ahead of me.'

'Yeah?'

'I start med school in September,' she says. But her voice is low, and she doesn't look at him.

'You don't seem convinced,' he says.

'I'm not. I don't know why. I've wanted to be a doctor since I was eight.' She shrugs again. 'Now, I'm not sure. Maybe I'm just tired.'

Rob finishes his beer and Lucy eats another fry.

'I know how you feel, I think. I'm supposed to be working toward being an architect, taking over the family business.' He picks up a fry, drops it.

'And...' she prompts.

'I'd like to be a historian.'

Lucy tilts her head slightly, listening.

'I told my father and he said, "Do you know how much teachers make?" So we settled on me taking a year off, and here I am. Nine months into my year. Still don't want to be an architect.'

Lucy looks at him. 'I can see you as a professor,' she says.

'You can?'

She nods. 'A white button-down, a grey cardigan. Wait till you have a few wisps of grey in your hair.' She laughs, takes another sip of her drink. 'What would you concentrate on?'

'Twentieth-century military history.'

'You're in the right place to absorb it,' she says.

'Tell my dad.'

'Maybe, while you've been away, he's started to make peace with it. Maybe you'll be surprised.'

'Maybe,' he says, not convinced. 'What about you? Why medicine?'

'I've always wanted to be a doctor, like my dad.'

'What was his specialty?'

'Emergency medicine.'

'You planning on going into the same field?'

'I was thinking of becoming a paediatrician for a while. More recently I was thinking of oncology,' she says.

'And now?'

'I just don't think I want to spend the rest of my life watching people suffer.' Lucy hadn't known this, until she said it. Now that it fills the air around her, she knows it is true.

Rob signals for another round and Lucy realises the evening has taken a turn toward the dark.

'What would you do instead?'

'I'm not sure. But I have been thinking I'd like to see a bit more of the world.'

The waiter appears with their drinks. Rob lifts his glass and says, 'I'll drink to that.'

* * *

The air is cooler as they walk back, and the sky is almost black. The church appears to be glowing from the flood-lights that break the darkness around it.

'Impressive, right?' Rob asks, as they stare.

'It's beautiful,' she says. 'It looks even bigger now.' She takes a step back, catching her foot on a jagged cobblestone and pitching backwards. Rob steadies her with an arm around her waist, holding her firmly until her balance returns.

Overhead a streetlamp springs to life, surprising them both. Voices from people she can't see make their way to them from the distance. They turn toward the shops, the ghostly light from the empty interiors falling into the street, creating a haunting feeling.

'I love the colour of the stone under the light,' Lucy says.

The sky is a rich purple now, like it's showing the bruises of the day. The evening has been so nice, she doesn't want it to end. Too soon they're back at her hotel.

Rob opens the door to the lobby, and Lucy steps inside the bright white foyer.

'What do you plan to do tomorrow?' he asks.

'I'm definitely going to see the church. Then I'm going to the library to find some maps of the town, before the war.'

'There's a historian in you, too,' he says.

She smiles. 'I like the sound of that.'

'I'm sure I'll see you tomorrow,' he says. Then he leans forward, holds her arm gently and kisses her lightly on both cheeks.

'Good night, Lucy.'

Lucy heads back to her room. Although it is dark outside, she feels so much lighter when she steps inside.

TWELVE
ESPERANCE, FRANCE. 1938

Something changes between them after Elise sends her thank you for the earrings. William's letters arrive more often, become more personal. He tells her about his day, his family, what he is reading. Walking on Boston Common. How the seasons look in New England. Elise relishes in the details about Cambridge, the town where he studies, and Boston, the city he loves. Elise starts to tell him things she has always kept to herself. About how different things were when Papa was alive. How Maman had laughed, been fearless in the face of those who thought her different and *too much*. How she wore bright colours and taught them all how to dance. How Philippe and Papa would spend hours talking about architecture, for Papa had wanted to study to be one. When William replies his letters are filled with both concern, and somehow a jolly tone that makes her smile.

Sometimes he mentions Germany, asks her what it feels like in France, but she ignores those parts. Who cares about fascism and all that stuff when there are books and poetry to read and lovely letters to receive? There is no kiss at the end of his notes but she thinks that one day there will be, and for now his letters, and this thought, are enough. They keep her going as she works and takes care of Maman. Occasionally Genevieve insists they meet for a drink. 'You must take care of yourself, too,' she says but Elise feels guilty when she sits still. When she spends money on herself. Genevieve does not.

Then one day when the bright October sun is shining, and the air is cool but still has the memory of summer, Elise receives a letter that is an answer to a prayer she could not remember saying.

William is coming to France!

There it is, in his straight up and down penmanship. 'I will be in Paris, taking care of some business for my father.'

Her heart dances.

Perhaps we can meet? I've not been in touch with Philippe, and it would be good to see him, too.

A crushing dread fills her. How can she leave the house, and her responsibilities?

Elise is thinking about his letter in her room, after a day that had been particularly difficult with Maman. She did not want to get out of bed, did not want to dress. Elise had insisted some semblance of normality must be kept, but Maman had flung her water glass at Elise, screaming, 'Get out!' and Elise had simply stared at the broken glass on the floor. Now, in the quiet of her room, alone at her desk, she looks out the window. She always thinks better looking at the stars.

Genevieve would know what to do, of that Elise is certain. The only thing is, she does not want to tell her too much about William. It is too special. Elise turns from the window and picks up her brush, running it through her hair. Genevieve had been urging her to get it cut, as is the new style, but Elise doesn't want to. She likes tying it back. Besides, everyone was running around with the same haircut. What was the point? She turns down the covers, getting ready for bed. The days are long and she looks forward to sleep. Sitting on the edge of her bed collecting her thoughts, she is startled by a noise from downstairs. A chair falling over. Elise sighs. How had she missed Maman getting up?

Making her way down the stairs, she tries to keep the dark thoughts away. Thoughts of leaving and never coming back, like Philippe. But duty and loyalty and love for Papa keep her rooted. She turns at the bottom of the stairs and sees Maman trying to pull herself up from the floor. Elise thinks about returning to her room and closing the door. Instead as she walks over to her, she decides that one way or another she is going to Paris to see William. She has had enough. It's time for Elise to look out for herself. To be happy. And William makes her happy. She has some planning to do. Find someone to look after Maman. She could not ask Marianne, not with the bakery and Michel to care for. Then she thinks of what Genevieve said to her, about taking care of herself. And she is the only person Elise knows who is strong enough, was more than a match for the woman who brought her into this world. But how to ask? And how much will she have to tell her about William?

* * *

As though fate is lending a hand, Genevieve drops into the bakery the next day. Elise can barely contain her excitement when she sees her friend, her hands trembling as she boxes up pastries. She can feel Genevieve watching.

'Is everything all right?' Genevieve asks.

'Of course,' Elise says, too brightly. But here is her opening. 'I have something I want to ask you about – perhaps we can meet after work?'

Elise can feel herself being studied. 'I will see you at three, at the new café across from the park,' Genevieve instructs.

'Thank you.'

For the rest of the afternoon, Elise thinks about what she's going to say, how she can ask. And then, at three, she pulls on her coat and walks to the café. Genevieve is already there. Taking a seat, Elise has a hard time thinking of how to ask for this favour.

'Whatever it is, spit it out, Elise,' Genevieve says, and it is the prompt Elise needs.

She takes a deep breath. 'I'm not sure where to begin., A little while ago I met this man, through my brother Philippe.'

'The American, William?'

'How did you know?'

'Elise, the whole town knows.' Genevieve rolls her eyes.

She pauses to regroup at this information.

Genevieve stares.

'William has invited me to Paris to visit.'

Across from her Genevieve leans forward, her eyes narrowing further.

'And I need... I'm hoping. Well, it's like this...' she flounders. She and Genevieve are friends, but not in the way she is friends with Marianne. Elise finds herself cautious around Genevieve. She can be intimidating, and

Elise does not like that. Most people don't. Besides, how does she tell her about her maman, when she has tried so hard to keep it all a secret? Genevieve was not born and raised here. She does not know Elise's family story.

Genevieve leans back in her seat. 'And you need someone to keep an eye on the house. Consider it done.'

Gratitude swirls through Elise. 'You will?'

'Of course. When do you need me?'

Elise names the dates. 'I can't thank you enough. But there are a few things you don't know.'

'That your maman has never gotten over your papa's death, never leaves the house, and depends on you for everything?'

'How did you know?' Elise's voice is low, a tiny bit of embarrassment, even shame, poking into her words, but mostly shock.

Genevieve gives a theatrical sweep of her arm. 'Same way I know about William. This town. But that is not important now. What's important is getting you ready to see William. Have you packed? What are you taking?'

'I haven't thought about it.'

'Let's get started on that, right now. I can meet your maman at the same time.' Genevieve stands, straightens her skirt, and motions for Elise to follow. Taking a last drink of her café, Elise turns and follows her friend.

'And I can give you a list of things I want you to pick up for me in Paris.'

THIRTEEN
NORTHERN FRANCE. SUMMER 2009

The church in the daylight looks like something from a fairy tale, during the happy parts, like when a curse is lifted or a princess marries her prince.

Lucy has never been inside a Catholic church. Does she have to cover her head? She waits outside the door and watches, looking for a clue, until an elderly woman approaches. Not just elderly, ancient. Like she could turn to dust any second. She is wrapped in a coat, wearing thick tights and sensible, ugly shoes. Lucy steps forward to help as she struggles with the enormous door, hampered by both the direction of the wind and the door's size.

Using both hands she tugs, and it gives way. She holds it open for her, and as the woman passes she looks at Lucy, starts to say merci and stops. Her expression goes from simple acknowledgement to confusion, to shock. Reaching out her hand, she places it gently on Lucy's arm. Not as a thank you, more like to make sure she is real.

Lucy attempts a reassuring smile, looking down on the

small woman who despite her age has full, thick and wildly curly grey hair, dotted with a few remaining streaks of her natural red. 'Is everything okay?' Lucy asks.

After a few seconds the woman nods, and as Lucy watches, she slowly, haltingly makes her way down the aisle, before stopping and turning back to look at her again. Lucy wonders if her jeans and hoodie are not acceptable attire but no. There is more to it than that. Lucy continues to watch until she takes a seat and bows her head. It seems wrong to watch her do something as private as pray.

The church is cool and although it is peaceful, slight noises, the flicker of flame, someone lowering a kneeler, echo loudly. A slight musty smell hangs in the air. The scent of history and time. A million old books. She walks softly, amazed at the height of the ceiling. The size and brightness of the windows. The colours sparkle, turning different shades of red, green, blue where the sun hits them.

It is beautiful, but it's the quiet she likes the most. She sits in one of the pews, folding her hands in front of her. Lucy is not sure how to pray. She's never gone to church. Granddad's family had been Catholic, but he always said religion was the cause of too many wars, so he told her to be a good person, kind to others and to herself. 'That's important, too, Lucy. You have to like yourself first.' Funny, the way the things he said keep coming back. She sits quietly, closing her eyes and thinking about what she wants – impossible things, like her parents to still be here. Granddad, too. This is harder than she thought. She tries again to get her thoughts organised. In the end, she decides to play it simple and safe. Closing her eyes, she whispers her prayer to the great space around her.

Hi, Granddad. It's me, Lucy. I'm here, in Normandy. I wish you were here with me. I miss you so much. I wish I had told you how much I love you more often. I wish I had asked so many questions. I wish I knew more about you, where you fought. If you were scared. I wish I knew more about my grandmother.

Tell Mommy and Daddy how much I love them. I hope you know how much I love you. I hope your coffee is strong and hot, and you get your eggs with peppers and onions whenever you want. Thanks for everything, Granddad. I love you.

She pauses.

If you could give me a sign, that you're okay. Please. And if you could tell me what to do about med school. That'd be great.. Thanks. And maybe if you could let me know a bit more about grandmother, that would be good, too.

She hopes it is enough.

* * *

When Lucy walks outside, it takes a moment for her eyes to adjust to the brightness. The air feels fresher, more alive. She stoops and picks up an empty bottle of water, and the wrapper for a candy bar someone has dropped. She looks around for a bin but can't see one, so she puts it in her bag, then she walks to the library. It's a small stone building not far from her hotel. In her best French, liberally peppered with English words, she says her grandmother lived here before the war, and she was wondering what the town would have looked like then.

The librarian pulls out a map from 1939 and Lucy

figures she must be used to such requests. 'Can I copy it?' she asks.

'*Oui*, madam,' she says. Lucy follows her to the copier. It takes a few attempts to get the contrast right on the old photocopier and the end result isn't great, but it's a start.

She walks around the small room that makes up the library, thinking about what to do next. She could ask about local history, see if they have a census from 1939, but Lucy has another idea. Thanking the librarian for her help, she heads to a small bistro. It's tucked away, almost empty. She takes a seat so she can think.

Lucy orders a glass of sparkling wine, something she's never done before. She wants to raise a glass to her grandmother before she starts this pilgrimage. She had to have been an incredible woman to have landed her grandfather, after all.

As she sips, she studies the map, locating the church as a reference point. She compares it to the map that shows the present-day town, again locating the church. Using the pen she has tucked into her new journal, she divides the area up into three sections, leaving the modern section until the last, if she has time. Today she will walk the southern part, a part she hasn't seen yet, away from the railway station and the pub where she ate with Rob. She'll save that part for tomorrow. She wants to explore the woods nearby. Rob told her there was a walking path, and that the houses near the station were the longest-standing, apart from the downtown core.

She wishes she had more time. She'd like to see Tours, and some of the nearby battle sites. But airplanes fly all the time, and already she knows she will be back. She feels a connection to this place. A sense of belonging. She feels so much better for having simply been here.

She pays her bill and heads to a part of the town she has not seen. It is time to start her own pilgrimage.

FOURTEEN
PARIS. APRIL 1939

Gare Saint-Lazare is overflowing with people. Noise. Energy. Elise loves it immediately, but fears William may not be able to find her. As she walks along the platform carrying her case, she can't believe they are in the same country. The same city! The same building even! Her smile deepens, further lighting up her already dancing eyes. The platform is almost at an end when she sees him. He's stopped, scanning the crowd, towering over the people who make their way around him.

And then they see each other.

'William, is that really you?' she says and then laughs some more. Oh, it feels good to laugh!

'It is I. And I would know you anywhere. You are as lovely as I remember.'

It was the perfect thing to say, and Elise is thrilled to her toes. He grabs the bag she struggled with, now weightless in his hand, and together they leave the station, dropping her case, borrowed from Genevieve, with the porter at his hotel. Elise would be staying at Philippe's. As they walk along Rue St Germain, her arm through his, William mentions he has seen him only once since arriving.

'I have not seen him in many months,' she says.

'Well, don't worry about him. I'm sure he'll turn up.'

'What shall we do for the rest of the day?' Elise's words are bright, her voice higher than normal. She feels overwhelmed by the excitement of it all.

'That is up to you.' His simple gallantry thrills her even more.

'In that case, I'd like to see the Eiffel Tower again.'

'Again?' he asks, playfully.

'Papa brought me here, for my birthday, when I was twelve. We had so much fun, just the two of us.' She pauses, letting the memory come. It hurts, but it is the good hurt, the kind that reminds you of being loved and better days. The promise those good days will return.

'Yes, I want to see the Eiffel Tower. It is time to make a new memory,' she says.

'Then that is what we shall do.'

* * *

After seeing the Tower and walking the Trocadéro, Elise suggests they find Philippe, as it is early evening. But he is not at his apartment, nor at the local bar he frequents. William remembers the place from when they studied together. They sit and have a drink; William has Scotch and Elise has lemonade. After an hour of searching and waiting, it is obvious that he is nowhere to be found. Elise is upset with her brother for being so unreliable, but more upset with herself for thinking she could depend on him to begin with.

'Let's check his apartment one more time,' William says as he pays the bill.

'Okay,' she agrees, praying her brother is now home. They walk silently, making their way through the sunny streets. And then they are at Philippe's. As they knock on his door, Elise sees the chipped and flaking paint, the old and splintered wood. Even with the door closed she can smell the stale air of his flat, seeping under the door, through the very walls. She crinkles her nose as William knocks, waits, then shoves a note under the door. Straightening, he takes her arm and they head wordlessly down the stairs, back to the street. The sunshine greets them, brightening the ugliness of her brother's selfishness.

'I'm sure he got tied up unexpectedly. We'll see him soon.' He squeezes her arm, trying to keep her disappointment and worry at bay.

Elise distracts herself by looking in the windows of the bakeries, looking at the big slabs of brownies and the plates piled high with food.

'Are you hungry? Would you like something?'

'I'm fine, thank you. Just seeing what Paris has to offer. The bakeries are so much busier here,' she says as people spill from the door of a large boulangerie, clutching the little paper sacks and boxes tied with string she knows so well.

'Do you still enjoy working at the bakery? You haven't mentioned it much in your letters.' He steers her through the door. A sweet, heady aroma of sugar and chocolate and warm bread greets them.

Elise nods her head. 'Very much. I love the library, too. The smell of the books, the quiet, the warmth.' She nods at William's selection of a buttery-looking tart but refuses a large square oozing chocolate. 'I do not care for chocolate, or rather, it does not care for me. I get headaches,' she explains, and he cancels the chocolate square.

William pays for the treats and then they resume their stroll, eating little bits of squares they break off with their hands. The world, at that moment, is a beautiful place. Elise knows this, knows what she has to return to, and works hard to remember every detail. The way the women wear their hats at a jaunty angle. The trees that line the streets, how the leaves tinkle in the wind. The smell of bakeries, coffee, sunshine – for sunshine, she thinks, has its own scent. As they walk and nibble, there is no place on earth Elise would rather be.

Just as they eat their last bit of buttery tart, they arrive at William's hotel. Elise is mortified as he signs for her room, across the hall from his, mortified that her brother has forgotten her and that there is no way she can pay. She has spent all of her savings on new clothes for this trip. She's also angry with herself. She knows her brother cannot be relied upon. She knows he is a drunk. But some sense of loyalty keeps her from acknowledging it, makes her pretend it's not true. An ill-placed belief he will snap back to what he was, a hope she has carried for years dies inside her at that moment. She can feel the flutter of it being replaced by something hard.

As they make their way to the stairs Elise says, 'I am sorry about this, William. I thought things with Philippe were settled.' She can feel the pinkness in her cheeks. William, seeing how upset she is, sets her suitcase down and puts his arms around her. 'Now I don't have to waste time commuting back and forth to see you.' It's the perfect response. Elise thinks of the other men she knows, her classmates, the boys she grew up with. They all seem so clumsy next to William. Is it age or an American thing?

He checks the key in his hand then opens the door for her, pushing it wide so she can duck under his arm, squeeze by. The closeness of him, the scent of his aftershave, thrills her again. So much hoping, and dreaming, and writing! And now here he is. It's like now is the time for her dreams to come true.

Elise walks into the room, the sunshine streaming in the wall of windows on one side.

'Are you tired? It's been a long day,' he asks, concerned.

'I'm not tired at all.' She crosses to the window and looks out on the city, sees Montmartre in the distance, the glow from the dome brightening the night sky. Ethereal, she thinks, delighted.

'It's a big day tomorrow... your birthday after all, and two years since we've met,' he says.

Elise turns and looks at him. 'You remembered.' Her voice is soft, and she feels as though she is glowing with happiness.

'I always remember the important things.'

'The book of poetry you sent. It was so sweet of you. It meant so much...' She hesitates.

'But?'

'I guess, I'm not sure how to say this, but why?'

'Why what?' he asks.

'Why the present, why did you get in touch?'

She can tell by the way his forehead creases he's trying to think of the right response. Elise had no intention of asking this question, didn't even know she was thinking it. Now, she's worried she's ruined everything.

'Just tell me.'

120

'I was saddened with how things were for you at home. How your brother had changed. You seemed, you are, so much better than that. I wanted to do something nice for you, at first...' His voice trails away. Elise is horrified to think he sent her the book out of some sense of charity, but she needs to know. She will not let him off the hook.

'And?' If he pities her she will stand up and walk out of the room this instant. She swears she will. Elise holds her breath. Everything depends on how he answers this question.

'And then, you replied. Your brother would not have, trust me. And what you said about *The Good Earth*, I thought it was so clever, cleverer than some I went to school with...'

Elise waits for the truth to come out.

'I have enjoyed corresponding with you. But...' He hesitates, plays with the pipe he has taken from his jacket. 'It is not right for a man my age to fall for a schoolgirl,' he finishes.

A feeling of joy washes over her, like bubbles in a nice hot bath. She wants to go to him, to hold him. To feel his arms around her. To feel safe.

'I'm not a schoolgirl anymore.' She cannot believe how bold she is being but Genevieve had said to hold her head high and exude confidence. Her friend had said, 'Men grow bored of starry-eyed girls who live and die for them. At least, the interesting ones do.'

Elise tilts her chin up, looking directly at him.

And then, he crosses the floor, closing the few steps between them with his long strides, and gently taking her in his arms, says, 'Elise, may I kiss you?'

She nods, not trusting herself to speak. And then, his

head dips, and his lips find hers. And for Elise, another dream comes true.

* * *

Elise wakes the morning of her birthday to knocking on the door. Perhaps it was not having to listen for noises in the night, or perhaps it was the very comfortable bed, but she has slept the sleep of a child. Deep, comforting, refreshing.

It takes her a few seconds to work out where the noise is coming from. When she does, she flies out of bed, throwing on her wrapper as she opens the door.

William is standing in front of her, holding a bouquet of white roses in brown paper. He's wearing tan trousers, a white shirt and a blue cardigan. His hair is still damp. He steps back when he sees her and Elise is aware of her wrap being half on, half off, covering a light cotton nightgown that has seen too many washes, her long dark hair tumbling over her shoulders, messy from sleeping. Oh, she must look dreadful!

'Good morning. I hope I didn't wake you?' His voice sounds oddly formal. Elise has no idea why.

'No, no.' She laughs. 'Well, yes, I can't believe I slept so late!'

He hands her the bouquet.

'Happy birthday.'

She flushes as she takes the flowers, still cool with morning dew.

'I was down to get a paper and saw them at a stand. I thought of you.'

'I like white roses the best,' she says, closing her eyes and burying her face in their scent.

'I'm glad. I'll leave you to get ready for the day.' He hesitates, then lifts his hand to her face, bends down and kisses her cheek. Then he steps away, moving down the hall. Elise closes the door, the sweet smell of her flowers filling her senses.

After a breakfast of croissants and café au lait, they make their way to the Jardins de Luxembourg where they stroll arm in arm under the tall trees that line the paths. Elise does not imagine that he walks closer to her today, and she is thrilled. The kiss they had shared, and more, so much more but not everything, the night before seems to have changed things, lined them up. They are a couple now. She squeezes his arm tighter at the thought. He looks over at her, and kisses the top of her head, as though in confirmation.

Spring has come early to France and the energy of it fills the air.

William motions toward a bench. 'Shall we sit in the sun?'

She nods and he places his handkerchief on the time-warped seat, creating a place for her to sit. A simple gesture but she feels the rush of pleasure from his attention.

'Any more plans for your studies? With your love of reading, I thought you'd go into teaching?' he ventures.

She thinks for a moment and says, 'I really wanted to train as a pastry chef, but there was no place nearby. And it's the same with teaching.'

Elise does not see William's frown.

'A pastry chef. I think that would require a lot of patience. Not something I could do.' He laughs.

'I don't know. You seem very patient to me,' she hedges, the lilt of flirtation in her voice.

'It doesn't come naturally. Trust me.'

They chat easily as the sun hits its zenith in the sky, before they make their way from the bench through the gardens and to the street. More people about now, motor-cars are going by. There's a smile of pure happiness on Elise's face. Her eyes glisten with pleasure, anticipation, interest.

'This city is magical,' she says, drinking in the sights and sounds, studying the people who pass, wondering what kind of life they live in Paris. They stumble on a market, and Elise is captivated. 'I think the entire population of my hometown is shopping here.' She laughs, making her way toward the tables and the wares. 'Perhaps I can find some-thing for Maman.'

William smiles. 'Take your time.' Elise passes a table stacked with dishes, teacups mostly, then makes her way to another table. She turns and smiles at him, and he makes his way quickly to her side.

'Find something you like?'

She picks up a rich emerald-green shawl, knowing it to be Maman's favourite colour. She thinks of how pretty it would look with a nice cream silk dress, like the one Elise and Genevieve sewed for this trip to Paris. But really – could a new shawl make her happy? Darkness falls over Elise and she straightens her back, prepared to fight it off. Nothing will ruin her day with William. She looks at the silky material in her hand. Maybe it will act as a catalyst. Make her feel pretty again. Maybe the colour will cheer her up. Elise is so happy, she wants everyone to be happy, too.

When she learns the cost she blanches at the number of francs the vendor wants. William steps forward to pay but Elise refuses to allow him to spend more money. Besides, it's stupid of her to think a simple shawl could make Maman happy. She thinks of the wrap the Allards gave her and how much she likes it. But Elise and her mother are two incredibly different people. It will take more than a slip of silk to bring her back to life. It will take a love she won't let into her life, Elise realises.

William offers one more time, a bundle of francs in his hand, but Elise is firm.

She slips her arm through his and says, 'Thank you for your kind offer. Now let's see what else Paris has in store.' She feels the warmth of him, the outline of his arm muscles through his shirt and sweater, and it thrills her.

They wander the streets for hours, talking, looking into the windows of bakeries, sharing a treat on the street in Montmartre. By late afternoon they are at Sacré-Coeur when William checks his pocket watch and says they must hurry. 'We have reservations.'

'Where?' Elise asks.

'It's a surprise. You'll have to be patient,' he teases.

'Oh, well, that I can do,' she replies with a grin, but her insides are on fire.

'And wear your favourite frock.'

* * *

Elise dresses, slowly, carefully. Genevieve had helped with her simple cream dress, and she sees now how perfectly she had done the top stitching, sitting at Elise's kitchen table, sipping on red wine as Elise prayed she didn't spill anything. Maman had sat and stared at Genevieve as though she was some exotic cat that had wandered into their home, and then she had gone to bed early, exhausted by the activity. She should get something for Genevieve, too. She likes large stones, Elise has noticed, but she cannot afford jewellery. Perhaps something will show up. The anemone earrings William sent her are sitting safely in the box. She has never worn them before, saving them for a special occasion. Now, here it is. Clipping them into place, she feels that same pinch, but they look so pretty, the pain is worth it.

Turning in front of the mirror, she drapes the wrap Marianne and Bertrand gave her over her shoulders. She is pleased with the results. In this light the deep burgundy looks dramatic against the cream colour and seems to darken her hair.

Precisely at eight William knocks on the door as Elise is pulling on her new spring coat, also bought for this trip. Genevieve had told her there was no way she could wear Papa's coat in Paris. 'People will think you are crazy.'

Elise remembers once wishing for someone to talk to, to give her advice. Genevieve has certainly fulfilled the last part.

Now William stands in front of her, his hair slicked back like Clark Gable, looking dashing in a grey suit and tie under a dark overcoat.

'You look lovely,' he says.

'Thank you.' Elise beams. 'Could I have a tiny hint about where we are going?'

'No. You just have to wait.' He shakes his head as he leads her to the lobby.

A car is waiting for them. They slide into the back seat together, and soon the driver makes his way through the streets, which seem to be even more alive at night. They pass by the Arc de Triomphe, head down the Champs-Élysées, across the Place de la Concorde. And then they are at Rue de Royal. The car stops, and the driver gets out, opening the back door for William and Elise. Together, on the sidewalk, he takes her small hand in his. Elise is thrilled to feel William's firm warm hand encircle hers.

They move toward a restaurant and Elise sees the sign: *Maxim's Restaurant.* Elise had heard about it, knows it is where the fabulously rich and famous eat, but didn't think for a moment she would ever go. Look at what is happening to her, all because Philippe brought a friend home for the weekend. Here she is on Saturday night in Paris at Maxim's. How different from her life at home! What would she be doing now? Getting Maman to bed, cleaning dishes. Probably rereading William's letters. Instead he sits in front of her now, a bottle of Champagne on the table between them. Elise has never had Champagne and is charmed by the dancing bubbles, the cold sweetness of it.

William, sitting across from her, reaches across the table and takes her hand.

'What do you think?' he asks.

'I don't know what to think. Being here, everything, it feels like a dream.'

'One of my favourite places in my favourite city.'

'I can't believe I live so close and have only been twice!'

'We'll have to fix that,' he says. His words give her a jolt and she looks at him, gently biting her lower lip, and says, 'Do you plan on spending more time here?'

'I'm expected to take over my father's company, so I'm not sure what the future holds. But I would like to, very much.' It feels to Elise like something more is being said.

Lively music fills the air around them, the air seems to

crackle with energy, with life. On such a night, in such a place, it is hard to believe that people can be troubled, swept low, broken by events.

|She is starting to think that, after a rather rough spell, the future looks very bright indeed.

* * *

They decide to walk back, arm in arm, along the Seine. They meet other couples, also enjoying the night, and each time they meet they greet one another, thrilling Elise, who feels like she belongs to this wonderful night, this wonderful life in Paris. The moonlight casts a glow that makes it all seem like it is already a precious memory. And then, as they cross a street, Elise catches her heel on a jagged stone, turning her ankle and stumbling.

'Careful,' he says, grabbing her by the waist, his arm steadying and supporting her. Elise could be embarrassed by her clumsiness, but instead she feels safe, as William holds her, under the lamplight, the gentle sounds of the river, the light tinkling of voices filling the air, wrapped around her like fine silk.

'Shall I get a taxi?'

Elise refuses, wanting the night to last as long as possible.

'I am fine, thank you,' she says. But she does hold his arm tighter as they walk.

It is after two when they reach the hotel. William opens her hotel room door for her as he ushers her in.

'I have something for you... I'll be right back.'

'William, no, the night has been perfect. I do not need anything else.' The hotel, the dinner, it had all been beyond anything she could have dreamed, and she had dreamed so much leading up to this trip. As he disappears to his own room, Elise takes off her heels, pads to the window and opens it up, letting in the night air. She is tired, but deliciously so. Walking through Paris all day, the excitement of being with William, of falling further in love, of thinking he is falling too, hoping, wanting to ask what he is thinking. It's all been heavenly. Hearing him at the door she turns. William has a package in his hand, and she knows for certain what it is.

'Really, William, it's all been so wonderful. But this is too much.' He waves away her concerns and motions her to the bed where they both sit. Elise unwraps the shiny blue paper to reveal another volume of poetry, matching the others. This time it is Tennyson. She runs her hand over the cover and turns to him. Their faces are so close. She closes her eyes and leans forward, whispers 'thank you' as his lips touch hers. As warmth spreads through her, the kiss deepens. Elise feels William's hand on her lower back and reaches up and wraps her hand around his neck, feeling the collar of his shirt and a small patch of smooth skin and the softness of his hair. She is scared, thrilled, exhilarated, as he moves closer to her, covering her lips with his. She responds immediately. But then, he stops. Has she done something wrong?

'You've had Champagne.' He loosens his hold as Elise tightens hers.

'I know exactly what I am doing.' She leans forward and kisses him again.

* * *

The wind blows softly their last day in Paris. The sky is a blur of blue and grey, and clouds gather in the distance. There will be rain by the end of the day.

William carries her bag as they walk to the station. Elise has her bouquet of roses in one hand, is holding William's arm with the other. They're silent; too many questions to even know where to start. So much between them unspoken, but perhaps words aren't needed to confirm what is happening.

'It's been a wonderful few days.' Elise breathes in his scent, thinking the word 'wonderful' is not up to describing what the time has meant to her. 'When will I see you again?' she asks, her heart beating furiously as she waits his answer.

He holds her hand as she steps onto the train, continues to hold it until the crowd separates them.

Shouting above the crowd vying for a seat on the train, William says loudly, confidently, 'We will see each other soon, somehow. I promise.' As their hands slip apart he yells, 'Though hell should bar the way!'

Elise leans out a window, tears shining in her eyes. She did not know it was possible to be so happy. To feel so much for another person. For all the books and poetry she's read extolling love, this is different, more profound. This is theirs, alone.

And then the train is leaving. He stands on the platform and waves. She blows him kisses until she can't see him anymore.

FIFTEEN
NORTHERN FRANCE. SUMMER 2009

Lucy can't sleep. Since her break-up with Hal she's had episodes where she slept days on end, and then had weeks when sleep was impossible, no matter how tired she was. But tonight, it is different.

Her mind is spinning. The walk had been nice, and she had seen a few things, but nothing had jumped out at her. She's not exactly sure what she had been expecting, but nothing happened. Absolutely nothing. It's like she was expecting someone to walk up to her in the street and say they are her long-lost relative and have been expecting her. But that hasn't happened, and in the darkness she wonders why she's here. She remembers how alone she is. The memory of what Hal did ebbs during the day but pulls her under the waves at night.

Turning her head, she stares out the stupid small window, searching for some light in the sky.

The minutes tick by. If she was home, she'd sneak out, go for a run. But she can't do that here. Can she?

At 5:05 she gives up even trying to sleep and gets out of

bed. Slipping into her running gear, she starts to think about a path she can take. She looks out the window. There's barely a hint of light in the air, and she figures she should stay in the town streets, where she will be safer. The quiet of the morning is its own presence, as Lucy makes her way to the lobby. Helene is still there, an omnipresent figure. She might have worked all night but she still looks fabulous. Lucy waves as she heads out the door, the smell of brewing coffee and baking bread greeting her like an old friend. She will treat herself, when she gets back. A café au lait and a croissant. She can taste them both already.

It feels like all of France is still asleep, except for Lucy and the bakers. She runs slowly, softly at first, as though her footfall might wake someone. The sun is moving up in the sky, causing shadows to fall along the road. As the stone buildings lighten under the rays, she settles into a comfortable pace. She was eleven when she started to run. It was sports day at school. When the teacher, Mr Roberts, put them together for the four-person relay, he said, 'Lucy is the fastest; she'll go last to make up any time needed.' Lucy had no idea she was a fast runner until it was pointed out. They came first and were given simple ribbons, mass-produced and cheap. But Lucy liked the deepness of the blue and how the silver lettering shimmered. She still had it, tucked away in a trunk at her grandfather's house. Her house, now.

She always thought running was something anyone could do; you just had to move your legs. But the more she ran, the more she learned about pacing and breathing. She loved the feeling she got when she pushed through a wall of exhaustion. Adrenaline kicked in, and she felt like she was flying. It was just her and the empty road ahead. She'd had to stop when she was fourteen and grew so quickly it caused problems with her knees. Had to stop but didn't for long. That was when she started sneaking out to run the beach. A night run, the crash of the waves for company. Granddad not knowing. The thought of it now makes her pick up her pace. Could she run to the coast from here?

Ahead of her she sees someone else out for a morning run. He has a nice gait, is an experienced runner. She picks up her pace but knows she will never catch him. He's taller, running at a quicker pace and with a longer stride.

As she watches, he stumbles, slightly, catches himself before he falls. Then he's bending over, tying up his shoelace. Lucy is close enough now she can see a small trail of sweat running along his backbone. It's Rob, she realises all at once. She watches, studying him. The way his grey shirt pulls across his shoulder muscles and hangs loose above his shorts.

He looks in her direction, alerted by her shadow in the early dawn.

'Fancy meeting you here.' He grins as he straightens up and Lucy falls in step beside him.

'You're a runner,' she says, like that isn't obvious. 'Nice stride,' she adds.

'Thanks.'

He dips his head and Lucy thinks he's blushing.

'Where are you running to?' he asks.

'No idea. Was going to run until I got tired and then run back.'

He laughs.

'I'd like to try for the coast. How far is that?' she asks.

'Twenty-two miles. Good for marathon training.'

They are silent, adjusting their strides to match, finding a rhythm.

The sun is higher in the sky now, and Lucy is running a bit quicker than usual. She can feel herself start to sweat. She's always loved that feeling, like all the bad stuff is exiting her body with each drop. Each pie, each cookie, each mean thought, each ugly shard of grief. Now, she hopes she does not smell near Rob.

'If you want to run to the coast, you should. I can pick you up and bring you back, if you tell me when you're going.'

'That's nice of you. I'll think about it. There's still a lot I want to see.'

'Any plans for the day?' he asks.

'Museum and library.' She's not going to tell him she plans on walking each street, hoping to pass by something important. To possibly retrace her grandmother's steps. To be guided to something from her past.

'You might want to take a trip to nearby Caen. It was almost completely destroyed during the war, and I tell everyone they should see it.'

'Caen – got it.'

'There's other places too. Want to have dinner tonight, and I can tell you?'

'Sure,' she says. 'But this time, I'm buying.'

'Okay.' He laughs.

They run in silence for a few minutes.

'You're speeding up,' he says.

Lucy feels like sprinting, and with a look over her shoulder at Rob says, 'Race you to the bend in the road ahead.'

'You're on,' he says, and picking up his own pace, flies

by her. But Lucy is very competitive and takes off after him with all she has. Moving over the street, with the quiet of the morning before the world wakes, she feels like she can fly. A few seconds after Rob hits the bend she bolts by him, and she feels almost invincible as they race along the path where so many have walked, including all those soldiers so long ago. But now, it is just the two of them, the wind in the trees, and the memory the land around them holds.

SIXTEEN
ESPERANCE. SUMMER 1939

'Elise, my dear, you are daydreaming again,' Monsieur Allard says as he opens the oven door and takes out a batch of bread.

Pink stains her cheeks as she blushes, caught again thinking about William, and that lovely time in Paris.

'Sorry,' she whispers, then returns to placing croissants in a basket.

He gives a playful frown, delighted to see her so happy. Hoping it lasts.

'I think we will make some lemon tarts. It is good weather for tarts. People like fruit when it is sunny. Could you start the filling, please? And pay attention!' he admonishes, making his eyebrows dip.

Elise laughs as she takes out the double boiler. She fills the bottom with water and brings it to a boil as she starts to mix ingredients. Elise detests lemon tarts, and they are a pain to make. So she thinks about William, now back in America. He had told her he planned the trip wrong, should have seen her at the start, so he could keep her in Paris with him. Elise relives that bit a lot.

Monsieur Allard is checking on Marianne, who has a cold and is in bed upstairs, when a customer comes in. Monsieur Dupont takes his time making up his mind, although he always gets the same thing. After Elise packages his cookies, rings up his purchase and makes chit-chat, she remembers the filling, and sails to the stove. It is boiling over, the smell of burnt sugar filling the space around them. Unthinkingly, she grabs the pot handle, which is red hot to the touch. Her hand sticks to the thick sugary mixture coating it, and for a long second it feels like her hand is melting onto the pot handle before she frees it, knocking the pot to the floor. It clangs and spins before coming to a rest. Elise knows it will scorch the wooden planks and grabs a dishtowel to pick it up. When she finally throws it in the sink, she looks at the mess she's made and sees the dishtowel is stuck to the burn on her hand. When she peels it off, a chunk of flesh is stuck to the cotton. The pain makes her cry as Monsieur Allard appears, having heard the commotion. He looks around, appalled.

'I'm so sorry about the mess, and the floor, and the pot...' Despite her best efforts tears spill from Elise's eyes – the pain is excruciating, flares of agony shooting up and down her arm. But Monsieur Allard is shaking his head, dismissing her apology as he grabs her arm, bringing her to the sink. He turns on the tap and pushes her hand under the cold water.

She flinches when the water hits the torn flesh but Monsieur Allard's large hand holds hers gently, firmly in place.

'I heard noise. What has happened?' Marianne sees

Elise and moves quickly to her. 'Let me see,' she says, stepping to the sink. She looks at the bad burn and blanches slightly.

'Oh, my dearest, this is going to scar,' she says. Then she is upstairs, quick as a flash, returning with a small white metal box.

'We have to keep it clean and dry,' she says gently to Elise, then: 'Fetch some brandy,' to her husband, who is hovering like a circus bear on a ball nearby.

'Yes,' he says, dashing up the stairs, making a solid thump on each step.

'How did you do this?' Marianne says, dabbing some cotton wool on the burn.

'I'm not... I'm not sure. The pot boiled over and I wasn't thinking...'

'Shhh, it is fine. A simple lapse in concentration,' she comforts. Then she reaches for a plant, breaks the end off. 'Some aloe vera. It will fix you right up.'

'You said it would scar?'

'It might be okay,' she soothes.

She is wrapping gauze around Elise's hand when Monsieur Allard reappears, a bottle of Calvados in his hand. He pours a great offering into a teacup and hands it to Elise, before tipping the bottle into his own mouth and taking a great pull. The dangle of bells announces a new customer, but he waves them away. 'We are closed,' he says, although it is still morning, and their busiest time.

The customer – Madame Theroux – takes in the scene and plants her feet. 'YOU are not! And I want my baguette.'

Perhaps it is the shock of what has happened, but

Monsieur Allard runs to help her as Elise and Marianne giggle.

'Have another drink,' she says, pushing the Calvados at Elise. 'It helps with the pain.'

Elise goes home, unable to work, wobbly from the shock and the liquid medication. The burn is the most painful thing she has ever felt.

Maman is sitting in a chair, staring out the window. When Elise checks on her, she does not notice her bandaged hand. Elise goes to her room, shuts the door. On the windowsill are the white roses William gave her in Paris. The petals are starting to turn brown, to wither. It surprises her to see this. She thought the flowers might last forever.

SEVENTEEN

NORTHERN FRANCE. SUMMER 2009

Lucy plans on walking all day. Her map is in her bag and her route planned in her head. She'll walk to the train station, where it all began, spend the morning walking the trail through the woods Rob has told her about. Then she will walk the streets and look at the houses. Maybe she will pass by the one where her grandmother lived. Maybe, somehow, she will know.

Lucy is almost to the train station when she sees the entrance to the path Rob had told her about. She starts to walk, taking deep breaths, listening to the sound of the wind in the trees. The whoosh is hypnotic. Little park benches begin to appear, simple wooden structures with small plaques, written in French. She reads each one as she walks by. Isn't that why people dedicated benches, so strangers would read their loved one's name, bringing them momentarily back to life?

Pour Monsieur Albert Lavoie
Mort pour la France

1919–1943

Albert Lavoie. Twenty-four when he died. Was he part of the Resistance? She wishes there was more information on the plaque. What was he doing, when he died for France?

Lucy moves along. The path winds through the woods, old-growth trees. She does not like to think about the ones cut down to lay the paved path, but the ones that remain are old, dignified. They remind her of her old neighbourhood in Boston. Another bench appears, and she tries to read the plaque. The bench looks older, worn. It is set in the direct sunlight and has been bleached by rays and time. The plaque is rusted. Lucy can't make out the name. *Un jeune fille.* Something about *jacinthes.* What could they be? She looks in her French–English dictionary. Bluebells. A young girl who liked flowers. Lucy takes out a tissue and tries to rub clean the plaque, but the rust won't budge.

It is sad, that this small memorial to someone long gone has been obliterated.

She sits, down, opens her journal, makes a few notes. Records the names on the benches. She has not been prepared for this trip, but when she goes home, she will get her grandfather's marriage licence, find her grandmother's last name. Write away for his military records. And she'll come back. That thought, and being here, brings her peace. Or maybe not peace, but a break from the darkness of reality.

Lucy pulls out her Thermos and takes a drink. She'll keep whoever this person is company for a spell. It's so warm, where she is sitting, and it is such a pretty day.

She takes her time on the wooded path, having a

conversation with a local man out for his daily exercise. It felt great to practise speaking French, and he was very patient with her. Lucy noticed again how elegant the French look, even while sweating. His trousers were the perfect length, his running shoes a smart black with cream-coloured soles. No oversize shirts that had been washed too many times, no knee socks with trainers. Her grandmother must have missed the French fashion when Granddad moved her to Providence, which wasn't exactly Paris when it came to style.

The trail ends and Lucy finds herself surrounded by old stone cottages. They are not joined together, like on the Main Street. They stand alone – very close, but alone. From the outside they seem flat, no porches, no garages, just perfect rectangles and squares. She'd like to see what they look like inside. Moving along, she reads the street signs, notices the subtle differences in the colours of the doors, the shutters. A house that looks out of place with the others appears. It is located in the middle of a bend in the road, facing the street at an angle. It looks like it's being pushed down into the earth. Not so much collapsing as drooping.

She is standing in the street staring when the door opens and a familiar figure appears.

'Lucy?'

Rob is on the step of the house, wearing a sweatshirt and jeans, bare feet, waving to her.

He's standing ten, maybe fifteen steps from her, but the unexpectedness of him has her questioning if she's seeing things. It's the second time that day they've run into each other, and Lucy wonders if someone is trying to tell her something.

As she waves, a drop of rain lands on her cheek.

'Lucy?' he repeats.

Another drop of rain hits the ground beside her. She looks at the mark it makes on the pavement, then to the sky, as if trying to understand the concept of rainfall. It feels like she's watching herself standing there, feeling the first few drops that herald a downpour.

EIGHTEEN
ESPERANCE. AUTUMN 1939

The first letter Elise receives after William leaves is different from the others. It arrives in the same light blue envelope, has the same straight up and down writing. But the words are different. They are not the scribblings to a schoolgirl, a friend's sister; they are not a note of thanks for a favour performed. They are words of love, passion, commitment. She is thrilled. And terrified. Something is not right.

She can't describe it, but a bad feeling fills the summer sweet air as Elise walks to town. It is its own presence, taking up more and more space each day. It's in the eyes of the people around her, the set of their mouths, the way their shoulders are raised, as if they are already trying to protect themselves from what is coming. Anxiety bounces in the air. She tries to concentrate on the ripe, full leaves on the trees, the sound of the waterwheel in the distance. The different shades of green of the grass. But everything feels off.

Maman is frantic, wondering what Hitler will do.

Terrified for her son. But Elise is not convinced. The effects of the Great War are everywhere. The families still mourning their dead, the men who returned sitting at cafés, armless, legless. How could the world forget so soon? How could it happen? And wasn't the last war fought to end all wars?

Bits of news float to her from the open windows of the homes she passes, the static from radios vying with the information from Paris.

She makes her way to the bakery, as she does each day, whether she is working or not. Some days she heads to her little spot in the woods and writes to William; some days she reads. Every day she checks the post office. She still thrills at the sight of the air mail envelopes, hardly believing William, her William, loves her. They love each other. The feeling of such love both strengthens and weakens her. This happens when you love someone as much, even more than yourself, she is learning.

Turning the corner she sees the familiar awning of the bakery and feels better, lighter.

The moment Elise steps into the shop, she knows something is very, very wrong. The baskets that are always filled with bread are empty. There is a half-iced cake sitting on the counter. And there are no people to be seen. The air is thick with dread.

And then, from the curtain that separates the shop from the stairs to the living space above, Monsieur Allard appears.

He is stark white and seems to have shrunk, like a soufflé collapsing on itself. Elise rushes forward, afraid he may collapse.

'Are you all right? Are you sick? Is it Marianne?

Michel?' She panics at the thought of dear little Michel being hurt.

He cannot speak. All he can do is shake his head for a few moments until, bending forward, pressing his large hands on his knees, he catches his breath. 'Germany has invaded Poland,' he gasps. 'My God, we are at war.'

The words hit Elise like a physical blow, and she steps backwards, leans on the counter.

'Are you certain?'

'It's the only thing on the radio.'

'I must get home.' Her eyes are wild, the news ripping through her as she stares at Monsieur Allard. What does this mean for Marianne, a German? How can all their lives be affected by an ugly little man in another country? William had been worried about this for years, but she didn't listen.

He nods, straightens his back. His chest puffs out as he gives Elise a nod as if to say, *I know how to handle this; we will all be fine.* Lucy nods back, showing belief she does not feel. The burn on her hand, healed but leaving a white patch of scar tissue, itches suddenly, and she scratches at it, feels the pain again.

They will both have a lot of pretending to do in the days to come.

* * *

The stink of cigarette smoke when she opens the door can only mean one thing.

Philippe is home.

'Hello,' he says when he sees her, as though they'd spoken the day before, when in fact it's been years.

He looks terrible. As though he's slept in his clothes for weeks. He has dirt under his nails and the wrinkles of a man twice his age. Elise would be shocked, if it wasn't for the news. That is all she is thinking about.

She nods and says, 'There's news.' She is gentle, as though a softness in language can change the meaning, change what is to come. Surely this news will kill their maman.

'I know.' Philippe seems to further shrink before her eyes, no doubt thinking about what this means for him. He pulls a bottle of Calvados from the cabinet, pours a large measure and sinks it in one go then refills the glass, wordlessly.

Already Elise cannot picture him as a soldier.

'You won't go fight, tell me you won't?' Maman's eyes are wild with fear. She grabs at Philippe's hand.

'I don't think I will have a choice.' He plucks her hand from atop his and returns it to her. Elise stares at her brother, trying to figure him out. He has never asked about her relationship with his friend William, and he must know.

Elise picks up a glass and pours herself a Calvados, for something to do. She takes a sip, winces at the sharpness of it, takes another sip, and begins.

'William thinks I, we, should go to America.' Her voice is low, calm. He had mentioned it in letters, but Elise had dismissed the possibility. Maman would not leave. There would be no more war. As she stands in their little house in France, she wishes she was in Boston already.

Maman looks anxiously around their home, as though it is the Taj Mahal. 'Leave France?'

Elise nods. 'I think we should. We must.'

'I cannot leave my home,' she says.

'It's a building, Maman, not even a nice one.' But she knows it is not the house. It is fear. Fear of staying, fear of leaving. If it were not for dear Papa, knowing how she would let him down, Elise would walk to Cherbourg and get on the boat today. What is keeping her here? Obligation. Duty. Hope, that this war will be short, over before a gun is fired.

She finishes her drink, pours another.

No one notices that Philippe is strangely quiet, staring out the window. Elise, so used to being alone, she forgets he is there.

She walks up the stairs and goes to her room. She had not made her bed when she woke, which is new for her. Sitting on the twisted blankets, she wonders what will happen, what will become of all of them. She had been so happy, thinking about being with William. A future together. A pretty home, babies that she would love fiercely. Now this war. It will change everything. She must convince her maman to leave.

The anxiety that had been filling the air has landed, covering everyone, everything. Elise falls into her unmade bed, her head on the pillow, her legs pulled up to her chest. In sleep there is oblivion. She closes her eyes.

Hours later, just after daybreak, she wakes. The stale air from endless cigarettes reminds her that Philippe is home. The news of the previous day hits again, and with it the confusion of it all. If her country is at war, what does that mean? And how can she get to William?

She makes her way the washroom, passing by Philippe's closed door. A splash of water on her face to wake her, then mindlessly brushing her teeth. Her morning toilette is cursory at best. She heads down the stairs to the kitchen, to make coffee. On the chair she sees her bag. It is open. And before she looks, she knows. The money she'd been saving is gone. She knows who took it and does not need to go upstairs to know Philippe's room is empty.

NINETEEN
NORMANDY. SUMMER 2009

'Lucy, come in, before the skies open,' Rob shouts to her.

Her words pull her back to reality, and she moves toward him. Once she's on the steps, he moves to the side, to let her into the house.

While the air outside has the sweet, heavy smell of a brewing summer rain, the inside of the house is heavier with scent. Lemon cleaner and paint fumes that can't mask the mustiness, the aroma of decay. And something else. Not a scent so much as a feeling.

She hears the door close behind her and then Rob is beside her, leading her into the main room, with a window that looks out to the street where she was just standing. It takes up most of the wall. No curtains. There's a sofa in front of the window that has seen better days. An oatmeal colour, with a hint of a sag in the middle.

'Hi,' he says.

'Hi,' she replies.

Lucy moves further into the room. There's a birthday card propped up on the mantel above the fireplace. Shelves beside the fireplace with a few books. A little room, a passageway really, connects the space to the back of the house, a kitchen and eating area in front of new patio doors.

It looks like someone turned an abandoned house into a temporary bachelor pad.

'Welcome to Casa Rob,' he says, carrying the dishes from the table to the sink. 'I wasn't expecting company.'

'Don't clean up on my account,' Lucy says.

'I was sitting here eating and saw someone standing in the street. I got up to look and was a bit shocked to see you.'

Lucy, standing by the table, turns and sees from where Rob was sitting is a clear view to the street.

'Can I get you anything?' His hand is on the fridge door.

'No. Yeah. Thanks.'

He laughs. 'Try again.'

'I have an apple in my bag. Could I have a drink?'

Rob looks at his watch. 'I'm having a beer. Want one?'

Lucy nods.

'Bottle okay?'

She nods again.

'This is not where I pictured you living.'

Her head peacocks around.

'What did you picture?'

She thinks of how he dresses and replies, 'Modern. Classic. So how did you end up here?' She waves her arm, indicating the house. It feels like her arm is cutting through something more than air and space.

'I walked by this place on my first trip here, when I was backpacking. You think it looks bad now? You should have seen it before I replaced the shutters, fixed the steps, cut the grass.

'Anyway, I saw a note in the window from the road and walked up to read it. My French was pretty appalling then, but they were looking for information on the owner, and there was a number to call. I thought it strange no one knew who owned the place, although I guess places are abandoned all the time. When I moved back, I called the number, and talked to the man who was taking care of it while they looked for the owner. We made a deal that I could live here rent-free, if I wanted to clean it up, but had to leave if he showed up. No one expects him to show up.'

'Why?'

'He's been gone a long time,' Rob says. 'The neighbours were delighted when I hauled out a mower. Not so pleased with the bin I had in front for weeks, as I ripped out old plaster. Or with the noise when I put in the door out back. I had to hire someone to help with that. But the place badly needed some natural light, and the door had rotted off and the wall was a disaster waiting to happen.

'You get to live on your own, and the place gets some TLC. Nice.'

'And occasionally beautiful young women appear in my street looking lost. It's a win-win.'

Lucy laughs.

'Didn't sound creepy at all, did it?' Rob winks.

She takes a drink of beer.

'It's like you were meant to walk by and see the place. Meant to save it.'

His head tilts slightly, and she can tell he's thinking about what she said. She likes that even more than his 'beautiful' comment.

'Do you believe things are meant to be?'

'You mean fate, or destiny?'

'I've never understood the difference between the two,' Rob says.

'Fate is what happens when you abdicate responsibility for your life. Destiny is when you get to a good end by making good decisions.'

'Abdicate responsibility?' He gives her a half-grin.

'A nice way of saying blaming fate for making bad decisions?'

'Like, I was fated to be a drug addict because I had bad parents?'

'That's the way I see the difference. I looked it up once, when doing a paper on *Macbeth*.'

'So what do you think?'

Lucy thinks about the decision to take a summer class when she could have gone to France. 'I think we all make the best decisions we can at any moment, but how we're raised affects the decisions when we're young, and memories and trauma affect them when we're older.'

'I like that. Makes sense.'

Lucy picks up her beer and moves around the room. There's a door that seems to lead to a room under the stairs.

'What's in there?' she asks.

'Old storage room. I cleaned some garbage out of it when I moved in and threw down bags of lime. It's very cold and very mildewed. It stinks.'

'No hidden bodies?'

'That's a bit dark.' He laughs.

'Be a great part of the story. If you found a murdered Nazi, or maybe a RAF pilot who succumbed to his injuries while being nursed by the homeowners.'

'Possible, but this place didn't see much action. Too far from the coast, nothing the Nazis wanted.'

Lucy stands in front of the door. It's old, wooden, with some metal reinforcements at the edges. She can feel the cold seeping through, likes she's standing in a draught.

'You can look if you want,' Rob says.

Lucy shakes her head. Moves away.

'My imagination is getting the better of me, as my grandfather would say.'

'No ghosts, no skeletons. I promise.'

Lucy laughs. But she's not certain she believes him.

* * *

They order pizza for dinner, and Rob opens a bottle of red wine. He lights a fire, seeing Lucy curled up on the sofa, her feet tucked under her, cold.

'Are you sure it's safe?' she asks after hearing about the house being in such bad shape when he found it.

'The fireplace?'

'Yes.'

'The house was structurally sound. Built back in the days when things were meant to last,' he says.

She watches as the flames catch, spring to life. A vague memory takes shape in her mind, of fires in her old house, before her parents died. She remembers burning Christmas paper after the presents had been unwrapped. She was wearing pyjamas with snowflakes and penguins. She lets the memory come, hoping for more, to see her parents, but just like that, it is gone.

'Lucy?'

'Lost in thought. Flames do that to me.'

'So what were you doing out walking today?'

She takes a sip of her drink.

'After the Juno tour, I started thinking about the local who noticed the border of flowers being disturbed. And it got me thinking about how my grandmother was a local. I started thinking that I could do a pilgrimage of sorts. Walk the streets and maybe retrace some of her steps. See the things she might have seen. Look for clues, I guess.'

'And there's no great-uncle or old aunt you could ask?'

'Nope. No one. My entire family is made up of only children and a lot of tragic deaths.'

She takes another sip as she waits for Rob to say something like, 'I'm sorry.' But he doesn't. He surprises her and says, 'Your grandfather sounds like a great man. Tell me about him.'

Somewhere deep inside, Lucy feels something that was broken being pieced back together. Like a handle being glued back to a favourite mug. It will never be the same, but you don't have to throw it out.

She turns to Rob and says, 'He was a good man.' Then she tells him about when she was very young, and he took her to Disney World. It's her favourite memory of him.

TWENTY
ESPERANCE, FRANCE. WINTER 1940

At first, nothing seems to happen. Some soldiers appear, which is startling at first. British and French soldiers. The British keep to themselves, but Elise sees them in the shops. It's an unsettling time, waiting for something, anything to happen.

At home, things are much the same, just with a new level of fear. And resentment. Elise is angry with her mother for not leaving when they could. Now they need papers to move anywhere. They cannot go to the US. They cannot even move around France.

They celebrate Christmas together, Maman waiting for Philippe to show, Elise knowing in her heart he is long gone.

But then it seems like maybe they will be all right. Maman insists de Gaulle would not get France involved in another bloody war. There is no fighting. She writes to William, cheery little notes, like everything is normal. But she does not hear from him, and this worries her. She wonders if the mail is getting through.

And then, on a warm, gentle spring day that made her feel like everything might be coming together, fighting breaks out. The Germans push through tiny Belgium, a country still reeling from the last war. The Maginot line is broken. France is overrun. Elise is both terrified and angry. How dare these people come into her country, her home?

One night, as she and Maman sit in the house in darkness, Maman afraid a light would bring the attention of soldiers, she says to the darkness around them, 'What about William?'

Elise is caught off guard.

'What about him?'

'Will you leave me to go to him?'

'We cannot go anywhere now,' she says, anger making her words brittle, her jaw ache.

Marie, her maman, looks around her home. 'This is all I have left of your papa. We were so happy here, in this little house. The war was over, and I thought the bad times were behind us. And he was so pleased, when Philippe was born. And you. I remember him holding you above his head, saying to me, "Just look at her!" as though I was not your mother, just someone new who popped by. You had a bond, from birth. He wanted a daughter.'

Elise finds herself afraid to move, in case she jars her maman back into the silence and sadness that had been her life for so long. She wills her to keep talking, wanting so badly to hear about Papa.

'When you were born, it was harder than with Philippe. I felt so sad for so long after. Papa got up with you at night, walked with you to get you to sleep. He would blow on your head to keep the mosquitoes away when you walked to the woods. He would take you over to sit with

Monsieur Gravel in the evenings. You would sleep on his chest.' Maman lifts her arm, as if cradling a sleeping baby herself. 'Your papa was a good person. A good man. Cared about people. Even old Monsieur Gravel who was so crazy.' She stops. 'He was a better person than me.'

Elise's heart feels like its own drum kit, a rhythmic pounding she can feel everywhere. She has no idea what is happening.

'It's all so very long ago now, but sometimes, when I look at the door, I can still see him walk in, take off his hat. Hear him saying, "I'm home!" before he even closed the door.' She nods in the direction of the entryway, and Elise tries to picture what she sees, but Papa is fading from her memory now. She has to think of him in context to picture him. And she has no memory of him announcing he had come home. She's not even sure it happened.

'I know his death hurt you, but us staying – that does not change things.'

'I think you should go to your young man, when you can. I will stay. Perhaps it is time I met the Germans.'

'You're talking foolishness now. Craziness. You can come, too.'

'Elise, I won't make it to Cherbourg, much less the US.'

'Maman, you're forty-six, not a hundred.'

'They say for every year you live through war, your body ages ten. So I am eighty-six.'

It takes Elise a second to think of a retort to this. 'Well, you look wonderful for eighty-six. What kind of face cream do you use?'

Maman's mouth drops open in surprise at her daughter's comment, and then she starts to laugh.

Elise watches as a bit of light comes back into the

woman's eyes, making her seem younger, happier. For briefer than a second she sees the beauty her papa fell in love with. And then, as though possessed briefly by a happy spirit she will not give a home, the laughter and the light disappear.

Elise waits to see if she will tell her more, but she is done for the evening. Tomorrow, Elise will bring up leaving, if and when they can. But maybe they will be lucky, and the British will fix everything.

TWENTY-ONE
NORTHERN FRANCE. SUMMER 2009

Lucy wakes curled up on the sofa, a blanket over her. She can feel the morning sun on her back, spilling through the window above her. It makes her feel warm and safe. It makes her feel alive. She doesn't want to move, but she needs some water. The bathroom. She wishes she had her toothbrush. Pulling herself into a sitting position, she looks around the room. A pizza box, an empty bottle of wine.

Hearing Rob on the stairs, she stands, wrapping the blanket around her shoulders.

'Good morning,' he says, appearing in front of her in chinos and a navy-blue sweater, like he just walked out of an advertisement. His hair is wet from his shower and forms a damp curtain over his eyes. They're a deeper blue in the early morning shadows of the house.

'Hi,' she says. 'What happened?'

He laughs. 'We were talking on the sofa, and you fell asleep. Mid-sentence. So I put a blanket over you and went to bed.'

'Mid-sentence?'

'Pretty much. To be fair, it was almost four. And we had wine.'

'And I guess I was boring myself.'

He laughs.

'Any chance you're making coffee?'

The floor is cold under her feet, despite her socks, as she follows him to the kitchen.

'I'd offer to make you breakfast, but I have nothing in the house. And I have to get to work. I have a tour.' He pours her a mug of coffee, handing her a spoon and the carton of milk. 'I don't have any sugar,' he apologises.

'I don't take sugar,' she replies, taking a big gulp.

'I gotta go. Don't rush. Pull the door closed behind you; it locks automatically. Do you know how to get back to your hotel from here?'

'Top of the street, turn left. Down the main drag, and another left.'

'That's it.'

'Have a good day,' he says. 'Don't forget to turn the coffee pot off.'

She follows him to the door.

'You're sure it's okay I stay?'

'There's nothing to steal. Just don't burn the place down.' He gives his trademark half-grin. Lucy can't believe how nice he is. And it feels real, like this is who he is, not a role he is playing.

She closes the door behind him, watches as he walks to the street.

* * *

The house feels different when he leaves. Less alive. Less welcoming. Cradling her mug for warmth, she looks around. The mantel of the fireplace is solid, a thick heavy wood that gleams from polishing and age. The floors need to be refinished, but Rob said it was too big a job. They look like planks of wood, covered in a greyish paint one too many times. She wonders if she'll get a splinter. Some cheap throw rugs are scattered about, but Lucy imagines the floors were once covered in handmade rag rugs. She tries to picture the place as it might have looked when a French family called it home. Did they curl up in front of the fire? Did children run happily about?

She runs her hands along the shelves Rob built. They don't hold much: a small stereo, a French brand he must have bought recently, judging by how new it looks. Some neatly stacked paperbacks. Raymond Chandler. Pierre Lemaitre, the same book in English and French. Stieg Larsson. P.D. James. The poetry of Emily Dickinson. Lucy picks it up, surprised Rob owns it. It looks older than the other books on the shelf, the pages water-damaged. It's a nice book, though. She loves Dickinson. There's more. Biographies of Napoleon. Someone called the Desert Fox. Amelia Earhart. The poetry doesn't quite sit right with hardcover biographies and she wonders if a girlfriend may have left it behind.

The dining table is old, scarred, solid. It might have come with the house. The kitchen is small, almost a perfect square. She opens the cabinets one by one, finds a bag of pasta, some tins of soup. More coffee and some tea. In the next, plain white plates, bowls and cups, all neatly stacked. She closes the doors, moves past the cellar door, down the hall to the stairs. She'd been upstairs to the bathroom a few times but had not seen the other rooms.

She's not exactly afraid but hesitates as she makes her way up each step, listening to the creaks, waiting to plummet to whatever is below. At the top of the stairs is the bathroom, and a small landing leading to three closed doors. Rob's, she knows, is to the right. She won't invade his private space.

She opens the door to the room across from it. It's much smaller, empty except for a wardrobe. An unpleasant smell hangs in the room. Must, and the vaguest hint of old cigarette smoke, caught in the very walls. A naked light bulb hangs from the ceiling, moving slowly, perhaps from the force of her opening the door. It is creepy, and Lucy pulls the door shut quickly.

The next room tells a different story.

At first it seems lifeless, the way unoccupied spaces can be, but there is a sweetness to the air, a scent of lavender, she thinks. A single bed frame with a wooden headboard is tucked against a sloping wall. There's a simple wooden desk in front of a window. As Lucy opens it to let some air in she pictures the curtains that once were there – lace, maybe. Something light and pretty. Birdsong carried on a gentle breeze of pure air comes into the room and she is still, enjoying the feel on her face. A wardrobe lines the other wall. She opens the doors, but it is empty. Behind the door, in the corner, she spies an old chest. Kneeling down, she lifts the lid. The hinges give a slight squeak, and a stale odour wafts up to her. Dusts motes dance in the air. Lucy sees a blanket, a wool blanket that might have been beige once, but now it's sort of brown, and sort of red, like somehow it managed to rust. She pushes it aside.

A bit of black leather appears, a book. She plucks it up and sees it is the collected works of Shelley. Not genuine leather, for it is flaking in her hand. Opening it gently, she flips the pages until she finds an inscription, written neatly in the top corner of the page. It is too faded to read. Moving to the window, she holds it up to the light, can make out what she thinks is a *W*. Wiping the dust from the cover, Lucy pulls the book against her chest, holding it there protectively. She sees two more in the trunk and hopes she can make out their inscriptions. But the books have been damaged by time and water. The words of Byron, her personal favourite, are too weak to read. She stacks them gently on top of each other. She would like to put them on the shelves but does not want Rob to know she was snooping.

There's one small box left, simple cardboard that looks like it holds jewellery. Lucy takes the cover off and there inside is a tarnished bracelet that was once silver with some blue stones, like sapphires. It's heavier than she expected when she picks it up, and although she's sure the stones are not real, it looks, and feels, valuable. Lucy wraps it around her wrist and fastens it shut. It fits perfectly. In the pale light sprinkling in the window the stones lighten, become the blue of the ocean.

She hesitates, then unfastens the bracelet, slips it into her pocket. She closes the trunk, and with one last look around, closes the door on the tiny, lavender-scented room.

TWENTY-TWO
ESPERANCE, FRANCE. DECEMBER 1941

Another year is coming to a close. Another year is gone. Soon it will be Christmas. There will be no present from William. No letter to keep her going. She misses the post so much.

Elise dresses in as many layers as she can. Food is rationed, and she has lost a great deal of weight. She is always cold now. Twisted with the cold, and emptiness.

Maman is sitting in a chair, facing the fireplace. A few flames burn dully, as if they too have been denied what they need to live. If the Germans could figure out a way to steal oxygen, Elise is sure they would.

'You are not going out!' Maman says. Her words might once have been sharp, but she too is thin, and what little energy she had is gone. Most nights she sleeps on the sofa, too tired to go up the stairs.

Elise looks out the door, scanning the area around her childhood home. She sees Monsieur Gravel's home, the wind chimes now silenced. Seeing no one, she steps out.

She walks quickly, purposefully, trying not to draw

attention to herself. Not wanting to be seen by people who were once friends. You don't know who to trust, now. Not wanting to see hungry children. Or those horrible yellow stars sewn onto once fine clothes. How naïve she had been to think war was impossible. But no one had anticipated this level of evil. How could they?

Turning the corner, she sees the church. Remembers that night, a lifetime ago, with William.

She stops. And thinks. Then she crosses the road, walks up the steps to the church. The large door will not budge, at first, and she thinks it is locked. It gives just enough for her to have a flash of hope. Looking around once, twice, a third time, she uses both hands to pull at the door. Thankfully it opens. Grabbing up the package, she steps inside. She is out of the wind, but it is somehow colder inside. Damp.

Her eyes adjust slowly to the dimness. Perhaps because life has been so very dark for so long. She moves slowly, trying to will forward the memory of her night here with William. A flame encompassed in a red glass holder on the altar beckons and she moves toward it. She is the only one in the huge building, and it feels like even the sound of her breathing echoes.

Taking a seat, Elise dips her head, unsure of what to do. Then she remembers, the France sisters, long gone now, seeing them kneel. Elise does the same. It is painful, her knee bones digging into the wood.

In the cool quiet, she collects her thoughts. What does she really want? For the war to be over. For the war never to have started. She could be married now, living in Cape Cod. But no, what could she have done about Maman?

She shakes her head and starts again.

Inside, she begins. *Thank you for William. Thank you for keeping us safe so far. We are scared, here in France. I'm sure you know that. We hear about camps. People disappearing. It has been very hard. Please, if the war could be over. Please. If William and I could be together, forever. Please. And Maman. It has been so hard. If she could please get better, strong enough to leave...*

A dark thought enters her mind, but she pushes it away.

Please. Let us all be safe and happy again.

She squeezes her eyes shut, as though this will somehow cement the deal. Struggling to her feet, as though she is old and not simply malnourished, sad, slightly broken, like a rag doll washed too many times. She sees the doors to the crypt and remembers the angel. Down the stairs, trying not to make any noise. What if someone is hiding below? You never know where the enemy might be. Even her neighbours, they were enemies now. Poor Marianne, vilified for simply being German. The thought makes Elise feel even heavier, even older.

And then, on the bottom step, it appears, the angel from so long ago. He's still there. She knew he would be, but still, seeing him, it brings comfort. There has been a church here for a thousand years. This angel has been here for that long. Faded, perhaps, even flaking in a few spots, but still there. It has not been erased or destroyed and this comforts Elise, gives her hope. She reaches out and puts her hand on the angel's chest, willing it to give her some of its strength. It feels cold, damp, but solid, too.

'Please get us all through this. Please send the Germans away.' She waits for a sign, but nothing happens. She lingers, would like to stay. The walls feel so solid, so protective. But she has been away too long. She makes her way to the door. It is easier to push it open from the inside. It is not until she is out in the street that she realises she did not say a prayer for her brother. It has been so long. He is more memory than person now. But then, that's what everyone will be, one day.

Outside, she looks toward the post office and the bakery, remembering the simple joy of going for post. Long walks in the woods. Now, Elise spends most of her time standing in line, as there are ration vouchers for everything. How she longs for those halcyon days when the aroma of baking bread filled the air, when the bakery was filled with energy and tarts and cakes. They were poor, and Maman was a handful, and Philippe was a drunk, a lost soul, she's not sure what to call her brother. But there was good food and the kindness of neighbours. That is gone, now.

The sound of the breeze in the trees that used to delight her feels like a warning. *Go back,* it says.

Everything is so strange these days. It is horrible when your home is no longer yours.

TWENTY-THREE

NORTHERN FRANCE. SUMMER 2009

The history marker outside the walls tell Lucy that Saint-Lô dates back to the Roman empire. Lucy can't believe she is standing in a city that old. A city where so much has happened. But then, Paris is that old, too.

The Vikings invaded and ripped the place apart in the 800s, and she wonders if that act of violence tainted it forever as she reads about its history. How it suffered during the Industrial Revolution. How a paper mill burned down in the 1930s. And then, how it was invaded in 1940 and occupied by Germans wanting to capture Cherbourg. She's read a lot about Cherbourg, and wishes she had time to see it now. She can't believe how quickly the time has passed.

Reading in the library, Lucy discovered that Saint-Lô was ninety per cent destroyed during the war, but a few houses survived. Lucy has the names of the streets written down in her journal: Rue du Neufbourg, Rue Croix Canuet and Falourdel, Rue Saint-Georges and Porte au Four. There is so much she wants to see here, a place she'd never heard of, until Rob told her about it. It's been pretty great, having her own personal tour guide. She wants to see everything, but the houses that survived and the church are the reason she is here.

People walk past her, the typical stylish French. Locals. She wonders if they ever walk through without being reminded of the past. If it is ever just a hometown. It must be. She lives on a beach that attracts tourists from all over the world, but there are some days she doesn't even notice it, she's sure.

Pulling out the map Rob gave her, she sees where she is in relation to Église Notre-Dame and then looks around for an indication of direction. A sign pointing to the church would be welcome, but she can't see one. Still, she's pretty sure she's heading in the right direction as she moves toward what looks like the busier part of the city. It is warm out, not too hot, just enough of a breeze so that everything feels fresh. Already she likes Saint-Lô, the feel of it. It has a strength and a dignity, perhaps because it has survived so much. It is peaceful now, like the city is relaxing, no longer holding its breath after so much violence, so many catastrophes. The Vire River keeps flowing. Life goes on.

She looks at the houses as she walks, their light-coloured walls. She knows they are all post-war construction, but they fit, blend in with the meandering roads and the sloping hills of the town. Lucy knows the US had barracks in Saint-Lô that have been turned into homes. She hopes she gets to see them, too, but thinks they are outside of the main town. Saint-Lô is bigger than her grandmother's hometown.

The church appears, not as regal as Notre Dame in Paris. Not as grand as the church near her hotel, but with its own shape, its own originality. Even from a distance she can tell it has its own story. Rob had told her about it, but seeing it is different. The original part the Allies bombed is connected to the new part with a wall of some kind. The modern part is made of a different kind of stone, so it stands apart, yet together. It tells a story of survival, connecting the past and the present. Lucy touches the cool rough stones as she walks around the church, seeing the outdoor pulpit, the unexploded bomb lodged into the wall. It makes her stand still, as though any movement might set it off. Old, imbedded in concrete, it is still terrifying to be so close.

She thinks, studies, trying to understand what it all means. What it wants to tell her. Surely there is a lesson here. That broken things can be fixed. That good triumphs over evil. That symmetry is not an absolute necessity for beauty. The church has a haphazard sort of appearance, but it is still magnificent.

She steps inside the church, amazed as always at the height of the ceilings, how churches always seem bigger inside than out. It is cool, slightly damp. The air, she thinks, is thick with memories. She finds a seat, sits down. For the second time in her life, she says a prayer.

Granddad, I'm sitting in a church in Saint-Lô. It has an unexploded shell lodged in the wall. It's been here since World War Two but I'm afraid I'm going to sneeze and set it off.

I am so sorry we did not do this together. How I wish I could change some of the decisions I made, but live and learn, as you say.

I love France and when I go home I'm going to find out all I can about Grandma, and I'm going to see if I can live here. Don't worry, I'm still going to medical school; I'm just not sure when. And I promise I will never tell anyone about what Grandma did.

I miss you, but you know that.

Lucy stops, and thinks for a second.

I'm sure you know about Hal now, and Molly. I don't like to wish ill on people, but if you could drop a piano on them, I'd like that.

She thinks for a second.

Okay. Maybe just give them both a bad rash.

She dips her head, says thank you, and then carries on with her day.

* * *

It takes a while, but she finds Rue Saint-Georges. The road, the houses on it, are one unit. They feel both solid and random. There's no symmetry to where the doors and windows are placed. It feels off balance, like it has been shaken and set down, everything settling where it landed.

She had expected something grander. Something that announced its strength and fortitude. In the US there would be billboards pointing out the history. That, she thinks, is the difference between her young, loud country, and the older grace of France. Here, there is no need to point.

As she gazes, she thinks about the people who lived inside its stone walls during the war. During the attacks that decimated the city. Did they cower inside, offering up prayers? She thinks of a photo she saw in a book once, of a soldier carrying a little girl through rubble, while another walked ahead with his rifle ready. The little girl was wearing a summer dress, and Lucy had thought about how a parent gets a child ready for a day that could bring liberation or destruction. Or liberation *and* destruction. It had bothered Lucy that her legs were not covered, thinking of all the glass and splintered wood.

Someone walks by her, a local man judging by his hat and shopping bag. Lucy can see bread on the top, sliced bread in a plastic wrapper, not from a bakery. She stops thinking about the house long enough to wonder why you would buy bread from a grocery store when you could go to a bakery. But seeing the man's slow gait, she thinks he probably went to the nearest shop.

'Bonjour,' she says.

'Bonjour,' he replies. Lucy watches as he slopes his way to a nearby house. Setting down his bag, he takes a key from his pocket, opens the door. As he bends to pick up his bag, Lucy is positive she hears his bones creak. She wants to go to him and help him, offer to buy him good bread, ask about his home, but while she thinks, he disappears inside. Lucy hears his lock click into place. Maybe he wants to keep out the weird girl staring at him.

With one last look, she heads down the street, back to the main part of the city. She has time to see the ramparts before her bus leaves.

TWENTY-FOUR
ESPERANCE, FRANCE. DECEMBER 9, 1941

The sky is black, with no hint of light, when Elise crawls from bed. She feels like a scarecrow wearing layers of too-often-washed clothing. It should feel soft but the cotton rubs against her, like burlap. Wire. Her feet and ankles are so cold she thinks they will snap like dry twigs when she puts weight on them.

Limping down the stairs, her short puffs of breath hang in front of her, like she's walking through a ghost of herself. Maman is asleep on the sofa, curled in a ball. She barely makes a ripple under the heavy old wool blanket. The fire has gone out. Lucy pushes the ashes to one side, puts in some kindling she collected from the woods. Funny, how she used to like to sit there and write to William. Now, it is where she scavenges. For wood to burn, for mushrooms to eat.

The fire starts. She reaches her hands toward it, her skin almost touching the flames before she feels the warmth. Her hands are old and cracked. She prays they heal before she sees William. If she ever sees him again.

She makes a cup of very weak coffee. Everything is being rationed, and coffee is scarce. When the war started, Maman sent her immediately to the shops, taking francs from a coffee can Elise knew nothing about. She bought everything she could find, even cycling to nearby towns. She thought it crazy at the time. Now she is grateful. The pantry had been stocked, but it is running low.

She sits in front of the fire, sipping. Maman wakes and rubs at her face. It takes her so long to sit up Elise thinks about getting up to help her but doesn't have the energy. Finally Maman ends up in a sort of sloped position, not quite sitting, not quite lying down. Barely alive.

'Another day in paradise,' she says. At first Elise is not sure she heard her correctly.

'Pardon?'

'Another day in paradise,' she repeats.

The omnipresent cold knot of fear that has lived in Elise's stomach for so long she has made grudging friends with it, grows colder, tightens.

Maman has finally lost her mind.

'I made a joke, Elise. I know that is not like me, but we can all change.'

Elise sits perfectly still, not certain what is happening.

'Judging by your reaction, it is probably best I don't try it again.'

The change in her tone snaps Elise back to life.

'Yes, it certainly is paradise,' she says. 'I'm about to happily wander the warm inviting streets to find some ambrosia at the bakery. I shan't be long.'

Maman, already receding into the darkness, nods.

Elise finishes her now tepid drink then starts to dress for the outdoors. As she pulls her dear papa's overcoat on, she wonders – not for the first time – about how ridiculous she must appear. She thinks again of her time in Paris, how carefully she had prepared what she was going to wear. Now, she'd wear the Christmas tinsel if it meant being warm. It was still in the attic, only because it couldn't be burned for warmth.

As she begins her walk to the bakery the first few shards of light pierce the dark sky.

The streets are as unwelcoming as ever. She has become used to the shutters on the houses being closed. A barrier to the cold, and to what is happening. Holding back the evil with the decaying bricks and mortar and dry wood of a house. Hoping to survive.

She trundles along, the stones of the street sharp on the soles of her old shoes. After a few steps she thinks something feels different. The shutters remained closed. The streets empty. But there's a new feeling in the air. A kind of electricity.

She turns the corner and is surprised to see the door to the bakery is closed, the building is dark. Bertrand should be making the day's bread rations. Elise knocks, once, twice, hoping he can hear, and that no one else is alerted to the noise she makes.

'Hello?' she whispers through the keyhole.

Footsteps on the stairs. The door creaks open. An arm reaches out, grabbing her.

'Quick, close the door. Come upstairs.' Bertrand is redder than normal, and it scares her even more.

Elise's heart is beating loudly in her chest as she races behind him, up the stairs.

One look at Marianne and she knows there has been

news. Good news, judging by the light in her eye, a light that has long been dimmed.

'Tell me, tell me!' she urges.

'We don't know all the details. But America has been attacked by the Japanese.

Elise feels like someone has picked her up and slammed her into a wall.

'What part of America? Has anyone been hurt?'

Bertrand looks baffled.

'What?'

Marianne moves past her husband, the three of them doing some sort of dance in the tiny space.

'Elise, this is good. America has declared war on Germany. We will have allies. They will save us,' she says.

But Elise is shaking her head. 'What part was attacked?'

'William,' Marianne whispers to her husband.

'Ah,' he nods. 'A place called Pearl Harbor. This was maybe two days ago.'

Elise looks at Monsieur Allard, his eyes wide, a tiny bit of hope, even joy, dancing in them. If the US joins the war, France, Europe will have a powerful ally. But William, her William. Of course, he will fight. And it feels like someone has reached into her chest and ripped out her heart.

'How do you know?' Her voice is strangely calm, considering how jumbled up she feels.

'I just do,' he says. Elise has never asked about his sources of information but knows messages have been passed in the lumps of bread they bake. No one pays attention to the baker with the bad leg.

'What on earth is a Pearl Harbor?' In her mind she pictures a waterfront shimmering with milky stones.

'A military base in Hawaii. Is that near where William lives?'

'I don't know. I've never even heard of Hawaii.' Elise spins in a half circle, arms out, like she is trying to get her balance back.

'An atlas. Do you have an atlas?'

'No.'

'Do you know anything else?'

'No.'

Elise pulls her scarf around her face. 'I must go.'

'Be careful,' he says.

She nods, already moving away. 'Start baking, before anyone gets suspicious.' She tries to whisper but her words come out anxious, her voice frazzled.

Outside, the sky is a hazy purple colour. Woodsmoke makes patches in the air, people still with wood to burn. Maybe furniture. You do not have the same emotional connection to your grandmother's table when you are freezing. Elise speeds down the streets, not caring who sees. She slips on the stone path to her house, righting herself before she falls.

Into the front room, the end table where the atlas rests.

Elise plunks the large book on the kitchen table. It hasn't been opened since she looked up Massachusetts and there's a layer of dust on the edges of the pages, nestled into the spine.

She finds Hawaii in the index, flips to the page, and lines up the number and letter on the pages. Using her fingers, she finds a series of dots: one that says Honolulu. She can't find a Pearl Harbor.

She flips to the index, finds a map of the US.

The entire country, a huge country at that, is between

this Pearl Harbor and Massachusetts, where William lives. Elise feels better, seeing this. She sits at the table, trying to make sense of it all.

For the rest of her life she would always think of the morning she learned about the attack on the US as the day Maman tried to make a joke.

TWENTY-FIVE
NORTHERN FRANCE. SUMMER 2009

She has three days left before she has to go home, and Lucy is scrambling to see as much as she can before she has to leave. She knows the town well. Has seen pictures of what it looked like before and after the war. Has stood in the very place where old photos were taken, thinking about her grandfather, her grandmother. What the war did to everyone. What it might have done to her.

In the morning she is biking to Sainte-Mère-Église. Holy Mother Church. She plans on getting up at five a.m. to bike to there, the first place liberated by American troops. It's a long trip and will take hours to get there and back. When she gets back to the hotel from Saint-Lô she takes a quick bath, gets her bag ready for the morning, then crawls into bed.

* * *

The morning light is still hiding, the sky a mottled purple as Lucy climbs on her rented bike. The saddle bag has water, a small baguette, cheese and an apple. Maps and her journal. She hopes to make it in two hours. Rob has told her to call him if she runs out of steam. Lucy will crawl on her hands and knees before she does that, but the fact that he knows where she is going is good. Granddad always wanted to know where she was. It's like he's checking in on her, via Rob.

The feel of the cobblestones under her bike tyres is familiar now. Funny, considering she's only been here a little over a week. As she pedals along, the town still asleep except for the dim light coming from the bakeries, she breathes in the clear air. It is so peaceful, the only sound is her pedals, the shifting of gears on her bike.

Something happens when she spends time alone. When the space is quiet. The world enters just a little, shows flashes. She's on a bike coasting through the French countryside when her parents come to her. She thinks about them at some point each day, but this time, it feels different. Like they're with her, coasting beside her. She slows down. She can't reach out and touch them, but they are very real to her.

She's never visited them at the cemetery. Boston was an hour away and she could have gone so easily. She knew Granddad arranged to have flowers sent. All the times he visited her, they never went together. She knows he did. She could not think about her parents lying in the cold earth. A small bend in the road appears, and Lucy flows with it, as sunflowers appear before her. She can almost see the dew on their yellow leaves. And she remembers the Van Gogh print of sunflowers her grandfather had in his study. He wasn't much for art, and the print always felt out of place. She wonders now if he had it because it reminded him of France. Or maybe had fought in the Netherlands, where Van Gogh came from. As she watches the tall flowers move in the gentle breeze a thought comes.

He didn't want to return to France. He felt he must. Felt he should. But he didn't want to. Funny. Duty was always so important to him. But she's certain now that was why he picked the two summers she was busy. Why it never became a concrete plan for her practical, get-it-done-at-all-costs grandfather. Why it was something they should do, would do, but never did. He had been putting it off, looking for excuses. Realising this makes her feel better. It was not a dream of his and she hadn't let him down. She feels a sense of peace at the thought.

She looks to her right, and her left, but she can't feel her parents with her anymore. It's like they delivered this message, then disappeared. It's not the first time it happened. She felt them when she was being bullied by Jocelyn Smith in junior high. When no one invited her to the Christmas formal. She felt them when she graduated from high school. When Granddad died, she did not feel them. She thinks now they were dealing with their own loss. They came back when she found out about Hal and Molly.

I wish you could come back, just for fifteen minutes. I have so many questions I want to ask you, Granddad.

As she makes her way to the main road, she wishes she had planned better. Taken the entire summer to backpack around. She's not even sure what she did in Boston all summer, or why she stayed, except that she wasn't ready to go. Wasn't ready for that part of university to be done. She didn't want to go back to the house in Florida. Wasn't ready to move to the Pacific Northwest, where in her heart of hearts she knows she'll be starting med school soon. That had been the plan for so long but now, she wishes she could travel more, see a bit more. Stay in France, away from Hal and those memories. There, she's admitted it, to the road she's travelling, to the hedgerows appearing, to the darkened houses she's passing, to the fields around her. She doesn't want to go to med school, at least not yet. But her apartment is rented, her life already in a storage unit there. Everything is in place.

She dips her head, pushing through a non-existent wind, and pedals faster, trying to outrace the decisions she doesn't want to make.

* * *

It's just after nine a.m. when she arrives in Sainte-Mère-Église. She stopped briefly for water, and now she needs to find a large coffee and a toilet.

She pulls onto Rue de Richedoux. *Doux* means soft in English. Richsoft Street. She likes the sound of that. Elegant and welcoming. Perhaps because it is a big road the houses are set back from the street. She sees the same greyish brick with cream-coloured wood. All the same, and yet all a little bit different. She pedals until she finds a place to rest, and the public facilities, in a little building close to the downtown. Even these remind her of her grandfather, who made them walk home to use the washroom. 'I had enough with latrines in the army,' he always said. Looking back now, Lucy sees this was the perfect start to any number of chats about the war. Why had she been so afraid to ask? Because she knew he didn't want to talk about it. To burden her.

She finds a café and gets a coffee, takes out her journal to write, but doesn't pick up a pen. Instead she looks at the map Rob gave her and double-checks her guidebook.

Sainte-Mère-Église has stood since the eleventh century. It saw battle during the Wars of Religion and the Hundred Years War. Lucy has never heard of the Wars of Religion, and jots down a note to look them up. As she flicks through the pages she sees a small photo of the town taken in 1944. It's an aerial shot in black and white. The way the buildings are laid out, it looks like a cross. She thinks about the churches she's seen, the paintings of the cross, and she wonders if it's a coincidence or part of the plan, to ward off evil with the shape.

Didn't really work, she decides.

It takes some doing but she finds a rack to lock her bike. Everything she wants to see is in walking distance, clustered together. She reads some of the memorials near the Hotel de Ville, which she's learned is city hall. Then she heads to the museum, a three-minute walk away.

She thinks the Airborne Museum is meant to look like a parachute. It's an interesting-looking building and as she studies it she wonders what Rob would think, with its white roof and glass walls. She walks by a tank on the lawn, pauses briefly to look at it. She remembers reading that the German Panzer was impenetrable when it came out, that the Allies' shells bounced off of it. They must have developed better shells or their own stronger tanks, or else they wouldn't have won the war. This is something she thinks she should know. Granddad, she is certain, would know.

Through the glass walls she sees a plane. They interest her more than tanks. She goes inside, and although there are many people around, it is quiet. Not like at Omaha, but still, a sense of reverence, of wonder, that this really happened, where they stand.

* * *

She spends half an hour in the museum, seeing the uniforms of the men who fought. As she looks at the itchy fabric sealed up in glass display cases, she wonders what happened to her grandfather's uniforms. He wasn't one to lose things, and they seem too important to have been thrown away. Another mystery.

The sun is shining through the museum walls, and Lucy moves toward the exit. She likes seeing the actual towns, the buildings, the streets. And there's a church nearby she wants to see. Like everything it is close, a few minutes' walk at best. She can actually see the spires from the museum, and heads toward it. She never thought the churches would be so interesting.

The church is smaller than she expected, a blend of Romanesque and Gothic styles. The stones are weathered, old, and she's not sure if they've gone from a darker colour to the now greyish sandy colour they are, or if they were lighter and have gone darker. She checks her guidebook, but it doesn't say. From the spire hangs a dummy, dressed like a soldier. In the guidebook she reads his name was John Steele and he was with the Parachute Infantry Regiment. His parachute got caught on the spires of the church and he hung there, pretending he was dead, as the fighting went on around him. If her grandfather was standing here, would he stop and stare, say he remembered when this happened? That's what interests her: the anecdotes, the stories. His stories, which she will never hear now.

She looks at the dummy and at the spire, then goes inside the church, where the air is cooler, heavy with time, history. She bows her head and takes a seat but she doesn't say a prayer this time, just sits quietly and enjoys the peace and the beauty of the old building that has witnessed so much.

* * *

It's four o'clock and for all she has seen, there is still so much more. But it's a long ride back.

She thinks about Rob as she pedals along, wondering what the historian in him thinks about the museum. About the new stained-glass windows in the church commemorating the soldiers of D-Day. He might say he wants to be a historian, but that doesn't explain all the work he's done on an abandoned home. Maybe he's not ready to step into his future, but Lucy thinks he will one day. She will, too. As she pushes against the ever-changing wind, the fields flying by, she realises she hasn't thought about Hal or Molly all day.

The thought makes her smile.

TWENTY-SIX
OMAHA BEACH. JUNE 6, 1944

The sounds started at daybreak. The earth rustling. Elise wakes, wondering if this is the end of the world. The entire house is heaving. As a crack appears along the wall next to her, she jumps from bed and flies to Maman's room. She is sitting up, wild-eyed with fear.

'The Germans?'

'I don't know. Quick! We must hide!' She grabs Maman's hand and they run down the stairs, down the hall, through the kitchen.

'The cellar!' Half-dragging her maman, Elise rips open the door as the house shakes. They stumble inside, hit instantly with the dank smell. Their eyes are slow to adjust to the darkness. Elise finds an old box in the corner, a packing crate, and turns it over, sitting Marie on it. The ground is cold but it is real, solid, and Elise presses her feet into the damp earth.

'What do you think is happening?' Maman whispers after what feels like days but has been less than an hour. The boom of artillery, the whistling drone of something.

Airplanes, maybe? What if something hits the house? They could be buried alive under the rubble, with no one to find them.

'I don't know, Maman,' says Elise. Maman grabs her, pulls her beside her. The crate is too small, but they manage. Elise puts her arm around the older woman's shoulders, feels her shiver through her cotton nightdress.

They wait. They listen.

'The Allies?' Elise ventures, although that has been a dream for so long it seems impossible. There had been leaflets dropped, telling people to go to the countryside. Elise figured they were in the countryside. All the Germans had moved to the coast.

Marie shakes her head. 'It's the Nazis. They mean to destroy us.' Her voice cracks and her legs are jumping, a grotesque dance of fear. Elise holds her closer, as if that will help. But then, a sharp pain fills her, like something has struck her chest. If she'd been standing it would have dropped her to her knees. She rubs at her chest, afraid she is having a heart attack, like dear Papa. She tries to breathe, but it catches, stays shallow, in her mouth. It's like something has pierced her chest and is radiating through her now.

Standing in the cold, she thinks of tea with sugar. The cakes they used to make at the bakery. How she will soon be twenty-three and she feels like she has lived forever. She has no idea what is happening outside this door although she can hear rumblings and feel the earth dance. She rubs her hands together, can feel the patch on her palm where she burnt it so long ago. She thinks of her friends nearby, Bertrand and Marianne and wee Michel, growing up during war. And William, well, William never leaves her thoughts. He carved out his own place inside her, the day they met.

They wait. And they wait. The sounds roar and fade away. Elise has no idea how much time has passed. Perhaps a day. No, more than that, for sure. Why did they not prepare for this? Why were there no blankets in the room, no food? They are cold, and hungry. Maman has wet herself, and Elise tears a strip from her own nightie for her to clean herself up. The war has reduced them as humans in a way she did not think possible. And she has had enough. The cold and damp are in her bones and she aches, but she stands, straightens up.

'I am going to open the door, Maman. I am going to see what is happening.' Elise's voice is controlled. If she's going to die it will be now, on her own terms, not hiding in a horrible little room.

'Elise, you mustn't!' Maman's voice is desperate, shrill, pleading – and without impact.

A calmness comes over Elise. Even if the house is filled with Germans she does not really care. She is tired of being cold, and hungry. Of being afraid. Of worrying about William. Oh, God, William. Did she dream him, too? Some days it feels that way. She rubs at her chest, the pain still there.

Maman backs up, hiding behind the shelves as though they can protect her.

Elise opens the door gently, surprised by the light. She walks down the hall, noticing a few broken bits of glass, things that have fallen from shelves. She approaches the window. She thinks she will see soldiers fighting, but she sees nothing. The streets are empty but the sky is filled with smoke. Planes fly almost directly overhead, so low she feels she could pluck one from the sky. There are fires burning in the distance, not campfires, not warming fires. Destructive fires. She can tell by the smell, something metallic and sulphuric at the same time. Not the comfort of woodsmoke on a quiet evening.

'Elise! Elise!' She hears Maman. Her voice floats to her, but she cannot turn around.

She's having a hard time moving. It must be from the cold. Her legs will not work as she wills them to, and her hands lie limp at her sides. It's as though all the life has been released from her. Like her heart has stopped, as she sits on the front steps of her childhood home, in her night-dress, wondering what could possibly happen next, where William is, and how she will ever find out.

It has been so long since she saw him in Paris, so long since she's had a letter. He has been her comfort, her solace, her passion for as long as she can remember. Her plans for their future are what has kept her going. With everything she has lost, surely she won't lose him, too?

TWENTY-SEVEN

NORTHERN FRANCE. SUMMER 2009

'So, Saint-Lô, Sainte-Mère-Église, and Mont-Saint-Michel tomorrow. You're getting around,' Rob says.

Lucy is sitting on his sofa drinking her third glass of water after six and a half hours of biking.

'I was thinking today, I wished I'd come for the whole summer. There's so much to see and do.'

'Why didn't you?'

Lucy thinks for a second. 'I thought I wasn't ready to close the door on my time in Boston. But really, my boyfriend of two years cheated on me with my best friend, and I think I was too traumatised to do anything. If my neighbour hadn't pushed me, I might not have ever come here.'

She can't believe she said it out loud. But she has. And he hasn't replied.

'Sorry, that was a bit heavy.'

'No, I'm just stunned. That is so much to go through, it's amazing you're standing, much less travelling through France on your own.'

'I had planned to backpack with him, believe it or not.' She shrugs, trying to make light of it all.

'I think being on your own, you're in far better company.'

This makes Lucy laugh. 'Instead of seeing more of France I slept a lot.'

'You can come back,' he offers.

'I can. I will. But it won't be the same.'

'Nothing ever is.' He gets up from the floor where he's sitting and goes to the kitchen. She hears him opening cabinets and poking around. When he returns he has a half-bottle of wine and two glasses.

As Rob hands her a glass she prods, 'That sounded ominous, what you said. *Nothing ever is.* What did you mean?'

'I just don't think you can ever go back to anything again. Time and experience alter everything. When you come back, and I hope you do, you'll have changed as a person, just from your new experiences. I'll have changed. It's just the way things are.'

Lucy thinks for a second. 'I get it. I feel changed by this trip. I mean, it's only been a few weeks, but I've learned things, experienced things. I've had these thoughts and realisations I wouldn't have had, staying at home.'

'Travel really changes you. It opens you up.'

'That's how I feel. I was thinking how cool it would be to be a travel writer, and that has literally never crossed my mind before now.'

'Same as me, seeing France and wanting to become a historian.'

Lucy thinks for a second, letting the little stenographer who lives in her head assess what she wants to say, and either give or withhold approval. When she gets the green light she says, 'I think you want to be a historian, but I think you want to be an architect, too.' She looks at Rob, wanting a reaction before she proceeds.

'You've been thinking about this?' He almost laughs, a spurt of delighted amazement.

'Look around this house. What would possess you to pour so much time and energy into this place if you did not see a structure that interested you? Something worth saving? Maybe you won't design the next Guggenheim or be the next Frank Lloyd Wright, maybe you'll be a restoration architect.'

'I don't think there's such a thing,' he says, a note of something happy, something light in his voice.

'So make it such a thing,' Lucy says.

'What about you, and med school?'

She shakes her head. 'We're talking about you now. You're the reason I'm going to Mont-Saint-Michel tomorrow. Tell me again why you love it so much and what I should see. And then I have to walk back to my hotel. I have another early morning.'

* * *

Lucy is up early, not quite sure where the place is where she is catching the shuttle to Mont-Saint-Michel. There's no bus, and although Rob had offered to take her, it's out of the way for him. She thought her legs might be sore from the marathon bike ride, but she feels fine as she makes her way to the coach, finds a seat by herself, and waits for the other passengers. The driver introduces himself, tells them the trip will take an hour and a half as he pulls onto the road.

She looks out at the window, wanting to commit the buildings, the houses, the shops, the very grass to memory. Thinking about what Rob said, about travel changing you. Who knows who she will be, when she returns?

They arrive at the abbey early, seeing the dark, formidable walls and spires standing straight up from the sea. For such a small country, France is filled with buildings and places that can only be considered wonders. Shifting her backpack on her shoulder, she listens to the sea as she moves toward the path that takes them across the channel and to the monastery. The bus has parked on the access bridge, and they walk the rest of the way in. She is the only solo traveller from the coach; everyone else is in groups of two and three. She hunches into her hoodie, the morning breeze from the channel making it cool.

The abbey is at the top, and lots of stone buildings seem to have sprung from the land leading up to it. They are all different, all weather-beaten. But instead of looking old they look formidable. It looks how she pictured the castle in Prague when reading Kafka. Prague, she'll have to go there, too. Lucy turns from the buildings and looks out to the water, can see the coach, already looking small on the bridge. The seagulls swoop and scream around them, and she can hear the waves. Not like horses galloping, as promised. Maybe she's here at the wrong time for that. Another reason to come back.

The abbey, Lucy learns, was built in 708 after Aubert of Avranches had a vision of Archangel Michael, telling him to build a church. When Lucy hears this she thinks of Ardenne Abbey. And she wonders about all the people who had visions back then. Maybe it was something in the water. Malnutrition. She does not believe in visions of any kind. Intuition, yes, but if someone appeared to her and told her to move someplace and build a church she's pretty sure she wouldn't start applying for building permits.

She thinks about the history as she walks the walls in the brightening light. First an abbey, then a prison, then a military garrison. Now, tourists walk it. There is a beauty in that, the evolution toward peace. Stopping to look out at the sailboat going by, she sees some flowers springing up through the rocks. Weeds she guess, but a pretty purple colour. Reaching over, she plucks one, studies its silky leaves, then she opens her bag, and her journal, and presses it in the pages.

It's small, Mont-Saint-Michel. Only fifty people live there. She's taking her time exploring, climbing the steps slowly, looking at the buildings, creating memories. A small café appears and she goes inside and orders a coffee. She needs a jolt of warmth. It is good, served with a little cookie of some kind. It's unwrapped, so she doesn't eat it – another habit learned from her grandfather. The walls are painted a soft blue and Lucy likes the feel of the place, the warmth and the cosiness. She orders a crepe, her first one since Paris. She gets it with raspberry jam and cheese. Granddad used to eat toast that way. If the waiter thinks it's weird he doesn't say anything. Maybe he learned it here, she thinks. And she smiles. When it comes its delicious.

When she is done she resumes her climb to the top. It doesn't take long; the whole place is only seventeen acres in total. She wonders if the soldiers who fought here, seeing it for the first time, stopped and stared. If they saw the beauty of it. She hopes so. Maybe it appeared when they needed to be reminded how long it had stood. All it had seen. A human life is fleeting, so easily snuffed out, but what is created lasts in some ways, forever.

From the top she looks down at the stone roofs of all the buildings she walked by. A Tudor accent on one of them stands out, and she is curious about British architecture in a French abbey. Or maybe it was French, too. Another question for Rob, she thinks. It would be nice to know a bit more about the buildings and the history.

She takes a final look at the water, lapping over the bridge in places, slapping at the sides of a boat moored midway between the walls and the coast. Then she heads back the way she came, stops and buys a pastry, and heads back to the bridge. She is so happy she came here, to Mont-Saint-Michel. To France. It may have once been torn apart by war, but the land has brought her peace.

She takes a seat by herself on the bus ride back, looks out the coach windows as the now familiar landscape rolls by. Funny, but for the first time since her granddad died, she doesn't feel alone.

* * *

As she steps from the shuttle in the hotel parking lot, a familiar figure appears in the early evening light.

'Rob?'

'Hi.' He takes her backpack from her as they walk to his van. It's dark out, and Lucy is both tired from the very long day and exhilarated by what she has seen.

'What did you think?' Rob asks.

'It was so beautiful. I don't know what to think,' she says. 'The sound of the waves, and the way it appeared, like it was rising from the ocean, like Neptune's castle or something.'

'I told you,' he jokes.

'You did.'

'Are you hungry?' he asks as he opens the passenger door for her.

'Not really, no. But...'

'But what?'

'Can we go to your house?'

'Um. Sure. Why?'

'I'd like to see it one more time, before I leave.'

'I told you, it grows on you.'

Lucy nods, but that's not it. She's not sure why she wants to see it, she just does. And she wants to come clean about opening the trunk, what she found. But not that she took the bracelet. That she can't explain. She's embarrassed by her actions, but she's not giving it back.

Rob pulls into the street, parks. The little house looks the same as that first day – innocuous, sad. Lucy studies every stone on the path, the steps, the front door, committing it all to memory.

He opens the door and she slips past him, breathing in the distinct smell in the air. She moves to the fireplace, running her hand over the mantel. There's a new book on the shelf. Victor Hugo in French. It all comes to her like snapshots.

She moves to the kitchen, turns and faces Rob.

He stands in front of her, hands in his pockets. His dark eyes and the small line on his forehead are not in harmony with his relaxed body language.

'What's up?' he says.

'I have to tell you something. The other morning, after

you left, I went upstairs, to the washroom. And I looked in the rooms, the empty ones, not yours.'

A half-smile warms his expression.

'There's an old trunk in the room upstairs. I opened it and found some books.'

'Yeah?'

'I just wanted to tell you I snooped, I guess.'

'Had to come clean, hmmm?'

'I did. And I'm sorry. But something else, too. The books I found, I think it might be nice to put them on your shelves.'

'Sure.'

He turns, and Lucy follows him up the stairs, to the room with the trunk. He has to duck to get through the doorframe. The room seems even smaller, barely able to contain the two of them. He bends and lifts the lid. Lucy reaches in and picks up the books.

'I knew the trunk was here, but never looked inside.'

'Weren't you curious?'

Rob looks around, as though seeing the room for the first time. 'I think I sort of forgot about it.'

'They're old, and there's writing in them. I can't make out what it says; I just think it's time they were put on display. They were important to someone, once.'

'Okay,' he says.

Lucy cradles the books in her arm like a schoolgirl as Rob closes the lid on the blanket and the memories of whatever it once held.

'The trunk is in great shape. Nice wood. It might be worth restoring,' he says, standing, as a crashing, ripping sound tears through the house. Lucy is sure the room shakes. She can hear glass smash, wood splinter. It feels like the sound will go on forever. And then, it stops.

'Stay right here. Do not move,' he says, jumping up.

'Where are you going?'

'Just stay here.'

She nods at him as he turns from her, and she hears the squeaky stairs under his light step.

She thinks about that horrible cellar room, and wonders what has happened.

TWENTY-EIGHT
ESPERANCE. 1944

The mail when it came, came all at once. Some envelopes so old, so worn-looking, Elise was afraid they may no longer hold a letter inside.

It felt like a small miracle, an answered prayer, as Amelie handed her the letters, as though they were sacred. Mail had been rare during the Occupation, and nothing had been received from America.

'Merci,' Elise whispers through her shock, her excitement. Amelie smiles, their hands both fastened on the pale blue envelopes. Her mane of red curly hair has thinned and a few grey streaks have appeared. Everyone has aged so much, but her smile of simple pleasure at the return of the post makes her look like the woman who handed Elise that first letter from William, all those years ago.

Placing the letters in her bag, Elise races to the street, past the bakery, the shops, into the house, up the stairs. Closing her bedroom door behind her she tries to catch her breath.

One by one, Elise lays the envelopes out gently on her

bed. Her heart is racing. All the time she has sat in this very spot, reading letters years old, for the hundredth time. Now, seven new ones.

Elise looks at the familiar writing, the ink faded but the hand that held the pen strong. She pictures that hand. Can feel its touch.

May 1940

Dearest Elise,

I write this letter not knowing if it will find its way to you, and that is not a pleasant feeling to have. How I wish I had seen this coming, how I wish I had made you leave France. I hate to think of you frightened, alone in that house. It makes me so angry to think of war being waged around you, and there is nothing I can do to help.

Father is glued to the papers, and we have great faith in the Maginot Line and the French army, and we all pray this is over soon. When it is, you will come here, to me, where you should be. We will bring your mother, too. And Philippe. How I hope he has righted himself by now and is taking care of you both.

Please stay safe, my darling. It seems wrong to write of books and art at this time, but these evil days will pass, and we will be together – I know this. I cannot imagine anything else. You are always in my thoughts, and if things are not sorted soon, I will swim to France if I must so I can hold you once again.

All my love,
William

She looks again at the date. Almost five years ago.

Before France had succumbed to the enemy. Before the real nightmare had begun.

The next letter is dated Christmas 1940. He speaks of the snow outside his window, the cold wind off the Atlantic. Of missing the scent of her hair. Of hope and prayers that the new year would bring peace. She reads quickly, wanting to learn what was happening with him, while she sat frightened and cold in the house she wanted so badly to flee.

Another letter is dated February, a simple love letter that makes her insides warm. A letter of love and devotion. A letter free of reference to the war.

Then another. A letter telling her about Easter. His mother had burned the ham, and they had ended up at a restaurant. His brother Aaron growing so fast they were almost the same height. She senses him trying to keep the letters light and simple. It was so easy to slip into the darkness, and even easier to remain there. She knows this too well.

The next letter she picks up feels different in her hand. Flipping it over she sees that two letters are stuck together. She pulls them apart and sees the writing is different. Larger than William's and loopier. There is a joy to the penmanship. A femininity. She is nervous opening it and scans it quickly.

Dear Elise,

I hope this note finds you well and safe.

I am writing to tell you that William, my silly son, has had an accident, and his arm is broken, so he cannot write. His leg is broken, too, and a few ribs. He had a road accident in his father's new car. He's in hospital and asked me to send you a letter so you would know why you are not hearing from him, if letters are getting through at all. Some he has written have been returned. Some have not, and he thinks they may have found their way to you.

I am looking forward to the world returning to normal, so you can come and visit us.

Best wishes,

Jean Hardwick

Elise feels numb at the words. Her William, in hospital, injured. A broken leg, arm, what else? She reads it a second and third time, as though new information will magically appear.

Despite her worry at his injuries, Elise cannot help but be pleased that William's mother knows about her, that he has spoken of her to his family. If the war had not happened, she would have visited by now. Perhaps they would be married. Her hands tremble at the thought.

The writing on the next envelope is weaker, slightly awkward. She cannot find the date.

Dear Elise,

How are you, my darling?

Please forgive the shaky writing. I've only just had the cast removed and am working to get strength back in my arm. It feels so strange to have gone from pounds of plaster on my arm, from fingers to shoulder, to having it removed. My arm feels as though it could float now, except for the fact that I have little strength and some nerve damage. I have some pain but not as much as Father had upon seeing what was left of his new motorcar.

Elise laughs at this. A small laugh that startles her. How long it has been since she laughed?

My school friends have all joined up, and Mother has gone from first being very worried about me, to being very angry with me about my accident, and now absolutely delighted that I cannot pass the physical. Each day she walks to the local church and prays for the war to end before I recover. I think my father does too, although he says nothing. Aaron, on the other hand, is desperate to go, but he's only fourteen. God help all of us if it goes on that long. But it won't. I'm certain.

I hope you can read some of these chicken scratchings. I will write again soon. Please know you are always in my thoughts, and I am counting the days until I can hold you again.

Love,

William

Elise tries, but can't make out the date on the next letter. She gives up and starts to read.

Dearest Elise,

How I hope this letter finds you safe and well. Mother has been sending care parcels, I know, but we both wish we could do more. Did you like the corned beef? Did the peanut butter survive the trip?

Corned beef? Peanut butter? Elise has seen neither. And this is not how he starts his letters, in such a detached, practical way. She feels a coldness creep over her, something dark pulling at her.

I went for a run on the beach a few days ago. It was wonderful to run again and I felt healthy and strong, fit as a fiddle. I am no longer 4-F.

Elise stares hard at the number, the hyphen, the letter. What on earth does it mean?

And so, I have enlisted. I am off to basic training soon. Will be there while you are reading this, I suspect, curled up in that little house I visited so many years ago.

I know this news must be hard for you. That, and seeing the look on my mother's face, were the hardest part when it came to making this decision, but you must know it was the only one I could make. I know you understand this is something I must do. Think of what has happened, to your country, to Belgium, to Poland. I must do what I can. The barbarity must be stopped.

The letter falls from her hands, the pages landing on the floor, making a fan of sorts around her feet. Her William, a soldier. She squeezes her eyes shut, trying to send the images in her mind into a dark void. William, getting shot. Having a leg blown off. Losing a hand. Dying on a battlefield, the earth leaching the blood from his body.

Her stomach tightens, her mouth goes dry. And she clutches up the pages.

I will write as often as I can and hope my letters make it to you, one day, when France, and the world, is once again free. When I get to hold you in my arms, feel the softness of you again.

With all my love and deepest thoughts,
William

She looks at the few pieces of paper that give a glimpse into his life in the four years they have been apart. Four years that could have seen them married, living in a nice house in America. Maybe by now she would have a baby, too. Instead, she waits and hopes to hear from him again. To know he is alive. To begin to live again.

TWENTY-NINE
ESPERANCE. 1945

The rain wasn't falling outside so much as it was being hurled down with great force. Elise, looking out her window, thinking, as always, about William, watches it pounding on her neighbour's roof. If it was coming down on a slant, she's certain it would shatter windows. The house has a damp feeling, she feels it burrowing deeper into her bones, but does not have the energy to light a fire, or even to pull a blanket around her. She doubts either would help, anyway. It was not that kind of cold. She will wait for it to stop, then try the post office again. It has been months since her packet of letters arrived.

She has spent so much time thinking about William, wondering. Ever since that horrible, wonderful day when the soldiers landed, she has felt differently. Disconnected, like a piece of her is missing. Still, she hopes, and she prays.

The rain continues to beat down, as if it is angry with the very ground itself. She tells herself it is letting up, as she wants to go to the post office. But if anything it is getting stronger.

Pulling a heavy cardigan over her nightgown, she tucks it into a pair of her brother's trousers that she had altered to fit her. Now they are loose again, and she cinches her belt as tightly as she can. Winding a scarf around her neck, she pulls on her own jacket, and her papa's over it. Grasping the door handle, she sees herself in the entryway mirror. It is too big, too ornate with its gold painted flourishes. It looks like something from Versailles and has never suited either the house or the space. But that is not what she notices today.

She looks old. Her lips are cracked, from the cold, from hunger.

For some reason, she can't get her legs to work. It's like she's caught in some sort of heavy web, or like hands are holding her back. She has to force herself to open the handle, step out into the storm. She opens her umbrella and listens to the rain hit it, the drops somehow twisting around and catching her, too.

The shutters are closed on the houses she passes. The lovely shops, the jeweller's, the leather worker's, all closed up. The bakery, too. They would have sold out of bread by now. How she misses the aroma of baking bread in the air, when the bakery was filled with tarts and cakes, energy and life.

She steps into the post office as a low rumble of thunder shakes the already unstable land.

Amelie is standing where she has always stood. Her crazy red curls are tamed by a large scarf, and the life they have been subjected to for so long. Her face is grey, aged by the war and marked by hunger. When she sees Elise she reaches for something, and she sees an envelope in

Amelie's hand – pale blue, with red. William used to send her such envelopes.

'There's been mail.'

Amelie attempts a sort-of smile, not of joy, but of softening, of support. A smile of nostalgia, for when post for Elise was the very best part of her life. Elise wonders why Amelie is not happy, as she usually is. Then she sees the writing. It is not his.

A coldness fills her belly as she takes the envelope, turns it over in her hands. Then slips it into her pocket.

'Thank you,' she says.

Amelie says something, but it's like she's underwater. Elise knows she is speaking to her but can't hear what is being said.

Forgetting her umbrella, she walks back into the street, past the bakery. Crossing the street, she moves to the church. The door is almost impossible to open, but she pulls and pulls until it gives, creating just enough of a gap for her to slip inside. Down the stairs she goes, to the crypt, to the pillar with her angel. She stands in front of him.

'I've had a letter,' she whispers. 'And I'm afraid. I don't want to read it. I think I know what it says already. But please, please let it be good news. Let William be in a hospital, nearby. I can go to him. Please. Let his arm be broken, and that is why he hasn't written to me. Please. Let him be alive. Because I don't want to live without him.' She closes her eyes. It is even colder in the crypt, and her feet can feel it from the concrete below.

Pulling the letter from her pocket, she looks at it for a moment. Then she tears off the edge, tips out the note inside. It is short, half of a small page.

Dear Elise,

I am not sure if this letter will make it to you but feel I must try.

We have just learned that we have lost William. It happened on June 6th. We don't know much else. All we have now is a telegram. He was killed in action in France.

William loved you very much, and I hope this gives you some comfort.

I hope you are safe, and your family, too.

If the world ever knows peace again, perhaps you can come see us.

Sincerely,

Jean Hardwick

Elise reads the letter a second time, and a third.

It is real now, although part of her has known all along. She felt something vital leave her body, that June day when the Allies arrived. She felt it. She knew.

She looks again at the angel. Tilts her head to study the figure. Sees it for what it is, a painting on a wall in an old building. A beautiful building, yes. But it has no power. Or maybe it does. Maybe Elise and her family are being punished for not going to Sunday mass for all those years.

She folds the letter, shoves it into her pocket, turns and climbs up the stairs.

The France sisters are lighting candles. Who knows how many francs they have put in that little tin offerings box over the years? She wants to tell them to stop wasting their money. Their lives have been as hard as hers. What have the candles, the prayers, done?

She can feel them watching her as she makes her way out into the rain. It is still falling, like it is trying to drown France. Why not? Everything else has happened to them. She walks home, opens the door. Lets her jackets slide from her, making a wet pile. Water splashes over the floor, makes a puddle that creeps across the old stones, making them darker. She walks directly to the cabinet, pulls out an ancient bottle of Calvados, given to her by Monsieur Gravel when she sat up with him when he had a chest infection. She opens it, takes a long pull directly from the bottle, then, tucking it against her body, moves up the stairs. She can hear Maman calling. She doesn't respond. No longer cares.

Inside her room, she closes the door and sits by the window. The rain is falling softly now. She stares at the puddles on her neighbour's roof, the only sign that the earlier rain had been so intense. Maybe she had imagined it, the storm. Maybe she had imagined everything, meeting him, the stars in the sky as they walked to the cathedral, Amelie smiling when she got mail from him, his letters a lifeline for her. Maybe she had imagined it all, a very pleasant dream. She blinks a few times, looks around her room, and sees the black spines of the books he'd sent her, solid, imposing. The basket where she kept the petals from the roses he'd given her in Paris. It hadn't been a dream.

It's funny, but she doesn't feel any pain. Instead she feels hollowed out, empty. Sort of like she is floating, just outside of herself. Around her, there is noise. Someone on the stairs. A knock. The door opens.

Maman, wearing a wrapper around her nightdress. Elise knows the clothes, but the woman looks different. Although stark white as though she's had a shock, gone is the fog in her eyes. Instead, in their place, is something alive, aware.

'Elise,' Marie says, reaching out with her hand. 'I have a bad feeling. Has something happened?'

'I'm all right, Maman,' she says. 'I would like to be alone.'

'But what is it?'

'Nothing, Maman. I'm tired.'

She cannot say the words aloud. Cannot. Will not.

Elise closes the door. Sits on her bed. The drapes move softly, even though the window is closed. There's a draught. She never noticed that before. She stares at the white eyelet curtains as though they will come to life and explain everything to her.

She takes a drink, and another. Then she puts her head down on her pillow, curls up in a ball, and lets the emptiness of her new grief fill her.

THIRTY
ESPERANCE, FRANCE. SEPTEMBER 1945

Time, for Elise, both stands still and goes on forever. She is unsure of the day, of what is happening around her. Marianne visits. She even brings Michel, who is thin and unhealthy, his childhood ruined by this war. But his love for her has not dimmed, and he hugs her, draws her pictures. She wants to thank him, hug him back, but it's like she can't wake up. Eventually, inevitably, Marianne stops bringing him. Genevieve comes, the first time with sympathy for her loss. The second time with sympathy flecked with impatience. The third time she stands at the door, and says, 'Shall I give you a haircut? You can take a bath and I'll strip your bed, remake it. We'll do your hair. Sit downstairs in front of the fire. You'll feel better.'

Her body had made way, fleetingly, for an additional emotion: anger. That her friend would think a haircut, a simple haircut, would make any difference to her now. Make her feel better. How?

'What do you say? Shall I help you to the bath?'

Elise shakes her head. Genevieve looks around for a

place to sit, and finally perches on the edge of her desk chair.

'I know it must hurt, to lose William. But you've got your whole life ahead of you. You are attractive and smart. You will meet someone else. But now you have got to get up and get dressed.'

Elise remains silent, wanting her to leave. As if Genevieve can tell, she gets up and moves to the door.

'I hope you feel better soon.'

Elise listens as the door closes behind her. She can hear Genevieve's heels click on the stairs.

She rests her head against the pillow, and sleeps.

Elise wakes to noise: cheers, horns honking, people singing. She sits up in bed. She knows the song, it's the Marseillaise. She sits up straighter. It is against the law to sing that song. What are people thinking?

Her door swings open with such force it bangs the walls and ricochets back, only to be caught by Monsieur Allard. Bertrand is standing in her room. Has the world gone mad?

'Elise, chérie! The war, it is over!'

It takes a second for her to grasp this. To understand. The Germans have been defeated. It is all over. Finally, it is over. But what does that mean, and what will happen next?

* * *

People will remember where they stood, what they were wearing, every single detail about what was happening when they heard the news that September day. It will become the start of stories told for years, decades, generations to come.

Elise will not have such a memory. She has been told Bertrand gave her the news, and she had been in her bedroom, she thinks. But why would he have been in her bedroom? Her memory couldn't be right. If she had stayed in bed, who had cooked, cleaned? Did she not go to work?

She remembers Maman forcing her to take a bath, following her into the bathroom where water and bubbles filled the tub, washing her back as Elise pulled her knees to her chest, freezing. It must have been October, maybe November then. Maman starting to dress her, but Elise balking, pulling on the pale blue nightdress she had set out. Brushing her hair, surprised by the number of tangles. She had pulled at each of them, aware of the pain in her scalp, her head, but not stopping even as her eyes filled with tears. The physical pain was nothing, a mere scratch, compared to what was happening inside her, the sharp blinding pain that struck from out of nowhere, hollowing her out to emptiness, before striking again. Grief, she has learned, is like the sea, with its own tides.

She rubs her scalp now, at the memory of that pain, as she sits in her room, trying to piece it all together. She sits at her desk where she had spent so many hours writing letters to William. Gently she opens the window, seeing her hands as though they belong to someone else. They are so thin, bony. The soft blue of the veins make stark paths in the white flesh. Somehow, she has her mother's hands.

There's a trunk in the corner of her room. She opens it, leaning the lid against the wall, and starts to fill it with the things she no longer wishes to see. Byron. Wordsworth. Shelley. Tennyson. The clip-on earrings. She does not stop there. The bracelet from Bertrand and Marianne. The letters. They mock her now, making her think about a time when she was so excited about life. Thinking things were getting better, but it was an illusion. The worst had still to come. Taking the wool blanket from Philippe's bed, she covers everything up and closes the lid. Shoves it behind the door in her room.

Then she goes downstairs, lights a fire, pours a glass of wine. Sits and stares into the blue flames.

* * *

A knock startles her awake. Elise has no idea how much time has passed. The fire has gone out, and the room has a chill. After pulling herself up from the couch she makes her way to the door. It will be Marianne coming back to check on her no doubt. She has been doing that a lot lately.

Elise is not prepared for what she sees. On the step, in front of her, is a soldier. An American soldier. For a brief, wonderful moment, she thinks that maybe there was a mistake, and that it's William, her William. But no. He's not as tall as William. Really, he looks nothing like him. It was just her mind playing tricks on her. It takes a moment to organise herself so she can speak.

'Yes. Can I help you?'

The soldier shuffles awkwardly, taking off his funny cap and clutching it in both of his hands.

'I'm looking for Elise,' he pronounces it so carefully, it comes out Ee-lease, and something inside her softens. The first real smile she has felt in over a year appears, briefly.

'I am Elise. Would you like to come in?'

He nods and wipes his feet on the mat.

Elise closes the door behind him. William. He must have known William. For a second her legs betray her and she grabs the chair beside her for support, grateful the soldier's back is to her.

'Can I offer you some tea perhaps? *Un café?*'

'I don't want to trouble you.'

'No trouble,' she says moving toward the kitchen. It gives her a moment to prepare herself.

Hands shaking, she sets the water to boil. Takes down the good mugs, and a tray. Elise runs her hands over it, flashing back to the first time she saw William, and how he carried that very tray for her. Her sixteenth birthday. A lifetime ago. When the coffee is ready she loads it onto a tray, and then carries it to the front room. The soldier stands when he sees her and takes it from her hands.

'Thank you.' He smiles at her, and Elise can't tell if he is shy or uncomfortable. They sit, an awkward silence, and something else, between them. Maman is napping, and she hopes she does not wander in. Elise does not have the energy to explain Maman to a stranger.

'I'm not sure where to begin. My name is Henry Corrigan – Hank – and I served with William Hardwick. He was a friend of mine.' His voice catches. She can almost hear his heart banging. 'I was with him, when it happened, and I just wanted you to know he didn't suffer. He wasn't in any pain. And he didn't die alone. I was with him,' he repeats.

Elise grips her mug, nods at the man sitting in front of her.

'His last thoughts were of you.'

Her eyes fill, but she does not cry.

He takes a sip of his coffee.

'June 6. Correct?' Elise remembers being under the stairs, in that horrible room with Maman. She remembers the feeling in her chest. She knew. William had died on a beach that was so close to her. A new hurt fills her, realising that her country's war brought him so close to her, only to take him away when they were in touching distance. If he had lived, it would be him sitting across from her now, not this soldier. This Henry Corrigan.

'Yes, ma'am,' he says.

'He didn't suffer?'

He shakes his head, no. 'We were in basic together. He was one of the older men and took me under his wing. We had... we had a lot in common. Came from the same part of the States.'

'You are from Cape Cod?'

'Close. Rhode Island. Different side of the tracks.'

Elise has no idea what he means.

'You must want to go home. The war is over. Why are you still here?'

'The military administers tests. Seems I'm good with details, so I'm in an administrative position now,' he says. 'And I wanted to come to see you. To pay my respects.' He stops speaking, looks away from her, toward the window.

'I plan to stay a few days. I'll take a room somewhere,' he hastens to add. 'If there's anything around the house you need fixing, I'm happy to help.'

Elise nods, understanding. William asked him to check on her. And that is what he's doing.

* * *

Hank stays across the street with Monsieur Gravel. Elise sees him cleaning out gutters, rehanging shutters, painting

the eaves at his house, when he is not doing similar work at
her home.

She wants to talk to him about William, but someone
always seems to be around, and Elise has discovered when
she speaks of him, people grow uncomfortable, fidgety,
wanting to change the subject. Monsieur Gravel has
warmed to the American, and a bit of life has returned
to him.

'Elise?'

Hank is standing in the doorway. His voice startles her.

'Could we speak, please?' She nods, makes tea, and sits
at her kitchen table. Hank sits across from her, laces his
fingers together, like it's a formal occasion and says, 'I have
to get back to my people, and I'm leaving tomorrow.
Catching a boat in Cherbourg and then one from
Southampton.' He's stalling for time. She can almost see
him looking for the right words.

'So if there's anything you need done, we need to sort it
today.'

'Thank you,' Elise says, but she knows that is not what
he wanted to say.

'It has been nice having you here, for Monsieur Gravel.
It has brought him back to life.'

'He's a good man,' Hank says.

Elise waits.

'I know you and William had plans. I know there was
talk of a future. I know he would want the best for you.'

'You know a lot of things,' Elise observes, with a trace of
something that could have been, at one time, humour.

It takes a moment for Hank to understand. He shrugs,
like he's trying to get out from under a burden, and starts
again.

'I know he wants the best for you. If there is anything I can do to help, please, let me.'

'You have done enough. And I am grateful.'

'When I get settled, you could come to see Cape Cod. I could show you around,' he tries.

'I don't think so, but thank you,' she says.

'If I can help...' he tries again.

'Thank you.' Elise begins to stand, to signal the conversation is over.

'I'll be off early in the morning, so I'll say goodbye. If you ever need anything, this is where you can reach me.' He hands her a slip of paper, with his parents' address.

'Thank you,' she says again. There's a brief hesitation, and then, he shakes her hand. It is awkward.

'Anything at all,' he says.

She nods and closes the door to his retreating back. She would like to see America, but there is no reason for her to go now. Maman is too frail, but there is more than that. The last time she saw William, when he took her to the train station in Paris, he had promised her they would be together, though hell should bar the way. It had. It does. Now he is buried in the land nearby. In a way he kept his promise. And she won't leave him now.

* * *

Six weeks after Hank's departure, Elise comes home from working at the library to see Maman sitting by the fireplace. Small flames crackle and hiss. Elise is perplexed. It is warm, and there is no need for a fire.

'Is everything okay, Maman?' She sets her keys and her satchel on the table and makes her way to the chair where

219

she is sitting. Elise can see the back of her head, the once glossy black hair grey and patchy. It needs a good brushing. She will talk her into taking a long bath and then fix her hair, it will make her feel better. And then, she notices how still she is, how her chest has not risen and fallen with each breath. The awkward angle of her head. And she knows.

She picks up a blanket from the sofa and tucks it gently around her knees, as though she is sick and not dead. Then she steps over to the fire. She looks into the dying flames and sees paper. A small scrap, but she knows her father's handwriting. The sight of it makes her heart race. Dear Papa. How different all of their lives would have been had he lived. She looks around, sees a box with paper inside. Maman had been burning his letters. Elise pictures her, young and vibrant, in love. How cruelly it had all been taken from her. So many ifs, so many buts. So many whys.

She hesitates for a moment then slowly commits the final piece of paper to the flames.

* * *

Three days after her death, when the sky is a bright blue without a hint of cloud, Elise buries her mother, next to her papa. Marianne and Bertrand and Genevieve stand with her. She does not know where Philippe is, but she keeps scanning the churchyard. It would be just like him to appear at the last moment. But it does not happen. They do not know if he is alive or dead, has not heard from him in years. Knowing him, he escaped the war, married, and is living off his wife's family now. Elise will never look for him again.

They walk back to the house, Genevieve holding her

arm. Inside the door Marianne slips on an apron and shoos her from the kitchen, telling her to sit. Genevieve brings her tea with sugar. Elise is very tired but she nods and accepts condolences. She nibbles at the food they bring her, like a mouse. People mean well but she just wants to be alone. For she is all alone now and must fill her time somehow. She could do anything, train to be a pastry chef. Move to the US, as William's mother suggests in the letters she sends. Jean uses the same blue envelopes to send her letters that her son sent. It hurts to see them arrive, for they remind her of William, and those days when the only thing that mattered was getting a letter from him.

The crowd thins out. Genevieve offers to stay but she doesn't understand. She thinks time will fix everything, but Elise knows that is not to be. Besides, she just wants to be alone, to sit with her memories of William. In her dreams he is still alive. Marianne cleans the kitchen, sweeping the floor, as Bertrand takes Elise's face gently in his hands and says, 'You come stay with us. Michel will love it.' His eyes are bright with concern.

'Thank you. Maybe in a few days, but right now I just want to be on my own. I'm fine. Trust me.' He pulls her into his chest, but Elise doesn't have the energy to return his embrace.

After closing the door behind the last guest, she moves toward the sofa, taking the pins from her hair. Tucking her legs under her, she looks around the room. She's not sure what to do next and rests her head against the back of the seat, closing her eyes. All she wants is to be alone. Good. Now she is.

THIRTY-ONE

NORTHERN FRANCE. SUMMER 2009

Rob is standing in the kitchen, staring at the floor, when Lucy appears by his side. He grabs her arm, noticing her bare feet.

'What happened?'

'The kitchen cabinets fell off the wall. All of them.'

Lucy walks to the front door, grabs her trainers and laces them on. In the kitchen, she picks through the mess, the broken dishes, the splintered wood.

'Be careful,' Rob says as Lucy pulls a green glass plate of some kind from the mess, and hands it to Rob. He takes it from her and puts it on the kitchen table as she digs out a matching glass dome and hands it to him. Then she stands, looks at them. A cake stand, she thinks.

'Where did it come from? I mean, I went through everything looking for a vase. It was not in the cupboards,' Rob says.

'It's old, an antique. The glass is so thick and heavy, you don't see that anymore,' Lucy says, inspecting it closely.

Rob looks at the grey square on the bare wall, where the cabinets had been for who knows how long.

'What are you going to do?'

'Burn them, I guess.'

'I'll get the broom,' she says. 'You start a fire.'

'I'll need to chop up some of them,' he says. 'The wood is dry, so it'll burn quickly.'

'Should you take pictures first, so your landlord knows it was an accident?'

'Yea, maybe. Although I doubt he'll think I ripped them off the wall in a fit of anger.'

Rob photographs the mess, the walls.

'I'll run you back to the hotel, then I guess I'll clean up.'

Lucy shakes her head. 'I'll help.'

'You sure?'

'Yes. Besides, I want to be here if something else crazy happens.'

Lucy pads back to the kitchen and begins gently moving the wood away, looking for anything else that might be trapped underneath.

'Be careful. I don't want you in the hospital when you have a flight to catch.'

Rob opens the back doors, letting in the cool breeze and the dark air of night. He carries a load of wood outside as Lucy keeps picking through, hoping to uncover another mystery. It is so quiet, she can hear Rob moving around, the swing of an axe. As she looks at the broken mess on the floor she thinks about cabinets. How they hide the business of day-to-day life. How people shove things in the back they don't want to see. Why would they have hidden such beautiful glass?

Rob appears, picking up another load. Lucy picks up

some, too. Nothing can be gained from staring at a mess for hours on end.

'Will the neighbours be upset about the fire?' she asks.

'They never have been before and I've burned a lot of stuff from that house. Old furniture, mostly.' As the fire gains power, he adds pieces of the cabinets and Lucy watches.

The flames crackle and hiss, jump, cast shadows. It feels like a November night in Rhode Island, not an August night in France.

'What do you think it all means?'

'What does what mean?'

'Everything smashes but an old cake stand you didn't even know was there.'

'That's the part I don't get. Why it didn't crack, and where it came from.'

'Could there have been some sort of top shelf you didn't see?'

'I'm six three. Not much is over my head.'

'It couldn't have just appeared.'

'I'm not sure how I missed it, but I did,' he says.

Lucy wonders what else has been missed as she sweeps up the mess on the floor.

* * *

She spends her second night on the sofa. After Rob leaves for work, she carries the cake stand to the sink, coats it with dish soap and scrubs away, filling the sink three times until it is clean. Drying it, she sets it on the dining room table, with the items from the trunk. She picks up a book, Byron, she sees, and opens it. There's a smudge of ink on the title page. Turning on the light, she studies it closely. A loop that could be an l. She carries the book to the patio doors, hoping the natural light might help. It doesn't. Setting it down, she picks up Wordsworth. The ink is stronger. She moves to the patio door, hoping for a clue.

Someone once wrote a note in this book. Perhaps it was a gift of some kind. But time has taken a toll, and no matter how hard she tries, she cannot make out a name.

PART 2

THIRTY-TWO
RHODE ISLAND. 1945

You carry the men who die with you. It's like some sort of cruel cosmic joke. You want to survive; you want your buddies on the line to survive. You have to cut down the enemy. The enemy has to cut you down. A death is a loss and a death is a win. It's a crap shoot as to who survives. It is sickening. It is war.

What no one told them in basic was how hard it was to see the men around you die. To see their eyes empty of light. To hear the strongest guy in the platoon gasping for breath, grabbing at the air like it holds the secret to life, because it does. Wanting his wife, or his mother. To see the sensitive guy, the kind-hearted guy, witness things no one should ever have to see. You want to step in and see it for them, because you know you are stronger. Then you start to think, maybe not stronger, maybe you lack some sort of vital piece of humanity. You have to get out of your own head.

You carry the dead with you. And they get heavier and heavier as you go.

Hank swore if he survived the war he would never, ever carry another goddamn thing on his back. What he didn't know was how heavy the memories would be.

* * *

The bus ride home, the shortest part of the trip, seems to be taking the longest. He wants a good shower, he wants to see his parents, he wants his own bed. He wants to burn this goddamn kit bag he's carried all over hell and back.

Hank has changed so much as a person, even he can feel it. Change happens, slowly, constantly. War makes it happen quickly, completely. You are never the same after you see a man die.

Looking out the window at the land he calls home, he tries to stop the dark thoughts. The day is fading and he's always loved a New England evening. The light is simply different here. More golden. More real.

They're on the outskirts of Providence now; Hank is shocked to see some new buildings. Happy to see every-thing standing. After all the ruined buildings, decimated villages and destroyed cities he's waded through, the fact that it's all intact makes him feel surprisingly good. They kept the threat from their own home. They did a good job.

The bus passes the store where Hank took his mother shopping, the day they heard the US was at war. She was buying poinsettias when the world changed forever.

The streetlights throw shadows into the path ahead as the bus turns into the station. It comes to a halt with a shudder, and the jerking sensation unsettles him for a second. Finally, he is home. Grabbing his duffel bag from the overhead rack, he shoulders it easily, and walks from the bus, pausing to feel the refreshing New England air envelop him. He pulls in a deep breath. It feels like a miracle.

'Right behind you, buddy. Move outta the way,' comes a voice from behind him, bringing him back to reality.

'Right,' Hank says, moving along.

Inside, the station seems smaller than he remembers. He looks around, thinking about walking the two or so miles home, or maybe seeing if there's someone around who will give an old soldier a lift.

That's when he sees an elderly man, sitting on a bench, in the middle of the station. His head is bowed over a newspaper, working on a crossword. First he recognises the hat, the way it is slanted a bit too far to the right. Brown, old and worn, still cared for. Still functionable.

Then he recognises the chin.

And the hand holding the pen, doing the puzzle.

Dad?

Hank is shocked to see his father, waiting at the station. He had no idea when he was going to be landing. How could his parents know?

His father looks old. Not older, old. Hank blinks, thinking maybe he is seeing things.

He sets the bag down and looks at the man, sitting on the bench.

As if sensing he is being studied, the man looks up.

A curious look that morphs into a shocked expression, before settling into one of both joy and relief.

'My boy,' he says. 'You're home.' He stands.

The two men embrace, Hank thinking his father has shrunk for a moment. But no, it's him. Hank is lean and wiry while his father is softer. He adjusts his embrace, loosens his grip. He is stronger than his dad now.

'How did you know I was coming in?'

'A feeling I got,' the older man says.

Father and son step back and study one another, as if trying to make certain they are both real, solid.

His father gives a little jump. 'Your mother. We have to get you home to your mother,' he says. 'She will be so happy.'

For a moment Hank simply feels good, coming home to so much. He's one of the lucky ones.

How did he get so lucky?

He throws his bag over a shoulder, and his other arm around his father, who throws his own around Hank. Like this, they walk from the station. Hank would never in a million years have thought this possible.

'Still driving the Packard?' Hank says, when he sees the car. He throws his bag in the back seat, climbs in the passenger side.

'There's no other car for me.' He laughs. 'I hope you're hungry, my boy. Your mother has been baking and cooking and freezing.'

'She's always been that way.' Hank laughs.

'More so recently.'

'Her care packages were a big hit,' he says. 'Especially the fudge.'

'She'd sit with her cookbooks in the evening, sorting out what would last the longest in the mail.'

Hank laughs. Does not tell him about the times the contents of the parcels went straight into the garbage as they were opened, rancid. It was the thought that meant so much to him. He knew the cost of postage meant a sacrifice somewhere for his parents. It would be better for them, now that he was back. Hank makes that decision as his father drives him back to his childhood home. His parents' lives would be better, and he would take care of William's girl. Maybe that was why he was spared.

They pull into the driveway, and Hank is shocked to see his house. It looks smaller, much like his dad does. But there's a warm glow coming from the living room window, and the light is spilling across the lawn where he played as a kid.

The porch light glows, and the familiar grey steps look liquid in its reflection. The door squeaks as he opens it for his father.

'Don't say anything; let's surprise her,' his father says, and Hank is shocked by his childlike excitement.

'Is that you, James?'

'Yes,' he says.

'Any luck?'

'Well, I found someone at the station.'

His mother comes scurrying around the corner. She stops so abruptly when she sees him; it's like she ran into an invisible fence. Her hands fly to her mouth, and she lets out a gasp that turns to a wail. As Hank watches she begins to shake.

He's seen so much shock, he bolts to her, as though she is a fellow soldier, not his mother.

'Jesus, Ma, I'm all right. I'm here, I'm here, I'm here,' he says. 'Dad, make some tea, with sugar,' he commands, over his shoulder. To his surprise, his father, who has never so much as made a piece of toast for himself, springs into action, making his way past them to the kitchen.

'No, no, I'm fine. Stop your father – he'll hurt himself.' She reaches out and touches him, making sure he is real.

Hank pulls her into his arms. He can feel her sniffle, trying not to cry. This is a house where no one cries, shows emotion. Hank knows what to do.

'I'm awful hungry, Ma. Could I get something to eat?'

It takes a second for her to let go. 'Oh, my goodness! Did the army feed you? You're skin and bone!'

She heads to the kitchen, looking over her shoulder to catch glimpses of him. He knows enough to follow her.

The same familiar scent is in the air and he knows for certain he's home. But it feels different. Smaller. Less permanent. Maybe he just needs some time to adapt.

He takes a seat at the kitchen table with his father, as his mother pulls a roast chicken from the fridge. Into the cast-iron skillet he knows so well goes a knob of butter, cold mashed potatoes.

He's definitely home.

* * *

Hank is opening drawers in the kitchen, searching for some writing paper, when his mother looks up from her tea, ready to jump into action. Since he's returned she's been waiting on him hand and foot, staring at him when he sits down, like she's trying to anticipate his needs.

'What are you looking for? What do you need?' she asks, hands in the air, at the ready. It is exhausting to Hank. He likes doing things on his own.

'Some writing paper. I need to write a letter,' he says.

'I'll get my writing pad for you.' His mother hurries to

the dining room, opens a drawer on the sideboard and pulls out a pad of paper and some envelopes.

'Do you need a pen? I'll get my pen, I think your father is using it for a crossword puzzle. JAMES! Henry needs your pen.'

'Ma, calm down. I have a pen. Let the man do his crossword.'

But his father is in the kitchen now, pen in his hand, ready to hand it over.

Hank sits at the table, takes out a page, setting the black lines that come with the pad under the piece of paper. He wishes he had such a strong guide for what he is about to write. He thinks for a moment, but no words come.

Reaching into his pocket, he takes out the piece of paper with William's address on it and sets it down beside him. He can feel his mother hovering behind him, twisting her hands, wanting to help, subtle as a UFO.

'I'll have a cup of tea, if you're making it,' he says. That might buy him some time.

He begins:

Dear Mr and Mrs Hardwick,

I hope you are well.

My name is Hank Corrigan, and I served with your son William. We met on the bus on the way to basic training and became good friends. We had a lot in common, and we got to know each other the way you only know the men you are in service with.

Hank thinks for a moment, back to his school days. Is it okay to end a sentence with 'with'? Is that a preposition? *Who the hell cares?*

He'd like to ask his mother what she thinks of the letter, but it might upset her. She seems so anxious, since he's been back. His father said once it's real to her, that the war is over and he's safe, she'll calm down again. Hank hopes so.

William spoke of you often to me. He had a real love for Cape Cod, and shared many fond memories of sailing, and runs on the beach. He made me promise...

Hank stops what he is writing. 'Made me promise before he died' is not something to write in a letter to a dead man's mother.

'Ah, hell.' He pulls out the page, crumples it up and starts again.

Your care packages were an event when they arrived, and we all enjoyed them. I want to thank you very much for the pencils and drawing pads you sent for me. It was a kindness much appreciated and a welcome reprieve from the time we were caught up in.

William was a good man, a good friend, a good soldier. While I was in France, I met Elise, and we spent time remembering William, and how important he was to both of us.

Will this make them miss him more? Bring back memories they are trying to forget?

Picking up the pad, he walks into the study where his father says he is working on a crossword but is in fact snoozing. This has been his weekend routine for as long as Hank could remember.

'Dad,' he says, gently, knowing it will do the trick. He's not a deep sleeper.

His father's eyes open and he grabs at the crossword.

'Yes, what do you need?' he asks.

'I'm not sure. I'm writing a letter to the parents of a man I served with, died beside me on D-Day. He was a good friend and I want his parents to know he is remembered. But I don't want to say anything that will hurt them.'

'Your mother is the letter writer,' his father suggests.

'I know, but... she's just so anxious. I don't want her to start thinking about what could have happened any more than she already is.'

'That's true.' He sits up in his chair. 'Read me what you have.'

Hank reads.

His father thinks for a second.

'I think if someone had good memories of my boy, knowing that would bring me a peace, and a joy. I think the worse thing would be to think he may be forgotten.'

Hank nods, folding up the paper. 'I won't ever forget him,' he says. There is something in his voice that makes his father's eyes narrow.

'Can I ask you something else?'

'Of course.'

'I was with him, when it happened. His last thoughts were about a woman he knew in France.' Hank hesitates.

'I'd like to tell his mother he felt no pain, and his last thoughts were of them.'

'And you're wondering about the lie?'

'Yes.'

'The God I believe in would be fine with it, I'm sure.'

Hanks nods, walks back to the kitchen.

I am not sure how to write this, and I hope it brings you some sort of peace, if that is even possible. But I want you to know I was with him when it happened. He was not alone, and he was not in pain. It was like he fell asleep. His last thoughts were of you and of Elise.

He ends up writing a three-page letter, putting it in an

envelope, sticking a stamp on it and putting it in the mail-box, before he changes his mind.

He thinks about writing to Elise, but he has no idea what to say to her, yet.

'I'm going out,' he says, taking his sweater from the peg by the door.

His mother appears, like he knew she would.

'Where are you going?'

'For a walk, maybe to the library,' he says.

'Will you be gone long?' She's anxious. He can see it in the move of her skirt, the way her hands move to her face.

'Christ, Ma, I'm a grown man,' he says.

His father appears and gives him a look.

'I'll be back for dinner,' Hanks says, softly.

Then he lets himself out into the cloudy grey day.

He walks to the library. It's his third trip since he got home, six weeks earlier, and his fourth trip in his entire life-time. When he was a kid he went once to get a book on drawing. He lost it and his father had to pay for it, and he never went to the library again. But William always had a book in his hand, and Hank had started to read. *The Grapes of Wrath. Great Expectations. The Hunchback of Notre Dame.* He likes a bit of action, a bit of redemption and reprieve for the characters. He does not need to be reminded how damn hard life is. He's not sure how long he's been walking, but one look at his watch and he knows he has to get to the library before it closes. He liked Stein-beck, and thinks he'll pick up another one. He remembers William telling him about someone named Hemingway, a book about the Great War. And he's heard about a French writer, Camus. He doubts they'll have anything by him. But Hank is pleasantly surprised to find an armload of books that look interesting. He checks them out, speaking to the librarian, Mrs McIntosh. He went to school with her daughter Doris, and her son Tom was two years ahead of him.

'Hello, Mrs McIntosh,' he says.

'Henry,' she says softly, a typical librarian. She is polite, but does not meet his eye, and the space around them feels off.

'Doris and Tom both well?'

She seems startled by his words, and he braces himself for more bad news.

'Dorothy is taking a secretarial course in Boston. Tom's not back, yet.'

From her words he knows not to ask any more about Tom. He has no idea what to say and stands in silence as she stamps the cards from each of the books, and hands them to him.

Taking the books Hank is dumbfounded by the brief look of hatred she gives him, before dropping her head.

'Thank you,' he says. She nods without looking up.

He is glad to be back outside, the sun warm on his shoulders. He's hurrying, remembering his promise to make it for dinner, when he runs into a man he went to school with, Jerome.

'Hank Corrigan, as I live and breathe,' he says, raising both arms in the air in greeting.

Jerome, Hank's mother often said, always had the Irish flair for drama.

'Hello, Jerome,' Hank says.

'How long you been back?'

'Six weeks,' Hanks says. 'You?'

'A year. Took a bullet in the shoulder.'

Only then does Hank realise one arm had drooped when Jerome had greeted him.

'What about you?'

'Got lucky,' Hank says. Embarrassed, suddenly, not to have been shot.

They stand on the street corner talking, and eventually move to a local bar. Rather seedy, but it serves its purpose.

'Where'd you see action?' Jerome says. He'd been in Japan, shot down over the sea, lived on a life raft for weeks. All this before being shot. 'I hope to God I never see the ocean again,' he says. 'The Japanese would fly over, and we'd jump in the water, flip the raft and hide under it, praying they wouldn't waste their bullets on the raft.' He pauses. 'How do you feel being back?'

'It feels unreal, like I'll be back over there any second.' The minute Hank says this, he knows it's true. He wonders if his nervousness was feeding his mother's.

In fifteen minutes he's talked about what happened more than he has with anyone. But if they didn't see it, they didn't need to hear about it. It didn't need to be spoken of, at all. But Jerome, he knew.

With that thought lodged in his mind, he finishes his beer.

They have another round. Someone at the bar sends over tumblers of Scotch, and Hank lifts his hand in thanks. It's not as good as the stuff his father has, but it does the job. He's feeling better than he has in a while. The knot in his back is gone. The constant wondering about how to help William's girl is gone, too. He'll figure it out. He always does.

* * *

Hank wakes with the sun cutting through his eyeballs like a kitchen knife going through stale bread. His head's pounding and he's never been so thirsty in his life. Eyes closed, arm thrown across them for extra protection he reaches around for his canteen, before he remembers he's actually home.

He's in his bed, fully dressed. The previous day plays out in snippets, like movie trailers in his mind. The library. Mrs McIntosh. The look she gave him sends a coldness through him although he's sweating. Meeting Jerome. The bar. Jesus. How did he get home?

It takes a second, then he remembers, a little flash of a waking nightmare. Standing on his doorstep, one arm over Jerome's shoulders. Jerome ringing the bell. His father, in his bedclothes, his dressing gown. Laying him on the sofa in the den. His mother in the background, until his father tells her to go to bed.

Waking up and stumbling to bed. Something breaking. He's not sure what.

Hank sighs. Feels like an idiot.

He pulls himself out of bed, opens his bedroom door, goes to the bathroom. A long hot shower to steam some of the poison from him. A cold shower to wake himself up. He shaves, forcing his hand to be steady and still cutting himself three times, then dresses and descends the stairs.

His mother is ironing clothes in the corner of the dining room. She always set the board up there, saying the light was better. His father is sitting at the table. The fact that he is not in his den is all Hank needs to know. Sometime today his father will have words for him.

Christ, he wishes he hadn't laid eyes on Jerome.

'You're awake,' his father says.

'Yes, sir,' he says.

His mother sets the iron down and picks up the skillet. Hank thinks for a second she might be fixing to hit him with it, but instead she turns on the grill, and he knows she's using it to reheat breakfast for him and cook a couple of eggs. She moves silently, which is unlike her. Every second that goes by without her speaking upsets him more.

'I'm sorry. I got a bit carried away last night.'

His father nods. His mother says nothing. Just a scrape of metal spoon against cast iron. It makes him wince. Well, something does.

'I saw Mrs McIntosh at the library yesterday. Doris is taking a course in Boston. Tom's not back yet.'

His mother hesitates, then cracks an egg.

His father looks out the window.

'Tom's missing in action. He was a paratrooper.'

There's a pause.

'Okay. It makes sense now.'

'What does?'

'She looked at me like she hated me,' he says.

His mother drops the spoon she's using to transfer food from the skillet to the plate. It hits the ceramic tiles and makes a clatter as loud as the bells of any cathedral he heard in France.

Hank stands up. Goes to the kitchen, picks up the spoon and puts it in the sink. He takes the plate from his mother and says, 'I'm sorry, Ma.'

Then he sits at the table and tries to eat his breakfast.

* * *

A few hours later, Hank realises his library books are missing.

'Goddamn it,' he says under his breath.

He lets himself out of the house, walking quickly, making his way to the bar. It's a shack from outside, and inside it is impossibly dreary. It's a little old man bar, a place where the bartender no doubt has a baseball bat at arm's reach and the cops know the address by heart.

'Get you a drink?' the bartender says. Same guy as the night before. Same clothes.

'No, thanks,' Hank says. 'I was here last night and left some books behind.'

He's using a filthy rag to wipe down the bar, and Hank feels nauseated at thinking he drank out of the glasses here.

'Oh yeah, I forgot about those,' he says, dropping the rag and disappearing. He comes back with Hank's stack of books.

'Thank you kindly,' Hank says, taking the armful and wishing he'd brought a bag.

A man sitting at the bar, head dropping and hair hanging in his beer, looks at Hank. Hank nods, leaving as quickly as he can, taking deep breaths outside to rid himself of the air of hopelessness inside.

It's not until he's home that he realises one of the books is still missing. He thinks about going back, then decides he'll pay for it instead.

In his room, he sets up the stack beside his bed, and starts to read.

* * *

One week after the event that has not been spoken of, Hank's father calls him into his den. For a moment Hank thinks they'll play backgammon, like they did before the war. His father had given him the board when he shipped out, but he left it behind, in England. No room in his pack. He feels bad about that now.

His father opens a bottle of Scotch and pours them both a drink. It's a brand-new bottle and Hank gets the sinking feeling it has been purchased especially for this moment. He watches his father's hands, scarred in so many places from his work as a pipefitter. He'd wanted to be a history teacher, but he did not come from the kind of family that sent their boys to college.

'You've been back a spell now,' he says.

'If nine weeks is a spell, then yes, I have been,' Hanks says.

His father gives him a look, and Hank knows he's pushed the envelope. 'Sir,' he adds.

'I've heard about this new government program. The Service Readjustment Act. Roosevelt's idea. Good man, FDR. The government will pay for boys like you to go to college.'

Hank perks up at this.

'It's something you should do.'

'I'll look into it tomorrow,' he says.

'I don't want you to go too far away. Not with your mother being the way she is with you. It might have been easier, if we'd had two or three, but you were a bit of a miracle as it was.'

Hank never knew this. 'Miracle?'

'Something wrong with the plumbing. You don't need to know. It's why she is the way she is, nervous like, with you. So be patient with her.' There's a change in tone, a new firmness to this, that confuses Hank.

'Sir?'

'Don't ever let me hear you sigh when she hovers again.'

'No, sir.'

'And this vulgar language you picked up. That ends now.'

Hank nods, embarrassed.

'I've read a lot about war, in my books.' He nods to the shelves that line the room, shelves his father made by hand, filled with books about Napoleon, Caesar, Alexander the Great, Atatürk.

'I know you must have seen some awful stuff. I don't know if talking about that sort of thing helps. Liquor doesn't.'

Hank thinks of the absurdity of his father saying this while they both have a glass of single malt in their hands.

'You need to put your life together, get working, get studying. Make the most of what you have before you,' his father says.

'I will, sir,' he says.

'Now finish your drink, look into the GI Bill, and leave me to my crossword puzzle.'

* * *

It's a Tuesday morning and Hank is out at a construction job when a parcel arrives for him. His mother has set it on the table, ready for him when he gets home.

Hank sees the parcel on the table when he walks in, carrying his empty lunchbox. He empties the paper used to hold his sandwiches into the trash, then rinses it in the sink, same way he saw his father do for years. But his eyes never leave the parcel.

'What's this?' He picks it up.

'I don't know, but it's a woman's handwriting.' If it were possible for his mother to sound coy, he'd say that was how she sounded.

He picks it up, and the return address, written neatly in the left-hand corner on the brown paper, jumps at him.

Cape Cod.

Holding it in his hand, he thinks he knows what it is.

Sliding a knife under the tape, he opens the parcel. The board is wrapped in cloth, to protect it, but already he sees the slightly worn brown leather, clear as day. On top is an envelope addressed to him.

He sits, and then opens it.

His mother, behind him, again.

The words his father said echo.

He opens the letter, and his mother walks away.

Dear Hank,

I want to thank you for your lovely letter. It arrived some time ago, and I should have replied sooner, but I found myself reading it over and over. For a few moments it seemed William was alive with us again, perhaps because he was being remembered by someone who knew him in a way that we did not. I want to thank you for that.

I never saw my son as a soldier. My husband promised me the army would see to it that he became one, but I had my worries. William was always such a sensitive lad. I guess what I am trying to say is that I was prepared, but that in no way changed my devastation at the news, or the pain I will live with every day for the rest of my life.

Hank stops reading, looks out the kitchen window. He might be sitting in the kitchen of his parents' home in Rhode Island, but that is just the meat and bones of him. The rest of him is sitting in a pub in England, staring at his friend, willing him to feel some meanness for the enemy, wanting to toughen him up, not knowing how.

The words on the page cut into him. Hank feels his failure a little deeper.

He looks back at the letter.

Even as a little boy, he did not play with toy soldiers or army men. He did not have any toy guns. He didn't even like to fish. I didn't want to send him off to war, but then no mother wants to. I had to accept that this was happening. But I knew.

Hank can hear his heart beating harder and harder. His mother comes into the kitchen, and he slides the letter away. He's read enough for now.

'Mother, you're not cooking tonight. We're going out to eat. How does Italian sound to you?'

The look of surprise on his mother's face, that he's just suggested something as outrageous as going out to eat on an ordinary Tuesday night, makes him laugh. Once he starts he cannot stop. His laughter is loud, and he can feel it in his belly. It brings his father from the den.

'What's happening here?' he says.

'He wants to go out for dinner,' his mother says, her hands clasped in front of her, like she is about to say a prayer for her son's sanity.

Hank forces himself to take a breath, to calm down. His peals of laughter turn to chuckles and end up settling into a big grin.

'Get your coats. We're going to Antonio's for lasagne,'

he says, knowing his father's unholy love for that very thing, something his mother never cooked in her life.

His mother looks sceptical, but his father is already getting his coat.

'I was going to make meatloaf,' she says.

'This way you won't have to spend the evening cooking and cleaning, Ma. You can do something nice for yourself.'

His mother's eyes dart around the room, as though something fun to do will jump out at her.

'I'll make some pies, for the church sale,' she says.

Hank realises his mother's entire life revolves around taking care of other people. He reminds himself to do something about this.

* * *

Hank has not been to Antonio's for years. The last time was when he graduated from high school, he thinks. His parents go on their wedding anniversary, and for his mother's birthday. Twice a year, they go out to dinner. The thought depresses him.

His mother has spaghetti, his father has lasagne, same as always. Hank tries something called gnocchi, a potato dumpling of some kind. It is good. His mother looks at it like it's some sort of magical crystal on his plate.

They need to get out more, Hank thinks. He'll have to work on that, too. Hank is discovering the busier he is, the easier it is to keep the dark thoughts that keep him awake at bay.

'Have dessert, Mother.' Hank pushes the menu to her. He has no memories of his mother ever ordering a dessert for herself. Come to think of it, she had just ordered the cheapest thing on the menu. That's got to change, too.

'Oh, I couldn't,' she says, but already she is glancing at what is listed. His mother loved sweets. He catches the eye of the waiter, and asks for a glass of Scotch, neat, for his father. He orders a coffee for himself. His mother orders something with ladyfingers and coffee and cream. For a moment, Hank feels a simple sense of contentedness as his parents enjoy the rare treat he has provided for them, from one of his own packets of wages.

At home, his mother decides to take a bath and go to bed. His father retreats to the den. Hank gets the letter from the desk drawer in the kitchen where he found it and starts from the beginning.

I am enclosing your backgammon game. William sent it to us for safekeeping, and it has not even been opened since it arrived. I like to think of my son having an escape from training and playing this game, although he was fondest of chess.

I know you are busy building a life in this new, post-war world, and I know your own mother won't want to let you out of her sight, but if you have the time, we would love to meet you.

Very best wishes,

Jean Hardwick

Hank picks up the backgammon board. On the day his father drove him to the train station to head to basic training, he'd given Hank a parcel and told him to open it on the bus. Inside were a dozen chocolate chip cookies and the backgammon board his father had taught him to play on. As a boy he'd had hot chocolate and they'd play at the kitchen table. As he got older, he moved to root beer, then one day he had a glass of Scotch, and hated it, went back to root beer.

In basic he'd played with William. In advanced training, they'd played in pubs in England. He remembers the day they were packing up to invade France, he left it behind, for the other recruits. There was so much stuff to carry. But that wasn't the real reason. The real reason was a lot darker. He didn't want it being returned to his parents with his blood on it, if something happened to him. William must have seen him and had mailed it to his own parents. He was that type of person. Thoughtful, like.

Holding the game in his hands, Hank walks down the stairs and into his father's den.

'Best two out of three?' he says.

A startled look turns to one of pleasure.

'Set it up. I'll get the drinks,' he says.

'I'll make a coffee, dad,' Hank says. He's had one drink since that bad night. But his desire for more is what scares him.

He opens the game, sets it up on the little table in his father's den.

War changed everything, except this ritual. There's a peace in that.

THIRTY-THREE
RHODE ISLAND. 1946

Looking around the classroom, Hank Corrigan is convinced he is the oldest freshman student ever. Until another man walks in the room. By the way his hair is styled, straight back with no crazy wave, the way his shirt is perfectly pressed, Hank knows a fellow soldier when he sees one. It creates a small sense of relief, and a bit of apprehension he was not ever aware he was carrying disappears.

Soon, he has a schedule, spending his time in four ways – going to classes, studying, working one of the three construction jobs he has, and running. Running, he's discovered, helps keep his thoughts in line. When he's at loose ends, that is when the rats tend to scurry around in his head. The only way to tame them was to tire them, keep them exhausted. His mother feeds him, does his laundry, cleans his room. He's seldom home, and when he is, he's exhausted.

They're having dinner one night when his mother says, 'Have you met any nice girls, any freshettes, at school?'

For some reason the simple question embarrasses Hank.

'No women in my classes,' Hank realises, for the first time. There are pretty girls all over campus, but he's always in such a race from one place to another, he doesn't really think about it. Sometimes, at night, a need for a physical release makes him think about them.

He can feel himself colour.

'Maude, leave the boy alone,' his father says, perhaps knowing why Hank is turning red while eating fish cakes, green tomato chow and boiled potatoes, one of his favourite meals.

Her comment gets him thinking about William's girl, the promise he's made and failed to fulfil. A bite of food gets stuck in his throat and he starts to cough. His parents watch him at first, until Hank bangs the table with his fist, causing the dishes to jump and his mother to grab some water. His father slams him on the back, but nothing is happening. Hank knows panic is the enemy here. How many enemies did he learn about in training? Dehydration, the Germans, the Japs, the cold, exhaustion.

His father is wailing on his back now and his mother is whimpering, terrified, until Hank stands, pushes his father away. Knocks over his chair. Making a fist, he finds the part below his ribs, over his belly button, and drives himself into the back of his father's still-standing chair. Once, twice, he's running out of time now.

The last time it feels like the chair might go clean through him, to his backbone. He coughs again, and again, a little trickle of air making him gasp. He feels like he's drowning. There's something still in his throat. Blood on the chair, the table. Running from his mouth.

His father is calling for an ambulance. His mother is praying. And all Hank can think is that it would be a helluva thing, to survive the war, and choke to death on a fishbone in his mother's kitchen.

* * *

It wasn't a bone. It was a fishhook that was missed at the canning factory. They keep him in overnight, worried about the tearing in his throat. It's sore as hell. Hank feels like he's cheated death, again.

The nurse on duty is kind to him, and he thinks she is a pretty little thing. Nina is her name.

He's survived again, and it's time to keep a promise.

* * *

It takes a few days, to come up with a plan. On his lunch break, he gets a bank draft for $100. He's not sure how many francs that is, but it's a lot of money to him. At home that night he writes a very simple note.

Dear Elise,

I hope this note finds you well.

I am back in the United States, living with my parents and attending college. I've wanted to write before now, but to be honest, I find it hard to think about what happened to William and am trying not to think about things too much in general.

I know it must be even harder for you, living in a country decimated by...

He stops. Doesn't want to use the word war and settles on *troubles*.

I hope the enclosed helps, until France gets on its feet.
Sincerely,
Henry Corrigan

He puts the letter and the bank order into an envelope and seals it up. It feels cheap, not like keeping a promise, but it's the best he can do right now. He posts the letter and tries to put it out of his mind, but like an itch, it's always there, hovering around him like a mosquito on a summer night.

Three months later, on a day when Hank is filled with a bad cold and not looking forward to classes or work, he gets a letter from France.

Inside is a small sheet of light blue paper with a half-page note.

Dear Henry,

Thank you for your recent note.

I know returning to a normal life in America must be hard for you. I wish you luck with that.

I am working at the library and at the bakery. My country is on the mend.

Best wishes,

Elise Lacroix

Folded inside the envelope is the bank draft. Hank looks at it as though for the first time, then puts it back in the envelope and slides it all into his pocket.

THIRTY-FOUR

RHODE ISLAND. 1949

It takes Hank three years to complete a four-year degree, taking summer classes and carrying an extra-full class load. His parents come to his graduation, his father in a suit, perhaps even the same one he got married in, and his mother in her best dress.

He wouldn't have taken the time for graduation, if it wasn't so important to his parents. He'd rather be working. In three weeks, he's starting a job with a local engineering firm. He'll do as much casual labour at construction sites until then as he can. He has very big plans.

He works and works and then one night, when he is having dinner with his parents, he tells them he is buying an apartment building.

His father sets his fork down with a clank, more than a clatter.

'You're what? Where?'

Hank tells him the address, and his mother pales.

'That's not a good area,' she advises.

'It will be, soon. The city is expanding. The population's growing.'

'And?' His father knows more is coming.

'I'm moving into one of the apartments. It'll be easier, being onsite. As a manager.'

'You're not leaving your job?'

'No, not at all. I can manage a property at the same time.'

There's a silence that Hank knows is filled with fear. People like his family don't buy apartment buildings. They might live in one, but they don't buy. Hank's parents are the only ones to own a home, and it was a sensation when they spent eighteen thousand dollars on it. A king's ransom, at the time. An inheritance from his mother's uncle made it possible.

'It'll be nice for the two of you, to have a break from me,' Hank cajoles. But he knows his mother will worry, no matter what he does.

'Are you sure you know what you're doing?' his father asks.

'I do, Dad. Trust me, I do.'

He moves into his own apartment on a late September day, when the leaves are just starting to show hints of yellow and red. He uses the second-hand pickup truck he bought, and his co-worker Joe helps. He's never seen his parents walk as closely together as they do once they get out of his dad's old car. The area they live in is blue collar, but it's pretty upscale, compared to this place.

His mother brought a bag of cleaning supplies and even though Hank objects, she gets to work in the kitchen of his two-bedroom apartment in the basement of the building. He plans to turn the second room into an office, like his dad's.

'So tell me how this works. You own the building, and the people pay you rent?' his dad asks, looking around sceptically.

'Which I give to the bank, for the mortgage,' Hank adds, hauling a box of kitchen items his mother has donated.

'I hope you know what you're doing.'

'Grab a bag, Dad, you're not that old yet,' Hanks replies.

* * *

A new plan begins to take shape. His parents' neighbours, they're all moving to Florida. A New England winter is hard on everyone, but it is particularly brutal on the old. So one April he drives to Florida with the intention of finding a small place for them in Clearwater, the only place in Florida he's ever heard of. Besides, he likes the name. Clearwater. The simplicity of it. The purity.

On the way he stops for gas, in a place called Saint Pete's. He sees a neighbourhood and drives through. A small white house with a wraparound porch and blue striped awnings catches his eye, and when he sees the For Sale sign, he pulls over and knocks on the door. The door opens and an older man appears, wearing grey flannel trousers on a day when you could fry a steak on the pavement. Hank knew the minute he saw him he'd been in the service and liked him immediately. Walking through the house, he could see himself living there one day.

'Can I ask why you're selling?' he asks the older man.

Edward's his name – as they sit on the back porch listening to the ocean.

'It's too much for me, and my daughter wants one of those fancy places in Miami Beach. There's not much around here to do. Suits me fine, but the younger ones are bored.'

Hank keeps his laugh to himself. There's not much around, but Hank knows it won't stay that way. The population is growing, and people will always need a place to live.

'Well, I'd like to take it off your hands. I think this is a little piece of paradise,' he says.

'I'll have to call my son. He's the lawyer.'

'Please do that. I'm here for the week and would like to get this all wrapped up.'

* * *

'Florida. Why would we fly to Florida?' his father asks, for about the fifteenth time since Hank said he'd bought plane tickets, and they were going. They do not know about the little house on the beach, yet.

'C'mon, Dad, it'll be nice for Mom to get some sun, relax.'

'Where will we stay for a week? How much will it cost?'

'Don't worry about that, Mom.' Hank wishes they would let themselves be excited. Be happy.

'Everything's taken care of. It'll be fun,' he says.

Neither have flown before, and both are terrified. His father's just hiding it better.

'My suitcase is heavy. I'm afraid it might fall through

the bottom of the plane,' she says, staring at the plaid case Hank never even knew they owned.

He starts to laugh. He can't help it.

'Planes are pretty durable,' he says. 'Don't worry about it.'

* * *

They land in the evening and take a taxi from the airport to the house. They drive by strips of hotels, gift shops, vacant lots and lots under construction.

'Are we driving back to Rhode Island?' his father asks, after twenty minutes.

'Relax, Dad. It's a big place.'

'No, it's not. I looked it up in the atlas.'

Finally, the driver pulls up in front of the house. The white glows softly, like a beacon in the darkening sky. Hank pays him, and they step outside. The sound of the waves and the aroma of the sea, salty and inviting, greets them.

His father looks around. 'Where's the hotel?' he asks as Hank pays the driver, who then carries the bags to the front steps. They're freshly painted but a bit warped and need to be replaced. He'll do that this week. You have to keep on top of things, when you own property.

Hank pulls the keys from his pocket and opens the door. His mother is still standing in the street, where the taxi dropped her.

'Ma, for goodness' sake. Come up here, now.'

'Henry, what are you doing?'

The use of his proper name makes him realise a surprise is not going to work. They're nervous.

He opens the door, turns on the inside and outdoor lights.

'I bought it, Ma. I own this place. Now come on in!'

Still, his parents don't move. Hank's a bit annoyed. He'd been looking forward to this moment, and they're acting like deer caught in headlights.

He takes a breath. Goes down the stairs and physically takes his mother's arm.

'Come see the house,' he says.

The light from the entrance only penetrates so far into the darkness of the small building. There are a few street-lights out front, and none in the back, just some wild grass, the beach, and the sandy slope into the ocean. Hank walks ahead, turning on the lights. When he looks back he sees his parents still standing in the entranceway.

They look like they're in shock.

Hank waits for them to put it together in their minds.

'You bought this?'

Hank nods. 'Winters are too hard, back home. I don't want you getting into cold cars, driving on icy roads. You can spend the winters here, when Dad retires. I'll rent it out the rest of the time.'

'But what will happen to our home?'

'I figured I'd live there, and you guys can come back when it's too hot here.'

His mother looks around. It's small, all on one floor, another reason he bought it. His mother was starting to struggle with the stairs.

'You want to see the kitchen?' he asks.

She nods. The kitchen is at the back of the house. There's a door to the back patio, but he plans to put in sliding doors, and a big window. Open up the space and let the beautiful sunshine in.

The kitchen is bigger than the one in Providence. Hank sees his mother's face light up at the new ice box, the row of cabinets.

His father follows them in, looks around. 'Open the window,' he says. 'I like the sound of the waves.'

Hank never knew this about his father. Already, it's all worth it.

* * *

Of all the things Hank thought his parents would love about Florida, he had no idea it would be the beach. The first day they sat and looked at it. The second day they walked down – in their shoes and all their winter clothing – and stood close to the water. The third day, his mother opined that if the weather was a dash warmer, she might like to stick her feet in the sea.

Hank thought for a moment she'd been nipping at the Christmas sherry when she said this. He wished he'd had a camera when she did it.

The house is taking shape. The kitchen now has a set of dishes, cutlery, a roasting pan for the turkey, a set of pots and pans. They have a table, too. The woman next door, Maggie, was a godsend. Took them to buy food. They spent sixty-five dollars at the grocery store, filling two trolleys. His mother was beside herself at the expense. Hank paid cash – carrying around a few hundred dollars at all times made him feel like he'd accomplished something. Then they went and bought a table.

Still, at some point every single day, he wonders about

Elise. Feels bad about her. He hopes by now she's found a nice man – after all she was a very handsome woman – and settled down.

He won't let himself contemplate her spending Christmas on her own.

'Hank?'

'He's lost in thought again, Maude. That's our real-estate tycoon.'

'Sorry, Ma. What were you saying?'

'We need to get some more towels, and I'd like to change the beds. When are we flying back home?'

'The second,' Hank says.

'Oh,' she says. Hank thinks he's heard a twinge of disappointment in that one syllable. And he's pleased, for a moment.

But something is not sitting right with him. He's not sure what it is. Maybe his mother is right, and he needs to settle down, find a nice girl. He thinks about Nina, the nurse who treated him when he choked. He'd thought a few times about calling her to go out, but something always stopped him. Never got up the nerve, his father would say.

But here's something else. He's not sleeping like he used to. The running, well, he can feel it in his left knee now, but it's not tiring out his mind the way it once did.

It comes to him, all at once: it's his promise to William. And it's time he sorted it out. It's going on ten years, after all.

* * *

It's bitter, the cold and the wind, when they arrive home.

Before going to bed, his mother kisses Hank on the

cheek, something she has not done since the day he set off for basic training. His father shakes his hand. 'Tomorrow, I'll beat you at backgammon,' he jokes. Hank notices both of his parents have nice colour, from the walks on the beach they took. Once, he saw his father hold her hand. It was unsettling at first – his parents were very reserved – but then, Hank was pleased. Married so long, been through so much. And they still love each other, in a gentle, genuine way.

Hank goes to the front room, where no one ever sits, and looks out the window, thinking. The street where he played ball hockey. The empty lot where they played baseball. The Dent house. He'd played with John growing up; they'd gone to school together. Now he was buried in France. The Sullivans lost a boy, too. And the Smyths. Three, on this street alone. But if he looks closely, he can see them all as lads, running the bases, fighting over who was safe at home, being called into lunch by their mothers. The endless games of bee bee bumblebee to see who went first.

Hanks know what he has to do.

Now that he has his parents sorted, it's time to help Elise. He turns from the window, from the memories of his childhood, and heads to the kitchen.

Sitting down at the table he starts a letter to Jean. He's been remiss there as well. He asks if she has heard from Elise, and if she is doing okay. Hank hopes she has married, and has a family, a life of her own. Hope, hope, hope. It's all he can do. No. It's all he has done.

He seals the envelope but can't post it until the morning. He goes to his room, changes into his running gear, and even though it will be freezing outside, he goes for a run.

Maybe he'll run into the ghosts of the boys they all once were.

* * *

It takes six weeks for Hank to get a reply from Jean. Her handwriting seems less certain, and he knows he's not done right by her, either. A letter here and there, but he still hasn't visited.

The note is not encouraging. Elise, as far as she knows, is in the same house. Never married. Doesn't hear from her as much as she used to.

I have visions of Miss Havisham, when I think of her, she writes. The sentence pokes at his heart – he knew the character because her son had got him to read *Great Expectations*.

Taking out the last three sheets of his mother's writing tablet, Hank begins another letter. Never wrote a letter in his life until the war, and now he's pretty good at it, even if he hates to do it.

He'll send another draft, and if he doesn't hear from her, he'll go to France and see what is happening for himself.

THIRTY-FIVE
NORMANDY. SPRING 1955

Hank always knew he'd return to France. There was no doubt. He never knew exactly when, but he knew he would. To pay his respects to the men who died. To see that goddamn beach that changed his life.

He has no desire to stay in Paris, so he goes straight to the train station when he lands. Paris was a city where they got up to some shenanigans, and even after all these years, Hank colours at what he did one night. He was young. He thought he could die at any moment. But he knew better. Poor girl, so broken by life. Both taking comfort where they could. He hopes she's okay, now.

He needs to find the train to the north.

The man he asks for help smiles at him.

'American?'

Hank nods.

The man sorts his tickets for him. He has to change stations, once, twice. Hank had learned a handful of French, but it is not helping him now. A woman behind them steps forward. She speaks French with the clerk, gives Hank directions in English.

'Merci, monsieur,' she thanks him.

'What?' Hank is baffled.

Whenever he speaks, he gets the same reaction. American? Canadian? They both fought on the beaches he is going to see.

He just happened to survive to tell the tale.

* * *

When he steps from the train, he knows exactly where he is going. He thought maybe he'd be confused – it was so long ago, and he was so tired at the time and so afraid of the journey ahead of him. He's not tired now, but he is afraid, for different reasons.

He'd written to her that he was coming, twice. But he wasn't sure she got his notes.

He lifts his bag and begins to walk. There's a bar on the corner, and some men sitting outside. They nod in his direction, plumes of cigarette smoke obscuring their faces. The remnants of some sort of meal on the table in front of them.

A man waves him over, and he moves toward them, not so much because he wants a drink, as he wants to delay what he has come here to do.

'*Américain?*' they ask.

'Oui,' he says. And one of them stands, quickly, the chair scraping the concrete it rests on. He calls for someone and a head appears in the doorway to the bar. Some quick words are exchanged that he misses, but Hank does catch 'Américain'.

A bottle of something appears and drinks are poured.

'*Santé!*' they say to him. He knows they are drinking to his health. He takes a drink, orients himself. He knows where the Channel is, and that beach, now.

He takes another drink as he thinks of William, the men who never returned. Ten years is but a blink of the eye, but for the men who died, it was time to build a life that was denied them.

Another drink is poured and Hank talks to the man beside him, asking about Elise. It is not a big place, and surely everyone knows one another? But the man shrugs. Hank is not a drinker and can already feel the effects of the alcohol. He thanks the men, shaking hands, and leaves.

Maybe it's the alcohol. Maybe it's being back, but he feels good walking the street that he knows leads to her house. A thought occurs that maybe she has moved, and he won't be able to find her. It makes him stop in the street. Would that be the end of it, then? Could he move on? But no, Jean says she is still there, and in his heart he knows she is.

* * *

The trees dance lightly as he walks down the street. Some wind chimes add to the sound of the magical tinkling of the leaves. He knows the house is around the small bend in the road. He turns, and there it is. The paint is peeling, the doorstep an accident waiting to happen. It is a sobering sight. He makes his way up the walk, but there's no way that step will hold him. It's sagging in the middle like a failed soufflé. Setting down his case, he moves along the side of the house, noticing the wood rotting in the window frames. Surely she doesn't live here?

He turns the corner, and there, at the back, he sees her. She's sitting in the sun, with a book. He watches her for a second. A fine-looking woman, beautiful even, if not for the wildness of her hair, the droop of her shoulders, like she's carrying something heavy. He raises his fist to knock on the side of the house, alert her to his presence, but she looks up and sees him just then, curled fingers in the air.

A look of alarm crosses her face, briefly, before being replaced by... resignation? He can't tell.

They look at each other, for a moment, maybe two.

'Elise?' he asks, although he knows it is.

'Oui, yes, it is me.'

She moves toward him, and he sees how old she looks, forgotten, slightly decrepit. Haunted. A bit like the house itself.

'It's Hank, William's old friend. We met...' His voice trails off. She must know when they met. And if she didn't, he had one helluva job ahead of him.

'Hank, yes. The man who sends me money.'

How she says it shames him. Like she knows about the promise. Knows he's trying to buy a reprieve.

'Would you like to come in for a drink?'

'Yes. Please.' He steps aside and lets her lead the way. The door to the back of the house is damn near off its hinges, the wood rotted through. A child could break in. He'll have to sort that before he leaves.

The house is clean – he'll say that much. Dated, old, falling apart, but clean. He's not sure if it's some sort of attempt at being house proud, or maybe something she does to pass the time. A kind of therapy, the way his mother was always cleaning his clothes, cleaning his room, cooking his meals when he returned. Like she was showing whatever force that saved him how good a mother she could be.

No, that was not the case here.

As Elise busies herself in the kitchen, he watches her.

'How have you been?' he asks, feeling foolish at the ridiculousness of the question.

'I am fine, thank you,' she says, like she is reciting a phrase she learned from a lesson book.

'I wrote that I was coming.'

'I do not go to the post office much.'

He doesn't know what to say to that.

'Did you come to mark the anniversary?'

He does not know if she means of D-Day, or William's death.

He says nothing.

She hands him a teacup filled with coffee and takes out a bottle of some sort of spirits. Calvados. He remembers now.

The smell reminds him of being here, the last time. Wanting to keep his promise. And not wanting to, as well. That hasn't changed, but this time, he has to do something to make it right. He owes that to his friend, forever asleep in a field on the coast.

'What brings you here?' she asks, refilling her glass.

He thinks, for a moment. 'It's time. To see the beach, to see the land.'

Her eyes half close, and her head dips briefly.

'I have not seen it, myself.'

'Why?' he asks.

'Because I do not want to.'

There is not much more he can say to that.

He tries to look at her as a human who is hurting. But he can't help but think... if she cut her hair, put on some lipstick, some fashionable clothes. Not that life is outward appearances, but she might feel better. How he felt better when he was in service, physically fit and having a purpose. Now, his middle is a bit soft. His purpose seems to be to make as much money as he can. But that too, isn't real. His tenants pay rent, that pays the mortgage. The house in Florida is leveraged against the apartment building. He's in it for the long haul, he knows.

'You and William. You lived close, in America. Have you visited his family, Jean, and his brother and father?'

He shakes his head. Maybe he should have, but would any mother want to meet the person who was with her son when he died, and didn't save him? He tells himself no, despite her invitations. Another reason to be ashamed.

'We've exchanged a few letters,' he says. He does not tell her about the backgammon game. Or his mother asking if her son was in pain.

'I used to hear from Jean,' Elise says. Hank notices the way she says 'William' sounds different, and it's not because of her accent. There's an energy, a force, a love behind it. For the rest of the world it might be ten years, but for her, it is yesterday that she got the news, learned of her loss. And it hits him: she has given up, refused to move forward.

He knows he has some work ahead of him and pushes his drink away.

'The house needs some work. I'm a pretty good handyman,' he says.

Elise starts to speak, and from the set of her jaw he's

pretty sure she's going to turn him down. But something changes her mind.

'Yes, the house needs some work. It is not something that interests me. Do you have a place to stay? You can have my brother's room, if you want.'

'What about Monsieur Gravel?'

'Died last year,' she says.

'Oh.' He bows his head, briefly.

'I left my bag outside,' he says. 'I'll get it now.'

* * *

Perhaps because Hank is naturally a man of few words, and Elise, it seems to Hank, too weak to speak, they communicate through food and chores. She's a good cook and feeds him well and he plans what needs to be done, ripping out old rotted wood and putting in new doors, new window frames, new planks in the floor. As he tears out and rebuilds he thinks setting a match to the place would be easier, but that's hardly something he can suggest. He works from first light to last, and in a week the place looks better. Not new, not fresh, not even able to withstand a strong storm, but better. As he hammers and saws he finds himself thinking about William. Mostly with sadness, a sense of loss. But sometimes, he wonders. How well had he known this girl?

The activity makes him feel good, and one night he suggests they walk into town. 'You've been cooking so much. Let me take you out to dinner,' he says.

'That is not necessary,' she says.

'Not much of the fun things in life are necessary, but they make life worth living. So let's go out to eat.'

She doesn't move. He can see her hesitation.

'Please?' he adds, softly.

'I will need to get ready,' she says.

'That's fine. I need to sweep up all the sawdust and get cleaned up myself. I'll use the basin in the kitchen,' he says.

Elise looks at him like she is trying to find an excuse, and Hank shoos her. 'Upstairs. Put on a nice dress. We'll have a good meal and you won't have to clean up in here.' He remembers saying these very things to his mother, and it gives him an odd feeling in his belly.

She turns and heads up the stairs, her footfall hesitant on the steps. Hank expects her to turn around, make excuses. But she does not.

When she returns to the kitchen, she is wearing a pink dress. Her hair is tied back in a knot, showing the beauty of her face without the grey curtain of hair. He's not sure if she's wearing makeup, but her skin has a soft glow about it. He likes to think it is happiness at the thought of going out, and not something from a pot or a tube.

Hank is wearing a blue button-down, tan trousers and a grey cardigan his mother knit for him. He didn't bring any dressy clothes with him, but he thinks he looks fine. Still, he wishes he had a sport jacket with him.

'You look really nice,' he says.

'Thank you,' Elise replies.

'Do you have any idea where you would like to go?'

'I do. There's a place near the waterwheel, if it is still there. It has been a while for me.'

'We shall try. And if it's not there, we will go someplace else.'

She pulls on a cardigan and even to Hank's untrained eye it does not match what she is wearing. But he smiles, pulls the door closed behind them, and as they walk down the path that leads from the decrepit home to the street, he offers her arm. She hesitates, then nervously slips her hand through the crook of his elbow.

The evening light shimmers, lighting their path as they walk the short distance to town.

'I've reinforced the back step, and the front. They're both safe now. I've replaced some of the window frames as well. I'd like to get an electrician to check the wiring, and then I'm going to plaster some of the walls. The damp has done terrible things to them. Some of the support beams might need to be replaced as well.'

He feels her stiffen beside him.

'Will this cost a lot?' she asks.

'No, no. Any costs, I'm happy to cover,' Hank answers quickly.

A moment of hesitation and then, 'Why?'

Should he tell her?

Hank stops in the street. The church is beside them, casting a large shadow across and around them. The sun is low in the sky, a brilliant ball of orange light compelling him to tell the truth.

'Because William was my friend. Because I was with him when he died. And because he asked me to look in on you. So please, let me do this. For my friend. And for you.'

Her head dips and Hank has a very real fear she may start to weep on the street. Instead, she lifts her head and says, 'He is still with me. I can feel him, you know.'

He nods, not trusting himself to speak.

They resume walking, passing by the church.

'When I first met William, I took him here.' She points. 'He loved the architecture,' she says. 'When he was fighting, I went there to pray for his safety.' She pauses, and when she speaks there is something new in her voice. Contempt. 'I have not been back since.'

Hank presses his arm, the one where her fingers rest so softly, closer to his body, pulling her delicate hand into his side. He reminds himself of how much she has lost and determines to do better taking care of her.

* * *

The bistro is still there, and Hank feels a new energy about Elise as she sees it. He assumes she visited it with William, the reason for all of her happiness.

'Would you like to sit inside or out?' he asks.

'Let's sit outside so we can hear the wheel,' she says.

Hank nods, helping her with her seat. There's a small cloud of black flies hanging over a green patch of stagnant water, and Hank orders them under his breath to stay where they are.

A waiter appears, and he seems to know Elise. Well, he kisses her on both cheeks, but that's just their way. No, Hank definitely sees a look of surprise on his face that turns to one of, if not pleasure, at least some sort of animation.

Elise is so thin, so delicate. If his mother saw her she would immediately start cooking.

'So, what is good on the menu?' he asks. 'Is there a national dish I should try?'

'Have you had moules frites...' He watches as she searches for the correct English words.

'Frites... fries.'

'Moules, a shellfish, we cook them with onions and tomatoes.'

'Mussels?' he asks. He has had them and is not a fan.

He orders a beef stew with beer and ginger, and Elise gets shrimp croquettes.

The food is tasty. The night is lovely, the sky still bright but with a soft purplish twinge to it. The waterwheel moves slowly, never speeding up or slowing down. Hank likes its constant, predictable rhythm. Snippets of laughter surround them, buzzy conversations. Hank feels a sense of peace that is rare for him. It feels nice.

'The food is good,' Hank says. Elise has not eaten much. She is a dainty eater, a nibbler, and part of him wants to tell her to clear her plate, as if getting some meat on her bones will strengthen her, both in body and spirit. It's her spirit he worries about the most, but there's not much he can do about that. He wishes she was a bit pluckier.

She is not at all how William described her.

He realises he is sitting with a stranger. A stranger he wants to bring back to the US. A change of scenery, to bring her back to life. The thought has always been there, but now that he has seen her, he can't leave her like this.

'The changes to the house. How long will they last?'

Her question startles him.

'How do you mean? Do you mean how long will they take? I'm only here another week,' he says.

Elise shakes her head. 'I mean, will the house be okay, for a few years, or ten? What will I need to do next?'

'There's a lot of upkeep with a house this old, but it should be fine for a spell, depending on how much I get done. And I can always come back.' He hesitates. 'Were you thinking of selling? Because I can...'

'No, I can't. The house also belongs to my brother, and we're not sure...'

Hank remembers William saying her brother had a bad drinking problem and disappeared when the war broke out. Another can of worms he does not want to open.

'The wallpaper in the living room, I really don't like it,' she says.

'Then we'll strip it, and put up new paper,' he says. 'We'll start tomorrow.'

'Just paint. I don't really like patterns. Or maybe, the stone. It must be under the walls?'

'That's even easier,' he says. 'I wish I had a car, I'd like to pick up a load of stuff.'

'My friend Bertrand has a car. I'm sure he'd let you use his, for a bottle of spirits, perhaps.'

'I'll ask, then.'

Elise looks like she is lost in thought. Hank waits to see what she's going to say.

'When you came to see me, you told me William spoke of me to you. Do you remember the things he said? I'd like to know.'

Hank feels the question in his stomach. For a moment he had thought she might be in the present, but the question tells him otherwise.

'He told me a lot of things. About visiting your brother and meeting you. That you both liked poetry. You wrote long letters back and forth for years. He said you were smart.'

She looks at him, wanting more.

'I don't like to think about it all now. I'm sure you understand.' It's the best he can do.

There's a pause. Around them the sky is leached of the

brightness of the day as the darkness of night settles in. The waiter lights candles against it.

'I can't think about anything else,' she says.

'He loved you. He told me so. He had no control over how he died. If he had the choice he'd still be here,' he says. 'Isn't it enough just to know that?'

'It will have to be,' she says.

* * *

Hank is up early, surveying the wallpaper she wants to get rid of. He is doing his best to be quiet, as he doesn't want to wake her.

He's making a list in his mind of things he needs, wondering if he can borrow her friend's car, when there is a knock at the door. The sudden noise in the still house startles Hank, and it takes him a second to sort the source of the thumping.

He opens the door to see a very large man, a man he recognises, standing on the porch.

'I can't remember the last time I used this step! Someone has been busy,' is the first thing he says.

He walks quickly, confidently, despite a bad leg, carrying a grocer's bag of food. Hank can see a baguette sticking out of the top. His stomach grumbles.

He closes the door, as the big man grabs him, kissing him on both cheeks, startling him.

'I've just returned from a trip, and heard you were back. Delightful news! Wonderful!'

So much for Hank being quiet; the people next door could probably hear this man.

'We've met before.'

'Yes,' Hank says, softly, hoping the man picks up on the cue. He does.

'Oh, oh, Elise is still sleeping, dear thing. Come, into the kitchen. I will make coffee and we can talk.'

Even whispering, you could still hear him outdoors. Hank follows the big man to the kitchen.

'I see you've been doing work in here. Lots of work. Good. The place is a dreary little piece of hell, but then it always has been, even before the war.' He glances at Hank as he says this. 'Nothing was done since her papa died, and Marie, her maman, don't get me started...' He rolls his eyes so hard Hank can almost hear them move.

He doesn't want to get him started. He wants to make him stop. His voice is loud, and now dishes seem to be flying around the kitchen. Hank is not much for noise. He opens the nearby window, to let in some morning light, maybe let out some sound, too.

'Here, eat,' the big man instructs as he opens the boxes filled with pastries, and pushes them toward Hank, who nods and takes a pain au chocolat. It's still warm. No one does pastries like the French.

'So, you are here for a little visit?' His one raised eyebrow makes Hank want to laugh.

'I wanted to know how she was doing, and she didn't reply to my letters. I hoped she'd met some nice man...'

'Pwah.' Bertrand's arms fly into the air. 'Wouldn't know a nice man if he knocked on her door. All wrapped up in her past, just like her mother.'

'How so?'

'Marie did the same thing, never moving on from her husband dying, as if she was the only person in the world to have something bad happen to her. I had hoped Elise would show a little more, how do you say, spirit? Yes, spirit.' He rolls the word around in his mouth, like he's committing it to memory. 'Maybe it's in her blood, but she's doing the same thing and I am fed up with her. It's been ten years.'

Hank thinks for a moment, gripped by a sense of loyalty to a man long dead, and a stranger he's trying to help. 'William was a friend of mine. He'd be a hard act to follow.'

'And maybe it was the love of a lifetime. But she was a starry-eyed schoolgirl with nothing else in her life to look forward to but letters from the dashing American. Maybe it would have worked. Maybe not. It is all a, how do you Yanks say, a crap shoot?'

There is no point going down this road now, although Hank knows come night, he'll be turning it all over in his mind, the way he always does.

'What's done is done. How do we help her now?'

The big man is shaking his head, and it looks to Hank like he needs the entire kitchen to do it.

'I don't know. Everyone who knows her speaks of it. So much bad luck has befallen the girl, there's like a myth around her. Like something from a crazy story my wife likes to read. People do feel sorry for her but...' He pauses, for a second. 'They also resent her. Everyone has suffered from the war. She does not own all the pain.'

The saucer rattles as he places a cup of coffee in front of Hank, who is digesting his words as though there may be some nutritional benefit to them.

'It is very sad but not necessary,' Bertrand sums up.

There's a creak from the stairs, and both men look at each other.

Did she hear them?

'She's awake,' Bertrand says. As they listen, they hear a bath being run.

Hank finishes the last of his coffee.

'I need to pick up some stuff, to work on the house.'

'My car's out front, let's go.'

'I'll leave a note,' Hank says, looking for a scrap of paper.

'At least she won't break her neck on that damn step now,' Bertrand says as Hank pulls the door shut behind them.

* * *

When Hank gets back, the kitchen has been cleaned. Elise is wearing a simple blue housedress that has been washed to within an inch of its life. Her hair is tied back severely from her face. Hank sees something different about her but is not sure what it is. She looks better due to the meal, getting out of the house the night before, he decides.

There are buckets in the living room, and he see she means business, getting the house sorted. Good, he can work with this.

'Your friend Bertrand stopped by this morning,' Hank says, carrying the first load into the house and turning back to the steps for another, his words trailing after his movements.

'He brought pastry,' he says over his shoulder. 'It's in the kitchen.'

'Yes, I had some. Did he tell you I used to work for him? Of course, you know that,' Elise says. Something about her words doesn't sit right with Hank.

'I worked for him, in the bakery. Took care of his son.

Stood up for his German wife when people turned against her, during the war.'

Hank sets the can of paint in his hand down, knowing he'll need all of his strength to deal with what is happening.

'Everything okay?' he ventures.

'I'm fine,' Elise says. 'Why wouldn't I be? Shall we get to work, putting the world to rights?'

Since he's arrived he's noticed Elise likes her wine, and her Calvados. He wonders if she's had a drink, but it's only eleven in the morning.

'I got some stuff to strip the wallpaper. We have to coat the walls and let it sit,' he says.

She stands, stares at him.

'Why don't you get some gloves, and we'll coat the wallpaper. Then I'm going to replace some of the treads on the stairs, reinforce the bannister. If you take the dishes from the kitchen cabinets, I can reinforce them as well.'

'I'll get the gloves.'

They work in silence, which is a relief to Hank. He's used to her being quiet. When he's finished with the stairs, he walks into the kitchen. All the dishes are on the table, neatly stacked. There's a pot of something on the stove, bubbling away.

'Smells good,' he says.

'Stew. You seemed to enjoy what you had last night. No meat – I hope you like lentils.'

'Sure,' Hanks says. He has no idea what a lentil is.

'I'll make some bread, when you're done here.'

Hank motions to the room under the stairs. 'There's a damp coming from there. I'm going to see what I can do.'

Elise is quiet, making Hank look up.

She's so white, even her lips have drained of colour.

'What is it?'

She sways slightly, and he moves to her, crossing the room in two steps. Placing his arm around her waist, he takes her weight with his own. His head pivots around, searching for a chair.

'No, I'm fine,' she says, pushing against his chest with her hand.

'Are you sick?'

She shakes her head. 'It's been so hard,' she says.

'What has?'

'Everything. Since I can remember.'

She moves away from him, walking toward the kitchen. He follows closely, in case she falls.

'I heard what you said.'

'What did I say?'

'This morning, with Bertrand. People feel sorry for me.' The words come out as though churned up from a well, deep inside her body. 'That people think I am like my mother.'

'Elise, I never said that. Bertrand was trying to help.' Hank racks his brains. What did he say, exactly? You get into a rhythm in a conversation, say things you don't believe to bring an awkward conversation to a close. You don't think about it again. But someone overhears, something is repeated. Hank sighs.

'I miss him so much.'

'I know that. I think about him, too. Every single day.' He does not say he wonders every day why he survived and good men, better men, men he called friends were killed beside him.

Elise looks at him, studying him, then wordlessly walks to the kitchen. He knows enough to follow her.

She moves to the room with the smell. Pulls at the door, trying to open it, but it's warped closed by damp and time. Another wrench and it gives. The smell pours out.

'This is where my mother and I sat during the invasion. D-Day, Overlord, whatever you want to call it. We were there for hours, an entire day, cold. Scared to death. This is where I was when he died. I know, because I felt it when it happened.' She touches her chest. Her words are softly spoken but are as potent as mustard gas.

Hank is silent, willing her words to release the poison that is killing her.

'My sadness hurts no one. If you don't want to see it, you do not have to.' She says this last bit with force, and Hank sees a flash of the spirit William told him about.

She looks at him, for a moment, then says, 'No one knows what I have been through. I do not know what you have been through. Enough with thinking you know me.'

Hank has the good sense to stay quiet.

'Is the wallpaper ready to come down now?'

'I think so,' he replies.

As she walks to the front room, he pulls the door to the room under the stairs shut, as quietly, and firmly, as he can. Later, he'll throw lime on the floor, paint the walls. Get rid of the smell. Smell is the sense most closely connected to memory. If he can't burn down the house, he'll get rid of as much of it as he can.

* * *

The floor is filled with soggy wallpaper, gone grey with water and time. Elise ripped it down like it had done something to offend her. Hank is putting it all in a box, wishing he had a skip out front. The work is so much harder without the right tools. Everything is.

By the end of the afternoon, Elise seems to have regained some normalcy, whatever that was. Perhaps her flash of anger was too exhausting to maintain. She has a steelier way about her now.

Hank does, too. Fourteen hours a day of manual labour, and Hank is feeling better. When he returns home he plans to make some changes. Too much of his time is spent sitting at a desk, and he doesn't like it.

He turns over the flower beds thinking Elise might want to plant something, even though he plans to ask her to come back to the US with him. Time is ticking by, and he's not sure what to do.

'The house looks good,' Elise says to him, as she serves dinner. 'Thank you for that.'

Hank forces himself not to pick up a fork and start shovelling in food. He's starving.

'I've become quite handy, keeping up the old buildings I've bought to rent out,' he says.

It's now or never, he thinks.

'If you wanted to come to the US to visit, I have plenty of space for you to stay,' he begins in a gentle way, not wanting to scare her. Not wanting to think there is more to this than there is. As he watches, she seems to be thinking. He decides to push a bit further. If she doesn't come with him, she's on her own. He cannot carry this load much further.

'Come back to the US with me. Just for the summer. A change of scenery.'

She looks at him as though he's crazy. 'But I work.'

'Ask for some time off,' he says. She has been to the

library for work a handful of times since he arrived. He doubts she is indispensable.

He waits, then tries again. 'If this is how you want to live, that is fine. I'll respect that. I'd like to help, but I can't force you to think as I do, that coming to the US, making a fresh start might be for the best.'

She turns away from him, glancing around the room that looks better, but is still the same place, the same walls she has stared at for too long.

'At any rate, the offer is there.'

They eat their meal in silence, and after cleaning the kitchen, Elise goes to bed. Hank sits at the kitchen table and thinks.

* * *

He is sitting on the sofa when Elise comes down in the morning. 'I am making coffee. Would you like some?'

'Please.'

'I'd like to turn off the water, and do some work on the plumbing,' he says.

'That is fine. I will be at work today,' she says.

He has one more day to sort out what to do. Because William got off the boat ahead of him, and turned back to help someone, while Hank kept on walking. Because he made a promise.

'I'm going into town, to pick up a few things. I'll be back soon,' he says.

She is stacking dishes at the sink. 'Yes,' she says, not looking up.

He lets himself out into the fresh morning air, looking forward to the walk, if not the purpose of his expedition.

He walks past the church, toward the waterwheel. There he stops, looks around. Sees it across the road, facing the little patch of green they consider a park. The bakery. He makes his way to the door, the tinkle of the bells alerting the workers to a new customer.

The first person he sees is Bertrand, talking to a small woman who Hank thinks is his wife. They both look at him as he ducks to clear the doorframe.

'Henri,' he greets him. Hank's not sure when he took to calling him the French version of his given name. Must have been when they were having a drink one night.

'Hello,' he greets Marianne. 'I'm wondering if I could have a few minutes of your husband's time?'

'Of course. Can I get you anything?'

'I'm fine, thank you, ma'am.'

Bertrand pushes past Hank, leading him to the tables and chairs outside the bakery.

'I have been expecting this visit,' he says. Hank knows Elise is still angry about the things she overheard Bertrand say. Bertrand knows it, too, and has stayed away.

'I'm leaving soon. I don't know what to do. It seems a sin, her living like this. I could give her money to relocate to Paris. Or she could come home with me. For a visit. I just don't know.'

'I wish I had advice, but the truth is, I don't know what to tell you. How does life get so complicated when all you want is the best for someone?'

'Don't ask me. If she was a man, I'd be straight with him, tell him he's wasting his life. If I say that to her, she will simply be more obstinate.'

Marianne shows up with coffee and a plate of pastries.

'It's been so lovely, having you here, Hank. And such a

lovely summer, too. But I hear in New England, they have wonderful autumns. With leaves that turn bright colours, and the children go out on Hallowe'en, collecting candy.'

'Yes, ma'am,' Hank says softly, knowing something more is coming.

'William wrote to Elise about how beautiful it was. Having an ocean outside his door, and seafood, and sailing.'

She looks at both men. They look back at her.

She sighs.

'Tell her you want to show her the places William wanted to show her. Tell her you promised him you would. Tell her his family wants to meet her. Don't treat her like she needs to be saved. No one wants that.' She gives her husband a look that makes the big man shrink.

Hank finds himself nodding. 'She won't do it for herself, or for me, but she will do it...'

'For William,' Marianne says. 'It's another way for her to keep him alive, and that is all she wants.'

Bertrand looks completely lost, but Hank has seen so much death. He understands.

THIRTY-SIX

RHODE ISLAND. SUMMER 1955

Elise stays in one of the empty units in Hank's nicest building. He furnishes it for her, makes sure she has everything she needs. She wants to speak better English so he stops by in the evenings and takes her for dinner. His parents visit and his mother spends time with her. One day his mother talks her into going to the beauty parlour and Elise comes home with a new hairstyle, shorter and dipping over one of her eyes, a soft golden-brown sort of colour. It makes her look younger, happier, more alive. Attractive, he finds himself thinking.

He takes her to Boston, to walk the Commons, which William so often wrote about. She is quiet, lost in her memories, and Hank tries to understand. How could she have built William up to such mythical proportions, that she is so devoted to him, ten years after his death?

Taking a seat on a bench, he says, 'The leaves aren't at their best yet. Give it another week or two, and the colours will be magical.'

'I think it is beautiful now,' she whispers, as though

speaking loudly might break some sort of reverie. There is a softness in the air, and the world seems a very gentle place at that moment.

'The university, where he studied?'

'That's another trip – outside of town,' he says. 'We'll go soon.'

They see Boston Harbor, and go to a restaurant for clam chowder. He sees her looking in a shop window at a cashmere sweater and insists on buying it for her. When was the last time she had something new? As he carries the parcel, she walks beside him, slipping her arm through his. She has not mentioned going home, and he has not mentioned it to her.

As they leave Boston the lights of the city reflect off the water, off the buildings downtown.

'It is so beautiful, this New England,' she says. 'Just like William told me.'

Hank feels a sense of pride that this land is his home.

One evening a few days later, while taking a walk through the local park and eating ice cream, when he thinks she is starting to settle into life, she says, 'I would like to meet William's family.'

The lick of ice cream in Hank's mouth turns to paste. He's been dreading this, for some reason he can't quite sort out.

'It'll mean being away overnight,' he says. 'It's a long drive.'

'I thought he lived close to you?' she asks.

'Close in France and close in the US are two different things. It'll take about four hours to get there. And mean staying overnight in a hotel,' he says.

'I want very much to see the beach he wrote to me

about. His favourite place. It is what I came to do, and after, I will go home. All I wanted to do will be done,' she says.

The way she says this, sounding so final, gives him a jolt.

Hank has already decided if she wants to go, he will send her back with some money and his best wishes. His promise will have been kept. He can move on.

* * *

It's a golden day in October, the air filled with the yellow-orange tinge Hank equates with autumn in New England. The leaves flutter in the light breeze. They drive in silence.

'I am nervous, to meet Jean. I don't want to bring back unhappy memories.'

Hank nods, thinks about how to respond. He's had such thoughts since William fell beside him. It is why he has not visited before.

'This is so beautiful,' Elise gushes, as Boston slips behind them and they make their way to Cape Cod.

The beauty is lost on Hank as he fears what Jean will say to him. Fears meeting William's father, whose name he can't even remember right now.

'It's still a bit of a ride. Let me know when you want to pull over and rest.'

'Oh, I cannot rest. I don't want to miss anything!' she says, staring out the window, like she is trying to memorise the land.

It has just gone noon when they arrive, finding the bright red door on the barn-style house Jean described in her letter, when they planned the meeting.

Hank parks out front, his truck pointed toward the ocean at the bottom of the street, just like William had described to him as they sweat their way through training, and to Elise in letters, as they fell easily in love.

It seems strange the house would be there, and the ocean, just as he had described, and that William would be gone.

Hank reaches into the cab of the truck, getting the flowers they'd picked up for Jean. They are walking up the stone path when the door opens, and a young man appears. He is the spit of William, and both Hank and Elise are taken back. It feels like the time he gave himself an electrical shock when he was rewiring an old lamp, and all of his senses are on edge. It's like his old friend is standing in front of him.

Elise rushes forward, and for a terrible second Hank thinks her mind has gone, and she will think it William. But no, already she is saying his name, 'Aaron! I've heard so much about you!'

Fair play to the young man that he takes her outstretched hands. Hank thinks a moment. Aaron must be in his late twenties now. Funny how you never think about other people getting older.

He smiles at her briefly before turning his head and saying, 'Ma, they're here.'

'For heaven's sake, Aaron, invite them in.'

Jean appears, smaller than Hank pictured her, and the three of them, Elise, Aaron and Jean are gathered on the front step, while Hank waits on the path, flowers in hand, the sound of the ocean filling his ears, no idea what to do next.

Elise and Jean are clasping hands like something from

Jane Austen. Aaron is looking at his feet; Hank can almost hear him wishing he'd not gone to the door. Finally a man appears, who looks like William would have looked if he'd been allowed to live, and shepherds everyone inside.

Hank steps through the red door and removes his hat. Putting it under his arm, he shakes hands with both men, then hands the flowers, wrapped in brown paper, to Jean.

'They are lovely. Thank you,' she says, although all she can see is some of the reds and gold of the fall blooms Elise had selected.

The house is big, with high ceilings and dark, expensive-looking furniture. Yes, William's people definitely had money. They move into the front room, where tiny sandwiches and cakes are laid out, and a china tea service waits. Hank gets the feeling that perhaps William's people might have been as nervous about this visit as he was. He can't speak for Elise. He cannot figure her out.

'Let me start the coffee,' Jean says, darting from the room. Elise moves to the mantel, as though in a trance, and Hank sees the photo of William, in a large silver frame, right in the centre. It's like an altar to his memory. Reaching out, she runs her finger softly down the side of the frame. Everyone looks away.

'Long drive. How were the roads?' Arthur says.

'Fine. Not much traffic.' Hank nods toward the window. 'That's a great view you have, at the bottom of the road.'

'It's a pretty part of the world here. We're very lucky.'

Jean returns with the coffee pot. 'Please, sit,' she says. The men do as they're told. Elise lingers on the photo, as though it will disappear if she turns her back. They wait, awkwardly, until she moves to the group of people gathered, the only thing they all have in common knowing, loving, the man who looks over them from the mantel.

Elise's eyes are shiny and bright and this worries Hank, wondering if she can withstand all the memories that are about to come out. She is so frail, inside and out.

'I want to thank you, for the pencils and pads you sent to me.' He does not say when he was fighting, during the war. He knows they will know. But Elise looks lost.

'Mrs Hardwick sent care packages, and sent me some pads and pencils,' he explains.

He flashes back to the day a care package came for William, and how his friend had pulled out the letter, read it twice then picked up the pencils and sketch pad and handed them to Hank.

'What's this?' he'd said.

'I told my mother you liked to draw. She likes to buy gifts.' He wondered what William said about him in his letters home. Hank never really thought to write about the men in basic with him when he sent short, sporadic letters to his own parents, but he started to after that. And he started to see the men he served better, from observing them. From sketching. A small gift but it made a big impact on his life.

The memory comes back like an old friend. A simple act of kindness, when they were about to face years of darkness.

'Do you still draw? William told us you had a lot of natural talent.'

There, it's done. His name has been said aloud. No one has collapsed. No one has started to wail. Elise's teacup clattered in its saucer, but perhaps only he noticed it.

'He helped me with technique. I learned a lot from

him,' he says. 'I wish I had the time now, to draw, but work seems to take up all my energy.'

'Hank owns several apartment buildings, and works as an engineer, too. And he has a home in Florida.'

Jean looks at him. 'What part? We have a place in Boca Raton,' she says.

'Saint Petersburg,' he says. 'My parents spend the winters there, now.'

The conversation changes to how harsh the winters are. Hank notices Elise trying to follow the conversation. Perhaps it is the accents. Perhaps she is waiting to talk more of William, but Hank can see his parents' grief is private. He is grateful for this.

After sandwiches and coffee, Elise asks if she can see the beach. Jean agrees, pulling on a jacket and boots for the walk, while Aaron pulls on a sweatshirt.

'I'm not much for the beach,' Arthur says, and Hank stays behind with him.

When they're alone, Arthur pours a glass of Scotch. The two men sit in lawn chairs out back, the sun catching their crystal glasses, making little rainbows of light appear.

'I thank you for coming and bringing Elise. It's important to my wife,' he says.

Hank waits, knowing something more is coming.

'I feel I need to do something, but I don't know what it is. With Elise, I mean.'

'I know that feeling,' Hank says.

'She's an attractive woman; she could meet a nice fella. I mean, I don't know how many men are left where she lives, but some returned from war.'

Hank's not sure where this is going.

'My wife sees it as this great love story. Maybe it is.' He

shakes his head, takes a drink. Hank follows. 'But they were both young, and things change. She needs to move on.'

'We can't force her to do that,' Hank says.

'I know. But I also feel, because of what she meant to my boy, I can't leave her to...' he searches for the right word '...disintegrate on her own.'

Hank turns in his chair. 'I have the same problem. If she wants to go back to France and live in that awful little shack of hers, then all I can do is fix the place up and give her some money. It's not the best solution, but it's all I can think of.'

'Why does she want to go back to France? I've heard she has no people?'

Hank is quiet, not wanting to say aloud what he thinks. That she wants to be close to the place where William died. Where he's buried. But this gives him an idea. Instead of being close to where he died, what about being close to where he lived? He wishes for a moment Marianne was nearby. She would know the right words.

'I think she's stuck in the past.'

'We'll help, with the money,' Arthur says. 'If it comes to that.' The idea of being stuck is alien to both of them.

The two men are silent for a moment, and then William's father, sounding nothing like his son says, 'Do you think the Red Sox will do anything next season?'

'It'd be nice to see them take a pennant,' Hank says. 'They've sure got some talent on the team.' He makes a mental note that if Elise stays for longer, he'll take her to Fenway. Everyone should see a ballgame.

Aaron comes back alone and walks toward the men. He has a bottle of beer in his hand.

'Where are the ladies?' Arthur asks, looking behind his son.

'At the beach. Talking about William.'

Hank looks at his watch, as though he's timing how long he'll wait.

'Leave them be,' Arthur says. 'Maybe they'll get it out of their systems. He takes out his pipe and lights it. Hank has never seen anyone smoke a pipe and likes the rich smell of the tobacco. It's a smell he will associate with this day for the rest of his life.

* * *

When the women return, it is obvious they've been crying. But they straighten up and wipe their eyes as best they can, and the men pretend they don't notice.

Jean moves toward her husband, sitting on the arm of his chair. 'I think we should go to the Lamplighter for dinner, the five of us,' she says, a smile on her face. 'You know how much William loved the surf 'n' turf.'

Hank stands. 'That sounds fine, but we should get on the road. We need to find a hotel.'

'I won't hear of it. Elise will have William's room, and Hank can have the spare room,' she says. Hank had been planning on getting a few hours of the drive done and getting a hotel. Truth be told, he would rather go home, sleep in his own bed, put this excursion firmly behind him. But when he sees the hope on Elise's face, he knows he's beat.

'If you're sure it's not too much trouble,' he says.

'Of course not. Now, one of you boys open a bottle of wine for us. Aaron, no more for you, you'll be driving,' she says. Aaron starts to object, but his father silences him with a look.

'Go to the cellar and get a bottle of white wine, Aaron,' his father instructs. Aaron lopes off. Arthur goes to top up Hank's Scotch, but he declines. Best keep his wits about him, he decides.

It's a good decision, because by the time they get to the restaurant, Elise, Arthur and Jean are all fairly well oiled.

The food is good, and Hank eats heartily, while the others drink and pick at their food. Jean is friends with everyone at the restaurant and people stop by to speak to her. She introduces Elise each time as William's girl, and Hank watches as people step back, shocked. The use of the present tense. The fact that a man ten years dead still has a girl.

He keeps eating.

Elise has never had lobster, and Hank takes it apart for her. She seems uncertain as she dips it in the warmed butter, but she loves it once she tastes it.

Hank rounds the group up and puts them all in the car.

At home, Jean and Elise sit in the living room. Jean has Aaron put a record on the hi-fi. He knows they will stay up for hours, talking. But Hank thinks he sees a difference in their profound grief. Unlike Elise who is wrapped in the darkness, Jean is doing all she can to find any shred of light. The way she chooses his favourite restaurant. The way she speaks of him. The way she plays music. He hopes the woman has a positive effect on Elise, who is still young, and has no one to help her.

He leaves them to their memories and goes to bed.

* * *

Hank is the first one up in the morning. Not wanting to wake anyone, he lets himself out of the house, walking the short distance to the beach. The sky is the pale blue of an early October morning, and he knows they'll have another day of Indian summer. He's pleased.

At the end of the road are steps that lead down to the beach. The sea, even as calm as it is today, sounds powerful.

He is startled when he sees someone sitting on the sand. The wildness of her hair in the sea wind takes him back to a garden in France, not that long ago. His mind hesitates. He's not sure what he's up for, but already his body is heading toward her. Elise.

'Hello,' she says, when she sees him.

'Are you okay?'

'I wanted to see the sunrise over the ocean.'

He stands for a second, wanting to walk, to move, then lowers himself next to her. He can feel the cool damp of the sand sinking through his trousers.

They sit in silence, the sun past rising, but still low, giving the water an ethereal sheen.

'William wrote to me of watching the sun come up here. He'd walk down with a cup of coffee, or when he took morning runs. I remembered every word he wrote about it as I watched it this morning.'

There is nothing Hank can think to say to that.

'I like to think I'm sitting where he sat, at one time.'

A moment passes in silence. Then two.

'I think land holds a memory. It's a living thing, and I think what happens on it, to it, around it, the land remembers,' Hank says. 'It holds the energy of the people who have passed by.'

Elise turns her head and looks at him.

'Thank you,' she says.

'For what?'

'For everything.'

The air is filled with sea salt, the sounds of the waves, the special promise each sunny morning makes that good things will happen.

'I don't understand why something I wanted so badly could be taken from me. I'm a good person, and it feels like nothing good ever happens to me.'

Her words cause a small flash of anger in Hank. He's fixed her house and brought her to the US, so she could sit on this very beach. But like a wave, his anger peaks and then ebbs away. She has lost so much. He has no idea what that is like. He has never been in love. And even he feels an aching nostalgia for the past when he watches the sun rise and set.

'Would you like to go back to the house or take a walk?'

'Let's walk,' she decides.

Hank stands and offers his hand to help her up. As they walk, she wraps her arms around herself, to ward off the cold. Hank shrugs off his cardigan and drapes it over her shoulders.

'Thank you,' she says.

Hank puts his hands in his pockets. As he walks along the sand he thinks about those last few moments with William, of the promise he is determined to keep. He should have planned this trip better and taken her sailing. He has no idea how to sail, but Aaron might. Another time, he guesses.

* * *

When they return to the house Arthur is in the kitchen, making coffee. They all have a cup, but there is an awkwardness between them, a return to the mundane reality of life after the anticipation of their visit. After the alcohol-induced frivolity of the night before. And something else. A realisation that their lives have continued while William is truly gone. They all feel it, but nothing is said.

Hank just wants to get on the road.

Arthur fries eggs and makes toast, and they're eating in the kitchen when Jean appears, in her dressing gown, smudges of makeup under her eyes. She looks older, perhaps because of the makeup. Maybe the wine.

'Goodness! Everyone up so early. Arthur, you should have woken me.'

'Nonsense. I'm capable of making breakfast.'

Jean sits at the table. Her hands shake as she holds her coffee. The sunshine filling the room makes her squint.

'We should go for a drive, later. Show you the sailing club William belonged to.'

'That sounds like a fine idea, but we must get back. I can't be away from my rentals for too long,' he says.

Hanks looks at Elise, thinking she will be upset with him, but he sees what he thinks is relief on her face.

'Yes,' she says. 'It's time to go back.'

He's not sure what she means. But he figures if he waits, he'll find out. She'll tell him, one way or another.

THIRTY-SEVEN

RHODE ISLAND. 1955

It's been a week since they've returned from Cape Cod and Elise has not mentioned returning to France. Hank knows the cold weather is just around the corner and does not want her travelling in a storm. When he says this, she says, 'Perhaps I can stay until spring?'

'If you'd like. I'll have to write to Bertrand about the house.'

He hesitates. 'How do you pay the bills in France?'

'There aren't any, really. The house was paid for, my father left some money, and my grandfather. And I've worked since I was sixteen. Fourteen, if you count babysitting.' She stops. 'Monsieur Gravel left me some money. And we've always been very frugal, too.'

Hank writes to Bertrand that night but doesn't seal the letter. He'll send a draft to cover any costs he might have. Who knows how long she'll stay?

As the winter winds start to bite, Elise buys some heavier clothes. Hank finds himself analysing everything she does. Does her new coat mean she plans to stay for more than one winter?

They have come to some sort of an understanding, or rather a routine. He goes to her apartment most evenings and has dinner. She cooks and they work on her English, which is better and better. They never speak of William, or of Cape Cod.

One night he goes to her apartment and is shocked that there are candles on the table, their flames dancing softly in some draught he's never felt. Elise greets him in a long skirt and bare feet, her toenails painted red.

'I love how warm it is here, even in winter.'

It's hot as hell inside, and Hank knows the heating bill is going to be enormous. But that's the least of his concerns. What is going on? Why the candles? Have her toenails always been painted bright red? He tells himself to stop looking.

He sees what the thermostat is set at and turns it down when she's in the kitchen.

'Something smells good,' he says. Familiar, too. They must have had it before.

Elise returns with a serving pot of some kind. 'Your mother said I could take some of the dishes from your house.'

'That's fine,' he says.

She sets it down on the table. 'Beef stew, like you had in France,' she says.

'I remember,' he says.

There is crusty bread, and mashed potatoes, too.

'What did you do today?' he says, tucking in.

Elise nods to the table by the sofa. Hanks sees a little stack of letters, waiting to be posted. He will take them with him when he leaves, to send. Elise does not like going to the post office.

'I wrote some letters and I went to the library.'

'How?' he asks, shocked.

'I took a bus,' she says.

'Really?' The girl he brought back from France could not have sorted a bus timetable on her own.

'Yes. It is one bus ride, and there are so many interesting things around the library.'

A sense of ease, something he's not felt in some time, fills him. A tension in his shoulders he was not even aware of leaves. She's pulling herself together. Relief washes through him.

When he leaves, she packs up the potatoes and stew for his lunch.

Hank doesn't know if he's being mothered or seduced. But he has work to do. He'll think about it later.

* * *

'Whatever you're eating smells good,' his co-worker says. 'But if you spill any on my blueprints, I'll thump you.'

'Got it.' Hank moves away from what he is studying.

Finishing his lunch, Hank remembers Elise's letters and walks to the post office. Waiting in line he looks through the stack. Marianne. A separate letter for their son. A card of some sort, perhaps it is his birthday. Someone named Amelie, and then, Genevieve. Hank looks closer at the letter. An address in Fort Walton Beach, in Florida.

He remembers that day, so long ago. He'd been young and exhausted at the time, nervous of meeting Elise, of the things he should tell her. Genevieve had shown up one afternoon, all red lips and stockings and perfume. Hank had taken one look at her and known she was bad news.

He posts the letters.

That night, over burgers at the diner around the corner from where he lives, Hank asks Elise if she would like to go to Florida, to spend Christmas with his family.

'That is fine with your parents?' she checks.

'Of course.'

'How will we get there?'

'The roads will be bad that time of year. We'll fly,' he says.

'How much will that cost?' she asks. He knows whatever money she brought with her must be dwindling.

'We'll call it a Christmas present from me,' he says. When she starts to object, he cuts in.

'I noticed your friend Genevieve is in Florida.'

'Yes, she married a man who has a business there. Well, not her first man.'

'Pardon?'

'She is on her second husband,' Elise says.

Hank doubts it will be the last.

'It's a fair piece from Saint Pete's to Fort Walton Beach,' he says. 'But we can work something out, if you want to visit.'

'That is not necessary. I don't really wish to see her.'

Hank is surprised at this. 'Wouldn't you like to see an old friend?'

'I have not seen or heard from her in years. She sent a letter to me in France, and Amelie sent it on to me. I had to reply.' She pauses. 'She did me a favour once, and I owe her.'

'Not a good spot to be in,' he says. He sees something

else in her eyes, in her look. A hardness. This is more than a favour being owed. He knows all about that.

'I will figure it out,' she says. 'Now please tell me about Florida, and about Christmas in the sunshine.'

Hank decides to let it go, figuring it is a case of an old friend from her village being a reminder of a traumatic time she wants to forget. He knows about that, too.

THIRTY-EIGHT
FLORIDA. WINTER 1955

A soft, warm breeze greets them in Florida. It is not hot but feels that way after the freezing temperatures of Rhode Island.

'This feels nice,' Elise says, loosening her coat as they make their way to the taxi stand.

'Are you comfortable? It's a long ride,' he says.

'Yes, of course.'

The taxi travels along the road that takes them across Tampa Bay. With the only light coming from the moon and stars, it looks like they're driving on top of the water. Hank rolls down the window to let in the night. It feels like a friend after the bitter cold of home.

Elise is fascinated. 'You mean that is all water, both side of us? Is Florida an island?'

'Close. It's surrounded by water on three sides.

'First time here, miss?' asks the cab driver.

'It is,' she says.

'Welcome to the Sunshine State!'

Hank makes a mental note to tip him very well.

* * *

His parents have waited up for them. He knows they find his friendship, for lack of a better word, with Elise peculiar but they are kind to her, indulgent to him. He can't ask for more than that.

'Hello, hello, hello,' James chimes as they walk in. His mother has been baking, and the aroma of shortbread and cinnamon takes him right back to being a kid. His mouth waters.

His mother is wearing an apron with Mrs Claus on it. Poinsettias are everywhere. Hank has never cared for them.

The tree is in the corner, and Hank grows momentarily nostalgic when he sees it has the same decorations it's had since he was small: knitted sleighs and wreaths and bells his mother made. Underneath are Christmas presents, wrapped and ready to go.

Hank carries Elise's bag to the spare room. He'll be sleeping on a roll-out in the den, since his mother has set up the other room for sewing. She's doing alterations for people. Hank is tickled about it. She's meeting new people, and now that his father is retired, she is the breadwinner. And he knows she loves it.

After Hank scrubs off the dust of the airplane, he heads to the kitchen, but no one is there. The back door is open, and he follows the voices and the tinkle of glasses.

They're all sitting on the back deck, drinking eggnog. His mother and Elise are planning on a shopping trip the next day, for a few last-minute things. He remembers being out on a similar trip with his mother when he learned the United States was at war. The news about Pearl Harbor. Funny, he'd been holding a poinsettia for her, following her through Murphy's Dry Goods. Too young, then, to fight.

His mother hands him a glass of the creamy yellow drink they only have in the few days leading up to Christmas.

'I thought I would miss Providence at Christmas, but I don't. It's so nice here, and on Christmas Eve, Elise, just wait and see. The locals all get together and light the streets with candles in little paper bags filled with sand.'

'That sounds so pretty,' she says, both hands around her glass, legs crossed at the ankles and tucked under her chair. Her hair falling in her eye. She is a blend of school-girl enthusiasm and reserved, damaged woman that he finds unsettling. So many faces, and he has no idea which one is really her.

'What shall we do tomorrow, Dad?' Hank asks.

'No plans, although I'm sure I'll get a list.' He grins at his wife.

'Oh, stop!' She giggles.

His parents still love each other, he realises. It gives him a warm feeling.

His mother makes him a plate with slices of pot roast, refried mash potatoes, carrots and gravy. Elise is not hungry but does nibble on one of the Christmas cookies his mother baked.

It's well after midnight when they retire. As Elise comes out of the washroom, Hank is in the hall, waiting his turn. Worst thing about the house was the one bathroom. He'd have to fix that.

Elise is wrapped up in a pearl-white dressing gown, her dark hair in such contrast to the silky material.

She looks at him and says, 'This is the nicest Christmas I've had since before my father died.'

'I'm glad, Elise.' Glad. Useless little word, but he had no idea how to respond.

Hank hopes, wherever William is, he knows she's feeling good, even if it is fleeting.

* * *

They go to a beach bar for New Year's Eve.

'I feel badly leaving your parents behind,' she says as they walk along the sand.

Hank laughs. 'They'll be in bed by ten. Trust me.'

Elise is wearing a dress with a skirt that swishes around her legs as she walks. The moon catches the creaminess of it, and Hank realises how much better she looks. The hollows in her cheeks have filled out some, and she looks healthier. Distant, yes, but not haunted. Still, she is very guarded, and has a remoteness to her. The girl William described, and Bertrand spoke of, is gone forever. But someone new has taken her place, and Hank finds he likes her. She is no longer simply a duty.

They can hear the music in the distance. Laughter. It mixes with the sound of the waves and Hank thinks it has to be the sound of happiness, or as close as one can get. For tonight, he's going to park his worries and his plans, and enjoy himself.

The bar is nothing more than a wooden floor, some posts and a roof made of planks and canvas. It's a bit like what he saw in the army. In the summer it's wide open, but now, there are shutters and plastic drapes of some kind. Christmas lights seem to cover every surface. There's a dance floor, a band. People are wearing paper hats shouting that a new year is upon them. Hank finds a seat for Elise and goes to the bar. A bottle of Champagne, a few glasses.

He returns to the table, where Elise is watching the band.

He hands her a glass, and Elise takes it, then stops. Stares at the bubbles. She pales, and Hank is not sure what is happening, for a second.

'It's Champagne. Have you had it? Would you like something else?'

'No, It's fine.'

'I can get you some ginger ale? It's almost the same thing,' he attempts a joke.

'No, no. This is nice. Very nice,' she says, taking a cautious sip, which somehow turns into a gulp. Hank hesitates then refills her glass.

'I haven't had Champagne since before the war,' she says.

The tone of her voice. She is caught in a bad memory, a bad place.

'I can get you something else?' he repeats.

She places her hand on his arm. 'This is fine. Thank you.'

The band is playing a lively tune, and Hank is not certain the floor will support all the stomping and jumping. But it's only six inches off the sand he figures. Maybe a broken ankle or two, but nothing serious.

Elise seems to be moving with the music, so he asks her to dance.

'I'm not sure I know how,' she says.

Hank drains his glass. 'We'll fix that!'

She shrugs, takes his hand, and Hank moves to the side of the dance floor and starts to show her the Jitterbug.

They dance, and they drink. They are both giddy, so unlike either of them, so often caught up in their own inner worlds. The air crackles with energy and simple joy. Everyone, it seems, is taking a break from their worries. When midnight hits, they count down with the rest of the bar, enjoying the moment to catch their breaths. As the clock strikes midnight, the bar erupts. Cheers, shouting, those paper horns that make such an appalling noise.

For a moment Hank feels sadness creep in. Sadness. Nostalgia. They're so closely connected, it seems. Then he feels a small hand on his face, cool, despite the heat of the room. He looks down to see Elise looking up at him, concerned. He will never know why, perhaps it was the emotions of the evening as 'Auld Lang Syne' filled the room, and people around them swayed together.

He bends forward, to kiss her on the cheek. But she turns her head, looks up at him and they share a kiss. He's not sure how long they stand that way until the jostling of the crowd, dancing once again, breaks them apart. Wordlessly, Hank takes her hand, and they make their way down the beach, the noise of the party absorbed by the waves with each step they take. It is isolated, on the other side of the bar. Most of the land is being developed but right now there is just darkness. There's a clearing, hidden by a cluster of trees. Hank looks around. No one will see them. His hand is in her hair; it is so soft. Her body is pressed against his.

'Is this okay?' He has to make sure.

'Yes,' she says. His hands move down her dress.

'No one can see?' she whispers.

'No, no one,' he replies, slipping off his sports jacket and laying it on the ground.

'It's just the two of us,' he says, hoping that for her it is just him, and not the ghost of what might have been.

THIRTY-NINE
RHODE ISLAND. MARCH 1956

They fall back into the same pattern, as though the night on the beach did not happen. Hank works, sees her some evenings, but not as often now. Elise, he has decided, is more capable than he thought. He has done what he can. The change of scenery has worked. Still, something pokes at him. He knows it is not enough. He thinks she is simply waiting for warmer weather to return home.

It's a bitter day, and he's looks out the window at the leafless trees in the street, their barks black with cold and frost. If he touched the branches he thinks they would shatter. He's wondering if he should visit her that night. Well, yes, he should. But he'd like to be alone. Like to read a book.

There's a knock on his office door, and he looks up. 'There's a woman here to see you,' Joe says. The look on his face, he knows what woman it is.

'Show her back,' he says. He sees the surprised look on Joe's face. Usually Hank meets everyone out front. But he feels they may need privacy here.

Elise walks in, not shyly, not confidently. Not curious about the new space – she has never seen his office. Hank suddenly feels nervous. She's come to tell him something important; he knows that. She wants to go back to France, he guesses. He feels a tiny bit of relief. And sadness. If she goes, he knows they will not see each other again.

'Hello,' she says softly, one hand absently brushing his desk.

'Hello, Elise.'

She nods.

'I'd offer to show you around, but there's not much to see.'

'It is not an easy place to get to – I took two buses.'

'No, it's not,' he says. He waits.

'I went to the doctor's,' she says.

'Everything all right?' Apprehension moves through him like a boat cutting through fog.

'We're going to have a baby,' she says, simply.

He does not know what to say to that.

FORTY
RHODE ISLAND. SEPTEMBER 1956

No one knows how to be a parent. They might know things they would not do, things they plan to do. But no one has the recipe for raising another human being. A careless comment, a flash of anger, something stupid said in the heat of the moment. Words running around getting bigger, darker, crashing into the fragile, hollow walls of a small being who hears and remembers everything.

No one knows what they are doing. You just try and do your best.

* * *

Nathaniel Anthony Corrigan enters the world on a spectacular New England September day. Eight pounds, eight ounces, in perfect health. Five months after his parents wed. Everyone knows, and no one says anything.

Hank, standing in the nursery looking at his son, is terrified. And delighted. And worried.

Elise had a difficult time of it, and is sleeping, mostly,

curled up on her side. Hank has gone to her room several times, brought flowers. Candy. Playing the role of doting husband. The nurse told him it was like this, sometimes. 'She'll feel better in a day or two,' she says gently. The woman reminds him of Nina, the nurse who helped him so long ago. Same hospital. It's crazy, but he wants to ask the nurse if she knows her.

Elise has not turned to face Hank. Has not held her son. He wonders if her heart is giving out, but surely a doctor would catch that.

More likely she is thinking about what this day would be like with a different man.

Sitting by her bedside, wishing things were different, he sighs.

It's a hell of a thing, building a life with someone who doesn't love you. He knows this.

'I'm leaving now, Elise. Visiting hours are over. I hope you feel better in the morning,' he says.

When he gets home, he pulls out the yellow pages, and starts looking for a nanny.

* * *

They've achieved a kind of peace in their living arrangements. Ned has done this for them. Hank loves his son fiercely, and when he's not working, he's with him. Elise is a good mother, in her way. But she seems nervous with Ned. So the nanny he hired stays on.

'She just doesn't trust herself yet. She will,' the nanny says to Hank. 'Give it time.'

And then one night, indistinguishable from the rest, the fragile peace is broken.

'Wake up, Hank. Wake up. You're having a bad dream.'

Elise is pushing at his shoulder, then scratching at his face. Hank is not sure where he is when he grabs her arms.

'HANK!' she screams, but he pins her arms, and he is yelling, too. Part of him knows he's in bed with his wife, but he can't reach that part, for most of him is in France getting the shit shelled out of him, his men, by German artillery. He covers his head as a tree explodes around him and Elise jumps from his hold, from the bed.

'Wake up!' she yells.

There's a baby crying. Who left a baby in this hell?

The shelling fades, stops. The exploding trees recede, even the cold he'd felt from the winter snow thaws, as his room comes into focus. He's confused, for a moment. Then he sees her, wild eyes, terrified, standing in the doorway. Hears Ned crying from his room.

He's sitting up, his face red from adrenalin, his hands shaking. Making noises that aren't quite words.

'What happened. Did I hurt you?'

'I'm fine.' She stands, staring at him, rubbing her arms. Her eyes have gone from wide shock to a narrow focus that cuts through him.

She turns, goes to Ned. Hank can hear her close the door to his room behind her.

Hank sits on his bed. A bad dream now, out of the blue. It makes no sense to him.

The next night, Elise sleeps in the spare room.

'You have bad dreams,' she says as she takes her night-gown from the hook behind the door.

Hank sees bruises on her arms and hates himself for it. But he doesn't say anything.

He hears her settling into the room across the hall,

closing the door. He thinks he hears her turn the lock. It's a bit much, he thinks, after one bad dream. She doesn't need to be afraid of him.

He turns off his light, reaches over and takes her pillow, places it on top of his own. He's always liked to sleep with his head propped up.

No bad dreams rouse him again.

* * *

Quietly, Elise sets up her own space in the house. Her clothes have moved from their shared closet to the one in her room. A few things she's never worn, a housecoat his mother gave her, stay behind, like she is attempting to say the move is not permanent. He doesn't pay much attention. He works. She makes his meals; his clothes are pressed. Ned is well cared for. He thinks about what his parents share, a genuine love and fondness for each other, but he can't magic that out of the air. Instead, he keeps busy.

It's a Tuesday and he's at work, back aching from leaning over tables filled with blueprints when he gets a phone call. It's a doctor in Florida.

While walking on the beach with his mother, his father had a stroke.

Hank knows his parents are getting older, but his father has always been so full of energy. So full of life. He pictures him in his long trousers, belt, perfectly ironed shirt over a pristine white undershirt, falling in the surf, and he thinks he might collapse himself.

'Is he going to make it?' Hank can feel everyone in the office staring at him as he speaks. The room that had been filled with scraping pencils, ringing phones, work chatter, is silent. The fear of what is happening fills the space around him.

'I'll be there as soon as I can.' He hangs up the receiver, in the cradle of the black phone. Then he walks into his office, gets his overcoat and hat, and walks straight out into the late morning light. He drives himself home, to the place where he was born, where his parents lived his whole life, before they made Florida their permanent residence.

Ned is sitting on the floor, playing blocks with the nanny. She stands when she sees Hank in the doorway. Ned starts to giggle and reaches up his arms. Hank scoops him up.

'What's wrong?' Diane, the new nanny, says.

'Little family trouble. I have to go to Florida.' He carries Ned into the bedroom with him. Takes out his suitcase and throws in some clothes. It's only when he's closing the door that he remembers Elise. Remembers he has a wife.

He calls the library where she works part-time, tells her what has happened.

'I'll get the next bus,' she says.

'You don't have to...'

'Your mother may need me. I'm on my way.'

Elise throws a case together. Diane has packed for Ned. They are on their way to the airport when she says, 'How are you, Hank?'

'Scared,' he says.

She reaches over the gear shift and sets her hand on his knee. He feels the touch travel through his body, like a shock.

They land at night, when visiting hours are long over at the hospital but Elise charms the nurses and Hank races to his father, the corridors never-ending, the hospital smell settling into him like a bad cold. The door is open, and there's a light coming from his father's room. He stops, straightens his shoulders, walks in. He never saw this happening. Other people's fathers died. Not his.

He's not prepared for what he sees. It's like his father has shrunk, barely making an impression under the hospital sheets.

His mother is sitting by his side, her back to Hank. He whispers 'Ma' softly, putting his hand on her shoulder. She covers it with her own.

Elise is standing at the door, not wanting to intrude. A sleeping Ned in her arms. Hank sees her hovering, the lighting in the hall showing the caramel threads of her hair, the paleness of her skin. She looks like a ghost, hovering between his family and her own place in this world, wherever that might be.

* * *

It is the first time they've shared a room since the night he had the dream. It's done wordlessly, knowing there is no way to explain separate rooms to his mother. But Hank thinks she knows. The older he gets the more he sees that his parents never missed a trick. And his mother has that female intuition. He remembers the look on her face when Elise did not want an engagement ring. She knew, then. And she knows, now.

Hank feels something sharp go through the middle of him as he realises something. She did not want a ring from him, because the only man she wanted a ring from was William.

He looks at her, unpacking her bag, and feels a coldness toward her he's never felt before.

Wordlessly he leaves the room, heads to the bathroom. As he takes a shower he thinks some more. He lets the water pound on him, washing away the germs, the anxiety, the sadness, the hopelessness. It's a lot to ask from a bar of soap, he thinks, and almost chuckles. All the emotions of the day. He's exhausted.

He steps from the shower feeling lighter, like he'd washed off a layer of cement, instead of some weightless airplane germs.

In his pyjamas and bare feet, he walks to his mother's room, taps softly on the door, not wanting to wake her if she's asleep.

'Come in.' Her words are faint.

She's sitting in bed, rosary beads in her hands. There's a grey colour to her skin he's never seen before.

Hank feels awkward. She's in some kind of blue night dress, but he sits beside her. She moves the covers up, out of propriety he guesses.

'How are you feeling, Ma? You must have got a shock.' His voice is still soft.

'I keep thinking about it. He was fine. We were walking along – you know how much he likes watching those little birds that race in and out of the waves – and we were talking...' She stops. 'I can't remember what we were talking about, but suddenly, he wasn't making any sense. I turned to look at him.' She turns in bed, and the book drops slightly. 'And his face. It looked like someone let the air out of him. One side just, collapsed.' She lifts her hand as though to show on her own cheek. 'He was trying to speak, and he was holding his arm. And then he fell on one knee.'

She stops speaking for a second, then, 'Thank God for that young lifeguard. He knew exactly what to do. I really must find out his name and send a letter to his parents.'

She starts to move, as though she is getting out of bed to do it that very minute.

'I'll do that, Ma. The city'll know who he is.'

'You promise, Hank?'

'I do. I promise. I'll see you in the morning. We'll go the hospital. He'll be all right,' Hank says.

He crosses to his own room, almost knocks on the door. Elise is in bed, reading. *Gone with the Wind*. She's read it a dozen times now, he thinks. Ned is beside her, asleep, sprawled like a starfish. 'How is your mother?' she asks.

Hank walks to his side of the bed, sits on the edge for a moment, then slides under the covers, lying flat on his back.

'She wants me to find the young lifeguard who saved my dad and tell his parents he's a good boy.'

Elise closes her book. 'That is good. She's not filled with despair.' She puffs up her pillow, curls up on her side, looking over Ned at Hank. 'How are you feeling?'

'Tired. Terrified,' he says, watching Ned sleep.

'He looked good, to me. Good colour in his skin. Your papa will be okay,' she says. Then she lifts her arm, and almost reaches to him, but changes her mind. Fixing the blanket over Ned, she then turns on her side, facing the window that is slightly open, the sound of the waves almost reaching them.

* * *

Hank wakes in the morning to the aroma of coffee and sunshine peeking through the window blinds. For a moment a sense of peace fills him. This house in Florida is his very favourite spot. Then he remembers why he's there, and a feeling of dread, like old cold grey porridge, settles on him.

He gets up, sees his dressing gown on Elise's side of the bed. He wonders where it came from. Pulling it on, he moves toward the kitchen, the comforting smell of coffee and bacon and eggs. With everything happening his mother is still keeping them fed.

It's not his mother at the stove, but Elise.

His mother is sitting at the table, Ned on her lap, and, Hank is startled to see, in her dressing gown. Drinking from a china cup.

'Good morning,' Elise says, then lower, just to him: 'Sit with your mother. I'll bring you your coffee,' she says.

'Good morning, Ma,' he says. 'Why the fancy cup?'

'Your wife remembered me saying I like to drink from a china cup. So she brought one from home for me and washed it up.' His mother is clearly touched by the small act of kindness.

Hank looks to Elise, but she is putting bread in the toaster, her back to him.

'After breakfast the two of you should go to the hospital,' Elise says.

'What about you?'

'I thought I might stop in later, after you see the doctors. If your papa is up for more visitors,' she says. 'He does not need to be overwhelmed. I thought I would take Ned to the park.'

Hank knows what she's doing. She's giving his mother time with just him. But she is also acknowledging that she is an interloper, an outsider.

He sticks a fork through his egg yolk. Maybe that was the way it was with all married couples. He did not know, as she had no family for him to meet.

'I don't like to think of you being alone all day,' his mother says.

'I won't be alone. I have the ocean to keep me company,' she says.

* * *

After two weeks in Florida, Hank has to go back to Providence. His businesses need him, and he needs the money to pay the bills. His father will need therapy, and his mother will need some homecare help.

Elise offers to stay, to get his mother back and forth to the hospital.

'Are you sure? I can't ask you to do that,' he says. In the back of his mind he's worried about Ned. He likes to have another set of eyes on him. Elise seems so far away sometimes.

'I'm offering. If your mother is comfortable with that,' she says.

'I'm sure she will be,' he says.

'You better check,' Elise says.

She has cooked all of their meals, cleaned the house, done the laundry. When his father woke, she was the one who thought to bring him his own pyjamas from home. She was the one who took his dirty clothes from the hospital and returned them, cleaned and pressed. She was the one who put fresh flowers in his mother's room. She knew what to do, and how to do it. But something was not right, still. Hank realises at that moment he knows what it is. Elise's actions come from a sense of duty, not love. He knows this feeling well and recognises it. He feels a hollowness in his chest at this realisation.

His mother is grateful for the offer of help, but Hank hears a sense of hesitation in her voice.

'She's hard to get to know, Ma, but give her a chance,' he says. Hank has always gone ahead of Elise, smoothing the way for her. He knows his mother depends on this.

Standing in the kitchen of the little house he loves, the sun pouring in the windows, his mother standing in front of him, she says, simply, 'I always have.'

Then she turns her back to him and walks in the direction of Ned's laughter.

FORTY-ONE

RHODE ISLAND. 1957

Elise and Ned return to Providence as the last few stubborn leaves blow from the trees. The rain is fierce as Hank navigates their way home from the airport.

They had not seen each other in seven weeks, and the kiss at the airport was perfunctory. Duty, more than anything else. Still, he has hope. It is no great love story, but they have Ned now.

'Hank?' she asks.

He did not realise she'd been talking to him.

'Sorry, what?'

'You seem distracted.'

'Just paying attention to the roads, trying not to get us killed,' he says. Ned is asleep in her arms. When the tyres on the truck catch on some ice, Hank's arm shoots out, covering his son's small head with his big hand.

'What were you saying?' he says.

'I was saying perhaps I could take over some of your landlord duties, so you could go to Florida more often. Your parents are going to need you more and more,' she says.

'I'll give it some thought,' he says. But he has no intention of doing this. His business is the only thing he can control. Besides, he's already approached Joe about carrying a bit more of the work.

'Is there food in the house? Do we need to stop for anything?'

Hank had no idea what was in the house. He'd been eating at the office, at the diner down the road.

'Good idea,' he says.

At the store, Elise tells him what to buy as she stays in the car with Ned, out of the bitter cold.

The wind is really picking up and a storm is coming. Hank hopes they won't lose power as he carries first Ned then Elise's case to the house.

Inside he turns to her and says, 'You stay out of the cold, put him to bed. I'll get the last load from the car.' He sets her case in the middle of the kitchen floor. He grabs the last load of shopping bags, struggling to close the car door behind him. He can't believe how quickly the weather has changed. He thinks they're in for a bad one.

Inside, he sees her case is gone. She's looking in the ice box, the overhead light catching the sheen of mist on her hair.

He takes off his shoes, hangs his coat by the door.

'Are you hungry?' she asks. 'I can make some eggs for us, or pasta, something quick,' she offers.

'That'll be fine. I'll just wash up.' He walks quickly down the hallway, toward their bedroom, knowing this simple action of hers is going to decide the fate of their marriage. But he doesn't really have to check. The light is on in the spare room, while their bedroom, his bedroom now he guesses, is in darkness.

Hank looks and sees the case open on the spare bed. He flicks off the light, steps into the washroom. Takes his time washing his hands and his face. He checks on Ned, asleep in his bed. He'd missed him so much.

'My boy,' he says, cradling his head.

Then he goes back to the kitchen, sits down and, as though they are sick, eats scrambled eggs and toast with his wife.

FORTY-TWO

RHODE ISLAND. WINTER 1960

The cold seems to have settled deep into the ground, buckling the roads and taking up residence in his bones. Summer is like a trick of the memory. There were days when the lawns were green and the sun spread warmth and light, days when you sweat walking from the house to the car. He knows that. But when it feels like your eyelids are going to freeze together while crossing a parking lot, it's hard to believe the world was once warm.

On a night when the cold has left an inch of hard frost on the windows, Hank looks out and sees the people across the way have left their dog out. He's seen him out before in weather not fit for man nor beast, but tonight, he puts on his coat.

Elise, sitting on the sofa with a book, her legs tucked under her and a blanket on her lap, looks up.

'Where are you going?' she asks.

'Across the street.'

'What for?'

'To get that dog before he freezes to death.'

He pulls the door closed behind him and strides across the street.

The house had been owned by the Bugliosi family for years. Their son Marco was the same age as Hank, and they'd played together as children. The first time he'd had lasagne was at their house. They'd moved, and now the family that lived there kept to themselves. They made a lot of noise and weren't too house proud, but Hank didn't care about that. The mutt freezing to death, he did.

'Hey, fella.' Hank keeps his voice low, not wanting to alert anyone inside the house. He doesn't worry about the dog barking, as they've been ignoring that for ages.

The dog has been neglected. His fur is matted. Hank crouches down, making himself as small as he can, then he slowly drops his hand, waiting in the cold, his feet freezing, for the dog to get used to his scent. His breath hangs in a frost cloud in the air. He feels it in his lungs. After a minute or two, Hank unsnaps the leash, picks up the puppy and, tucking him under his arm, jogs back to his house.

The door opens as he comes up the step. She must have been watching him.

'Put some water in a bowl for him, will you?'

'Should I warm it up?' she calls over her shoulder as she heads to the kitchen.

'Just room temperature,' he says, setting the dog on the floor and pulling a blanket from the sofa. He tucks it around him.

Elise returns with the water. 'Poor little guy.' She reaches out and tenderly strokes his head, and the look the little thing gives her could thaw the roads outside. 'What kind of dog is he?'

'A terrier mix of some kind I think,' he says.

Elise turns her head and whispers, 'He does not smell too good. Perhaps a bath would make him feel better,' she says to Hank.

'Why are you whispering?'

Elise looks at him. 'Not to hurt his feelings?' she says and starts to laugh.

Hank laughs, too.

He can't remember the last time they laughed together.

The puppy, resting between them, looks up, moving his head to watch both of them.

'All right, run the tub for him. We'll give him a bath, and then I'll have to find a bed for him.'

'We will need food, too,' Elise says.

The dog picks up his head and rests it on Elise's knee.

Hank might have rescued him, but from that moment, he is Elise's dog.

'Does he have a name?' she says.

'Maybe, but I don't know what it is.'

'What shall we name him?'

Hank studies him for a second. 'He looks like a Floyd to me,' he says.

'Floyd? No, I don't like it. Albert. I shall name him Albert.'

'We might have to give him back,' he says. 'I did just steal him,' he says.

'Albert is mine now. Those horrible people across the street will not touch him.'

Hank, carrying the newly christened Albert, follows her to the washroom, where the tub is filling with water. Elise turns off the taps and Hank lifts the puppy into the water.

'God, he does stink.'

'Hush,' she says. 'Albert is sensitive.'

Hank laughs. When she's like this – funny, relaxed – he feels such tenderness for her, and he thinks they could make it. But these moments are few and far between. And he has no idea how she feels.

He watches as Elise lowers herself elegantly to her knees, pouring shampoo on her hands. He folds a towel and bends down beside her. 'This floor'll kill your knees. Lift up,' he says.

She does, and he slides the towel under her.

Leaning over, she starts to rub the suds through Albert's fur.

The scent of shampoo fills the air, overpowering the smell of stinky, wet dog. Honeysuckle, jasmine, strawberries.

'We can't let him out smelling like flowers. The other dogs will laugh. He'll get beat up,' Hank says.

'No one is going to touch Albert. I won't allow it!' she says as though he was a baby.

After he is rinsed, and Hank lifts him from the tub, soaking his shirt, Elise towels Albert dry. The tub is filthy and Albert himself looks both thinner and brighter. His fur is a lovely golden-brown sort of colour.

'Well, aren't you a handsome thing!' she says as the dog licks her face.

'You'll have to go to the shop, Hank. We need some dog food. And get him some treats, too.'

As Hank leaves, he looks at Albert's old home. Even the light from the kitchen looked depressed. He wonders how long it will be before they even notice the dog is gone.

He doesn't have long to wonder. Three days later, as

he's getting out of his truck, a man appears at his shoulder and says, 'You got my dog.'

Hank is startled by his proximity and the fact that he did not hear him approach.

'What dog?'

'I seen him looking out your window. He's mine, and I want him back.'

Hank runs through his options in his mind.

He looks at the man's shoes, with their split seams. The frayed cuffs of his trousers that are shiny at the knees from wear. It's too dark to see his hands, but Hank has always judged a man on how clean and well-trimmed his nails are. The smell of booze coming off him, enough to peel the paint off his truck door, tells Hank what to do.

'My wife has taken a shine to him. They get along well, and he enjoys being in the house.' A not so subtle dig.

'I want my dog.'

Hank reaches into his pocket, pulls out some cash.

'I'm sure you love Albert...'

'Who the hell is Albert?'

'The dog.'

'His name is Champ.'

Hank ignores that and counts out some bills. 'Like I said, I'm sure you love Albert...'

'Champ.'

'But he's taken a real shine to my wife. He's happy. Would fifty bucks make you happy?'

'He ain't for sale.'

Hank sees him eyeing the bills and pulls off a few more.

'Eighty?' he says.

'I'm awful partial to that dog...'

'A hundred bucks, and Albert stays here.'

The man sticks out his hand. Hank pays him and he nods, walks away.

When he opens the door she is waiting for him. Albert is at her feet, and if it is possible for a dog to look concerned, he's mastered it.

'Everything okay?' he asks. 'Where's Ned?'

'Playing in his room.'

Hank has never seen her so nervous. He takes his coat off, hangs it by the door.

'Albert's owner knocked earlier. I didn't open the door. But Albert barked.'

Both of them look down at him, and Hank swears the dog knows something is going on.

He squats down, and gives the little pup a pat. He's a cute dog.

'He's yours now, fair and square. I paid for him,' he says.

Elise bends down and pats Albert, giving his little silky ears a scratch. 'Hear that? You get to stay! Thank you,' she says to Hank.

'You're welcome.'

He heads down the hall. A light is glowing from Ned's room, a baseball nightlight in one corner, a train nightlight in the other. Both gifts from his grandparents.

He's tucked into his bed on the floor. Walked at ten months, crawled out of the crib at fifteen. Too young for a bed, but they were both terrified he'd hurt himself climbing in and out. Elise had taken to sleeping on the floor by him. So Hank bought a single mattress, put a mat underneath it for insulation from the floor.

He kneels down beside him now. Reaches out and

strokes his downy soft hair. Albert barks, and Ned gives a little jump in his sleep, but it doesn't wake him.

His boy is healthy. He has money in the bank. A wife who took care of his parents. A dog now that rounds them out.

He's a lucky man, he tells himself.

FORTY-THREE
RHODE ISLAND. CHRISTMAS 1962

For the first time in the six years they've been married, they spend Christmas in their own home. Hank plans to go Florida for a few days, but Elise says dragging all of Ned's presents to Florida is too much work. And she won't put Albert in a kennel again.

Hank agrees. His father has recovered from the stroke, mostly. When he speaks it sounds like he has a marble in his mouth, but he's fine. Hank always has something to do at his buildings, and with the office closed for the holidays, maybe he can get all caught up. That's been the dream for as long as he can remember.

He spends the afternoon of Christmas Eve painting an empty unit. Makes plans to call the cleaners, as the hallways aren't what they could be. Changes a light for a woman who has lived in the building since before he bought it. She gives him a tin of Christmas cookies, like she does each year.

Hank gives her a Christmas cactus, like he does each year.

On his way home, he stops and buys flowers for Elise. A Christmas mix with roses and carnations and a bunch of other flowers he doesn't recognise.

The air is crisp and cold, but not too cold. When he lets himself into the house, Ned runs to meet him. It's the best part of every day for Hank.

'Hey hey!' he says, scooping him up.

'Where you been, Daddy?' he asks, putting his hands on Hank's cheeks. 'Your face is cold!' he says.

'I've been out working, like you should be doing now!' he says, setting him down.

Hank gives him the flowers to give his mother.

'Mommy!' Ned yells, running through the house.

Hank watches him go, then looks around the kitchen. Elise has been cooking, and the aroma of something fills the air. He hears Elise say, 'For me? They're beautiful!' Then they're in the kitchen, Elise getting a vase for the flowers, Ned and Albert right beside her.

Hanks gives a sigh of appreciation. It's a good day. Elise has some energy about her. Ned is happy.

He walks over to join his family in the kitchen.

* * *

When Ned finally goes to sleep, Elise brings his stocking from where she's hidden it, and gives it to Hank to hang. She can never find the little nail on the fireplace that his own stocking used to hang from. Hank can do it blindfolded.

He looks at the tree, a reindeer of some kind made from cardboard hanging from one of the branches.

'This Ned's handiwork?'

She nods. 'He made it at school. You're getting something similar for Christmas. Act surprised.'

She takes a sip of her eggnog. Hank sits on the chair across from the sofa where Elise rests, her legs tucked under her as always. There's a coffee table, and a whole world, between them.

'I was just thinking. It's Christmas Eve. I have one family member left, and I have no idea where he is. Haven't since 1939.'

Hank has no idea where this is coming from. She's never mentioned her brother. Hank can't even remember his name. Pierre, he thinks.

'He may have a wife. I may be an aunt. He may be dead.'

Hanks waits.

'It doesn't seem right, that I don't know. But even if he called right now. I don't know if I could speak to him.'

Hank remains silent. Saying the wrong thing to fill the space – he's learned silence is better.

'I've never told anyone this, but the day we found out about Poland, he was home. Maman was in shock. I went to bed, thinking Philippe could watch over her. When I woke, he was gone. He took all of the money I'd been saving in a little purse in my bag.'

Philippe. Not Pierre.

'No one knew what was going to happen. If we would open the window and the Nazis would be in the streets. And my brother stole my money.'

Hank does not know what to do with this information. He does know to listen.

'He fled. And to the day she died, he was my mother's favourite.'

Venom, anger, hatred coat her words, but underneath, hiding behind the ugliness, is the hurt, which she's carried all of her life.

'I am sorry. I don't know what got into me,' she says, setting her drink on the table.

'It's a lot, what you've been carrying around,' he says. He thinks for a second and says: 'Philippe is the only person I ever heard William speak badly about.'

Elise looks at him, eyes wide. They've not spoken of William since they visited Cape Cod, all those years ago.

'If it had not been for Philippe, I would never have met William.'

'If I learned anything in service, it's the arbitrariness of life.'

They look at each other. Maybe for the very first time. Hank sees a tiredness in her eyes, a resignation.

'I notice you got a Christmas card from Genevieve,' he says. He'd seen it shoved beside the breadbox, not on display like the other cards they'd received.

'Yes.'

'What happened between the two of you? You were friends for a spell, weren't you?'

'We were, yes. I don't know. She said some things I could not forget, not forgive,' she says. Her gaze drifts toward the window, her eyes dim, and Hank knows not to push.

'All right, do I need to assemble toys? Shall we have another drink?'

'Yes, to both,' she says.

Hank jumps up from his chair, grateful the crisis was averted. Maybe, just maybe, she's getting better. He reminds himself again of how much she's been through.

That night, she sleeps in his room. He holds her as she rests her head on his shoulder. He doesn't say anything, not even when he feels her tears on his skin.

* * *

Christmas Day, and things are back to normal. Elise is efficient in the kitchen, efficient with Ned. She seems to avoid Hank, but he was expecting this. It happens after people let you see them raw, exposed.

They watch as Ned tears through his presents. They both express delight at the candy cane reindeers they receive from him. Hank gives Ned a little box to give his mother – earrings his secretary picked out.

Elise gives Ned a parcel for him to give Hank. A fleece jacket for his worksites.

Albert is not forgotten, with several chew toys and a bag of treats that he rips open when no one is paying attention.

After lunch, Hank suggests a walk, to burn off all the turkey and gravy he says, but really, to get out of the house. After the presents and the lunch, there's a let-down sort of feeling in the air he's never cared for.

'It's not a cold day,' he says, snapping the leash on Albert as Elise ties a scarf around Ned.

The sun is bright, melting some of the snow and ice on the road. Ned's wearing his snowsuit, and it's making little swooshing noises as he walks. Albert growls at the house where he once lived, and Hank knows if he gets near it he will lift his leg and urinate on their drive, so he holds tight to the leash.

They walk to the park, even though the city has

removed the slides and swings, and all that stands is the metal structures that support them.

Elise looks around the wide space they have only to themselves and lets Albert off his leash.

Hank's not sure it's a good idea, but keeps his mouth shut. Why ruin the nice time they're having? He makes a little snowball and throws it at Ned, who laughs. Hank waits while he makes one to throw at him. Then Hank teaches them all how to make snow angels.

Lying in the snow, Elise picks up her head, looks around for Albert. When she can't see him she stands.

'Hank, where's the dog?'

Hank stands up, looking around.

'Albert!' he calls, spinning around looking for him. He jogs to a clump of trees, saplings when he was a boy, thinking the dog might be doing his business.

Nothing.

He studies the fence, but there's no way the dog could have gotten over it. Hank moves along it, wondering if he got under it.

When he turns back, he can't see Elise or Ned.

He heads for the entrance, seeing all of their tracks in the snow.

He hears a crunch. A whimper. And then a scream.

* * *

The driver of the car who hit Albert was blinded by the sun. He's standing there apologising as the little dog lies in a heap, silent. Not moving.

'Jesus Christ,' Hank mutters, under his breath. Ned

walks out into the street, and both the driver and Hank sprint to grab him.

Elise doesn't move.

Hank holds Ned, moving him away from Albert.

He wants to tell Elise to take Ned home, so he can deal with Albert, but he doesn't trust her with his son. Their son.

Hank takes off his coat, rests it on the ground, and lifts Albert onto it.

'Ned, take your mother's hand. Walk ahead of me, the two of you,' he says.

'What's wrong with Albert? Is he asleep?' Ned says.

'Walk with your mother,' Hank says.

'I'm so sorry,' the driver says.

Hank nods, moving toward the house. They walk silently, Hank not even noticing the cold as he holds Albert close to his chest. When they get home, he puts the dog in his truck.

Then he takes Ned by the shoulders and says, 'Go in your room. Okay? Play with your toys. Do not leave your room until I get back. Okay?'

'What about Mommy?'

'Mommy is fine. You just be a big boy and go sit in your room. Okay?'

'Will Albert be okay?'

Hank feels like someone punched him in the gut.

'I hope so,' he lies. He knows the dog he left in his truck is dead.

He locks the door behind him and drives to the vet's. Looking at Albert on his coat beside him, Hank tries to hold back the tears. But he can't.

* * *

When he gets home, he sits in his truck, not sure what to do. If it wasn't for his worry for Ned, he might have sat there forever. At last he opens the truck door. Steps out. The temperature has dropped. The snow is hard, and crunches under his feet. The noise seems to echo in the twilight of the Christmas Day.

He unlocks the back door, lets himself in. Goes straight to Ned's room. He's sitting on the floor with this train set.

He looks up at Hank and smiles. 'Hello, Daddy. Where's Albert?'

Hank wipes his face with his hand. Then he plucks Ned up and sitting in the rocking chair in the corner, sets the boy on his knee.

'There's a place in the sky, where all good dogs go when their time here is over,' he begins. 'It's a great place with lots of space to run and lots of treats to eat.'

'When's he coming back?'

Well, I'm making a mess of this.

'He's not, Ned. But you know what? He's always alive here.' Hank draws a circle over Ned's heart. 'And here.' He touches his head.

Ned looks at him, confused. Hank doesn't know what else to say. He gives him a hug, kisses the top of his head.

'Let's go see the tree,' he says, because he can't think of anything else to distract him.

Elise is nowhere to be seen, so he figures she's in her room. He pulls some of Ned's new toys from under the tree. When he's playing, absorbed in a toy tractor, Hank stands up.

'I'm going to check on Mommy. You stay here.'

Hanks walks down the hall, pausing in front of the door to the spare room, well, his wife's room.

He knocks. When there is no answer he opens the door. He's prepared for tears. He's prepared for anger – he was the one who suggested they go for a walk.

Why did he not tell her to put the dog back on the leash?

He pushes the door open softly, afraid he might scare her. Afraid of what he might see.

She's sitting on the bed, looking out the window. Her skin is as white as the snow falling outside. She looks like a marble statue, the kind you see in a church.

'Elise?' he says.

She turns to him, in slow motion. Looks at him, through him. Stays silent.

'I took him to the vet. It was quick. He didn't suffer.' He doesn't tell her he paid to have him cremated. That he cried, too.

'If we had gone to Florida, he would have been in a kennel. Safe.'

Hank opens his mouth to say she can't think that way. To utter a platitude. But he closes it when she puts her hand up to stop him.

'If I had stayed home with him, and let you take Ned for a walk.'

A single tear falls down her cheek, and Hank thinks he's going to fall apart himself, just seeing it.

'If I had left his leash on...' But she can't get the words out. The noise that comes out of her is a wail, like an animal caught in a steel trap. Hank pulls her to him. To comfort, yes. But he does not want Ned to hear her cry like this.

She sobs against his shoulder. He feels her heart pound, like the sobs might break her in two. She cries until there are no more tears. Then she leans away from him. The warmth from where she rested against him cools quickly.

'Why don't you take a bath? I'll feed Ned. Don't worry about us.'

She nods. When it's obvious she won't be saying anything else, he moves to the door, lets himself out.

'Everything I love dies,' she says.

'What?' Hank didn't catch her words.

But she shakes her head. 'Nothing.' She turns back to the window.

It had started out as such a nice day.

FORTY-FOUR
RHODE ISLAND. APRIL 1963

Hank is anxious for May, when the sky is a pretty blue, and everything starts to bloom. He's hoping it will help Elise, too. She has stopped working at the library. Rarely cooks, and almost never leaves the house. Today is her birthday, and he suggested Italian. She said no. Hank bought flowers for Ned to give her. They're beside him on the truck seat now.

Most days he picks Ned up at school and takes him back to the office with him. The secretaries make a fuss, and the boy does his homework. Draws pictures. He has a good eye. Today he's with a friend. Elise had arranged a play date for him. Hank took it as a good sign.

He often thinks about what Elise said as he was leaving the room that day Albert died. Something about things she loves. He's not sure.

It's just past twilight, a hint of light in the air. In minutes it'll be dark. Hank steps from his truck and looks at his house, catches himself wondering if his father ever had the feeling of dread he had seeing his front door. Somehow, he doubts it.

Hank hesitates, just for a second, thinking about going to the bar down the road for a drink. In the end he takes out his keys, unlocks the door.

The house feels different, quieter. The door from the kitchen to the hall is closed. It's never closed. There's a stillness to the air, and Hank hopes she's out shopping. He left money for new clothes for Ned. He glances at the table to see if the money is still there. It is, and something else. An envelope. His name in her writing, with black ink. Funny, it looks stronger than usual. He can see how her writing has eaten into the pages.

He pours a drink, takes a seat, and looks at the letter. She's left, that has to be it. And that's fine. But she's not taking Ned anywhere.

The envelope is sealed, and he pulls out his pocketknife, slitting it open, and begins to read.

Dear Hank,

By the time you read this I will be gone. I am sorry it has come to this, but we've both been unhappy for so long, something has to change, if not for us, then for Ned.

I don't want to put him through what my own mother did to me. I see the two of you together, and you are so happy. You get each other. I am in the background, because I've always been afraid to love him too much. The men I love are all pulled from me early – first my papa, and William. Even my brother. Every man I have ever loved has died young.

He stops reading, even though there is more. A coldness enters his body, and he realises the heat is not on in the house. Why would she turn it off? But that is not what is making him cold. Something is very, very wrong. Setting the letter down, he moves through the kitchen. Takes the stairs three at a time. Before he reaches the top, he sees her.

She's wearing a plain cream dress; one he's never seen her wear. There's some sort of pink material at her feet, which are unnaturally still.

He's seen enough death. He knows. He rights the chair next to her, tucking it into the corner where it belongs. Already wanting things normal for Ned.

He carries her to the spare room, sets her on the bed. Sits beside her. Stares. He can hear the second hand on the clock in the hallway, filling up the empty space around him, the seconds crashing in on him, like waves.

The clock seems to grow louder as he thinks about what to do. Finally, he stands.

'You are a stupid, selfish woman. And you should have used your goddamn head once in a while. Maybe you and William would have gone on to a beautiful life together. Maybe, and maybe not. I never thought I'd fight in a war, and I never thought I'd survive it once I was there. I thought once I was home everything would be okay, but all I saw came back with me. I've carried all of those dead men with me every single day. Who are you to say your losses were worse than anyone else's? And what have you done to your son?'

He stops, realises he's arguing with a dead woman.

'I hope he was worth it,' he says, staring at her, waiting for her to sit up and defend William.

William. He hadn't thought about him in a while. Now, he remembers it all, so real and so loud he wants to cover his ears.

'I did my best,' he whispers. 'I'm sorry I never took her sailing.'

Then he goes to the kitchen, picks up his Scotch, and calls the police.

PART 3

FORTY-FIVE
RHODE ISLAND. 1966

It's a beautiful September afternoon. Ned's tenth birthday. Half the kids in the neighbourhood and some from Ned's class are in the backyard, eating burgers and waiting for cake. He'd taken them all bowling as a birthday present, and now they're having a barbecue. Some of the parents are there as well. Joe's wife had bought decorations and there are balloons and streamers. There's always someone to remember the stuff he forgets, and he's grateful for that. He watches Ned laughing with his friends, chewing with his mouth open. He'll have to talk to him about that later. He's a good kid. Has good friends. Laughs a lot.

They had a few years, Nate wondering where Mommy was, Hank's parents in a state – the gravity of the situation shown in his father disregarding medical advice and flying, and his mother letting him. They'd stayed for six months, and were an enormous help, but it was the little dog sitting next to Ned now that pulled the boy through. Skipper. He knew his job the moment Hank brought him from the pound. He never left Ned's side.

He flips the burgers, filling a plate. Joe's wife Eleanor opens a bag of buns.

'We should bring the cake out soon. The boys will need to get home,' she says.

Hank nods, but he's in no hurry for the day to end. Parents arrive to pick up their sons, but Hank offers food, drink, and the men have a beer. Eventually the cake is served and everyone sings happy birthday. Hank feels a softness inside him as he watches his son awkwardly sitting on his hands, a big grin on his face. It's the time of night when he feels nostalgic, and he finds himself thinking of Elise. If he could have helped her. He used to think at least he tried to keep his promise to his friend. Then he thought some promises were better off broken. But lately, watching his son grow, he's started to think everything happens for a reason.

It was easier to think of life as having some sort of framework, instead of thinking how damaging and destructive the choices you make with the best of intentions could be.

His friends head home as darkness looms. Eleanor helps him clean up. When she and Joe have gone, Hank tells Ned to take a bath.

'I don't need one,' he starts, but Hank gives him a look.

'Yes, sir,' he says.

'And use soap!' Hank shouts to his retreating back.

There was a time when he loved bubble baths. But then one day he said he was too old and wanted to shower. He seemed to think that meant the end of bathing entirely. But Hank taught him how to use the taps, then stood outside the door Ned insisted be closed, heart in his throat, ear pressed to the door, afraid he'd slip in the tub.

Being vigilant and invisible. A bit like being a soldier.

FORTY-SIX
RHODE ISLAND. 1979

Being a parent was a helluva thing, Hank thought, as he sat looking out the window onto the same street he'd looked onto since he could remember.

All he wanted for his boy was a happy life, free from the struggles he'd had. When, in med school, he thought about becoming a psychiatrist, Hank worried it was to deal with his own problems, and almost drove himself crazy trying to figure out what they could be, as Ned never told him anything. All he got was, 'I'm fine, Dad. Don't worry about me.' It made Hank think of when he came back from war, and his own father would try to get him to talk. He wishes now he'd known what the man was thinking. Hank could have said, 'I'm having flashbacks to hiding in ditches, feet away from men who want to slit my throat.'

Ned grew up in a nice home, with a father who made enough money for him to do the things he wanted. He was good-looking, smart. Popular. It always came back to Elise.

Hank worried every single day that the lies about his mother's death would be revealed. Thought every single day about it being a mistake to go that route, but his own mother was firm. Elise might not have been Catholic, but they were. Mortal sin. Hank thought it was a sin, all she went through. And that told him a lot. You don't marry someone because you feel sorry for them. He used to get mad at her for not being able to move on, but now, he thought there was more to it than that. Now, he thinks she was afraid to be happy. Whenever she was happy, whatever she loved was always taken from her. Like she wrote in her letter. Her father dying so young. Her mother failing to be a mother. Her brother. William. Or maybe he just told himself that to feel better. Life was about creating the story you could live with.

He'll never forget the letter he got from Genevieve after she learned of Elise's death. Most notes had been expressions of condolences. Marianne and Bertrand had been devastated, and it took months for them to be able to go to her old home, locked up for so long. Marianne told Hank that Elise had asked her to mail William's letters to her after she had decided to stay in Rhode Island. They'd gone missing in the post, he learned. Another time of depression for her, he guesses. There was nothing else in the house to send, she'd told him. Nothing of value. One of these days he'll have to figure out what to do with the eyesore.

But it was the letter from Genevieve that stood out. She said she was sorry for everything he had gone through. 'I told her many years ago you were a good man, that pining over a man long-dead, whom she barely knew, was ridiculous. She never spoke to me again, but I do not regret what I said. I hope you and Ned carve out a new and happy life for yourselves,' she'd written. He found himself liking

Genevieve more. After the letter. She had been brave enough to say to her face what he had only yelled at what remained of her, that day long ago. He had asked Elise a few times why she was no longer friends with Genevieve. Now he knew.

'Let's go out and throw the ball around,' Hank says. Ned is lying on the sofa, reading a book. He's home for a visit during summer break, and Hank is enjoying every minute of having his boy around.

'Sure,' he says, getting up.

'Then we'll go to Mario's for a pizza.'

Ned's reaching for his glove in the hall closet but he stops, mid movement, arm stretched for the box on the top shelf where his glove and assorted balls and frisbees were kept. They used to accumulate by the back door, until Hank tripped on them one night bringing in groceries and lost his mind when a carton of eggs smashed all over the floor. Really, it had been the twist in his knee, reminding him that he was old, but Hank used it as an excuse to talk about the cost of food and to haul out the old parental nugget of children starving in Africa.

'Is something wrong?'

'No, why?'

'The last time we went to Mario's, we put Skipper down.' Ned speaks the name of his dog softly, even after all these years. He'd been eighteen then.

Hank flashes back to that day, the trip to the vet's. Skipper resting on Ned's lap, too old to pick up his head and look out the window.

Ned stroking his ears, his hands so similar to his mother's.

Hank feels a lump in his throat the size of a traffic cone just thinking about it.

'Didn't mean to scare you – just felt like pizza,' Hank says. He realises they've gone out for pizza for all the milestones in Ned's life – both good and bad. When he graded. When he didn't make captain of the hockey team. When they put Skipper down. But that had been a bad decision, and Hank had ended up getting the pizza to go.

Hank takes his spot at one end of the backyard. When they started playing catch, Ned was barely more than a toddler. Hank remembers throwing the ball to him while on his knees. After a while they moved further apart. Hank stood but was mindful of how tall he was. One summer Ned had to get a new glove. He'd outgrown the one he had. Hank noticed for the first time how tall and lean the boy was. A swimmer's build, more than a hockey player, but he did both. Hank believed keeping him busy and tired would keep him out of trouble.

The sun is sending shards of light that seem to be aimed right at Hank's eyes, and he misses the ball twice. The third time it happens Ned says, 'Let's switch sides, Dad,' and Hank's embarrassed.

'No need for that,' he says, not willing to bow to time or the sun.

They play for a few more minutes. When Hank misses the ball in the sun and it ends up cracking him in the head, Ned lets out a roar of laughter, then sprints across the yard, graceful as a deer, to check on his father.

'You're gonna have a welt on your forehead tomorrow,' Ned says.

'Hell with it. Let's go for a pizza.'

At the restaurant, Hank is holding a glass of ice water to his forehead when Ned says, 'Can I ask you a question?'

'Shoot,' Hank says, feeling his spine straighten. No simple question ever came prefaced in that way.

'What did Mom die from?'

Hank can feel his heart banging around in his chest. He thought the question might be about a girl. He knew something was on Ned's mind.

'Where's this coming from?' Hank asks.

'She's my mother. I have the right to know,' Ned replies.

'I never said you didn't. I'm just wondering why you want to know now, what more you think I can tell you,' Hank hedges.

'You said it was her heart. Her dad died young of a heart attack. I'm reading a lot about cardiovascular health, and I wonder if I am predisposed to heart problems.'

Hank lets himself relax, for a second.

'You seem to take after me, and you couldn't kill me with an axe. I know. The Germans tried their darnedest.'

Ned laughs at that. And for a second Hank thinks he's skirted this particular landmine. But he can tell when Ned grows silent and looks up at him with his head dipped down, exactly how his mother once did, that there is more to come.

'We never talk about her,' he says softly.

'I know. That's my fault. I've always tried to put the bad stuff out of my mind,' he says.

'It's not fair. I want to know her,' Ned says.

'What would you like to know?'

'Did she love me?'

Hank's heart breaks a little, like a crack appearing in a frozen pond when a skater slices over it.

'Of course she did. Why would you question such a thing?'

'There's no pictures of us together. When I was a baby, learning to walk, nothing. I notice now, at my friend's houses. At Mike's house and at Tommy's, growing up, I mean, the whole house was full of baby pictures with their moms. There's not even one of me and her at our house.'

He sounds so young, it breaks Hank's heart.

'That's my fault,' he lies. 'When she died, I put all the photos of the two of you away. Out of sight. And I don't know where I put them.' Hank begs a God he doesn't believe in for his son to let this go.

Ned is older now. And Hank needs to stay on his toes.

'How could you lose them?'

'I thought they were in the attic. Then I thought maybe I gave them to your grandma. And a lot of things got lost when your grandparents passed away,' he lies. Hank has never lost a thing in his life.

'What was she like?'

Hank knows defeat when he sees it. He's stubborn. Elise was stubborn. So it makes sense the young man sitting with him would be, too.

Hank closes his eyes for a second, memories racing through his mind, as he searches for the right words.

William. Her brother. Albert. Genevieve.

'Loyal. She was loyal. And very smart. Loved to read.'

All the time he's spent shutting out the past, working so hard not to think about the what ifs and why nots, and now he's trying to remember, to find some good things, for his son.

'Grew up in Occupied France and survived. That's no small thing. Was very good to your grandparents, when your granddad had a stroke.'

He sees a slow smile and the light of interest and love in Ned's eyes. Hank will have to do his best to keep that alive. A boy needs a mother, even if she's gone. Hank should have remembered that.

FORTY-SEVEN
RHODE ISLAND. 1984

There were things in life you always remembered. Your own birthday. Christmas. Where you were when you heard the world was at war. When Kennedy was shot. There were things that lived in Hank's memory that were as real as the toast he had for breakfast, or the wind that howled through the trees in November. He didn't speak of those things.

When Ned brought Amanda home, he knew he'd remember what he was wearing and the dishes stacked by the sink, the way the light bulb flickered in the hallway.

She stood in front of him, in a dress that looked like it was going to fall off her, with a smudge of some kind of dirt on the front, and the hem dipping in the back.

He'd call her a hippy, but they'd been gone for twenty years, he thought. Fashions were much looser these days. At least she wasn't wearing those ridiculous trousers and all kinds of crazy purple eye makeup.

A nice girl. Little bit odd in how she dressed, but that wasn't important. She looked at Ned as though he was the air she breathed. And Hank let himself relax. Felt good, even. His boy had found love.

So when Ned showed up at his office and suggested pizza, he knew what was happening.

'Sounds good,' he said, grabbing his coat.

They walk the familiar route to Mario's, the Italian restaurant on the corner. The owner lifts his arm in a wave of greeting when they enter. He can't remember his name, but he's always reminded him of Bertrand Allard, the baker who had helped him with Elise. He'd had a few letters from Marianne after Elise died, but he'd not seen them. He regrets that now. He should have taken Ned to see where his mother was born. He should have gone to see where William was buried. Once things settle down, he'll go, he decides. It's time.

They take a seat in the back, a booth. It's too hard cramming into a small table, and Hank hates being jostled by people.

'The worst thing about...'

'This place is too many tables,' Ned finishes his father's sentence.

Hank laughs, setting his jacket on the seat. 'They make great sausage and mushroom pizza,' he says.

'They do.'

Hank settles in. 'Okay. Shoot.'

'Dad, I'm getting married.'

'Well,' Hank says, sitting back in his chair, all the emotions he's feeling taking up space.

'Good,' he says. It seems weak, but it's all he can think to say. Doesn't trust himself with much else. 'When?' he asks.

'Summer, maybe even next summer. I'm leaving that to her. I have to work.'

Hank watches as Ned folds his pizza in half, taking an enormous bite, the way he always has.

'The ring?'

'Man, those things aren't cheap,' he says.

Hank wonders what happened to Elise's wedding band. He thinks his mother had it. Maybe he has lost things.

'We'll have to go out and celebrate.'

They eat their pizza. When they are done Ned pays the bill. They walk out into the street, a street filled with honking cars, hurrying pedestrians. A jackhammer is ripping up cement and Hank can feel the noise and the vibrations in his teeth.

A man bumps into him as he makes his way by. Hank looks at his silent retreating back and says to Ned, 'The world was a better place in my day, before all the noise and hurrying. We had manners.'

'Yes, the good old days of a global war and women vacuuming the house in pearls. Isn't that when the Valium crisis took hold?'

'Ha ha,' Hanks says.

Ned looks at his watch, the one Hank gave him when he graduated from medical school. 'I gotta go, Dad,' he says. He pulls his father into a hug, right there in the middle of all the hustle and bustle.

Then he turns and walks away, following the path of the man who banged into Hank and never apologised.

FORTY-EIGHT
RHODE ISLAND. 1984

They're getting married at her parents' home a sprawling affair near Barrington. Hank drives himself to the house. It's been in the family for generations and was impressive once. Looking at it, he wishes he'd brought his toolbox. The place looks like it needs tightening up before it blows away.

Hank parks the car under an old oak tree and makes his way to the house.

Amanda's father greets him at the door, his hearty handshake and wide smile showing pure joy for the day.

'Hello, Hank!' he says. 'Come in, come in! The kids have a great day for it, not a cloud in the sky.'

'Couldn't have asked for better,' Hank agrees.

'Ned's in the back room, staying away from the bride, superstition and all that. The wife's in the kitchen with the caterers.'

Hank moves to the back bedroom, toward the sounds of male voices.

Hank knocks once and opens the door.

'Dad,' Ned says, and Hank is delighted there is joy in his son's voice, and in his eyes.

Ned's in a blue suit, no different from one he might wear to someone else's wedding. His son was not a man for tuxedos or flash. Hank's suit is grey, newly purchased for the event. He wanted a suit he hadn't worn to a funeral for his son's big day.

Ned sees his father's reflection in the mirror where he's fixing his tie.

'Dad, you're here.' He and Ned shake hands, then his son gives him a hug. His best man George, his old college roommate, shakes hands with Hank as well.

Amanda's mother comes in. Standing back in her pink wedding finery, hands on her hips, she surveys them and declares, 'I swear, it's like looking at those handsome Kennedy boys.'

She takes a boutonniere from a box and runs her fingers along Hank's lapel before fixing it in place. Hank can smell the wine on her breath. She's as lit as a Christmas tree. But she's happy. They're good people.

After she leaves the men have a drink of Scotch before George says, 'All right, Corrigan – let's get you married!'

George walks out ahead of them, perhaps thinking Ned and Hank might want a father-son moment. Hank puts his hand on his son's shoulder and squeezes. It's enough for both men.

FORTY-NINE
RHODE ISLAND. 1988

Lucy Eleanor Corrigan – named for not one, but two Beatles' songs, is born on the kind of spring day that makes everyone feel happy just to be alive. The kind of day when winter's icy grip has finally been broken and the sun rises higher, bolder, in the pale blue sky.

Hank is pretty much floating as he makes his way to the nursery – the same nursery where he first laid eyes on Ned, all those years ago.

She's six pounds, six ounces of perfection, and he falls hopelessly in love the moment he sees her, wrapped in a blanket, quiet and regal among all the screaming babies.

Ned is beside him, tired from being up all night with Amanda.

'Isn't she beautiful?' he says.

'Prettiest baby girl ever,' Hank says.

The two men stand side by side, neither taking their eyes off Lucy.

'How's Amanda?' Hank asks.

'Exhausted.'

'I won't bother her. But tell her I stopped by. I hope she's feeling better.' He hesitates. 'Give her my love,' Hank says.

'Baby got you all mushy?' Ned jokes, then, 'Thanks, Dad.' He takes another look.

'I'll be here if you need me,' Hanks says, staring. When the nurse taps on the glass he figures she's telling him to move along, he's giving her the creeps. But she waves him in. 'First grandbaby?' she says.

'Indeed she is,' he says.

'Take a seat in the rocking chair. I'll bring her to you.'

Hank thinks his heart is going to jump from his chest when the nurse hands him Lucy. He holds her gently, pulling her in close to keep her warm. Sitting in that nursery, for the first time in a long time, Hank Corrigan's world makes sense.

* * *

Hank would never forget the day he walked into his office with his granddaughter strapped to his chest. Of course, he couldn't have gotten away with it if he didn't own the place. Amanda wanted to get her PhD and Hank volunteered to help out. Truth be told, having Lucy around made him feel better than he ever felt.

He moved a playpen into his office, stocked up on formula, and Lucy became the youngest employee of Corrigan Enterprises.

At lunch he took her for walks, and the women in the office all pitched in. He got a swing, and some toys. He talked to her as he worked.

After Amanda graduated, she went to work as a town planner, although Hank did offer her a job with him.

'Working for my father-in-law? Not a chance,' she joked, as they ate pizza and drank Champagne.

He's proud of his son's wife.

When Lucy starts kindergarten, Hank walks her there each day, and picks her up after. He goes to the school plays. Takes her to ballet class. They are best friends.

But the winter bothers him now. Arthritis has set into his hands and feet. So when Lucy is eight, he decides to move to Florida. She can come for school holidays. He'll be back and forth for work.

They'll make it work.

* * *

It's hard, watching the real-estate agent hammer a For Sale sign into the patch of grass outside the house. A young man, a friend of Ned's. He waves to Hank as he climbs into the car, hammer still in his hand. Hank guesses he's thrown it onto the passenger seat as he watches him back onto the road.

Times have changed, and so have property prices. Now it's all about location, and Hank has that on his side. His little house is a find, because it's close to the city centre. It's been listed at over fifteen times what his father paid for it. Wouldn't Hank love to see his father's reaction to that. Of course, the place he bought in Florida is worth thirty times what he spent on it. That was the best investment he ever made.

Financially, he's done well.

He walks through the house, like he's already saying

farewell. The front room, where his mother once had plastic on the old sofa to 'keep it nice' even though no one was allowed to sit in there. He was going to throw away the set, but Ned said it was made of solid wood, so he should get it reupholstered. What's old is new again.

He opens the hutch, sees all the glasses his mother loved, the way the blue glass has different shades in the shadowy room. He turns on the light inside the cabinet and watches the purple, green, red, and orange glass shimmer. His father had bought her one for every special occasion. Royal something or another. He'll have to pack those well. He picks one up, looks at the stem of the glass. They look so fragile but are surprisingly heavy.

Putting it back, he catches his knee on something. Looking down he sees a handle. He gives a snort of surprise – he never knew this thing had a drawer. Bending down, he opens it. When he sees the contents, his heart gives a thump.

A letter, in a white envelope, his name in his mother's hand. My God. How long has that been there?

My boy,

I hope you read these words when you are ready. I have always feared you selling this hutch before you found this, but I had no idea where to put these things.

Hank looks in the drawer and sees below where the letter rested is a small box.

He plucks it up. You never know people. And you never know a house.

We are so proud of you. You've done so well for yourself, and you've done it while being a strong, ethical man. That is what makes us the proudest.

I will never forget the day you gave us the little house in

Florida. I was terrified to be away from everything I knew, but it gave us a new lease on life. Thank you for making our last years so wonderful.

I want you to know that your father and I tried our best with Elise, but it is not easy watching your child marry someone who doesn't love them the way they deserve to be loved. We tried very hard to understand your choice. We tried very hard to appreciate the good things about her, and she was wonderful after your dad had the stroke. But there was a distance to her; she had an aloof way about her. Even with Ned. That's what bothered me the most. And then, how she chose to leave us.

Reading the letter, Hank can picture his mother struggling over each and every word. He wonders how long it took her to come up with that euphemism.

I always thought if I had a daughter-in-law, I would have a friend, someone who loved my boy as much as I did. But Elise did not want to be my friend. Your father said she didn't want to be anyone's friend. After, we talked about how we could have helped her. Your father says she was always beyond help. Your father never misses a trick, and I think he was right.

I'm leaving the emerald ring your father bought me for Ned's wife. I should have given it to Elise, but I just didn't want to. I hope you understand.

Love,

Mom

Hank folds up the letter. He hopes wherever his mother is, she's at peace. The ring is sitting underneath, in the old box it came in. He looks at it now. It seems so much smaller than he remembered it on his mother's hand. His father had put it on layaway, paid it off over time for their anniversary. The only piece of jewellery his mother ever owned.

He puts the letter in his suitcase, and the ring in his pocket, until he can figure out where to store it.

He only has a few days left, and he has so much to do.

FIFTY

FLORIDA. 1996

The first thing Hank does when he moves into his parents' old house in Saint Pete's is open all the windows. The air is musty, hanging like some sort of ugly cloud, and he wants it all gone.

He cranks up the air conditioner since it is such a hot day and opens them all wide – even the patio doors. To hell with the cost.

Hank has never been afraid of hard work, and despite the dull ache in his knees, he fills a bucket with hot water and pours in a healthy dose of some lemon-scented cleaner. It's the scent of his childhood, for his mother was always scrubbing something.

He starts with the cabinets, the countertops, then moves to the floor. Kitchen sorted, he continues, replacing the water and cleaner each time he changes rooms. He attacks the walls, using a sponge mop. He'll repaint them soon enough. Then he looks at the carpet. That had to go. He'll rip it up and lay down some wooden floor. Lucy has such bad allergies, and carpets bothered her. Wooden floors made more sense here, anyway.

He picks the room at the front of the house, a small room where his father did his crosswords and dozed, as his office. He has a business manager now, but Hank still knows everything that is going on in every single one of his properties. With every single one of his investments. There might be more to life than money, but so far, money is the only part of his life that makes sense. Besides, he wants to make sure Lucy has everything she could ever need, and with the cost of college going up and up, well, that is keeping his mind busy now. He makes a mental note to buy some hangers for her closet, then, picks up a pen and writes it down. These days his whole life is recorded on to-do lists.

Unpacking his suitcase, he finds his mother's ring. Looking around, he tries to figure out where to put it. He decides to have a safe installed in his office. Something else for the to-do list.

The neighbour, Maggie, pops over with banana bread. She's still a handsome woman. Her husband's been gone ten years, but she's still on her own. He finds that strange, although he's been on his own since Elise died. But then, he was on his own when she was alive, too.

The house is sparkling. He feels settled in, for this, the last part of his life. He pours a small glass of Scotch, sits on the back deck and watches the sunset.

He is a lucky man.

FIFTY-ONE

RHODE ISLAND. 1996

'Lucy has made her Santa list. She wants a puppy, which she is not going to get. A pony, ditto. And a stuffed panda bear.'

Hank laughs.

'I've left that up to Amanda. But the next part is on me.'

It's the last week of November and Hank is sitting on his back deck in a pair of shorts, drinking some Mexican beer with a lime in it. Maggie and her new man, Butch, introduced him to it.

'Okay,' Hanks says, thinking he'll go out later and buy a panda bear for his granddaughter and pushing away his drink.

'The third thing on her list is to have you come for Christmas.'

Hank pulls in a breath, releases it slowly.

'You mean she asked Santa for me?'

'I don't think Lucy has ever believed in Santa – she's too practical, a bit like her grandfather.'

Hank doesn't trust himself to speak, just thinking about how much he loves that little girl.

'And since you're such a hard man to shop for, not wanting anything, I was thinking I could buy you a plane ticket, as a Christmas present to you and to my daughter.' He pauses. 'It'd be good to see you, Dad.'

'What's Christmas without snow?' Hank says – his way of agreeing to the trip.

Hank looks at his watch; if he hurries he can make it to that big new toy shop with the funny name. What is it she wants again? A panda bear. Surely he can find one of those.

* * *

Ned and Lucy meet him at the airport. When Lucy sees him she screams and claps her hands, running through the crowd to get to him. Hanks drops his bag, bends down and grabs her up in his arms. He feels tears coming, the good kind, from when you think your heart is going to burst with happiness. He doesn't even try to blink them away.

'My girl,' he says, feeling her small arms around his neck.

Ned appears and picks up his bag. 'She's too big to carry, Dad.'

'Hello to you, too,' he says. 'And hush, she is not.' But he sets her down, and she slides her small hand into his. With his free hand Hank shakes his son's as Lucy jumps around beside them, too excited to stand still. Life is very good indeed.

* * *

Ned's house is in College Hill, a lovely part of Providence. Home to the students of Brown.

Amanda opens the door wearing a set of felt reindeer antlers.

'How festive!' Hank laughs, giving her a hug. She's so small he has to practically bend in half and is careful with his embrace.

In the corner a tall tree is blazing with lights, surrounded by presents. The green and the gold combination of tree and baubles reminds him of his mother's ring, and he wishes he had brought it for Amanda. Next trip, he tells himself. Lucy is holding his hand and jumping up and down. He's never seen her this keyed up.

'Come on. Let's get you fed, Dad,' Ned says.

'Then can we open a present, Granddad?'

* * *

Lucy gets two panda bears – Hank couldn't figure out which one she'd like more – and little gold studs for when she gets her ears pierced. She also gets a plane ticket for Florida, and a week at Granddad's. Hank figures he better milk the Disney bit for all it's worth, because soon she won't want to spend time with her grandfather.

He can't believe how big she's gotten since he saw her, just four months earlier. He thinks she'll be tall, like him. Like Ned. Although she looks an awful lot like Elise.

Ned's done okay for himself. A healthy, happy little girl and a wife who looks at him with adoration.

The week flies by, and as Hank packs his things, he's already planning a return visit. He'll come back in the spring, help with the work that needs to be done to a house in New England after a hard winter.

Amanda has bundled up Lucy and is pulling on her own coat. They're stopping by to visit friends after they drop him off.

'Okay, guys, everyone in the car,' Ned says, carrying his father's suitcase, trying to move them along.

Hank stops in the drive, looking into the sky. The air has the faintly metallic smell it gets when snow is coming. A few flakes start to fall, and he gets a bad feeling.

'Maybe I should take a taxi,' he begins.

'What? Why?' Ned asks.

They're piling into the car, Lucy sitting in the back with him.

He makes sure she's wearing her seatbelt.

'Can we go back to Disney when I visit, Granddad?' she asks.

He laughs, knowing what story she wants to hear. 'Remember when I took you to the Country Bear Jamboree?'

She starts to giggle.

'Walked out in your sock feet! "Where are your shoes?" I ask, and you said, "I took them off." I don't mind telling you, I was stumped. Had to go back into the ride and find your shoes. Turns out, at the start one of the bears...'

'That would be Big Al,' Ned interrupts, knowing the story word for word, but still loving hearing it.

'Said, "Sit back, relax, take your shoes off".' Hank chuckles, getting ready for the wind-up. 'I said, "Why did you take your shoes off?" And Lucy says, practical as you please, "He said to, and I thought he might check!"'

Everyone in the car laughs. Amanda turns around in her seat and smiles at Lucy, and at him.

The snow is really falling now, small flakes coming down on a slant, which is not a good sign. Hank sees Ned leaning forward, huddled over the steering wheel, the pellets coming at them like an attack.

'I can't believe how quickly the weather turned. I wonder if your flight will even go.'

'If it doesn't, I'll take a room near the hotel. I don't want you back and forth on these roads.' Hank wishes now he'd called a cab like he suggested. He'll be worried the entire time they're on the road back home.

'So yes, Miss Lucy, we'll go to the Country Bear Jamboree when you visit. Only if you keep your shoes on.'

She laughs, so happy.

There's a crunch, a crash. Something barrels into the driver's side of the car. The windows of the car explode. Hank's neck snaps back. His arms reach out, grabbing for Lucy.

Screams fill the car as it spins in a circle before something slams into them again. Sparks are flying, like at a welder's bench. The cold takes his breath away as he tries to cover Lucy's body with his own, his seatbelt holding him in place.

Then everything is quiet.

* * *

Someone is shining a light in his eyes. He's strapped to a board. His arms start to move, searching for his gun, until he realises he's not a soldier anymore. The war is long over. What has happened?

The airport. The car. The snow.

Ned.

Lucy.

He's frantic now, arms flailing, grabbing for something, someone. He knows his mouth is moving but he can't hear anything. Can't hear himself.

A nurse grabs his arms. 'Easy, Mr Corrigan. Easy.' Her voice is soft and soothing and then she turns, and says with some urgency, 'I need some help here.' He can feel a jab; someone has given him a shot. He fights the drowsiness that descends, like a curtain bringing a play to an end, for as long as he can. Lucy. He has to know.

* * *

Hank will always remember the young doctor who told him Ned and Amanda didn't make it. He'll always remember the way the sun was falling through the window blinds, leaving slashes of light on his hospital bed sheet. Daggers of brightness on a cold January day. He felt like he died inside.

'Lucy...?'

'She's fine. A few bumps. But she's fine.'

The doctor, who knew Ned from the hospital, makes a point of telling Hank they died on impact, so there was no pain involved. Hank flashes briefly to the times he's said something like that. To Elise, saying William felt no pain and his last thoughts were of her. To Jean, the same thing. He wasn't in any pain, and his last thoughts were of his family. Hank knows he is lying. He heard the screams in the car.

'The Country Bear Jamboree,' Hank says, lifting his heavy eyes to the doctor.

'What's that, Mr Corrigan?'

'The last thing we were thinking about... the Country Bear Jamboree.'

He feels the young man settle his hand on top of his as he closes his eyes.

* * *

Thirteen stitches in the shoulder and his face, from the glass. A sore neck they thought might indicate spinal issues – why they kept him drugged up he guesses. That's it. His son, and Amanda, two feet away, injuries unsurvivable. Like the men who died beside him in the battlefields of France and Belgium, while he remained unscathed. Lucy with a bump on the head. Hank sees the scratches on his hands from where the glass hit, as he covered her head. She has stiches next to her eye. Thank God she didn't lose it.

He takes a white shirt out of the closet. A neighbour asked what they could do to help and Hank said, 'I need a suit. Navy blue or black. Plain. Forty-four long.'

He remembers saying it, but he doesn't remember when it appeared.

He sits on the edge of his bed. If he hadn't come for Christmas. If he'd stayed at home. If his flight had been the day before, or the day after. A few hours earlier or later. If he'd called a cab.

He rubs his face with his hand, mindful of the bandage. He's seen enough blood. A knock at his door.

And there she is, her little face. He sees a look of fear in her eyes that goes straight through him.

'Granddad?' she asks as he tries to fix his face into an expression that takes the fear away from hers.

He pats the bed beside him and she sits. Her little feet in their Mary Janes can't touch the floor, and her legs, in their grey wool tights, swing.

She's old enough to know her parents are gone. But Hank is not so sure she realises the finality of it all. He's not even sure he does.

'How are you feeling, sweetheart? Did you have any breakfast?'

'I had a pop tart. Blueberry are my favourite, the ones with frosting.'

Hank lets it go, for now. Later he'll have to see about getting a good meal into her. Part of him wishes his mother was here; she'd have them all fed and organised. But it's good she did not live to see this. It would have been too much for both of his parents.

He thinks of Elise, and her belief that all the men she loved died young. It's happened again,' he tells the ceiling in his room. He feels something inside him harden against her.

Hank stands, gets a tie and starts to put it on.

'It's going to be a hard day, today,' he begins. He's not convinced she should be going to the funeral at all. He doesn't know what to do. Ned's friend seems to think she needs the experience. He's a psychiatrist, so Hank listens to him. Still.

'Do you want to stay home?'

'Will you be here?'

'No, sweetheart, I have to go.'

'I want to be with you,' she says, her little shoulders giving a shrug.

'Get me your hairbrush, sweetheart,' he says.

Lucy hands him the brush. He is gentle, as he pulls out the tangles. When he is done he tells her to get her hat and her coat.

He takes her small hand in his, and they go into the kitchen, where Ned's friends are waiting.

FIFTY-TWO

FLORIDA. 1997

When he thought about it, Hank realised he parented mostly on instinct. He kept Ned busy with sports to keep him out of trouble. He taught him respect for himself, and for others. But when his granddaughter came to live with him, that all went out the window. A girl. His granddaughter. He loved his son, but his love for her, well, that was a whole new level of love. And of responsibility. He was raising someone else's child. He had to get it right.

He sits down and makes a list.

Ballet, of course. Swimming lessons. They're in Florida, after all. Ponies. The thought cuts into him. She'd asked for one for Christmas. Could he get her a pony? Not yet. He sets the pen down and wanders into her room. She had made the bed, but the blankets are uneven, hanging on the floor. The teddy bears are arranged, resting on the pillows. He opens the drawers in the small chest. A few T-shirts. A few tops. Not much. She'll need clothes. Where does he take a girl her age to buy clothes? He picks up the phone and calls Maggie.

As he explains his predicament, Maggie listens. 'I'll take her on Saturday. We'll make a day of it, go to the mall and have lunch. It'll be fun.'

'I can't ask that,' he says.

Maggie laughs. 'You didn't ask. Besides, I get to shop and spend someone else's money – that's a good time for me.'

Hank feels a sense of relief work its way through his back muscles. He must buy Maggie a bottle of wine. And a case of beer for her new man to drink while he watches football in the garage. What was his name? Butch.

Then he picks up his pen and continues with his list.

* * *

The days pass. Hank sits with the grandparents when he watches her swim, at her dance recitals. They muddle through. Together they mark the milestones. First birthday, first Christmas. First trip back to Providence. That was rough. She seemed fine. He was proud of her, but he didn't know what she was thinking.

He makes an appointment with a psychiatrist for her. After her first visit, they stop at IHOP and have pancakes. After the second visit they do the same. After the third, she tells him she doesn't want to go back.

'Why not?'

'I just don't,' she says.

'Do you not like the doctor? We can find someone else,' he says, cutting up a pancake.

'It's just... He never met Mommy and Daddy. And I don't want to talk about them with someone who never even met them.' She shrugs her shoulders, her way of saying it makes complete sense to her, so why all the questions?

'Okay,' he says. 'Fair enough. If you want to talk to someone, let me know, okay? We'll find someone.'

That night he calls Ned's friend, asks him what he thinks.

'Children are more resilient than we give them credit for. I wonder though, if someone telling her not to talk about people behind their backs has confused her.'

'I hadn't thought of that.'

'Lucy knows me. And I was fortunate enough to know her parents. If she needs to talk, have her call me.'

'I appreciate that,' Hank says. He doesn't want to make the same mistakes he made when Ned lost his mother.

Hank suggests they go to IHOP one morning, to talk.

Lucy looks up and says, 'Can we go to Denny's instead?'

'We can go wherever you like. Why Denny's?'

'I like their hash browns,' she says.

All he can do is watch, and pray he'll see the signs if she's in trouble. He watches and waits. But nothing seems out of the ordinary. Some fallings-out with friends, a bit of bullying another parent told him about, a kid named Jimmy who made fun of her for 'living in an old house with an old man'. Hank wanted to knock the hell out of the little bastard but then he met the kid's father and knew where he got it. So he sat Lucy down and told her that when people are mean to you, when they say mean things to you, or about you, that it was really their own unhappiness. Their own stuff.

'So when Jimmy calls you old he means he's old? That doesn't make sense.'

'Okay. I'm not explaining this too well. But Jimmy is not a nice kid because his parents aren't nice. And they aren't nice because they're unhappy. So when he says mean things, it's really because he's hurting inside, and wants other people to hurt, too. Do you understand?'

'I think so. And I don't care when he says stuff about me, but when he says stuff about you I really want to beat him up.'

Hank smiled at Lucy while he melted inside. God, how he loved his girl.

'Just ignore Jimmy. Life will sort him out eventually. Years from now you'll be walking down a street and bump into him and one of two things will happen. One, he'll apologise for how he treated you, or two, he'll still be an idiot. Either way, just ignore him for now.'

Nothing more was said. And that was the end of Jimmy.

The early teens had their moments, but overall, they were doing okay.

And then, Lucy was turning sixteen.

For her party, she asks if a handful of kids can come over, and if they can have a barbecue on the back deck.

'Sure thing.' He's delighted by how normal it all is. Until he remembers he is not the fun granddad. He's also the parent.

'There won't be any drinking at this event?' He lowers his voice, sounding stern.

'My friends aren't like that.' She sounds indignant and he has to smother a laugh. The patio door slides open, and she lets herself outside, a book under her arm.

* * *

He's had it easy with Lucy. Despite the worrying, the waiting for the other shoe to drop, she seems to have emerged well-adjusted and strong. Excels at school, a few loyal friends who are always underfoot, it seems. Likes to read in her room, too. He's grateful.

He looks at her, sitting on the back deck reading Jane Austen. Swap Mr Darcy for Sherlock Holmes and she's her father, through and through, and he couldn't be more grateful for that.

He opens the deck door and steps outside. She looks up from her book and smiles at him and Hank feels it in his chest. The feeling you get when someone you love is simply happy to see you. There is no better feeling in the world.

'We'll have to buy some groceries for your friends coming. And what kind of cake would Miss Lucy like for the big day?'

He knows what she'll want, but he asks anyway.

'A Pepperidge Farm red velvet cake,' she says. 'In the freezer section at Publix.' She has the same cake every year. They're always on sale, but she only gets them for her birthday.

'Are you sure? It's a special occasion.'

'Yup.'

'Okay. Tomorrow night, we'll go to Juniper's, just the two of us.'

Lucy gives a little nod of delight. 'I love Juniper's.'

'I know, sweetheart. Now, I'm off for a spell. You okay for a few hours on your own?'

'I plan to read,' she says.

'Good girl. Keep the doors locked. If anyone wanders up from the beach...'

'Go inside and bolt the door. Call you on your cell. You'll come right home.' She finishes for him. 'Honest, Granddad, you say that all the time. No one has ever wandered up from the beach. I'm fine!'

'Keep your guard up, Lucy...'

'There are some crazy people out there,' she finishes for him.

Hank allows himself a simple moment of pride, in her and for himself. They've both done well.

* * *

They're in his pickup, driving to the restaurant. He thought about getting her a car, but she has shown no interest in getting her licence. For that he is both happy and sad. Happy he won't need to worry about her driving, sad because he's certain it is connected to her parents' deaths.

Lucy is wearing a blue summer dress, short, with tan sandals. Her hair is long, a golden-brown colour, almost like the sugar. She has large blue eyes, like her father. Like Elise. Hank thinks she's the most beautiful thing he's ever seen.

At the restaurant he parks the truck and they step into the late heat of the day. He opens the door for her, feeling the wall of air-conditioned air. She'll be cold, and he sees she hasn't brought a sweater.

'Do you want to go across the street and buy a sweat-shirt?' he asks, already taking out his billfold.

'I'm fine. Let's eat!'

He smiles to himself.

After the plates are cleared away and before the cake

comes, he takes a small package from his pocket, setting it on the table in front of her.

Lucy has a thing for old movies and loves Audrey Hepburn. The first time he let her stay up past ten was to watch *Breakfast at Tiffany's*. He laughs to himself, at Lucy wondering why the white actor was spoofing a Chinese person. She thought it was horrible. Times have changed, he told her. Now, he places the little box on the table in front of her.

'Oh my God... goodness,' she corrects herself. He was strict about bad language.

Her hands are shaking as she opens the little blue box and sees the earrings.

'Diamonds from Tiffany's!' she gasps, tears filling her eyes. Lucy gets up from her seat and gives him a hug, squeezing him so hard he jokes, 'Enough!'

'I love, love, love them!' Her voice is so loud Hank thinks about hushing her – he knows people are looking. What the hell, he decides. Happiness is fleeting. He lets her have her moment.

Lucy takes out the small blue stones she's wearing, and with a hand that is still shaking, puts on her new earrings.

'I need a mirror. I have to go to the bathroom,' she says, getting up. She hugs him again.

The waitress brings the cake. 'Someone's excited.'

'My granddaughter's turning sixteen,' he says.

'Aw, how nice.'

She takes out a lighter and the candles are glowing brightly as Lucy comes back to the table.

After she blows out the candles, and after the applause, Lucy looks at him and says, 'I wish Mom and Dad were here.'

Her words are a physical blow to Hank at first. But then, he's pleased. They're on her mind. And that keeps them alive.

'Me too, sweetheart,' he says, then after a pause of silence in his memory, he says, 'Show me your earrings.'

Lucy smooths her hair out of the way so he can see the shining stones.

Then the waitress brings the leftover cake, and the bill. Another of life's big moments wrapped up for the two of them. What's next? Prom. Sending her off to college. Pre-med in Boston. Like her father. It will kill him to see her go.

'You all right, Granddad? You seem a bit sad.'

They're walking to his truck, capturing the last few minutes of light before the sky fades to black. Hank is silent, trying to think of how to answer the question.

'I'm just thinking that pretty soon you won't want to spend time with your old granddad,' he equivocates.

'Never gonna happen,' she says, then she links her arm through his and gives it a squeeze.

'Have I told you how much I love my earrings?' she sighs.

Hank smiles to himself. He had thought about giving her his mother's ring, but that, he decided, was for something bigger.

He drops her off at her friend's, then drives home, the little blue box on the seat beside him. When he gets home he puts it in her room. Sees the cover of a romance novel peeking out from under her pillow. How long has she been doing that now?

He sits down and pulls it out, reads a few pages just to check. Then he remembers she's sixteen now and puts it back where he found it.

In the kitchen he pours a glass of Scotch then stands on the back deck, looks out over the water. The day has come to an end, and night is upon them, but still there is a streak of light spilling from the sky, creating a pool of light in the water. Hank is not a man to believe in signs, but still he lifts his glass to the brightness in the dark and says, 'She's a good girl. The two of you would be proud.'

The beam of light seems to grow, expand, vibrate with life, then the sky swallows it up, and the reflection on the water dissolves into the waves.

FIFTY-THREE
FLORIDA. 2006

It's the last summer before Lucy goes off to college. Hank is so proud he thinks he could burst, and a nervous wreck at the same time. She's a little girl, and he's sending her off to a big city on her own. He knows she has a good head on her shoulders, but the world is a mean place at times. He goes to the safe in his office and spins the dial. A code he did not need to write down – a day that changed the course of history, and of his life, too.

He finds himself spending more and more time in the past, when he was a young man and had the physical strength and energy to push through anything that got in his way, whether it be German artillery or keeping a promise or building a life that had more than its share of tragedy, and more than its share of success.

He often thinks of that young man who saw a problem as well as how to fix it. Now, making decisions take as long as it does for him to get his old body going in the mornings. Some days it never really did get going, just sort of idled, creaky as an unoiled motor, barely turning over. Still, he has no real health problems. He's just old.

Peering into the safe, hunting for one small box, he sees the paperwork that documents his life. Wills, insurance policies, certificates of ownership and bank statements. They're all neatly stacked to one side. Moving them, he sees the other papers that represent the other part of his life, the one that did not line up as neatly as a profit and loss statement. While he knows he's done well financially, he doesn't think he's quite broken even with the other part of his life.

He pulls out the letters he received during the war. Mostly from his mother. A good woman who he knows had a good life. The envelopes that originated in Providence, in that old house he grew up in. The house he returned to after the war. The house be brought Ned to, straight from the hospital. Where Elise... well, he won't think of that now. Sold it for a fresh start. Hank was old enough now to know there was no such thing as a fresh start. The only people who could put the past behind them were people with no conscience. He learned that in the war, too. A lesson reinforced by life.

He sets the letters on his desk. He'll read them later. Now, he has something he needs to do. He digs around in the safe, it's not that big, and he's starting to wonder when he feels the small box under his hand. Plucking it out, he opens it to make sure it's the right box, even though he knows it is.

Lucy is standing at the fridge guzzling water after a long run when Hank walks into the room.

'Take a seat at the table,' he says.

Lucy is soaked in sweat but does as he says, sensing something important is happening.

'This is from your great-grandparents. My mother and father.'

He hands her the little worn box, and she opens it, letting out a small gasp when she sees what's inside. Gently, she takes out the emerald ring his mother wore every single day of her life, after her father bought it for her on their tenth wedding anniversary. He had planned to give the ring to Lucy when she graduated, but if Hank has learned anything about life, it's that plans can change, and planning too far ahead was never a good idea.

Lucy holds up the ring, a square green stone surrounded by small diamonds.

'I know it might not be to your taste, sort of old- fashioned like,' he starts.

'That's what I like about it,' she says. 'It's gorgeous.'

'You be careful with it.'

Lucy slips the ring on. It's too big for her ring finger but fits her middle finger perfectly.

'It's like something from an old Hollywood movie,' she says. 'And you know how I feel about old movies. I love it.'

She looks up at him with the kind of happiness you see on someone's face few times in life. And it does his heart good, knowing how much she loves it. She always did like old things, come to think of it.

Hank wills himself to speak. There are so many things he wants to say. How much he loves her. How much he loved her father, and how much he misses him. She reminds him so much of Elise, not just in appearance, but mannerisms. But he won't tell her about Elise. Can't. What is there to say? Besides, in all the ways that mattered, she was her father's daughter.

He'd like to tell her about William. But he can't do that without telling her about Elise. It bothered the hell out of him to think there was no one left to remember his sacrifice. His friend's parents were long gone, and his brother was just a boy when William died. What memories did he have, other than the ones of sadness at his loss, of his parents being broken? By not speaking about him all those years, that was like a death, too, he sees. No one to remember is somehow worse.

Not for the first time he thinks about the coincidence of it all. William was a friend. A real friend. And a good man. Hank knows he's a better man for having met him.

Lucy is still looking at her ring.

'Did Grandma ever wear it?'

Hank is startled by the question.

He hedges his bets. 'It belonged to my mother, who was your great-grandmother.'

'I know.'

'No, my dear. She passed away before your grandmother could give it to her.'

'What was she like – Grandma?'

Hank searches for the right words. Remembers all the lies he told Ned. He hopes he did the right thing.

'She was very sad, and very beautiful. You look so much like her.'

'You told me that, once. But I'm taller?' She obviously remembers that morning, when he suggested they go to France one day.

'You are. You get that from your dad, who got it from me.'

Hank is silent, letting her lead this conversation. He's old. The words said won't rattle around in his mind as long as they will in hers. He feels like he's treading water, waiting for her to speak again.

'Why was she sad? What did she die of?'

Hank has a chance to tell the truth. Or to keep up the ruse. But Lucy is the only person who will ever know.

'She killed herself, when your father was a boy. I never told him.'

Lucy is silent, pale. He wonders if he's burdened her with too much.

'Why?' she whispers.

'She had a hard life. Suffered a lot. I don't really know why, but sometimes bad memories get to be too heavy to carry.'

'Dad never knew?'

'No. I told him she had heart trouble.'

'Wow,' she says, looking at the ring. 'That must have been so hard for you.'

Hank is caught off guard, that her first thoughts are of him.

'And I look like her?'

'You do. Very much. Same eyes. Same hair.'

'Do you have a picture?'

Hank flashes back to his son asking this question. What had he told him then? They were lost, he'd said. Truth was, there were no pictures.

'No.'

'Did you love her?'

In for a penny, Hank thinks. 'I did, in my way.' His words jar something loose in him, something he's not let himself think about. He could have loved her, would have loved her, if she had let him. Maybe she was afraid to. He'll never know.

Lucy looks out the window, taking a thoughtful sip of water.

'She was from France. Paris?'

He shakes his head no. 'A place in Normandy, called Esperance.'

Lucy thinks. 'Esperance? That's French for hope.'

Hank gives a little snort of surprise. 'I never knew that.'

'How did you meet?'

'She was the girl of a friend of mine. He died in service, and I checked in on her. He was the best friend I ever had.'

Hank is careful not to say too much. Lucy is smart, but she also broods, much like him. He doesn't want to put something in her head that she will think on for years.

'We'll have to go to France someday. I'll show you where she lived,' he says. 'Now go take a shower. You stink.'

There is so much more he could have told her. But what was the point, now?

FIFTY-FOUR
FLORIDA. 2008

Hank has always loved September. Growing up he loved the way the leaves changed, how the days started out cool and grew warmer as the day progressed. He loved the scent of woodsmoke in the air. It was different in Florida, where if you lit a fire in the blazing heat people would think you'd lost your mind or were maybe getting rid of evidence.

Lucy's back at school for her final year. She's doing well. Seems happy. She's dating a boy Hank can't warm to. Hal's his name. It's been work, keeping his mouth shut about him. He's been polite enough but Hank knows he has no integrity. Too showy. He hopes it runs its course.

A week after Lucy left he'd called the doctor. Gone through so many tests, had so much blood drawn he thought they may have emptied the tank.

Now he's going for the results.

Inside the doctor's office he waits. Other people might have a spouse, a child with them for support. Hank realises as he sits there he's always done the big stuff on his own.

He prefers it that way. Lucy doesn't need to know. Until there is something to know.

The doctor comes in, and the way he's fixed his mouth, can't quite meet Hank's gaze, he knows it's bad. But then, he's known that since the first pain in his belly that went through to his back. He knew it wasn't a strain.

'How long have I got?' Hank says.

The doctor turns, startled. 'That's pretty direct,' he says, pulling up a chair and opening a file.

'It's my death, and I'd like to know what I've got and how long I've got left.'

'Pancreatic cancer,' he says. 'I'm sorry. It's not good.'

'And?'

'Six months, maybe. The treatments are...'

'I'd like to stick around for my granddaughter, but I won't have her putting her life on hold while I go through hell to maybe get a few more months out of life.'

'Still, we should talk about options.'

As the doctor speaks Hank watches the tree moving in the breeze outside the window. He's always loved the sound the leaves make, a sound like no other. The ocean made a sound that couldn't be replicated either. Whoever or whatever put this world together, they put some thought into it, Hank thinks.

'I'll get back to you,' Hank says, rising, shaking the doctor's hand.

The doctor writes a few prescriptions. 'For the pain, now. We'll have to talk about that again soon.'

Hank thanks him and steps out into the day. A day that looks the same but feels so different, now that he knows this is the last September he will ever see.

* * *

Hank has successfully talked Lucy into not coming home for Thanksgiving, and he is delighted. To be fair, she's so busy studying, it didn't take much convincing. He doesn't look so good, and he knows they are in for a rough conversation at Christmas.

He orders Thanksgiving dinner to be delivered to her from a restaurant she likes, enough for a crowd of them and leftovers, and goes to Maggie's for his dinner.

Maggie knows he is unwell. Everyone does, except Lucy. He's made them all promise no one will call her or send her one of those crazy emails or texts that are so easy to shoot off these days. He arrives with a bottle of Champagne and a big bouquet of flowers, slightly winded from his walk across the street.

Maggie takes his offerings and leads him to a seat by the window. They do not have the view he has, but the house is warm and cosy. He's been blessed with neighbours.

He hears a pop and knows his Champagne is a hit. He refuses the glass brought to him at first, but then realises it's the last time he'll have Thanksgiving with his friends. He takes the glass.

It's a good day.

* * *

Hank has never not picked Lucy up at the airport. He's never lied to her before he got sick, well, tiny family lies, but everyone has those. But now he's got to work to keep the lies straight.

Maggie is picking her up. They'll be back any minute. Hank looks in the mirror at his loose grey skin. He's lost so much weight his clothes are hanging off of him. She's in for a start when she sees him. He feels bad about that.

The tree is up, the same one they've always had. There are presents underneath. Maggie picked out most of them, wrapped them. Set up the tree. Lucy will have to go buy groceries on her own. Hank doesn't venture out much anymore. The last trip to the doctor he took a cab – cost him almost thirty dollars. He thought the shock might kill him right then and there.

He has on two T-shirts under his sweater, and a big fleece Maggie got him. He's cold, but he's trying to look a bit bigger, too.

He opens the patio door and lets the cool evening breeze come in. The air smells sweet and he relishes the feeling of the air on his skin. The moon is glowing in the sky, and Hank swears he can see the surface of it, the tracings of purple in the yellow, like he never has before. Funny, he's never really stopped to look at the moon since he was in the army. Then it made him feel like there was some harmony to the world of madness he found himself in. Now, he sees the permanence of it. He will be gone but the moon will still wax and wane, glow heavenly over this beach he loves so much. The waves will still sing.

He must have missed the sound of the car pulling up, the door open, for when he turns back to the house he sees Lucy, standing in the doorway, her skin white with shock, her mouth open but wordless.

Hank curses himself. This is not what he wanted to cause.

'It's okay, sweetheart. Everything will be fine,' he lies.

He wraps his arms around her, a kind of hug he has never given in his life, willing what little strength he has into her. She stays that way, wrapped in his arms, motionless, as the sea ebbs and flows with life behind them.

* * *

'Why didn't you tell me?' Lucy asks. She's sitting on the sofa, legs pulled into her chest, arms wrapped around her knees. It looks to Hank like she's trying to hold herself together. And he feels worse, witnessing this, than he did when he got his diagnosis.

He poured her a glass of port, for the shock, and she gulped it down. The empty glass is on the table in front of them, the crystal catching the blue and green lights of the Christmas trees. Hank finds the colours, the beauty, comforting, in the midst of this darkness.

'You had school, and so much on your plate,' he offers. It made sense to him at the time, to spare her. But what has he done to her now?

'I knew something was wrong when Maggie picked me up. I thought maybe you'd broken a hip the way old people do. I thought maybe prostate trouble. But that is treatable. How could you go through this and not tell me?' Lucy uncurls herself, plants her feet on the floor.

She is angry with him, and Hank feels better about this. Anger is a motivator. Anger is energy. Grief, sadness, they suck everything out of a person. She is rallying. She is his girl.

'Maybe I made the wrong call, but I didn't want, don't want what I'm going through to mess up your life.'

'What you're going through? This is not some rite of

passage, some wobble in life that will correct itself. Pancreatic cancer kills. You're dying!' Her eyes blaze with indignation, hurt at his perceived weakness of her. Fear of losing him. He can't tell.

'I want to see you accomplish as much as you can, while I'm alive to see it,' he says. 'I didn't tell you for purely selfish reasons.' He's lying again, but this sounds like a good lie. He's almost proud that it has come to him.

'Baloney,' she says.

Hank looks at Lucy. The set of her jaw, the way she tilts her head up, just a bit, the narrowing of her eyes. He knows she's thinking hard. He just doesn't know about what.

'You're here for almost two weeks. We have plenty of time to talk about this,' he says. 'Why don't we have some eggnog. You know how much you love it.'

Lucy stands up and goes to the kitchen. He can hear her opening the fridge, the carton of eggnog. Hears her open the tin of cookies Maggie brought over.

When she walks back into the room he knows by the way she moves that she's made up her mind about something. Handing him his glass, she walks back to her seat. Then she looks at him and says, 'Forgive my language, Granddad. But there is no way in hell I'm going back to school in two weeks' time.'

He hears her, on the phone that night. Trying to talk through tears. She's talking to that boy. Hank thinks of the first time he met him, at that lovely restaurant on the harbour. He didn't stand when Lucy excused herself from the table. Okay, that might be old-fashioned, but still. Lucy liked old-fashioned things, like manners. Shouldn't he know that? Hadn't offered to pick up the cheque. Hank wouldn't have let him, but still.

He listens, even though he knows he shouldn't. Lucy will need Hal and Molly, and Hank hopes he's wrong about Hal, and that Molly finds a compassion he hasn't witnessed so far.

Hank waits, and watches. What would he have done, in Hal's shoes? Come to visit, to offer support. Sent flowers. None of those things happen.

Hank sighs. He wishes he had taught his girl how to pick good friends.

* * *

Hank doesn't need to open his eyes to know Lucy is in the room with him. He can feel her presence, as bright as sunshine, as real as the morphine dripping into his arm, keeping the physical pain at bay. The pain of leaving her is another thing.

He doesn't know how long he's been in here. He got up to go to the bathroom one night and collapsed. Can remember her appearing in the doorway, embarrassed to be seen the way he was.

When she holds his hand he can feel the ring his mother used to wear. He liked that feeling, the two of them somehow with him. Then the orderlies moved a cot in for her. He wanted her to go back to school, but he feels better, knowing she is near.

He can hear when Maggie comes in, telling her to go have a shower, to have a good meal. They broke the mould when they made Maggie, he thinks. But Lucy hasn't left in a day or two now.

Hank wishes someone would open the window. He'd like to hear the birds sing one last time. Wishes he could hear the ocean. If he'd known that last night at home how he'd end up, he'd have sat on the deck and listened to the ocean one last time. Had a glass of Scotch. What harm could it have done?

His arm twitches, he's lost control of some of his fine motor skills. The movement seems to alert Lucy. He can picture what she's doing as she stands up, lowers the railing on his bed – he hates that. It's like you get old and sick and revert to being a baby in people's eyes.

Then she's sitting beside him. He can feel her resting her hand on his arm.

'I'm here, Granddad.' Her voice is soft, but he hears the tiredness. He hopes she won't get sick. So many worries, so many hopes. That she gets a good job somewhere she likes, finds a new man to build a happy life with. His girl deserves the best. He twitches his hand on purpose, and she takes it gently in her own.

'I should have brought a radio,' she says. 'You always liked to listen to the news. And Dean Martin. You always liked to listen to him.'

She pauses and Hank wonders what she's thinking. Wishes he had the strength to talk to her. There's so much he wishes he had said now. About life, and love, not settling. Being careful about the promises you make. Being scrupulous with your word. About the war. About William and even Elise. He feels a gentleness toward her now. Perhaps William was the love of Elise's life the way Lucy was his.

How very much he loves her, his beautiful granddaughter, who has made all the bad worthwhile. He tries to pull in a deep breath. Wills his mouth to form the words, to speak. He wants her to know. But he has no dominion over his body. His best friend has betrayed him.

Lucy leans closer to him. 'What is it, Granddad? Are you in pain?'

He squeezes her hand, and she scoots from the bed, off to get a doctor. That is not what he wanted. He wanted her to know how he felt about her.

He feels a tear escape. Gravity moves it from the corner of his eye to the bed.

Lucy returns. A nurse says they can't give him any more pain medication.

That's not what he wants!

'Please. He's in tears.'

The nurse says he's fine. Hank is grateful for the soothing tone she is using with Lucy, who is crying now. All because he wanted to tell her how much he loved her and can't.

He falls asleep.

In the early hours of the next day, as the night is easing away to the light, Hank feels himself give a jolt.

Lucy, in the chair beside him, wakes.

'It's okay, Granddad,' she says, sitting beside him on his bed.

He feels her soft hand brush the hair from his eyes.

My girl, he thinks.

Lucy lies down beside him, puts her head on his shoulder, wraps her arm over his chest.

'It's okay if you want to go. Dad's waiting for you, and it's been a long time since you've seen each other. I'll be okay.'

He knows she is trying not to cry, and he is so proud of her.

'I'll be fine.' She kisses his cheek softly.

'I love you, Granddad,' she says.

Hank's body gives a jolt, a shake, a rattle. The last sensation he has is his granddaughter's arm over his chest, and the feel of her head on his shoulder.

FIFTY-FIVE
NORTHERN FRANCE. 2009

Cradling a cup of coffee in her hands, Lucy looks around the sad, broken house that now looks so different. Like it's surviving, not dying. Funny, she had thought it only good for a wrecking ball when Rob first showed it to her.

Stacked next to her backpack are the books she found in the trunk and put on the shelf. She's going to ask Rob if she can take them with her. She did not tell him about the bracelet. Already she has packed it with her things.

The front door opens, and she knows he's returned.

'Hello,' he says.

'Hi.'

She sees the time. 'You're early.'

'I want to take you somewhere, show you something.'

'Omaha?'

He looks at her, curious. 'How did you know?'

'A feeling I got,' she says. 'And I was standing here wishing I could see the Channel again.'

'I'd like to show you where my great-uncle is buried.'

'You visit his stone, don't you? I saw you that first day, with your hand on a marker.'

'I visit him each time I go, mostly for my grandfather.' Rob shrugs.

'That's nice. I'd like to see it,' she says.

* * *

The drive to Omaha and the cemetery is much shorter than she remembers. But then, the closer it came time for her to fly out, the faster time seemed to move.

The hedgerows are flashing by. Rob is driving faster than usual, aware maybe that time is running out for them.

'Do you think you'll come back to France anytime soon?'

'I know I'll be back. I'm just not sure when.'

'Christmas is pretty beautiful here.' She hears a hint of something in his voice.

'That an invitation?'

'Yes.'

'We'll keep in touch?'

'I will start the first letter tomorrow night.'

'I like the idea of getting a letter in the post,' Lucy says. She thinks for a second.

'I'm changing my phone number when I get home. I'll text you the new number.'

'Does that have anything to do with your ex?'

'Yes. It's time to move on.'

Lucy feels better than she has felt since that December day she went home and found her grandfather bundled up in layers of clothes that did not hide that he was wasting away.

'So, any more thoughts about medical school?'

'I'm going.'

'What changed?'

'In the past three weeks, it feels like everything.'

'Like I said, travel has a way of changing things.'

Lucy looks out the window at the almost familiar landscape, remembering this same journey just ten days earlier. Even then it had felt both like a new road and a path trodden before. She can't quite figure out that feeling, but she will, perhaps, in time. Maybe the secrets of the past will be revealed to her if she pays attention.

Rob pulls into the parking lot. It feels smaller now to Lucy, seeing it for the second time. He parks and they get out of the van, closing the doors quietly, already mindful of the space.

It's not as cold at the cemetery as it was that first day, or maybe Lucy is just dressed for it. Maybe she's used to it. She breathes in deeply, the aroma of seawater, of the beach, filling her up, making her strong. The beach back home brings her peace. This one brings her strength.

They pass the reflecting pool, making their way among the clean white markers. Rob walks quickly, purposefully, Lucy matching him stride for stride.

'A lot of people would think this was weird,' he says, just loud enough for the wind not to take his words.

'What is?'

'Taking a girl you like to a cemetery.'

'If I learned anything in high school, it's that people who think others are weird are usually pretty fucking boring.' Lucy's hand flies to her mouth. 'I'm sorry,' she says to the stones around her. And she is. What a time to start to swear. Granddad would be horrified.

He squeezes her arm before stopping and ushering her ahead of him.

Lucy moves slowly, reading the names as she goes. She wishes she had time to read all the names in the cemetery. She might read the name of people who knew her grandfather, fought with him. In saying his name, he would be with them all briefly, even if just for a second.

Rob stops, places his hand on the top of a stone.

Lucy looks at the marker.

William Hardwick. Age 25. Massachusetts.

'He was my grandfather's brother. So, my great-uncle.'

Lucy places her hand on the stone. 'William. I wonder if people called him Billy?'

'From what I hear, they didn't. He was a proper gentleman. Studying to be an architect. Voracious reader.'

Something twigs for Lucy when he says that – it sounds familiar.

'All those dreams, all that potential, taken away.'

'We never met, I know, but it bothers me sometimes, to think about him dying. I hope he wasn't scared, or in pain. I hope he didn't die alone.'

A leaf, a shade of green she's never seen before, lands on top of the stone. Both she and Rob look into the sky, wondering where it might have come from.

'Another mystery,' Lucy says. Then she picks it up, places it in her pocket. With her index finger she traces a tiny heart on the top of William Hardwick's marker. And then she walks away.

ACKNOWLEDGMENTS

Thanks to my agent Hannah Schofield at LBA Books and everyone at Aria and Head of Zeus for believing in me (and Hank and Lucy).

Enormous gratitude to the brave souls who read my first draft and offered advice: Kerry Andrew, Katherine Armstrong, Christine Bridger, Roberto Pastore, Heidi Pentz, and the wonderful Bill Buckley, who fought in World War II and shared his stories with me. Bill, you are a legend.

Thanks to the Faber Academy and Richard Skinner.

Huge thanks to Marla McAlpine for being my biggest cheerleader and to the friends who have helped in all sorts of ways: Anne Mackie, Dan Foster, Lee Walton, Simon Frost, Diana Marrs, Treena Muck Pixner, Michael Callanan, Pamm Sullivan, Philip Gwyn Jones, Christopher MacLehose, Simon Rees, Jo Harcourt-Smith, Becky Lucas, Catherine Gladstone, Harriet Copland, Felicia Sinusas and Lydia Gard.

Much gratitude to my sister Anita Pentz and to my brother-in-law Bob Pentz for many reasons.

Thanks, Dad. I miss you.

ABOUT THE AUTHOR

MARINA McCARRON was born in eastern Canada and studied in Ottawa and Vancouver before moving to England. She holds a Bachelor of Arts and a Master of Publishing degree. She has worked as a reporter, a freelance writer, a columnist and a manuscript evaluator.

She loves reading and traveling and has been to six of the seven continents. She gets her ideas for stories from strolling through new places and daydreaming. *The Time Between Us* came to her as she stood at Pointe du Hoc on a windy June day and asked the magical question, what if...?

Hello from Aria

We hope you enjoyed this book! If you did, let us know, we'd love to hear from you.

We are Aria, a dynamic fiction imprint from award-winning publishers Head of Zeus. At heart, we're committed to publishing fantastic commercial fiction – from romance to sagas to historical fiction.

Visit us online and discover a community of like-minded fiction fans.

You can find us at:

www.ariafiction.com

🐦 @Aria_fiction

📘 @Ariafiction